CW01083550

DON'T DIE ALONE,
ALONE,
LUCAS COOK!

DON'T DIE ALONE, LUCAS COOK!

GEORGE LESTER

CLOUDY DAY
PUBLISHING

ALSO BY GEORGE LESTER

Boy Queen

———

PRAISE FOR BOY QUEEN

A funny, sparkly, and joyful celebration of drag! I loved it!

Alice Oseman, author of *Heartstopper*

It's full of fun, sass, and heart. Hang on to your wig because it will be snatched!

Dean Atta, author of *The Black Flamingo*

BOY QUEEN has drama, charm, and warmth, and George Lester has created a cast of characters you'll miss as soon as it's over.

Justin Myers, author of *The Last Romeo*

A lovely, inclusive book with very likeable characters, and a must-read for fans of drag

Sophie Cameron, author of *Out of the Blue*

Funny, warm-hearted, packed full of joy and spectacular glamour! Utterly delicious!

Simon James Green, author of *Boy Like Me*

To Chris and Jon - thank you

———

ISBN 978-1-0687670-0-5 (Hardback)
ISBN 978-1-0687670-2-9 (Paperback)
ISBN 978-1-0687670-1-2 (eBook)

The characters and events portrayed in this book are fictitious. Any similarity to real persons, living or dead, is coincidental and not intended by the author.

Cover Artwork by BAKA.RASU
Interior Illustration by Nicolae Negură

Published by Cloudy Day Publishing

———

CONTENT WARNINGS
Grief, Parental Death, Anxiety (Mild)

ONE

INTRODUCTIONS
Notes On How Not To Die Alone

Congratulations on picking up this book. What a moment this is. We're going to become very close over the next few hundred pages, you and I. I'm here to help you reach your true potential, help you really take control of who you are and what you want, and make sure that you don't die alone surrounded by a bunch of cats. That's the fear, right? Yeah. Me too. We've all been there.

It's not going to be easy; I can promise you challenges and low points, but I can also promise you rewards. All you need to do is take that leap. Are you ready? Deep breath now. Let's go.

I CAN'T BREATHE.

It's the last thing I expected to see on my first day at work. But I've barely set foot in the staffroom at Buttons Café and Bookshop when I see someone lying across the sofa, feet up on the arm of the chair, reading a copy of my dead mum's long-forgotten relationship manual.

This has to be a joke, right?

If Max has set all of this up just to spite me, I will kill him.

"You lost or something?" The girl stares at me from behind a pair of green-framed glasses, hazel eyes narrowed as she tries to figure out who the bloody hell I am.

I'm standing in front of her in a purple apron and a name tag that says "LUCAS (He/Him)" on it. If she thought it through, maybe she'd clock that I work here. Then again, I am staring at her, mouth hanging open, not talking.

Say something, Lucas. Say something.

"It's my first day?" I say. It comes out like a question, like even I'm not sure. I'm sweating, my heart running a hundred miles a minute, and I hate that not only am I being confronted by first-day jitters but also Mum's book.

The girl folds over the corner of the page, the sound of a thousand booksellers screaming bloody murder drowned out by my heart pounding in my chest. It's as she puts it down that I get a full look at it.

It's a white, glossy cover with bright pink writing across the front reading "DON'T DIE ALONE!" with the subtitle "How To Find Love And Actually Keep It!". Some of the gloss seems to have peeled off the front, and the corners of the cover are a little bent and worn. I would have said it was a well-loved copy were it not for the big red sticker in the top right-hand corner obscuring the author's name, Olivia Cook, and marking it as "On sale for £2."

Mum

I feel like I'm about to pass out.

"So, you're the new June?" she says.

I blink. I know the words, I just don't know what they mean in this context. "I'm what?"

"And you've met Maria?"

Is this thing on?

Maria is the manager. She's the one who interviewed me last week. She's sort of equal parts fearsome and kind. One minute she's making a joke with you, the next it's like she's going to tear you a new asshole. Showing up barely on time this morning probably didn't help that.

"Yeah, I'm Lucas," I say, suddenly nervous about saying my last name, given that it's plastered across the front of the book she's reading.

2

Why is she reading it? Where did she find it? These are questions I desperately want the answers to, but I'm too afraid to ask.

She looks at me like she doesn't quite believe me, getting up from the sofa to take me in fully, still in the doorframe, wishing the ground would swallow me whole.

She's short. Well, shorter than me, which isn't saying much considering I barely scrape 5'10". Her dark brown hair is cut into a bob that hits just past her shoulders, and those hazel eyes that were already narrowed in curiosity, now have a distinctly judgemental glow about them.

"Nice to meet you, Lucas. I'm Vicky Morales-Jones," she says, flapping her name tag at me, showing off "VICKY (She/Her)" with a Spanish flag next to her name, before returning to the sofa and the book. Whatever test it was she was giving me, I seem to have passed. Victory, I guess. "There are lockers through that door, keys are in them. Just pick a free one."

"Sure thing. Thanks," I reply, finally stepping into the dingy little staffroom. The lighting is unflattering, washed out to the point of almost being grey. It's a far cry from the aesthetically pleasing café and bookshop no less than twenty steps away.

I find the lockers, shoving my bag and jacket in one before slamming the door and locking it, just like I try to slam the door on my feelings.

If there's one thing I've learned about grief, it's that it never just goes away. You don't forget, you just learn to cope with it as time moves on. Some days everything will be fine, and you won't think about how much it hurts that someone so important to you is no longer there. Other days, a complete stranger will be reading their book and you'll wonder if you're about to unravel in front of them. I am pleading with myself not to unravel right now.

"Don't I know you from somewhere, New June?" Vicky calls out.

I turn to see that she's watching me, the book in her hand. It's only as she's holding it from this angle that I can see the back cover, and my face goes red hot.

Right on the back of the book is a picture of me, Mum, and Dad. I can't be older than four or five. I'm cheesing at the camera and wearing the brightest pair of red dungarees you have ever seen in your life. I forgot about the picture. I think Nana took it. She had it on her mantelpiece. Pride of place. We look happy. When was the last time Dad smiled like that?

Jesus Christ. Deep breaths.

"Do you go to Southford Secondary?"

I try not to let out a heavy breath. "Yeah, I do," I say, a sudden wave of guilt hitting me as I realise I don't recognise Vicky at all. Though, now that I'm seeing her without the haze of panic and sweat, maybe there is something familiar about her. The glasses feel like they should be a bit of a giveaway. "You too?"

"You don't recognise me?" she says, hand at her chest, mock (at least I hope) offended.

"I mean, sort of?" I reply, somewhat hopefully. "You look familiar, but if you asked me to pick you out of a lineup, I'd probably have to pass."

She laughs. I don't expect her to laugh. It's enough to put a smile on my face.

"That's fair," she says. "If it helps, same. I sort of feel like I know you but can't place it. Figured it had to be school."

There is a mirror near where the lockers are, and I look at myself. My brown hair is usually a little bit swoopy and fluffy, but looks wilder than I intended this morning. I do my best to smooth it out, to make myself look presentable. My eyes look tired. Blue, usually a little on the sparklier side, they look grey today, and the heavy bags under them don't help. The lighting in here is homophobic. This is not a good place for selfies.

"Lucas?" Maria's voice booms down the corridor. A pale brunette walks into the staffroom, a collection of papers in her hand. She's wearing a purple apron like the pair of us, her name tag fixed to it reading "MARIA (She/Her)" with several flags after it. Maria speaks a lot of languages.

"Lucas Cook," she says with a bright smile. Her face must ache from it; she smiled when she greeted me this morning and I'd wager she's not stopped since. "Contract here."

"Lucas Cook?" Vicky says, raising an eyebrow at me before turning back to the book in her hands.

Oh no. Here it comes. She shows me the back cover of the book,

Mum looking glam, Dad looking…like Dad, me with my bright red dungarees and same wild hair. The more I look at it, the more it looks like the kind of bold fashion choice I would never make today. A shame.

"Is this you?"

My name is beneath the picture: "Olivia, Matthew, and Lucas Cook; A Happy Family."

I have two options here. I can lie to preserve my identity, something Vicky will likely figure out anyway, which, if I lie to her about it now, would make the embarrassment worse. Or I can suffer the consequences of her knowing, of everyone who works here knowing, of everyone at school suddenly remembering, and me having to pick up my entire life and move to Canada, so I never have to suffer this again.

"Lucas? Vicky?" Maria is still in the doorway, staring at us like we're…well…like we're holding her up from opening the café. Which we are.

I nod. "Yeah, it's me," I say, ignoring the slight crack in my voice. "Shall we?"

———

"WERE YOU GOING TO KEEP IT FROM ME?" VICKY ASKS SUDDENLY.

It takes me a second to calibrate what she's talking about. As soon as Maria opened the doors at 8:01 (Christ, it's early), customers poured in.

I'm pretty sure I screwed up more orders in that first hour than anyone has in the history of this establishment. But nobody yelled at me, which feels like all I could ask for given that I'm so frazzled.

"Keep what from you?" I ask as I head out onto the floor, armed with a bottle of cleaning spray and a cloth.

Henry Leung arrived at ten, so they are manning the counter while Vicky and I clean. Maria looked like her head was going to explode when she saw the state of the place.

"That you knew who wrote the book I'm reading?" she asks, following me out from behind the counter with a dustpan and broom. "That you know her quite well, in fact."

We make our way through the far-too-close-together tables, inching around chairs so we can get to the back of the café.

"It's awkward," I say. "It's my mum."

"It's cool!" Vicky replies loudly enough that a couple of customers look at us. She doesn't seem to care. "Bare minimum, I'd call it fascinating. Your mum wrote a book. How can you not be excited about that? Her name is on bookshelves and stuff. Did she write anything else? What is she like?"

I open my mouth, but I'm not entirely sure how to respond. I could tell her what she was like, that she was kind, loving, but she was away a lot. The first book did well, but not super well, and she was always chasing the next thing, the next bit of success. Ambitious, I guess. But I've already almost lied once to Vicky this morning and, even though I'm about to make things really awkward, I feel like the right thing to do is say this out loud.

"I think she wrote other things, but nothing published." *Deep breath, Luc, here we go.* "And if she were alive, I'm sure she'd still be writing. No idea what, though."

I see it land. Watch as Vicky's mouth drops open. "I am... Oh my God, I am so sorry," she says. "I'm so stupid."

"You are not!"

"No, this has to be some kind of record for me."

"You didn't know," I reply. "It's honestly fine."

"I'm still sorry," she says quietly. "I mean, first day at work and you're having to talk about all that? I didn't mean to bring it up."

"It's not your fault," I say. "It was a long time ago."

"How long?"

"Seven years," I say. "So, much as I can tell you that she was lovely, and a great Mum or whatever, I...don't really remember. I've got snapshots of her." And that's the truth. They feel like they fade more and more with each passing day. "Why were you reading it, anyway?"

"I run a blog," she says. "It's called Love Me Nots. It used to be with my friend, June, but she went to Uni so now it's just me." I get the impression that the June topic is off limits. "We write about romcoms. We analyse them and how their dating techniques work, marking them on a Love It/Love It Not scale."

"Cute."

"And I was reading the book because…well, it was my idea of expansion," she says. "I've read a few dating guides and written about them. They're fascinating and surely had to have worked for people once upon a time or they wouldn't have been so popular."

"Or people were just desperately looking for love?" I offer.

"Cynic."

I shrug. "Maybe." If she'd met my dad, she would probably understand why. He's not dated since Mum died. He just…stopped believing in it.

"If I'd known you were coming in, or had any idea who you were, no offence, I wouldn't have done it, okay? I don't even know you; I wouldn't want to hurt you or anything. I only started asking because…well…it's an interest of mine. But I'll stop now, and I won't bring it up again."

"It's just weird to see someone with the book, I guess," I say. "Definitely not how I thought my first day would start."

It's a surprise Vicky even knows about it. It was a modest hit. Very modest. It stayed in print and my mum did events, but it didn't set the world on fire.

But the book was never really something that factored into our relationship. I mean, she died when I was nine, so her writing about relationships didn't really come up in my life until after she passed. Kids asked what my mum did for a job, and I said she wrote books. That was it.

There was a time in Year 7, only about a year or so after she died, that kids caught wind of what she did. I was trying to figure out who I was, and I had bullies at my school quoting paragraphs of it at me. Specifically, the parts that related to sex. Of course. They'd leave ripped-out pages of it on my desk or stuck to my locker. It was mortifying. The only thing that stopped them was my best friend Max stepping in and telling them she had died. They didn't find it so funny after that.

I can tell Vicky has more questions and there is a part of me that really wants her to ask them. It's been so long since I've talked about Mum. I don't bring her up with my friends. Dad never brings her up anymore, like at all.

7

When she first died, I know he made an extra effort to talk about her, to keep her present in the house as much as he could, to stay in contact with my nana so that it didn't feel like she was gone, so we could support each other, but with time that faded. The pictures of her vanished, the copies of her books disappeared, and mentioning "Mum" in a sentence was met with frost. I don't even feel like I can bring her up anymore. I can't remember the last time we saw my nana.

"Have you read it?" Vicky asks. Maybe she can sense my curiosity.

"What?"

"The book," she says. "It's fascinating. The way they met, the things she did to 'get' your dad. It's incredible."

"No, I haven't," I reply. When Mum first died, I was way too young for it, and now I couldn't even tell you where her books are in our house.

"How can you not have read it?"

"It's about my mum and dad," I reply. "It's weird!"

"It's her legacy," Vicky says. "It's your parents' history. And it's your mum, and...you know...it might help you get a...friend of some indeterminate gender."

"A boyfriend?"

"Didn't want to assume," she says with a wink. "But...have you ever thought about it?"

"I...I don't even know where the copies are," I say. "They're in the house, probably gathering dust in the attic."

"I'm on my second read, taking notes for the blog," she says. "You can borrow mine if you want."

She's being serious. There's this genuine, open look on her face, wide eyes, a big smile. She is trying to help me, trying to bridge the gap, trying to help me feel closer to my mum. And there is a small part of my brain that is itching to take her up on the offer, itching to see what my mum wrote.

"Sure," I say before I can stop myself. "That would be...great. Maybe I can—"

"Darlings," Maria calls from behind the counter. I turn to look at her, the use of 'darlings' not hiding the fact that her face looks a few shades short of murderous. "Customers! Let's get moving. Henry is good, but they only have one pair of arms!"

Henry looks up at us, a sheen of sweat on their forehead, an apologetic look on their face. It's their way of telling us that they didn't ask Maria to step in. We quickly make our way back behind the counter, my brain trying to shift from talking about Mum to thinking about coffee and what the hell all these buttons do.

But I can't help drifting back there during every lull, thinking about what's within the pages of her book and, for the first time in a while, thinking about Mum. And, I don't mind it one bit.

TWO

ANYTHING WORTH HAVING DOESN'T COME EASY

You're about to start a journey that many fear, a journey of self-discovery, of self-reflection, of change. This is also the story of how I fell in love. How I found my man and lived my romcom life.

You have to kiss a lot of frogs before you find your prince, and when I tell you I went through the ringer with some absolute toads, I'm not lying. There were times when I thought about jacking it all in, thought about giving up and getting those cats. But as the title of this section suggests, nothing worth having comes easy. It's going to be tough, but you can do this.

GROUP CHAT

SOPH

Anyone here? Max and I are early

JASMINE

On our way.

KRISH

Be there in ten

JASMINE

Snap.

MAX

Lucas???

SOPH

Luc? Are you coming?

MAX

Paging @Lucas Cook?

...

LUC & MAX

MAX

Just checking in. Are you okay?

...

On my way! Promise!

GROUP CHAT

Sorry, sorry, sorry, running late. Be there ASAP.
Sorry!

Despite leaving work in what I thought was good time, I'm running late to meet my friends. There is tiredness in my bones. A full day on my feet and I am absolutely spent and, honestly, the last thing I want to do is travel halfway across town. I want my bed. Mostly, I want the book that's burning a hole in the bottom of my bag.

Vicky handed it to me before I left—I didn't even remind her, she just gave it to me—and it's been calling out to me ever since. There is a part of me that wants to take it out on the bus and dive into the pages, but I don't want people to look at me funny. I don't want people to recognise the cheesing kid on the back and clock that it's me, or see me reading a dating book in public. It's weird.

Instead, I put my headphones in and try not to think about the book as I ride the bus over to FUNTERTAINMENT. No, that really is the name.

Saturday nights here are practically a ritual for the kids at my school. It's got everything you could possibly want. There's a cinema, a bowling alley, restaurants, coffee shops, clubs, all sorts. It's a giant entertainment complex on the side of an A-road.

I see some of my friends before they see me. Sophie and Max are outside Lamberti's, practically joined at the hip. Soph sees me first, waving excitedly before tapping her wrist and rolling her eyes. She looks dressed up. They both do, at least compared to me, having bolted here straight from work.

Sophie Thompson—bestie, icon, moment—is wearing a pair of figure hugging jeans that hit every single curve and swerve of her body, her brown skin glowing, her hair pulled back into a severe ponytail with a lot of curl in the back. She's also wearing her boyfriend's leather jacket, which actually suits her look better than it does his.

"Thought you were ditching us," Soph says, before pulling me into a hug. She squeezes me tight. Christ, she even smells good. I probably smell like coffee and deodorant right now. "This shirt is nice! I love you in this."

"Coming from you, looking like a glamour model," I say. "Also, Max, this jacket suits her better."

"Like hell it does," he says with a wink. And I won't lie, I melt a little bit.

Max Carter. Soph's Max. My Max. Well, when he wants to be. All perfect teeth and perfect hair and perfect fresh-off-a-winter-holiday tanned skin. He looks annoyingly good right now.

He pulls me into a hug and it's the best thing. I don't get enough Max hugs these days. Call me needy.

We've been best friends for the longest time. He was the one who was there for me when Mum died and for every little breakdown about it since. I was there for him coming out as bi, he was there for me coming out as gay. We lean on each other. I don't know what I would do without Max. Although, since he and Sophie got together a year or so ago, I'm steadily learning what it's like to be without him.

"Seriously, what's with the lateness?"

"Buses suck," I say. "Besides, no Krish and Jasmine yet. I'm practically early!"

"Nice try!" Krish says from behind me as he and Jasmine exit the restaurant.

Krish has his arm around Jasmine's shoulders, looking every bit the definition of tall, dark, and handsome. I mean, dictionary definition. Black hair that is all sorts of swooshy, and gorgeous, dark eyes that you could literally get lost in if you stare for too long, and the height… I mean, he makes Jasmine look even more petite than she already is. The boy is a giant.

Krish flicks his wrist, showing that he's not wearing a watch, but definitely making a point. "Who had twenty past six?"

"I think that was me," Jasmine chirps. "Sorry, Luc, you have priors."

"I'm not always late!" I protest.

"The lie detector test determined that is a lie," Max says with a laugh.

"I hate this," I say. "Can we go in and eat? I'm starving."

"We're waiting for a table," Jasmine says, holding up a little buzzer. "Figured we'd be waiting a while, so decided to get straight on it."

"I was late off work," I say, "the buses were running late, it was a perfect storm. But I'm here now, so what's the harm?"

They look at me like I've grown an extra head.

"Work?" Soph says. "Since when did you have work?"

And that's where the shocked expressions have come from. Shit.

"Oh yeah," I say. "I started work today. Surprise."

Soph and Max are still looking at me funny, while I get some halfhearted congratulations from Krish and Jasmine. This has gone down like a lead balloon and I can't for the life of me figure out why.

"Since when?" Max asks.

"Today," I say. "I'm working at Buttons, the café near school."

We've been there a couple of times as a group, sat in the booths, indulged in way overpriced iced beverages. Well…they have. I usually go for something a little less pricey.

"I'm so confused," Soph says with a nervous laugh. "Why didn't you say anything?"

"Um…" My brain seems to have suddenly gone into overdrive as four pairs of eyes stare at me, and I'm so sure that they all hate me because I've kept this from them. "I…needed to get a job. It was a chat I had with my dad. Money's tight…"

Now it's even more awkward. None of my friends have side jobs. None of them need them, as far as I know. Dad talked to me about it the other week, about getting laid off from his job, so I did the sensible thing and found something so I could help out.

"It came about pretty fast," I say, trying to make it better, trying to diffuse the tension. I know I'm trying way too hard.

"How many people did you spill coffee on?" Krish asks, a smile tugging at the corners of his mouth.

"Not one!" I say, eternally grateful for him cracking a joke, even if it is at my expense. "And I am not that clumsy."

Krish's eyes widen at me. I can feel a story coming on. My face is probably bright red. It's certainly still sweaty from a combination of rushing from the bus stop and the awkwardness I feel. As he starts telling them about the time I went arse-over-tit in the canteen and covered myself and a bunch of teachers in pasta, I can still see the confusion on Soph's face and I hate it.

"Soph, I—"

Jasmine yelps, and holds the small black rectangle above her head. It's buzzing, green and red lights flashing all over it.

"Table's ready," she says, nodding over her shoulder to the front of Lamberti's. "Shall we?"

Krish walks in with Jasmine, his arm still over her shoulders.

Max follows them, but Soph hangs back for a second.

"Do you have to wear an apron?" she asks.

"What?"

"Those cute little purple aprons. Do you have to wear one?"

"I have a name tag and everything," I say. "'LUCAS (He/Him)' And it's all completely adorable until you're clearing up the coffee some child has thrown on the floor."

"I'm going to come in and send all my drinks back," she says.

"You think they let me make drinks?" I say. "Were you listening to Krish? Clumsy. I pretty much fell into the interview; I don't think they're going to let me near any machinery, apart from the till point."

"That's definitely wise," she says. "You could have told me, you know."

I shrug. "I was embarrassed," I say. And she's so busy with Max, I didn't really get the chance. That's what I'm telling myself anyway.

She points her finger at me, ET style. I press my finger to hers. It's our thing.

"Besties tell each other things."

"I know," I say, my cheeks definitely going pink again. "I meant to, I just…didn't."

"Okay," she says. "Next time?"

I take a breath, knowing I can rescue this.

"Hey bestie, you'll never guess what!"

Soph laughs, and it calms my aching heart that she might not totally hate me.

"What?"

"I got a job."

She gasps, her hand flying to her chest. "No way, go on, babes," she says.

"You two are adorable, but I think they want to seat us," Max says, appearing at Soph's side and pulling her towards the restaurant.

I follow them in, a neon sign over my head that says, 'Fifth Wheel!' God, I love being me.

THREE

"TABLE FOR FOUR?" The host is smiling broadly. She takes in my friends and then turns her gaze to me, looking me right in the eye like she's wondering if I've accidentally wandered in with these people.

"Five," I say, but even I don't sound sure about it.

"Five!" Her turn to sound unsure. Is she waiting for one of them to say that I'm not with them? Jeez. Who hurt her? "Sure thing, follow me!"

It's crowded, and so loud that I can barely think as we cross the floor. But the way this place smells is next level. This is almost always our restaurant of choice because the food is just…I can't describe it. You know how there is no such thing as bad pizza? Just a sliding scale of good? This place has convinced me that there HAS to be bad pizza, because nothing compares to the stuff they make at Lamberti's. Not a damn thing.

"We've got you set up just here," the host says, a big fake smile on her face. "Menus are on the table, and your server will be with you shortly. Have a great night!" She quickly scoots away, and I notice something's wrong.

We're at a table for four. Four chairs. Five people.

Max and Krish sit on one side of the table, Sophie and Jasmine across from them, and I am just standing there. None of them seem to notice. I'm starting to wonder if I died on the way here and am about to live some kind of paranormal YA fantasy, when someone clears their throat behind me.

"Excuse me?" A waiter has appeared, a sheen of sweat across his brow, a chair in his arms. "Do you mind?"

"Sorry." I move out of his way, and he puts the chair down at the end of the table, practically running away.

I squeeze onto the chair, barely enough room between Max and Sophie. The table leg is also there, so I'm having to sit, legs apart like some manspreading monstrosity, just to get close enough.

Someone walks by and brushes against my back. I flinch. It's only as I look that I see my chair is positioned pretty much right on the aisle. Someone else walks past, knocking into my chair. I apologise. I don't know why. I feel like I'm in the way and my brain can't take it right now.

Soph's hand appears on my arm. "You good?" Someone else knocks into me. I flinch. "You want to switch?"

"So you can get knocked into? Pass," I say. "I'll be fine."

As I bring my attention back to the table, trying to shake this off, Max has turned his body away from me to talk to Krish, and I can barely hear what he's saying because of the noise all around us and the sound of my blood pulsing in my ears.

Someone else crashes into me. They apologise. I apologise. Why am I apologising for existing? Get it together, Lucas.

"You're not fine," she says as she turns to the others. "Shuffle the table over."

Max blinks. "Huh?"

"Shuffle the table over. Luc is practically sitting on the aisle."

Max looks at me now, a smile cracking across his face. Cut to me, melting.

"You should have said something," he says. "As a unit, one, two, three."

It's the loudest scraping sound imaginable, pulling the focus of practically every diner and every member of the waitstaff. We collapse about into giggles. This is why I love them so much, because that tension I was feeling is gone in a flash and I can breathe again.

"Oooh, sharing starters," Jasmine squeaks, looking over her menu at Krish. "Want to split something?"

"Sure, what do you think?"

"Can we?" Sophie asks Max. "I've been looking forward to the garlic bread all week."

Max agrees to it and I keep my eyes on the menu, trying to figure out what I'm going to order for me. This is another thing that happens when we're out. When the ordering begins, I'm reminded that I hang out with couples, and couples split things. Don't get me wrong, I would love to share a starter. I would love even more to have somebody I could share it with.

I shuffle about in my seat, crossing my legs, accidentally knocking the table as I read through the mains. I definitely cannot afford a starter, sharing or otherwise, the main will be fine.

Suddenly, I feel something on my leg. I look down and see that Max has taken off his shoe, which, first of all, public place, gross, and is running his foot up and down my leg. Does he... Does he know what he's doing right now?

There is a smile on his face as he looks at his menu. I look over at Sophie, who is pretty neutral as she looks at hers. I want to scream.

"Max?" I say. He doesn't hear me. Maybe it's the volume in here, maybe it's the focus he's putting into running his foot up and down my calf. I lean forward and tap his arm. He looks up at me, the attempt at footsie stopping. Obviously not a multi-tasker. Poor Sophie. "Can you stop that?"

His face twists in confusion. "Huh?"

"The..." I incline my head to where our feet are. "The...the rubbing."

He looks at me blankly, it taking a couple of seconds to register. His eyes bulge in panic.

"Oh my God, Luc, I'm so sorry," he stammers.

"I get it, whatever," I say, uncrossing my leg to keep it away from him.

"Stop that," he says quietly. "That's not what I meant."

We're best friends, but even so, I have a complicated relationship with Max. There's always been something there, at least there was for me, and when he came out a couple of years ago... I don't know, there was a part of me that thought something might happen.

Then he got with Soph last year, who I love. She's also my best friend, but…I think he knows I had feelings for him once upon a time. And that stuff doesn't just go away, which is why the tension seems to have gone up at the very suggestion of something vaguely sexual between us.

"Why didn't you tell us you got a job?" he asks, shaking me out of my head. "I mean, it's great and everything, but like…"

"I just didn't think to," I reply, shrugging. "And I was embarrassed. None of you work."

"True, but it's nothing to be embarrassed about."

"It happened really quickly," I say, lowering my voice. "You know how things have been. Dad lost his job and…we need all the help we can get." Max knows my family situation better than most. He knew the second Dad lost his job because…well…I tell him everything. It's what friends do. I just didn't tell him this. "And, I don't know, it just seems boring, you know? It's just a job, right?"

"It's exciting," he says, smiling at me. "You'll have extra money coming in, which will be great."

"You sound like my dad." I laugh.

He raises an eyebrow at me. "There are too many jokes in there."

"Eww, stop it."

"But you're good?" he asks. "Everything's good?"

This isn't the time or the place to have this conversation. I forget the last time we had any time that was just the two of us. He's usually with Soph. I'm usually…well…not.

"I'm starving is what I am," I say, focusing back on the menu.

Max reaches out a hand and puts it on my arm, giving it a quick squeeze. It's not a lot, but it's something. He's letting me know that he's there. Even though sometimes it feels like he isn't.

When the food arrives, I have to lean forward to get close enough to the table so I don't end up dropping pizza all over the floor. It means I'm bumping shoulders with Max, feeling like I'm in the way. We laugh it off, but I can't shake the feeling of not belonging here.

They're talking about sharing desserts and I definitely can't afford to get a dessert, at least not if I want popcorn or something at the cinema. I tell them I'm not sure about dessert, then I excuse myself to go to the bathroom. Apparently everyone else had the same idea because I have to join a queue just to get in.

While I wait, I pull out my phone to kill time. My thumbs acting before my brain can properly register what I am looking for. I find my way to LOVE ME NOTS.

There is a strong logo at the top of the page, two cartoon doodles of Vicky and who I assume to be June. It's exactly what she said it was, reviews of romcoms ranging from the heyday of Nora Ephron to the modern Netflix Christmas trash-flick that's like a Hallmark film on acid. They analysed the dating techniques, the romantic scenes, and gave it a rating on a sliding scale of "LOVE IT" to "LOVE IT NOT," which each rated differently, Vicky clearly the more diehard romantic than June.

There are other books that were reviewed too. One about men and women being from different planets, another about men loving "bitches" which feels a little, I don't know, much. So this is what she's planning to do with Mum's book. On both of these she's gone through their advice, analysing it and trying to apply it to the modern world. Given that Mum's book is twenty years old this year, I dread to think what kind of advice she was giving to women of the early noughts.

I bookmark the page, promising I will actually check back, unlike everything else that's sitting in there unread. There's a part of me that wants to know what she'll say about it. I haven't even read it myself. Maybe Mum's got some tips for me.

When I get back to the table, desserts have arrived, both couples sharing a giant ice cream sundae. I slide back into my awkward chair at the end of the table and watch as they 'Lady and the Tramp' their way through the desserts.

When the meal is over, and the bill has been split three ways— Max paying for Soph, Krish paying for Jas, and me paying for myself —we walk out of the restaurant and into the cold of the January night. It's kind of blissful after how stifling the restaurant felt. Even though the walk to the cinema is short, they've not wasted a single opportunity to reattach themselves at the hip as we walk. Two couples. And me.

Getting in my own head, party of one.

"Max!" The voice is coming from somewhere in the distance. I look past my friends and my jaw practically hits the ground.

Grayson Murray.

Everything grinds into slow motion. From the way he shrugs his jacket back onto his shoulders, to the way he waves as we approach. He grins at us, biting his bottom lip.

Seriously, biting his lip? He has to know that looks hot. SURELY! GOD HAVE MERCY!

And I know I'm staring, but I can't help myself. When it comes to Grayson Murray, the lust is real.

His hair is ginger and a little messy where he's been battered by the wind. In the light coming off the restaurant signs, the paleness of his complexion looks ghostly, and my stomach flips. He's a ten. No ifs, no ands, no buts, he's just a ten.

There are a few people behind him, people I know he hangs out with at school. Dylan, Madhuri, Laurie, others whose names I forget. He's chatting to Max and Krish, making jokes with Soph and Jasmine, making them all laugh. And I'm standing at the back like I'm basically not even here. They're all talking. Why am I staying silent? Why am I stood on the edge of all of this? Why can't I find the right words to say?

"We're going to see that too," Grayson says to Max, and I realise I've missed something key here. "Mind if we tag along?"

Grayson looks around at us until his eyes find me. There's a moment where I see that he's trying to figure out where he knows my face from, trying to remember which of Max's *other* friends I am, that we've been in classes together for the past four years, to remember that he once pulled a dickhead bully off me in Year 9, to remember that our lockers are literally two columns apart, and that is the closest I've ever been to interacting with him.

Everybody loves Grayson Murray. He's attractive, he plays rugby (hello arms), and he's gay. What are the chances? He came out in Year 8 to such fanfare that it made me feel a little more comfortable doing it myself, albeit more than a year later. In case I hadn't already been admiring the gorgeous red-headed rugby boy with the killer smile and the big shoulders, and wondering what those eleven-year-old feelings were, I crushed on him. Hard.

Have I ever spoken to him?

"Sure," I say, my voice squeaking a little. This would probably be the second time. The first being when I said, "Thank you! I'm sorry he ripped your shirt, but thank you!" when he decided to play Knight in Shining Armour back in Year 9.

"Smooth," Max says under his breath, nudging me.

"The more the merrier," Krish announces to the rest of the group.

"It'll be fun," Max says, turning back to face me for just a moment. There is a flash of concern on his face and I realise I'm likely giving away too much, so I quickly smile at him. "You okay?" he mouths.

Before I can even respond, we've started walking again. Grayson has moved ahead with his friends. Soph, Max, Krish, and Jasmine following closely behind. Me behind them.

Why am I like this?

We buy tickets and head into the cinema to see a film called Chasing Love because, of course, let's hammer the point home that I'm not chasing a damn thing here. Normally, this would be right up my street. I love a good romcom. But tonight it's the absolute last thing I want to do.

Grayson is in the same row. I can see him out of the corner of my eye. He's watching the film intently. And I wonder what it might be like to be sitting beside him, to be holding his hand like Jasmine and Krish, to be leaning on his shoulder like Soph is on Max.

As we watch the closing scene, as the heroine doesn't get the guy she's been after for the whole film, but her best friend who is quite obviously perfect for her, I'm left wondering if it could ever be me. I take one last look at Grayson. No. Definitely not.

Everyone is saying their goodbyes as we make our way outside, rushing to be picked up by parents. Sophie hangs back to link arms with me, which isn't the worst thing in the world.

"What did you think of that?" she asks.

I shrug. "It was fine."

"You love romcoms."

"Yes."

"So, why are you being grumpy?"

I blink. I feel like I'm being called out.

"I'm not," I reply. Squeaky voice again. Liar. "I've had a long day. And…I don't know…" I don't want to say it. I really don't want to say anything that's going to make this evening awkward. I watch

Grayson say his goodbyes to Max before he heads out into the night. "Romcoms just make me feel lonely sometimes."

She leans into me as we walk, our pace slowing a little. The others have pulled ahead, and I'm glad of that because I don't want them to hear me being a massive sad sack.

"You know you can find someone if you want to, right?" she says. "I'm not saying you have to, nobody has to, but, like, there are gay guys at our school." She pauses and gives me a quick squeeze. "You didn't say a word to Grayson tonight."

"Not true," I reply. "I said 'Sure.'"

"Bringing your grand total of words said to him to around twelve," she says.

"I can't do it," I say. "He's too pretty."

"Lucaaaaaaaas, you're so stupid," she whines. "You need to do something!"

"What?"

"Anything?"

"Helpful!"

"I can help." She looks excited, an idea literally forming in her head in the moment. "We all could. Why not? It would be fun!"

"And turn me into your project?" I say with a laugh.

"Who is turning who into a project?" Max asks, appearing out of nowhere. "You okay?"

"Fine," I say quickly, willing the subject to be dropped.

"You think if I write about it I can submit it for biology?"

"I'm out of the loop. What's happening?" Max asks with a nervous sort of chuckle.

"I want to set Lucas up with Grayson."

"Grayson?" Max says, raising an eyebrow at me. "You seriously like Grayson? Did I know this?"

"*Everyone* likes Grayson," Soph says. "And are you blind? He drools over him every time he sees him."

"I thought that was just…well…Lucas being nervous around new people."

"Going home now," I say.

"So you like him? Like, *like him* like him?" Max asks. There's some-

23

thing in the way he is saying it that makes me tense. "Do you even know him?"

"What?"

"Grayson," Max says. "Have you even spoken to him before?"

I hesitate. "On occasion."

"On occasion?" Max repeats. "I don't think I've ever seen you talk to him."

"Max—" A warning from Soph.

"Are you trying to warn me off him?"

Max laughs. "You can do what you want," he says. "I just think it might be worth talking to a guy before you set a wedding date." He turns his attention to Sophie. "Mum's here," he adds. "We should…" He nods towards the car that's just pulled up.

"See you Monday, Luc," he says, clapping a hand on my shoulder. It's not the slightly more sentimental goodbye I was hoping for, but I'll take it.

"Bye," I say as he walks away before I turn my attention back to Sophie. "I hate you."

"You love me."

"I love you and that's why I hate you," I say. She pulls me into a hug, squeezing me tight. "What's this for?"

"That's for you," she replies. "And to remind you that if you want my help, you can have it. Though, I will go full parent on them and have to ask what their intentions are with my dear sweet Lucas."

"And I will be forced to combust on the spot; sorry about that."

"Ah, my beautiful little pile of charred remains, whatever has become of my Lucas."

"I mean, maybe Soph, I just—"

"Soph!" Max calls out from his mum's car. It pulls Soph's focus off of me for a second, a smile bursting across her face. She's gorg. Truly gorg. She turns back to me.

"You're okay?"

"Fine," I say. "See you Monday."

She kisses me on the cheek and hurries over to Max, who offers me a wave as he heads out the front door of the cinema, closely followed by Krish and Jasmine.

I wave as Max's mum pulls away, taking them back to Max's

house, and Jasmine's mum picks up her and Krish, taking them back to Jas's house. Suddenly very aware that I'm on my own, I make my way to the bus stop.

Cue dramatic musical solo.

I'm definitely in my feelings. Maybe I'm tired, maybe I'm just in my head, maybe it's the day that I've had, but whatever it is, I'm noticing things more acutely than I have before.

Sure, they've not ignored me all night, they're not treating me badly, it's just… Have you ever been to a party or been out with your friends and felt like it wouldn't make much difference if you weren't there? Like, if you hadn't shown up, nobody would miss you? That's how tonight felt, and it's all sealed as I skip past any remotely upbeat songs on my phone to find something a little more reflective of the moment. Double points if it's an older woman singing a sad musical theatre ballad. Sondheim is normally a good place to go for things like that.

Everybody around me seems to be coupled up and happy, from the people stumbling out of the cinema and to the club, to the girl throwing up in the bushes not three feet away. A guy, who I assume is her boyfriend, is holding her hair and rubbing circles on her back. Why am I jealous of a girl who's vomiting?

I need to do something. Sophie was right. I don't know what it is, but I need to do something.

Oh yeah, that's it. Go home and cry. That's the one. Perfect.

FOUR

GETTING TO KNOW YOU

You might think you already know yourself coming into this book, and that's fine. But I'm about to tell you that you don't. You never really know yourself until you start looking at yourself with an outside eye. That's what we're going to do in the first section of this book.

Section One is all about you. Before you can think about yourself with someone else, you need to look at your life, at your choices, see you who are. If you don't think you can do that, you're already lost.

"DAD?" I call out as I step inside.

Nothing. He must have picked up some extra hours tonight. Dad has worked as a roving chef for as long as I can remember. Conversations about 'tightening our belts' since Mum died have been pretty common, but now, it's serious. Things are drying up. A restaurant that he'd been steady at for most of my life is closing and we're in trouble.

A dinner a couple of weeks ago started with words like "redundancy,"' and "cutting my hours to the bone," and "wouldn't know a good chef if it whacked them in the face with a frying pan, and I might," quickly descended into why I needed to get myself a job and kick in a little bit. He's been picking up shifts all over town, calling in favours from buddies, working every shift under the sun.

Anything to keep the house he's called home since before I was born.

"Dad?" I try again, just in case.

Nothing.

At least if he isn't here, I don't have to talk about tonight. And if I don't have to talk about tonight, maybe I can avoid overthinking it. Not likely, but a nice thought, at least.

I head to the living room and switch on the TV, letting the sound of it wash over me as I go horizontal on the sofa, immediately taking out my phone.

Vicky's website is still open in the browser. And Mum's book is in my head again.

I go get my bag and bring it to the living room. I take the book out. Why the hell am I shaking? It's a book, not a bomb. But somehow in my hand, it feels explosive.

I half expect the doorbell to ring or thunder to crack in the sky. The only cracking is the spine as I open it. It's deafening. And there she is.

Mum.

We look nothing alike. We have practically nothing in common in that department except her eyes. It's the first thing people who knew her notice when we meet. It's in the blueness of them, or the way they go all squinty when I smile.

She's smiling in this picture. I smile back at her. I can't help myself.

I've been told that I look more like Dad than Mum. He used to have the same swooshy hair that I've got now, the same chubby cheeks, the same teeth that only look like they do because of a retainer and a little light prayer. His hair has got darker over the years, now more salt than pepper, and he's a lot leaner too. When people say we look alike, I don't really see it.

I stare at the picture a little longer. The book itself looks dated, the fonts on the cover very much frozen in time and, in a way, so is this picture. I think it was taken before I was even a thought in her head. It was only her and Dad.

I sit on the sofa and open the first page to an introduction, "Notes on How Not To Die Alone," which feels a bit rich. The irony and tragedy of it is not lost on me. Mum was killed on the side of the road seven years ago, knocked off her bike by a dangerous driver on her way to pick me up from school. That she, technically, died alone, kills me. The fact that she died before anybody—Dad, Nana, me—found out, sucks.

And there are tears in my eyes. What the hell am I doing? Why am I opening this book?

It's her legacy! Vicky's enthusiastic words reverberate in my head.

I keep going.

I can sort of hear it in her voice. Well, what I remember of her voice. It's become a lot more distant as time has gone by, but there is an echo of it there, reading it to me.

"Are you ready?" it reads. "It's time to take the leap. Let's go."

I'm about to flick through it when I hear a noise at the door, Dad's keys jangling in the lock. I leap from the sofa, standing in the centre of the room with a copy of Mum's book in my hand. I debate sprinting upstairs, but I'm too late. Dad is walking through the front door.

I throw myself back onto the sofa, tucking the book behind me. The corners dig into my spine. This is fine. Absolutely fine.

"Luc?" Dad calls out.

"Hey, Dad!"

"Marco!"

"Polo!"

"Marco!"

"Living room!"

I hear him chuckle as he hangs his coat up, the shuffling of fabric, the sound of his shoes hitting the rack. He pops his head around the living room door. He's in the process of trying to grow a beard, black and grey stubble lining his jaw that he rubs as he takes me in. His eyes look tired, heavy bags hanging beneath them, dragging him down.

"You alright?"

"Good, yeah," I say, trying to ignore the book that feels like fire against my back. "How was work?"

I see him wince. He tries to hide it, rearranging his face into a weak approximation of a smile.

"Work was...work," he says. "Oh wait, what about you?" He makes his way into the room, plopping himself onto the sofa across from me. He seems excited now, the grin a little more genuine. "How was it for you?"

"My feet hurt."

He laughs. "The sign of a hard day's work," he says. "You'll get used to it. You back there tomorrow?" I nod. "Great. You're back early."

"You're back late," I parry.

"Touché!" he says. "Some of the guys wanted to stick around for a drink after work. I stayed for a little while to chat. They're all…pretty gutted about the restaurant closing. And there aren't enough shifts going around to keep us all afloat."

"You'll find something else. Places are opening all the time; someone will take you."

"Fingers crossed," he says, before narrowing his eyes at me. "You dodged before. Everything okay?"

"What?"

"Your evening," he says. "You avoided the question. Your friends alright?"

"Yeah," I say. "It was fun. We had dinner, saw a film. Max and Soph say hello."

"Hello back," he says, his eyes still trained on me.

He's clocked that something's wrong with me, something's on my mind. I have no idea how I'm supposed to respond.

He seems just as clueless. His mouth opens and closes like a fish, and I just wait for him to find whatever words he's searching for.

"Anything else to report?" he asks.

Maybe I should tell him about Vicky reading Mum's book, about that very book currently digging into my spine.

"It was a good film," I say. "Don't know if it's your kind of thing, but…it was nice. What about you? Anything else to report?"

He shakes his head. "No," he says. "Just work being…work." He is eying me carefully. "Is everything okay with you and your friends?"

"They're fine," I reply. "They're head over heels in love with one another. It's nice…for them."

Dad takes a breath and runs a hand through his hair. He seriously considers what he's about to say next, and I can already feel myself dreading it. And this is how our conversations often go. The silences when it gets serious are long, like there is a canyon between us and we are shouting across it to each other.

"Well, they're young," he says. "These things happen."

I blink at him. I don't even know what that means. "Huh?"

"They're kids, they'll fall in love, they'll fall out of love," he says with a shrug, nonchalant. My Dad, the romantic. "Maybe you will one day. Who knows?"

This isn't what we talk about, this isn't what we do. Unless he's getting a call from the school to find out I'm being shit (which has actually happened once or twice) it's just business as usual, nothing too deep.

We've never talked about dating or me being with someone. I came out, and that was kind of it. He doesn't know I've never kissed anyone. He doesn't know that I don't know the first thing about talking to a guy I like, or how bloody hard it is to do that when you're gay, especially if you're still in school. And he doesn't seem to want to open that door.

He's not dated since Mum. I don't know if he ever will.

The conversation has stalled and neither one of us seems to know where it's going to go from here. Dad slaps his thighs and gets to his feet, like that's the answer to something.

"I'm going to get a cup of tea," he says. "Do you want anything?"

"I think I'm just going to head up to bed," I say. "But thanks."

"Well, goodnight then," he says, awkwardly standing in the door-frame like he wants to do something like hug me or plant a kiss on the top of my head. But he doesn't do either of those things, instead he gives me a thumbs up and leaves the room.

When I'm sure he's made it to the kitchen, I pull the book out from behind me and make a break for the stairs, calling a quick, "Good-night!" to him on the way. I hear the TV volume go up before I shut my door, and I know that I'm safe.

When I'm ready for bed, I crawl under the covers with the book, turning to the contents page. "It's All About You: Level Yourself Up." "The Rules of Dating." "Oh, My Man, I Love Him So: Finding Your Partner." In my head I hear Barbra Streisand singing "My Man" from Funny Girl, the song it's a quote from. Apparently, the musical theatre love is buried deep in my genes. And I feel like I can hear Mum in it, too. She used to sing a lot around the house.

That's what it was like before she died. There was always music in the house. She'd hum random tunes or play Barbra at full volume and sing along.

It isn't altogether surprising that the next bit of text my eyes lands on is, "You're Never Fully Dressed Without A Smile." It's from Annie. I watched that with her far too many times, and it was a song that always stuck out. She used to hum that around the house too.

Before I know it, I'm reading the entire chapter on how you should smile at the person you're trying to win over. How something as simple as a smile can brighten someone's day and how they're catchy too. You smile at someone, and it puts a smile on their face and it's contagious. It sounds like just the kind of thing Mum would do.

I keep reading.

My husband, Matthew, (who might read this or might not, I don't know) has the most wonderful smile.

I stop short. It's about Mum and Dad and it feels like I'm prying.

Her book sold well at the time, especially when books like that were all the rage, but it faded eventually. But enough people were interested that Mum kept doing events for it over the years. Whether about her book or about other people's, moderating panels at festivals and what have you. There are tonnes of people who know this story. Why not me?

And he often said the same of me. I would always respond with how my teeth are crooked or how my eyes go all crinkly when I smile and lament that I'll have crow's feet when I get old. And he told me he would love every line on my face if it was there because he'd made me smile.

That's what you need to find. So smile, smile, smile. A smile can do a lot of things. It can win a man over, it can catch his attention, but if nothing else, it will make him smile too. It's one of the things you can do so he doesn't forget you.

I put the book down. I can't even imagine Dad saying something like that to anyone. I don't think he's ever had anyone but Mum to say it to. But I guess I didn't know him then. I know him now.

I can't even imagine Dad smiling. When was the last time he smiled? Like, properly cheesed?

How hard can smiling be?

I think back to what it was like seeing Grayson at the cinema today. I could barely string a sentence together, let alone smile. I just stood there, dumbstruck by...him.

I try to picture a world where I can walk up to someone like Grayson, or maybe even actually Grayson (imagine that) and say a coherent sentence that maybe results in some light flirting, and maybe the chance to hang out in a non-school setting. Or even just to smile at him.

I read the rule again: You're Never Fully Dressed Without A Smile. I could smile at him. If I can push the nerves down long enough, maybe I can smile at him, maybe I can make it seem like I'm not a total disaster.

I pick the book up again and keep reading. A guy can dream.

FIVE

YOU'RE NEVER FULLY DRESSED WITHOUT A SMILE

Would you go and meet your potential suitor naked? I would say no. Coco Chanel always said that before you leave the house, look in the mirror and take one thing off. As someone who loves accessories, I always struggled to do that. But allow me to add to it. Take one thing off and put on your smile. Keep it friendly, not strained, let it infect you and brighten your day. Maybe you will brighten someone else's.

THE BOOK IS GONE when I wake up.

I've torn my room apart, but I can't find it and now I'm definitely going to be late for work again. I'll have to find it later and make an excuse to Vicky today if she happens to want it back. Surely she won't. Who reads a whole book in a night?

"Lucas? That you?"

"Yeah, just about to head out," I say, carrying on down the hallway and towards the door.

"Can you come to the kitchen for a second?"

"Dad, I really should—"

"Literally a second."

I pull my shoes on, silently screaming to myself. Late late late late late.

Dad is standing at the kitchen counter making tea, putting some of it in a flask. He hands it to me and I feel like the biggest arsehole in the world.

"Thanks," I say. Did he get up early to make me tea before work? I look over at the dining table and see his computer, some papers and mail next to it. How long has he been up? "I should be done by five. Are you working tonight?"

"I'm going to see if I can pick up a shift somewhere," he says. "But if not, I'll see you tonight.

"Great." I am about to leave when I notice what's on the counter in front of him. The book. I look back at him.

"Want to tell me about this?" he asks.

"Not really," I reply.

"Where did you—?"

"I got it from work," I say, not wanting to get Vicky in any trouble. "It's a bookshop. I saw it and…"

"And what?" he asks.

A beat. A hesitation. "I wanted to see what it was about," I say, a little fire igniting in my chest. "Like, is that a crime?"

"Lucas—"

"What, Dad?"

"I don't want to pry," he says, in a way that tells me he's about to. "But when I came upstairs last night to go to bed, your bedroom light was on and…I don't know what made me do it, but I went in to check on you." He takes a heavy breath. "You seemed off when you got in and I thought you were still awake. But you weren't. You were asleep and…you were reading your mum's…you were reading this."

He can't bring himself to pick it up or even say the words, and there's this look on his face like I've just punched him, like he's crumbling from the inside out. It's in his eyes, the way they look a bit watery, like he's been crying. A wave of guilt crashes over me.

I look back at the table, the papers, the computer. Has he been up all night because of this?

"Yeah, I…" I don't know what to tell him. I was curious? I wanted to know more about it? Why do I feel like I did that time I got caught looking at gay porn? This shouldn't feel like that. She's my mum. "I just wanted to see it."

He smiles at me. It's a sort of sad smile and I can see how much it's hurting him to even have this conversation. We never talk about her, and just having the book in the room with us is throwing him back to seven years ago. It's like no time has passed. He's still feeling all of it.

"I didn't think I'd ever see it again," he says, his voice cracking on the words. "Though, I guess I'd see them if we had to move. They're only in the attic."

It was another thing that came up during the 'tightening our belts' conversation. The house is still being paid off. If Dad can't cover it, we have to move, and I don't think either of us wants to do that.

"You can ask about her if you want," he says. "I know we don't talk about her very much."

Ever, I think. *We don't talk about her ever.*

"But…we can…" That same sad smile is on his face.

All that I feel is guilt. I shouldn't have taken the book, I shouldn't have read it, and I certainly shouldn't have been stupid enough to let him catch me reading it. Because now he's hurting. We're both hurting in different ways, I suppose. He's hurting because I brought her up. I'm hurting because he never does. An impasse.

But I've been fine up to now. What's changed? I'll go back to not talking about her. I'll give the book back to Vicky. I'll let it go. I'll just have to let it go.

———

"Hey there, what can I get you?" I say, for what has to be the hundredth time already.

It's been relentlessly busy since we opened, busy enough that my brain hasn't had a chance to focus on anything other than pressing the right buttons on the till and not upsetting anybody by getting their orders wrong. It's a blessing and a curse. My legs hurt, but my brain doesn't—a pretty fair trade-off, I would say. And it means I haven't had a chance to fall headfirst into the pool of guilt that appeared after speaking to Dad this morning.

Oh no, wait, there it is. Time to dive in.

We are without Henry today (they don't work Sundays) so it's only Vicky and me on the floor, which doesn't seem wholly responsible given we're both teenagers, but Vicky assures me that if the shit hits the fan, then Maria will be out here in a heartbeat.

"So, how was last night?" Vicky asks as we venture out from behind the counter.

My mind flicks back, snapshots of it reappearing in my head. The awkwardness with my friends, the awkwardness with Grayson. I don't know I even want to talk about it.

"It was fine," I say. "Was out with some friends. You?"

"I was doing blog stuff," she says. "Nothing too exciting."

"I looked at it," I say. "Your blog."

Vicky's eyes widen. "You did?"

"Yeah! I hope you don't mind. It's great. I loved it. Dissecting my favourite films, the dating techniques, that kind of stuff. Though your ratings seemed to be higher."

Vicky shrugs and goes back to sweeping. "June is a tougher critic than I am," she says. "I'm a hopeless romantic. I get swept away with it all and before you know it, I'm giving it tens across the board. Nothing wrong with a bit of romance."

"Seconded," I reply. "We saw Chasing Love last night. Seems like it would be up your street."

"Who were you out with?"

"School friends," I say. "Sophie, Max, Krish, and Jasmine."

"Okay," she says, eyeing me carefully. "So you hang out with two couples?"

"Most of the time."

"That must be...fun."

"They're my friends!" I say, but even I know I'm not convincing anybody, least of all myself. I don't know if it's because she's right or because she's looking at me pointedly, either way, I don't like it. "Everything's fine!"

"Sure, Jan," she says. "You said the night was fine. What was fine about it?"

"It was all fine," I say. "The food was fine, the film was fine..." Grayson showing up out of nowhere was fine. I mean, he was fine, but a totally different kind of fine.

"But the company wasn't?"

"Not what I said!"

Vicky waits. She's not going to let this go.

"I felt spare," I say. "That's all. I think I was just tired, you know? A full day here, then out with them. Then it felt like the whole world was conspiring to make me feel really, really single."

"Well, that's going to happen when you hang out with couples," she says. "I used to hang out with June and her partner, right? And it was great most of the time, but there were definitely times when I just felt like they wanted to be alone. Know what I mean?"

I know exactly what she means. How many times have they just wanted to be alone or to just be two couples and they can't because I'm there?

"Your silence is telling me yes," she says, looking over her glasses at me. "It's fine, it happens. You're not a bad person for thinking it, and they aren't bad people for doing it. They're just in love."

"But what do I do about it?"

She shrugs. "Get a hobby," she says. "Or new friends, or a relationship, I don't know. Break them up!"

"Vicky!"

"Kidding!" she says. "Just something that takes you away from it." She eyes me carefully. "I could help you out," she adds.

I try not to sigh. Why does everybody want to suddenly turn me into their pet project?

"Don't look at me like that," she says.

"Like what?"

"Like I want to turn you into my pet project," she says, as if she'd read my mind. "Look, I know stuff. I've read books, I've watched movies, I have a blog. I could help you find somebody."

She says "somebody" and my mind immediately goes to Grayson Murray. Grayson Murray, with his big arms and his swoopy ginger hair. Grayson Murray, and his gorgeous laugh and his *lights-up-the-entire-room* smile.

"Or maybe there already is a somebody," she says. "Who are you thinking about?"

"No one," I say quickly. "No one at all."

"You're blushing."

"It's hot in here."

"You're basically a beetroot!"

"I don't want to talk about this anymore," I say quickly. "Let's talk about you. What did you get up to last night?"

"Nice subject change."

"Thanks."

"I barely noticed," she says with a laugh, reaching the broom beneath the table to sweep out some wrappers. "I was working on your mum's book," she adds.

"Ah."

"Well, you did ask."

"Um...same actually," I say.

"What?"

"Well...not working on it, as such. Reading it. I've not thought about it in the longest time and seeing it there, and then my crappy evening...I..."

The truth was, I wanted my mum. But I wasn't about to say that to this person I've barely known for twenty-four hours.

"And?" Vicky is on the edge of her seat.

"What I read was fine," I say. "I don't know. You're the love expert."

"I have a blog."

"You were using that blog as leverage to help me a minute ago."

She snorts. "Fine. Now I'm being modest," she says. "I think it's pretty great. It has its moments where it's a bit awkward and potentially damaging, but that's because it's old. The science is there."

"The science?"

"Love languages, how to engage with somebody," she says. "With a bit of careful updating, it might work." She is staring at me intently. "I'm being serious, you know."

"About what? The book being good?" I ask. "I mean, it had to have something to it, right? It got published. It didn't sell loads of copies, but it did okay, enough that Mum kept pushing it and—"

"I don't mean that," she interrupts, stopping to fix me with a semi-serious stare. "I meant about helping you."

"Vicky—"

"Hear me out," she says. "I know you're saying there isn't anybody, but let's just say, for argument's sake, that there was. I want to try this book out because I think it will work AND it will give me

38

something to write about for Love Me Nots. You don't want to be a lonely, sad sack, right? You don't want to die alone—"

"Wow, kick me while I'm down."

"Maybe go on a few dates or something," she continues. "That sounds like two people who could help each other."

"It sounds like a recipe for disaster," I say.

"It sounds like you need my help."

"It sounds like I'm going to ignore you now."

"Lucas!" Vicky says, her voice almost whiny. "Come on, if it doesn't work out, it doesn't work out. What have you got to lose?"

"Um, my dignity!"

"What dignity?"

"Rude."

"Well?"

"You being rude isn't helping your cause," I say.

"Look, I'm just saying, what if this book could help you?"

Am I supposed to believe that a twenty-year-old book, where one piece of advice was smiling, is supposed to change my life? The temptation is there. To try something new, to get out of my comfort zone or something. But the way Dad has been absolutely obliterated by losing Mum and the way he was looking at me this morning when we talked about it... I can't do that to him. It's too hard.

"It couldn't."

"Well, what if we combined the book with my years of romantic experience?"

"You've had relationships?"

She shakes her head. "I'm talking cinematically here."

"Okay, sure, yeah."

"The two things combined could be golden for you," she says. "I mean, if you asked me, and the book would back me up here, I would tell you that next time he's nearby, just smile at him."

You're never fully dressed without a smile...

"You really think it's that simple?" I ask, the song playing on a loop in my head.

"I think it can be," she says. "It worked for your mum, didn't it?"

It did. But I can't help thinking about how hurt Dad looked this morning. I don't think I can do that to him.

"I'm sorry, Vicky. It seems like a great idea for your website," I start. "Actually putting the book into action with somebody sounds like a hit to me. But I'm not your guy. I'll just… I'll figure something else out." Or I'll just die alone. Most likely the latter. "I brought the book back, by the way. I'll give it to you at the end of my shift."

She opens her mouth to speak, but then goes back to focussing on the broom. I hope I haven't upset her.

"Vicky, I'm sorry, I didn't mean to—"

"Lucas—"

"No, look, I—"

"Customer."

"Sorry, is anyone serving?" There's a pointedness to their tone that makes me immediately feel tense. God. Not this. "I just want to grab a drink if that's okay?" I turn around from the table I'm clearing, trying to ignore the fear gripping my chest at the thought of a pissed-off customer, and am brought face to face with Grayson Murray.

My mouth drops open. If it wasn't connected to my face, it probably would have hit the floor.

"Hey…um…yeah…sure… What can I…? I mean, I can't actually get…They've not…" I make a noise that sounds like something between a groan and a cat being stepped on, and turn to Vicky.

She is trying her best not to laugh.

"Do you want to come over to the counter?" she says. "Lucas, come on."

I follow Vicky over to the counter, my eyes fixed on the floor because if I look at him, I think I'm going to combust. I am fucking this up. I am fucking this up so much. If he sees me at school tomorrow and remembers what a weirdo I am, I will never live this down.

My palms are sweating, and my heart is pounding so hard it might as well be pumping out of my chest like I'm a cartoon. Is it warm in here? It feels warm.

I clear my throat. "What can I…uh…What can I get you?" I ask.

I steady myself and look up at him. He's not looking at me yet. He's looking at the menu behind me and he looks exasperated. God. He hates me. Shit.

"Tea and a latte," he says, still not looking at me. "To go. My Mum's outside."

I remember what Vicky said. I take a deep breath, and I smile.

"Will that be all?"

Then his eyes find mine. And suddenly he's smiling. He's smiling at me. And it's not a mean smile, not mocking. It's a sweet smile that convinces me to calm down a little. I mean, my body is still on absolute fire and I am sweating profusely, but I haven't died.

I can almost hear my mum's voice singing, "You're never fully dressed without a smile." It steadies me a little. I can't place why, but there it is. And we're just smiling at each other. It feels like it lasts an eternity, but is probably only a second or so.

"Yes, thank you," he adds quickly. "That's all."

"O-okay," I manage, tapping it into the till point.

Vicky makes the drinks in record time and, before I know it, he's walking towards the exit, drinks in one of those little cardboard carrier things. They must have a name. I should probably find out what they're called.

He waves to me as he gets to the door. "Thanks so much, see you later!" he calls as he heads out.

I wave back half-heartedly, my hand lingering there as he heads out into the late afternoon. My hand is still there like I am frozen in time, a lazy smile on my face.

Vicky nudges my side.

"What?" I say.

"Well, there's your somebody," she says.

"Grayson Murray?" I snort. "You've got to be joking. I don't stand a chance with Grayson Murray."

"Why not?"

"He's Grayson Murray!"

"And you're Lucas Cook!" she says, like that actually means anything. "I'd say you need my help."

I open my mouth to respond, to tell her that no, I do not need her help. That I do not want to go through my mum's ancient dating manual to try and get with the guy I've been having very slash-fic thoughts about for the past three years. Or that I don't want to hurt my dad by bringing Mum up. But I don't. Just sharing that smile with

Grayson has lit a strange sort of fire in my chest. I like it. I want more of it.

I turn to Vicky and take a shuddering breath.

"I'll think about it," I say.

She smiles so wide it looks like she might explode. "You will not be sorry!" she squeals before going back to cleaning.

What have I let myself in for?

SIX

SECTION ONE
It's All About You: Level Yourself Up

This book is about more than getting the guy (and keeping him). This is about you getting to live your full romcom fantasy life, just like I did.

The first person to think about is you. That's right. If you're looking for someone else, you need to think about yourself first. What can you do in order to become the very best version of yourself? That's what we will discover in this section.

"YOU'LL BE KEPT ANONYMOUS," Vicky says as we make our way off the shop floor at the end of our shift. She's not stopped talking about it since I said I'd think about it. The one benefit of her constant chatter is that I haven't spent the rest of the day thinking directly about Grayson...just indirectly...and of what might be...

"What if people find out it's me?"

It's one thing to have Dad know about it, that would probably break his heart, but for Max and Soph, the rest of the school...

She stops and stares at me. "Do you know what anonymous means?"

"I'm not even going to dignify that with a response," I say. "What if—?"

"They won't," she interrupts with a confidence I do not possess. "Look, barely anyone at school knows I exist," she adds. "The blog is something people are aware of, but nobody really cares about it. It was just me and June. Now it's just me."

There is a strange sadness in the way she finishes that sentence. I really want to know more about June, but we barely know each other. On the other hand, since the second we met, my life seems to have been on display. Now, I suppose even more of it will be.

"No names, not even descriptors," I say as firmly as I can. "If you're Gossip Girl-ing my life right now, I'm not having any initials pointing out who I am."

"Spotted, Coffee Boy absolutely freaking out over the thought of dating another boy."

"I hate this."

"It's going to be great!"

I take my bag out of my locker and look at myself in the mirror. I look absolutely exhausted, it has to be said. The bags clawing at my eyes are heavy, the way my hair is falling over my forehead tells me that it is in desperate need of a wash. I am not looking my best. Do I really think Grayson would be interested in this?

Vicky pokes me in my side. I flinch. "What?"

"Stop that," she snaps.

"Stop what?"

"I can see you over-analysing and semi-hating yourself," she says. "I'm not having it."

"You're wrong," I say with a triumphant smile. "I was fully hating myself. You think you're so smart."

"I *am* so smart," she says, dead serious. "But maybe hold off on that and focus on the fact that you managed to say two words to Grayson Murray without your head exploding. You also smiled at him."

"And he smiled back," I say, unable to stop the rush of excitement buzzing around my entire body.

She nudges me again, softer this time, looking at us in the mirror. I am so much taller than her, it's actually ridiculous. Being around Krish and Max all the time, I'm not used to being the tall one. This friendship might be good for my romantic life and my ego. How nice.

"Okay, so the first piece of advice was a freebie," she says. "This is going to take work and, for scientific purposes, we are going to need to start from the beginning of the book and follow it to the letter."

"Okay."

"You've got copies of the book at home, right?"

I open my mouth to reply and realise I've not really explained to her what happened last night and this morning with Dad. I'm not even sure that I want to. He's dealing with his own stuff right now, I don't want Vicky to have to think about that as well.

"We do somewhere," I say. "I'm pretty sure they're buried somewhere in the attic, though."

"Okay," she says. "Follow me."

She grabs her bag and heads out of the staffroom. Before I have a chance to ask her what she's doing, she leads me back out into the café and through the now stacked tables and chairs all the way into the bookshop.

"Where are we—?"

"Shh!"

"What do you mean, shh? It's a bookshop, not a library!"

"Just follow me," she hisses, speeding around a corner to what has to be the most disorganised-looking shelf in the entire shop. The books are mismatched in height, stacked both horizontally and vertically from floor to ceiling. Unlike the quiet, calmness of the shelves in the rest of the store, this one feels loud and alive, bright red signs all over it reading: "CLEARANCE!"

Vicky grabs a book and puts it in my hand. Mum's book. It's not quite as battered as the copy that Vicky was reading yesterday, but it would certainly be in the running. There is a little tear on the top right-hand corner, minuscule really, and the edges are a little bit bashed. But it's all there.

OLIVIA COOK.

"What? This one not good enough for you?" she asks. "There's a whole shelf if you want to get a different one."

I look at the shelf she's gesturing towards. She's not wrong. At least half of the middle shelf is copies of Mum's book. It's a strange feeling seeing them all there together. It's like a little marker to remind me that she was real once upon a time. I might not have seen her in seven years, but on this clearance shelf, tucked away at the back of this bookshop, my mum is alive and well. Weird.

"Hello?" Vicky says, trying to catch my attention. "You okay?"

"Yeah, yeah, fine." I look down at the book. Now, this really doesn't feel real. If I'd made a list of all the things I expected to do this year, buying my dead mum's book wouldn't even have made it into the top fifty. But here we are.

Vicky drags me to the cash desk so I can pay for the book. She makes sure to remind the handsome bookseller with the purple hair that I work in the coffee shop so should get a discount. He winks at me. I turn into a puddle on the spot. This book had better be worth it.

He rings it up at £2, the employee discount meaning that owning a piece of my mum's life and potentially getting to kiss Grayson Murray costs me no more than £1.80, which I have in change. Cool.

"So, you're all set," she says. "For tonight, your homework is to read the opening—"

"I read the opening last night," I say.

"Read it again," Vicky says with a smirk. "And start filling in the diary section at the back." I open my mouth to make an excuse, but she fixes me with a stare that tells me to shut up. "Problem?"

"Not at all," I say. "I'll figure it out."

"Good," she says, taking out her phone. She taps on it a few times before handing it to me. "Number?"

We swap numbers before heading our separate ways. The sheer weight of expectation on this book feels like I am carrying a boulder all the way home rather than a paperback.

Despite reading that opening section last night, the diary section had definitely slipped my mind. And Vicky seems pretty set on me doing all of this properly. Dad can't know about this.

Should have thought of that before buying the book.

I'll keep it from him as best I can. Maybe keep the book in my bag, and definitely make sure I don't fall asleep while reading it. If he found the book and saw I was writing in it, he'd have questions.

Online.

Vicky said that no one really pays attention to her blog, apart from the romantics. So who would read a blog about this? Certainly not Dad. He'd never look for anything to do with Mum's book, and if I disguise it well enough, no one will know it was me. And who knows, maybe Vicky will prefer it this way. It can all be part of her case study.

I carry on, headphones in but nothing playing, my mind playing out scenarios about what could happen over the next couple of weeks. Eventually, I find my way back to Grayson smiling at me. The next step, surely, is him knowing my name.

Who says I ask for too much?

SEVEN

BE ACCOUNTABLE
Fill In The Diary Section Of This Book

I've kept diaries pretty much since I was at University, journals that tracked my day-to-day life, many of which I've returned to in order to write this book. All the details of when I first met my now-husband, Matthew Cook, are in there, so I have used them to create this.

I'm not saying you have to show them to anyone, or that you have to use them to write your own book, but it is a way of keeping track of everything that you do while you're out in the dating world.

Hopefully, one day you will look back on all of this and be able to laugh about it, or even be able to share with your new husband all the things that you did to get with him in the first place. As I said in the introduction, this is just the start of your story. In the pages at the back of the book, I want you to tell it, warts and all.

DAD

Got a shift tonight. Won't be back until late. Don't wait up.

There are leftovers in the fridge. See you tomorrow.

Thanks. See you tomorrow.

ON ANY OTHER NIGHT, I would probably call Soph or Max, see if they wanted to come over and watch a film, or do homework together. But after last night, and with that book in my bag, I don't want to.

I turn on the oven to heat up the leftover lasagne Dad made on Friday night and head upstairs to grab my computer. I set myself up at the breakfast bar, Mum's book to one side, and a blank Word document on my screen. I take a deep breath and open the book to the first page.

Notes On How Not To Die Alone

That stings a bit.
Here we go.
The second I start reading, it's like I can hear Mum's voice all over again. It's faint, but it's right there, like just by reading the book it's waking her up again in my mind.

Mum was quite well spoken. There was still a bit of Essex in her accent, because you can take the girl out of Essex for a national book tour, but you can't stop her fake tanning and dropping her Ts and pronouncing her THs as Fs. Every now and then it would slip, usually when she was around Nana, who is as Essex as they come, or around some of her old school friends.

She'd always go a bit posh when she was doing book stuff. She'd be on the phone to her editor or someone at the Guardian with this fake proper accent that Dad would always take the piss out of her for.

It gives me an idea.

I'm only a little way through the opening when I put the book down and start to search the book online. There's an audio edition, but it's read by somebody else, and looking for that leads me elsewhere. Why have I never thought to Google Mum's book before? Before I can stop myself, or question if it's a good idea, I am down a YouTube rabbit hole all about Mum. There are radio interviews that people have ripped and uploaded, videos from book festivals taken when I couldn't have been much more than a toddler.

There's even an interview she did in a theatre, in front of what has to be a crowd of at least five hundred people, and she is heavily pregnant. She's up on stage next to a bunch of other writers in a comfy, red armchair, her blonde hair yanked back into a ponytail, her belly sticking out in front of her. Her hand is resting gently on it, cradling me while she answers questions.

There are questions about Dad, a few questions about the book, and even a question about me, which is strange. She's talking about me before she even knew me, holding onto me as tight as she can, the smile never leaving her face, not even for a second.

"I wrote the book because I wanted people to find love, the same way I did," she says. There is a murmur of approval from the audience, presumably from people who have achieved just that. "I never expected it to be adopted by so many people. So I want to thank you all for taking me into your hearts and putting me onto your bookshelves. Who knows? You might find your happy ending one day too. And when you do, you must tell me about it. I love nothing more than a romance with a happy ending."

I turn the video off and the kitchen suddenly feels silent without Mum's voice filling it. Now that I think about it, it's the truth of the past seven years of my life. This isn't a happy ending. The house sits in a constant state of quiet, unless I turn something on in the background. Dad is always working, trying to keep us afloat, and when he's out, I'm here, trying to fill a space that, since Mum died, is way too big for the two of us. She was a big personality, and it hurts when I think about how empty things feel without her.

My phone buzzes on the table, loud and gritty enough to push me out of my sadness spiral.

VICKY

Have you started yet? Not to pressure you, but to put pressure on you, I've started talking about it on my blog and people are very intrigued. :P

A knife of anxiety goes straight through my chest.

What did you say?

That I'm going to start experimenting with a new book soon, actual real-life experiments. People are going nuts.

How many people?

OMFG, anxious, calm down. It's literally four people, but they are buzzing. You're still in, right?

I still have Mum's voice echoing in my head about wanting people to find a happy ending, to find love. She really believed in that. Why shouldn't I?

Of course I am. First accountability post is going live tonight.

YES! YES YES! Send it when you're done!

EIGHT

IF YOU CAN'T LOVE YOURSELF...
Learning To Love You

It's an age-old saying, but one that rings somewhat true. I was always told that I needed to learn to love myself before I learned to love somebody else, and I just never thought that was true. Loving oneself is not an instant thing. It's an ongoing practice and not something you can acquire overnight. Even as I write this book, I do not love every part of myself.

What I am preaching to you, dear reader, is that you start to appreciate yourself and take care of yourself a little more. Buy yourself the nice dress that made you feel gorgeous. That is what I mean by loving yourself. Treat yourself to that pastry you saw in the bakery window this morning. That is loving yourself. Change your hair if you want to. Upgrade your wardrobe. Walk tall. Take up some space. This is loving yourself.

I HATE MYSELF.

Posting the blog last night set off a low-level bubbling of anxiety in my chest, one that kept me awake way past the point when my head hit the pillow. What if someone found out it was me? What if it got out? What if everyone finds out my mum wrote this book and I end up having to go into hiding?

But there were no views on it this morning. Not one. So now not only am I anxious and tired, I'm also snubbed. Love that for me.

Headphones on, volume up as loud as it can go, I make my way to school. Once upon a time, I would have walked with Max, because he doesn't live all that far away. We used to walk to primary school together when our parents first let us; it became our thing. Then he started going out with Soph, and…well…he started walking with her instead.

Southford Secondary School is okay as far as schools go. It's a hodgepodge of different coloured buildings, with teachers who look like they lost the will to live about a year and a half ago. I can hardly blame them.

I head straight to my locker, grabbing my English notebook that I stupidly left here over the weekend. Thankfully, the homework was to read the first few chapters of Pride and Prejudice. No, I didn't do that either.

"Morning."

I freeze at my locker, key half in the hole. It's a voice that I could probably pick out of a crowd if someone asked me to. I look over to see Grayson a few columns down, his locker open, a smile on his face.

Is he…is he talking to me?

"Morning, you twat!" The voice behind me happily confirms that he is not, in fact, talking to me. Dylan Wilson bounds forward, slapping Grayson so hard on the back even I wince at it. He laughs it off. They all seem to.

By all, I mean the rest of Grayson's friends. Like I said, Grayson was always pretty popular, even more so after he came out. Grayson, Madhuri, Dylan, and Laurie. Inseparable. Insufferable. Feared and loved by all.

I find myself watching for a little bit too long. Grayson doesn't even look over at me. He's talking to them, he's laughing with them, he catches sight of himself in the glass of a door at one point, fluffing his hair, pouting a little, and, honestly, if I looked like that I'd check myself out too.

Laurie notices me staring and gives me a quick up-down look before whispering something to Grayson. He laughs, checking himself out again before going back to what they're talking about.

I turn to my locker and take my books out, trying to block out the conversation happening very loudly next to me. They're planning a party. When are they not? There's always something happening with them.

Maybe it's the tiredness speaking, and I don't know what I was expecting to happen, but it was obviously more than this. Apparently, if I'm not the one standing between Grayson and his caffeine fix, I am invisible.

They head down the corridor towards their form class and I stay where I am, bathing in the silence for a second. I watch as he walks away, the red of his hair easy to spot from the opposite end of the corridor. This is the boy I'm trying to get the attention of. Am I completely out of my mind?

"Another party, is it?" I practically jump out of my skin as Max appears at my side. He looks annoyingly fresh-faced for first thing on a Monday morning, his hair is just the right side of swooshy, his brown eyes are a little bit sparkly, and there's a big old smile on his face as he enjoys the fact that he scared the shit out of me. "You going?"

"I won't be invited."

"Everyone goes."

"I won't be invited."

"'Repetitious and repetitious,' said the New York Times."

"Piss off," I groan as I slam my locker. "How was the rest of your weekend?"

"Someone is in a bit of a mood this morning," he says. "You okay?"

"Fine," I reply. "Just tired."

He pulls me into a hug and I find myself falling into him. Max is a great hugger, and when I'm this knackered, this is exactly what I need. He gives me a big squeeze before he lets go.

"Come on," he says. "They'll be wondering where we are."

We walk down the corridor together, heading in the direction of the Geography block where we usually hang out. There's a small seating area and a couple of tables, and it's pretty out of the way, so it's often quiet, which is a blessing. When it's summer, we'd be out on the field trying not to get hit by the lads playing football, some of those lads being Max and Krish. But in the dead of winter, there is no way on this planet I am sitting outside in the freezing cold. I'd rather shove bamboo under my fingernails. And, blessings aplenty, Sophie agrees wholeheartedly with that sentiment.

"Wait, why aren't you with Soph this morning?" I ask.

"She came in early," he replies quickly. "Something about having work to do or meeting Jasmine."

It occurs to me that we could have walked in together, and I'm suddenly saddened that I've missed out on some precious Max/Lucas quality time. We don't get a lot of that anymore.

"Good morning, stranger," Sophie calls out as we round the corner. "See? Told you it would be Luc. And Max!" She smiles at me sweetly, sitting next to Jasmine and Krish, who are so entangled they're practically attached to one another. "Morning, bestie."

"Just so you know, she tried that on about four different people before you showed up," Krish says. "That's four people she said good morning to before it actually landed with the right person."

"Well, those people are blessed with a good morning, thanks to me," Sophie retorts. "Where have you been? Mr Marshall will be here to drag us into our form class in mere seconds. I thought you'd got lost."

"Had to swap books over at my locker," I say. "Bumped into Max."

"Oh?" She says.

"And saw Grayson."

Her eyes widen. "Oh."

"No 'oh,' I'm just telling you," I say.

"So you didn't…" She waves her hands around, like that means anything.

"What?"

"Try and talk to him?"

"I'm sorry, have we met?" I say. "I was just relaying the information."

"Oh, God," Max says. "You were serious on Saturday?"

"Deadly," Soph replies. "So you didn't—?"

"No," I reply, pulling my planner out of my bag. "I was swapping books over. I didn't forget any homework, did I?"

"Apart from reading for English, I don't think so," Jasmine says, absentmindedly running her fingers through Krish's hair. I'm ninety percent sure it's putting him to sleep. Jealous.

"How are you getting on with Pride and Prejudice?" Soph asks.

I mock-think about it for a second. "Well, I think I'm enjoying the pride part of it rather a lot, giving properly queer vibes," I start, taking a seat on the floor next to Krish's chair. "The prejudice part, though? I dunno. It's making me feel a little uncomfy. So five stars for pride, two stars for prejudice, rounding it out to about three point five."

"Shall we say four to be generous?" Soph adds.

"Let's!"

"You've not read the book, have you?" Jasmine says.

I look at her. My face deadpan. She can't be serious.

"What gave you that idea?" Sophie says. It's enough to diffuse Jasmine and for the subject to drop. "Good weekend?"

"Fine," I say. "Was back at work yesterday, so more of the same. What about you?"

There's a moment of hesitation, an uncertainty, a glance between her and Jasmine. She quickly rearranges her face and starts to talk about her lazy Sunday, how she hasn't read a page of Pride and Prejudice either. At least I'm not alone in that.

The bell rings and we make our way into our form class, Max helping Soph to her feet before they walk in side by side. The two couples take seats next to one another, while I take a spare seat at an empty desk behind them, pulling out my phone while we wait for Mr Marshall to arrive.

> Saw Grayson this morning.

VICKY

> And?

> Absolutely nothing. I might as well be invisible.

> *eye roll* What did you expect? That he was going to fall at your feet first thing this morning?

I hesitate. Hard no. But also a hopeful yes. We had a moment yesterday, didn't we?

> Your silence speaks volumes.
>
> We've not even started yet, so chill out.
>
> We'll have him obsessed with you in no time.

I am about to put my phone away when it buzzes in my hand again.

> Great first blog post by the way.

It's enough to put a smile on my face. One view. Good for me.

I open my phone and start scrolling while I wait. And there it is on Jasmine's story, clear as day. A photo from last night.

Max and Soph, Krish and Jasmine, crowded around a table in a different restaurant from where we went on Saturday night, mid-laughter. Jasmine is holding the phone, and I can't tell if it's a fake candid or if they're all actually laughing. But I'm not there, and that sucks.

All the more reason to throw myself into this thing with Grayson, right?

I'm about to respond to Vicky when Mr Marshall walks in, locking eyes with me as he steps through the doorframe. He gestures for me to put my phone away.

"Morning," he growls, as he strides over to his desk.

I'll talk to her later. Like she said, we haven't even started yet. I've got nothing to worry about. Not that I've ever let that stop me.

NINE

GROUP CHAT

SOPH

Going to the canteen to grab lunch with Jasmine, does anybody need anything?

Brought stuff from home.

JASMINE

Can you save our spot in Geography?

Sure

SOPH

Boys?

KRISH

Football

Gross.

SOPH

Seconded. Not this. See you in form

———

I'm waiting in the Geography block, looking at the book as secretly as I can when I hear Jasmine and Soph approaching, deep in conversation. I practically throw the book back into my bag.

"I just can't figure him out half the time," Jasmine says, her eyes quickly finding mine. "Hey, Luc."

"Who can't you figure out?" I ask.

"Doesn't matter," she says. "Just…boy stuff."

I narrow my eyes. "I'm a boy."

"Yeah…" she says, "I know that."

"Ask him," Soph says.

"Ask me what?" I say, suddenly nervous about what I'm getting myself into.

"Oh, come on, I don't want to do this now," Jasmine says. "I'll figure it out. Subject change, please."

Soph rolls her eyes and turns her attention to me. "She's having Krish troubles, and you know him, you know what he's like."

Jasmine slaps Soph on the arm and makes a groaning noise. "Say it louder, the people on the table halfway across the block didn't hear you."

"She can't figure him out," she says.

"What's there to figure out?" I ask, turning to Jasmine, waiting for some kind of clarity. Sophie and I both know Krish well, but whatever her advice is for Jasmine, she doesn't trust herself enough to give it.

"He's just…I don't know…distant?" she says. "I feel like I can't get to him a lot of the time, you know?"

"Have you told him that?" I ask.

"Huh?"

"That you want to reach him?" I say.

"Well…no."

"He's a lot more sensitive than he looks, you know," I say, trying to keep in mind they haven't been dating for all that long and me and Soph have known Krish for years. "You like him?"

"Of course."

"Tell him," I say. "He wants to hear it."

I'm reading heavily into what I've seen of their relationship. Jasmine is very closed off with me, with Max, not so much with Sophie, but I can only assume that she sometimes keeps Krish at arm's length too. Sometimes, Krish needs to be reminded that you like him and want to be friends with him. There is a lot of bluster, a lot of hyper-masc bollocks that comes from him being part of the football team and being good at PE. But he's a way more sensitive soul than his exterior projects.

I relate to Krish in that way. Some people would call it needy. I call it, "I hate myself too much to believe that people actually like me." It's deep, and it's real.

Sophie nods. "That's what I thought," she says. "See? She should have asked you. You're good at this stuff."

"Your turn," Jasmine turns to Soph.

"What do you mean, my turn?"

"You said you wanted to talk about something," she says.

"Why are you turning the spotlight on me when I was ready to start in on this one for telling you to tell Krish how you feel when he won't do the same for Grayson?"

Jasmine turns to me, eyebrow raised. "Good point."

"Different situations."

"How?"

"You're dating Krish. I'm not even on Grayson's radar."

"So get on his radar," Soph says.

"You make it sound so easy," I reply. It goes quiet for a moment, each of us taking a moment to eat. "So, what did you want to talk about, Soph?" I ask. "Everything alright?"

"Um, well—" The bell rings, interrupting her. How this half an hour has vanished so quickly is beyond me. She laughs and shakes her head. "Saved by the bell. Maybe later," she says. "It's nothing, I swear."

Jasmine links arms with Soph as we all stand up, the two of them walking into our form class together and sitting next to one another. I'm about to turn around and engage Soph in the conversation we almost started, when Mr Marshall walks in and pulls my focus back to the front of the room.

Krish and Max come in red-faced and out of breath, both looking hot in both the sweaty way and in the other way. They're talking way too loudly about something interesting that happened in their game that I do not follow and do not care about.

I half expect Jasmine to move and sit next to Krish, but she doesn't, still talking deeply with Soph even when the guys try and get their attention. Whatever it is, it must be serious.

They even walked together to English after form, pretty much leaving me in the dust like we weren't all heading in the same direction. And even though I know I'm not entitled to know anything about it, I feel a bit shit that Soph has someone to confide in that isn't me.

————

MAYBE IT'S A CLICHÉ, MAYBE IT'S JUST SCIENCE, BUT THE BOND BETWEEN English teacher and gay boy is unmatched. Mrs Leighton and I are basically besties. She somehow manages to make a dusty old book like Pride and Prejudice seem fun, and that takes skill. I had Mr Goldberg in Year 9 and fell asleep more than once. How he teaches A Level students is beyond me.

"You okay?" I whisper to Soph as we sit down. She's at the desk next to me, but across the aisle—a futile attempt by Mrs Leighton to stop us from talking to one another.

I've interrupted whatever she was saying to Jasmine, which earns me a sharp look. Not from Soph. Soph just doesn't seem to be here right now. She turns to me, her eyes a little glassy. The ghost of a smile makes its way across her face.

"Fine, Luc, why?"

"Just checking in," I say.

"You're sweet, just…life stuff, you know?" she says, giving me nothing more than that same smile before turning back to Jasmine and resuming their conversation. I try not to take it personally, try to convince my brain that she hasn't suddenly decided to hate me. It's not working.

Should I ask her about yesterday, about them all hanging out without me?

"Okay." Mrs Leighton gets to her feet and dramatically claps her hands. Her white-blonde hair is pulled up into a messy bun, a couple of pencils sticking out of it to let everyone know she's an English teacher. She is ready to go, and if she mentions the pages I'm supposed to have read, I think I'm going to combust. "Pride and Prejudice!" she announces. Apparently, she missed her calling as a drama teacher. "How are we finding it?"

I sink into my chair. I do not need this right now. I one hundred percent do not need this. She is looking right at me, and I can feel that she's about to call on me.

"Grayson, how are you finding it?"

I feel a heavy breath leave my body as Grayson answers. She eyes me carefully, and I know that she knows. I start taking serious notes while Grayson talks about how much he's enjoying it, the themes and so on. It sets Mrs Leighton off for her lesson, and I think I might have dodged a massive bullet here. Definitely need to read the bloody book before Wednesday.

When the bell rings, I have more notes than I usually would because I've been avoiding her gaze by looking extra studious.

"Lucas, can you stay behind, please?"

My heart sinks. Soph gives me sympathetic "Sorry" eyes as she leaves with Jasmine. She waves on the way out.

Mrs Leighton gestures to the chair by her desk. I'm in trouble. And the worst part about feeling like you're in trouble and not fully knowing what you're in trouble for, but sort of knowing, is the anticipation.

"How are you, Lucas?" she asks, offering me a sweet smile. She's my fave, but I'm instantly suspicious.

"Good," I say. "Working hard, you know." She raises an eyebrow at that, I barrel on regardless. "Started a job over the weekend, so that's new. And just, you know, trying to keep up with everything."

"You know why I'm talking to you," she says, looking over her glasses at me.

I nod, bracing myself for the onslaught.

"Okay," she says, pulling a few loose sheets of paper from her top drawer. "The Creative Writing Group is gathering on Wednesday after school," she continues, handing me the sheets of paper. "This is the reading material. There's a little prompt at the bottom to get you going and—"

"Hold on, what?" I say. "That's why you kept me behind?"

She looks surprised. "Yes," she replies. "Why? What did you think?"

"I thought I was in trouble."

She laughs. "What for?"

I open my mouth to respond, but quickly stop myself. No point putting myself in danger here.

"I don't know," I say. "That's why I was so confused."

"Well, then we seem to have our wires crossed," she says. "You know I run the group. I just thought, given everything I wrote on your school report last term, that maybe now would be the moment you'd want to join us."

She's mentioned it to me a few times, brought it up at Parents' Evening once or twice, but I've always declined because...well... because of Dad. Why did she think I would have changed my mind now?

"Why?" I ask, and it comes out so much harsher than I intend. "I didn't mean—"

"I enjoyed the pieces you submitted for assessment last term," she interrupts, still smiling, albeit a little weaker than it was a moment ago. I'm an arsehole. "I mentioned them in the report, and I really think you could have a future in writing if you want it. You're talented."

"Thank you."

She looks at me. Then she looks at the papers that I am clutching quite tightly in my hands, the nerves of getting caught out still not having faded. She's hoping I'm going to say yes, but I am going to have to disappoint her. Which I hate.

"I'm sorry, Mrs Leighton, I don't think it's for me," I say. "But thank you for these." I try to hand her back the sheets of paper. She pushes my hand away.

"Hold on to them," she replies. "In case you change your mind. We're currently working towards a presentation at the end of the half term, and I think it would be good for you. If nothing else, you should come and watch. Everyone is welcome. See you on Wednesday, Luc," she adds, turning back to her computer.

The reason I keep saying no to Mrs Leighton about the Creative Writing Group comes down to Dad. She mentioned it to him at a

Parents Evening last year and the second we got back into the car, he made his feelings on it quite clear.

"Unsteady life, that," he said before I'd even had a chance to put my seatbelt on. I didn't even know what he was talking about at first. "Your Mum always said she wished she'd done something a little more secure. She was always chasing the next thing. You don't want that, do you?"

It was a leading question, but it's always stuck in my head. Do I want that? I don't know, but I know my dad doesn't want that for me. And whenever it's come up since then, he's always mumbled something about Mum and the conversation has finished.

I look at the piece of paper she's given me, a single-page piece with a prompt at the bottom, a reminder in big red letters that they have a presentation right before half term, people reading their pieces out loud to an audience. It sounds like hell, but maybe I'll go just to keep her happy. It might distract her when I inevitably still haven't read Pride and Prejudice.

I pick up my things and head out to the now-empty English corridor. Sophie and Jasmine didn't wait around. I pull out my phone to see a message from Soph on the lock screen saying she had to run. I quickly respond to tell her it's fine, before seeing another message pop up.

VICKY

You ready to get started?

The honest answer is "absolutely not." But I don't see Vicky accepting that, not for one second.

Meet you out front.

TEN

DRESS TO IMPRESS AND YOU DRESS FOR SUCCESS
Don't Be Afraid of Standing Out!

Your clothes are your first impression. I know you're going to hate to see this in print, but everybody judges each other by their appearance. In a perfect world, this wouldn't be the case, but this is not a perfect world, this is not an episode of Blind Date. What you wear makes a statement. Look at what you're wearing right now. What kind of statement are you making? Think about what that statement says to the man you're trying to attract.

This is all about The Turn.

"I'M NOT sure I see the point," I say to Vicky as we're walking into town.

"What do you mean, you don't see the point?" Vicky asks. "It says here, you need to dress to impress."

"But I only ever see Grayson at school," I say, lowering my voice. "What am I going to do to impress him? Wear a jazzy tie clip?"

"Pretty sure a jazzy tie clip would go against the dress code," Vicky says flatly. "Also, I would bully you if you wore a jazzy tie clip."

"Noted," I say. "But I'm serious. He only sees me in school uniform."

"But the plan is for him to see you in more than just a school uniform, Luc," she says. The eye roll is implied in her tone. "Think it through. You go on a date with him. What are you going to wear?"

I can't help the goofy smile spreading across my face at the mention of going on a date with him, the anxiety in my stomach erupting so hard it's like I've had the breath knocked out of me.

"Earth to Lucas!" Vicky barks.

"I have shirts," I say quickly.

Vicky stops in the middle of the street and stares me down. "You have shirts?"

How does she manage to make that sound like an insult?

"A nice checked one," I say. "I could wear it with jeans."

"This isn't about settling for what you have," Vicky says. "It's about upgrading yourself. You know how in romcoms there are always those big makeover scenes where they go into the changing room and come out a new person?"

"I don't want to become a new person," I say.

"I'm not saying you do."

"I definitely don't have the money to become a new person."

"And I'm not saying you need to break the bank either," she says. "This is about finding a style that makes you confident, makes you happy, and maybe makes you standout a little bit. You want to have The Turn."

"The Turn?"

"The Turn," Vicky says again. "Honestly, have you read the book? She talks about The Turn in the section about clothes."

Christ, not me getting told off for not reading something. I thought I'd dodged this bullet.

"I've read the beginning. I didn't know we'd be diving into me learning how to love myself so quickly," I say. "I feel like I need more time. What the hell is The Turn?"

"The Turn is the moment when the main character walks into the room and everyone turns to look at them," Vicky says. "You are transformed, you are made new, the leading man sees you for the first time in your final form."

"Like a Pokémon?"

Vicky sighs. "Yes, Lucas, like a Pokémon."

66

We continue into town until we reach the shopping centre, Vicky leading me past the crowds and towards Hansen's. It's big and bright, a gorgeous glass-fronted shop with the name in bright purple letters over the top of the door. There are screens everywhere with beautiful people modelling the clothes, and I feel fifty shades of intimidated.

"What are you drawn to?" Vicky asks.

"The exit."

"Lucas!"

"What?"

"You're not even trying," she says, grabbing me by the arm and pulling me into the thick of it. We start looking at shirts that are hanging near the front of the men's section. There are a couple of nearby mannequins dressed in muted colours, browns and blacks, navy blues, moss greens. But the thought of going in the opposite direction and standing out makes me feel nervous.

"What is it?" she asks.

"Huh?"

"You're not even really looking," she says. "You're touching all this fabric and none of it is speaking to you?"

"If the fabric starts speaking to me, I think that's a sign to leave," I say, a desperate attempt at a joke.

"Stop trying to deflect."

"I'm not," I say. "It's just…none of this looks like me."

"Which version of you?"

"Huh?"

"The version of you that is here right now, or the version of you that you want to be?" she says. "It's all about upgrading yourself, isn't it? So what does the upgraded you look like?"

"I…I don't know."

She narrows her eyes at me, folding her arms as she steps back, really taking me in. I don't know what it is she is looking for. I'm wearing my school uniform. This is the furthest I could possibly be from my upgraded self. My shirt is half untucked, my tie is loose, my top button is undone. This is the last thing I would wear if I were going on a date with Grayson. Mostly because I'd be riding there on my flying pig.

"What are you scared of?"

I blink. "All of it."

"Give me specifics."

"I'm scared of looking stupid," I say, looking over to where there are a couple more vibrant shirts, stripy tees that catch my eye. "I'm scared of what people are going to say. I'm scared of not looking like myself. You're supposed to be helping me. This book is trying to change me, isn't it? Surely, the last thing I want is to get Grayson by pretending to be someone I'm not."

Vicky shakes her head at me. "You're right," she says. "But I think you've misread what we're trying to do here."

"Have I?" I say. "Because we keep talking about upgrading, and a new wardrobe, and 'The Turn,' and all of that makes me think that I'm going to come out of this a different person."

"You are," Vicky says. "But not because you're changing everything about yourself. I don't think that's what your mum means at all."

There is a strange pang in my chest when she mentions Mum. I don't know what it is, a sort of claw gripping my heart and squeezing.

"I think, on the surface of it, that's what it looks like, but if you really dig into what she's saying, it's that you find the best version of YOU."

"By changing my wardrobe?"

"No," Vicky says, exasperated. "You're not changing your wardrobe, you're buying the things you've always been too scared to pick up. You said you prefer to wear stuff that's plain, but is that because you want to wear plain stuff or because you don't want people to look at you?"

"Can't it be both?"

"I think you're scared of what might happen if people actually pay attention to you, Lucas," she says. "You've spent way too much time playing second fiddle to your coupled-up friends. This book is about you becoming a main character and having main character energy. Main characters grab the clothes that they want to wear and damn the consequences."

"Yeah, but if a queer character does that, they're probably going to get beaten up at some point."

"Lucas," Vicky snaps, firm, frustrated. "I'm being serious here. I'm trying to help. Do you even want to do this?"

Of course I want to do this. I agreed to do this. The thought of not having to fifth wheel forever and maybe, just maybe, getting to kiss Grayson Murray is what made me agree to this. I just need to stop being so scared all the time. How the hell do I do that?

"Pick something out," she says. "Something that scares you."

"But I don't even know what Grayson—"

She puts a hand on my arm. "This isn't about Grayson. Not yet, anyway. This is about you. What do *you* want to wear?"

I walk away from the main menswear section, where all the colours are muted and boring. There is nothing in there that stands out to me. I think of the boy in the red dungarees cheesing on the back of Mum's book.

I spot a red checked shirt that has my name all over it. Vicky is looking at me with wide, expectant eyes. I keep going. I grab a green shirt in the same style, some of the striped tees that are in cute pastels, a few more shirts. I have so much in my arms at this point that Vicky has to help. She might have created a monster, but she isn't about to stop me.

I try things on. The striped tees are definitely a little bit out there for me, but I like them. The shirts are nice too, the red one in particular is vibrant and a little bit lumberjack-esque. I have no desire to go and chop wood or be outdoorsy in any way shape or form, but I don't mind wearing a shirt that looks like I do. I almost look, dare I say it, cute. And for me to think I look cute, this shirt must have some kind of magic powers. Which might be why the price is as high as it is. Christ, can I even afford this?

I send pictures to Vicky from the changing room, getting heart-eye emojis and responses in block capitals saying "YES!" and "GET THIS ONE!" Her enthusiasm is infectious because I pick up the things she suggests, things that actually might look good on me. I even post them on my story, struggling to believe that's me in that more-vibrant-than-usual shirt.

Feeling emboldened by her comments, I send the pictures to Max and Soph as well. They're probably together right now, but I want them both to see. I actually think I might look good.

There is no way on earth I can afford to buy all of it, at least not without rendering my first pay from the coffee shop null and void. I give a couple of the tees back to the attendant at the entrance to the fitting room, keeping the green shirt too. This will be the last of my birthday money. A couple of tees and two shirts will be enough. My wallet feels suddenly light in anticipation of the spending.

"See?" Vicky says, after I've paid for my shirt. "You can already feel it, can't you?"

"What?" I ask.

"You like it, don't you? That you're making moves?"

"It feels like something for the blog," I say. "What I'm feeling, I mean."

"Explain."

"Well, I think it can be misconstrued as changing yourself when, like you said, it's about being a bit bolder, right?"

"Right."

"And, I don't know… If I want him to notice me, then I need to be bolder."

"Certainly bolder than you've been so far, yes," she says, linking my arm as we walk out of the shop. "We'll have you talking to him before you know it!"

The thought makes my stomach flip.

ELEVEN

SOPH & LUC

SOPH

WHAT?!

DO MY EYES DECEIVE ME?!

> What?!

YOU BOUGHT CLOTHES!

> I did!

Can't believe you were in Hansen's today. You HATE clothes shopping.

> Yeah, I know. I went with Vicky from work. Just wanted to get some new things. For once! Ha!

I would have come shopping with you if I'd known you were going. Could have helped you dress up for a certain someone!

> STOP IT! Hahaha! I didn't even get that much, some t-shirts, a couple of new shirts. Some new jeans.

That's a spree for you. I need more pictures. ASAP. See you tomorrow! xx

LUC & MAX

MAX

Stunning! <3

> Thanks Max

The lumberjack shirt is perfect.

> <3

<3

"Lucas?" Dad calls out as I open the door.

"Hey, Dad," I call back. "Good day?"

"Long day," he replies. "You're late."

"I went out with a friend," I say.

"Max?"

"No."

"Soph?"

"No, Vicky."

"Vicky?" he calls back, it hangs in the air, a giant question mark over her name like he's wondering if I've made her up. "Do I know Vicky?"

"Not yet," Vicky calls back.

"Oh! Sorry!" I can see Dad's face in my mind's eye, beet red, embarrassed at the thought of embarrassing me. But Vicky is absolutely cracking up, silently cackling to herself in the hallway.

"Marco!" I call out.

"Polo!" Dad calls back.

I follow the sound of his voice all the way to the living room where he's on the floor with his laptop, surrounded by papers, his glasses balancing on the end of his nose. There is a light flush to his cheeks.

"Lucas, I didn't know you were having a friend over tonight," he says. "Sorry, Vicky, I didn't mean to—"

"Don't worry, Mr Cook, I was just messing around," she interrupts. "I'm only here because we're working on the book. I won't be here too long. I've got to get home."

Dad perks up. I feel my heart fall out of my chest.

"Book? What book?" He turns to me. "You're writing a book?"

"No, no, it's not that," Vicky says. "I'm talking about—"

"A school project," I interrupt, automatically starting to sweat. It feels like someone just turned the heating up from something liveable to the fiery pits of hell. "We're working on a school project. The book is a collection of essays and poetry. You know, that thing I'm always looking through over the weekends when I'm doing homework. Big. Blue. Landscape on the cover that looks like a postcard."

"Ohhhhh," Dad says, nodding knowingly. "I mean, you say that, but I can't remember the last time I saw you doing homework."

Because you're at work, I think. *But also because I'm definitely not doing it.*

"Vicky is helping me," I say.

"You're struggling?"

"No," I reply. God, when did he suddenly decide to start playing the parent card? "We just need to work together. It's a script. Like scene work."

Dad nods, making an "Ah" sound as he turns back to his computer.

"Well, we should probably get started," I say. "We'll be upstairs."

"Dinner is in half an hour," he says, not looking up from the computer. "That's what smells so good."

"You're in tonight?" I ask.

Dad turns to me. I didn't mean to sound so surprised, but he looks taken aback by it.

"Yes," he says. "You weren't planning a house party, were you?"

I snort. "Yeah, a sixth former is coming round with the booze in a couple of hours and someone else is bringing the drugs. Can you make yourself scarce?"

"Alright, funny man," he says. "Half an hour. Be hungry."

"Yes, sir."

Vicky and I head upstairs. I can feel her eyes burning a hole in the back of my head all the way to my bedroom, but she has the good

73

sense not to call me out on my blatant lie until we're out of earshot from Dad.

"What was that all about?" she asks.

I let out a heavy breath. "I've not told Dad that I'm following Mum's book," I say. It's the simplest version of the answer, the version that maybe means I don't have to go any deeper. "That's all."

Vicky folds her arms. "And?"

"What?"

"Come on, Lucas, you're a horrible liar."

"I am not, I fooled Dad."

"You didn't. He'll know something is up, parents always do," she says.

She doesn't know Dad. I'm the last thing on his mind. If I've told him everything is fine, he'll think everything is fine.

"What is it?" she asks.

"When he saw me reading your copy of the book the other day, he got sad and weird about it," I say. I shrug it off like it's nothing, but Vicky is staring at me, waiting for me to continue. "I didn't tell him it was yours or anything, so don't worry about that. But we never talk about Mum. And then he saw the book and talked to me about it yesterday morning and…and he looked so hurt. But I want a shot with Grayson, so…I figured if I just do it in secret, then he doesn't need to hear about Mum and nobody gets hurt."

"Hence the blog, rather than you writing in the back of the book."

"Hence the blog."

She's thinking about it, trying to figure out what to say next, and I am so sure that I don't want to talk to my newfound friend about my dad's hangups about my mum. It feels too deep, and if I tug at that thread, I know that only pain awaits me when it unravels.

She takes a breath. I brace myself. Here it comes.

"Right, we need to talk about your hair," she says.

I blink. The subject change has given me whiplash. "What about it?"

"It's the next section in the book," she says. "We're taking pride in our appearance, so now it's time to talk about your hair." She smiles at me. It's soft and understanding, and in that moment I am incredibly glad to have met Vicky Morales-Jones.

"I like my hair," I say. "What's wrong with my hair?"

She rolls her eyes and we both pull out our copies of the book, hers from her bag, mine from beneath my mattress, and start to read.

We spend some time fussing with my hair. Ultimately, I like my hair a little bit longer. I like the way it frames my face. I like the way it makes me look, so getting a completely different haircut is out of the question.

I catch sight of my reflection in the mirror. Sure, my hair could do with a little styling. The most I usually give it is a bit of a brush before I leave the house. I don't want it to look like I've been dragged through a hedge backwards. That's what Mum always used to say when she'd collar me to drag a comb through my mop.

"Read what your mum is saying," Vicky said, for what had to be the fifth or sixth time. "She isn't telling you to change your hair, she's telling you to enhance it. Drag a brush through it, use some styling product, see what happens."

By the time Vicky leaves, and Dad calls me down for dinner, I feel pretty good about myself. I have new clothes, and an idea of what I can do with my hair. Even though it was all superficial, the outside at least looks good. And that outside is what's going to get Grayson's attention.

At least, I hope it is.

TWELVE

"WHAT'S GOING on with your hair?"

They are the first words that come out of Jasmine's mouth as I round the corner into the Geography block.

I was kind of gutted that Grayson wasn't at his locker this morning. Not that I'm saying my hair would have resulted in The Turn, but imagine if it did? Instead, I'm faced with Jasmine, who looks confused.

"I'm just…trying something," I say. "Something different. You all know Vicky, right? She works with me at Buttons."

They all say their hellos to Vicky, who says Hello back.

"It's nice!" Soph says. She looks to Max for support, but he's looking at me like I've grown another head. "It suits you!" she adds. "Max?"

He looks at Soph, then back at me before he gets to his feet. He positions himself in front of me and starts to fuss with my hair, moving it, playing with it, so close to my face that I can barely catch my breath for a second.

"What are you—?"

"Shh," he says, still moving it, getting it to a point where it sits just right. "There," he says with a smile. "Slightly more well-placed chaos, than just chaos."

"Rude!" Vicky snaps.

"Sorry, did you do it?"

"I helped," she says. "It was mostly Luc. It suits him, right?"

"It's great," he says.

"I've been trying to get him to do more with his hair for years!" Soph says, now also on her feet. She links an arm through Max's and gives him a quick squeeze.

"Why does everyone hate my hair?" I protest.

"We don't hate your hair," Vicky says.

"No, not at all. But this looks good!" Soph says. "Not that you need me to tell you that you look nice but, come on, new clothes, new hair, Lucas 2.0 is in full effect."

"Oh my God, stop. It's hairspray and a couple of new shirts," I say.

"It seems like someone is trying to get someone's attention," Soph says, sitting back down. "Am I right?"

Max looks at me sharply, his face a picture of surprise. That my friends seem shocked that I would do my hair is not making me feel good.

"I'm trying something different," I repeat. "It doesn't matter if someone else notices."

I can feel the red in my cheeks and it's enough to elicit excited claps and giggles from Soph. Max looks at me, confused. I'm now desperate to change the subject.

I take a seat next to Soph, Vicky sitting nearby.

"What did you want to talk about yesterday?" I ask Soph quietly. "If I'd not been kept back yesterday, we could have talked about it on the way home."

"I went back to Jasmine's," she says. "So we would have been going the opposite way."

"Still."

"What did she keep you back for?" she asks. "Did she clock that you'd not read it?"

"No, thank Christ," I say with a laugh. "Just hassling me about the Creative Writing Group again."

"Wow, relentless."

"Truly," I say, and wait for her to return to my question, but she's turned her attention to her phone. "So…everything's okay?"

She looks over at me, her face twisting in confusion. The penny drops.

"Oh, yeah, fine," she says. "It's…um…it's sorted. Mostly. Nothing to worry about, I promise."

"So Wednesday night," Max says. "What are we thinking?"

Wednesday nights have been our thing for as long as I can remember. We usually go to Max's house, sit around, do homework, eat food, and then end up watching a film until everybody has to go home. It's become a tradition, and it's pretty much the only way my brain can focus enough to get work done. Something about the quiet competition of other people being around.

"I have to work," I say. "My contract is one afternoon and weekends. But I can come after."

"Definitely come after," Max says, his hand falling on my shoulder and giving it a squeeze.

It sends a strange sort of chill through my body. My mind flicks back to him being stood inches away from me, playing with my hair. Bloody hell, Luc, get it together.

"You should come too, Vicky," he adds. "If you want to, no pressure."

Vicky is about to respond when Max's attention gets pulled towards the entrance to the Geography block. There is a flurry of noise as Grayson Murray and his friends walk past, loud, obnoxious. I'm staring up at him. He waves. But he's not waving at me. He's not even looking at me.

I look to see that Max has caught the wave, even Krish and Jasmine have. It's just me who is sitting here, like I don't even exist.

Grayson beckons him over. Max hesitates. He beckons again.

Max sighs, annoyed? Is he annoyed? "One second," he says, getting to his feet and going over to talk to Grayson. Krish follows. I watch as they walk away, the two of them engaging in conversation with Grayson. And before I know it, the bell is ringing and I've been staring at Grayson for what has to be at least five minutes. He didn't even notice me.

"Don't you dare spiral," Vicky says as we get to our feet.

Grayson says his goodbyes to everybody, quickly exiting.

"Too late," I say.

"The hair works," she says.

"He didn't notice."

"He hasn't had a chance to notice," she replies. "Homo wasn't built in a day. We'll get you there. It's going to take time."

"Vicky—"

"If your hair isn't like this tomorrow, I am one hundred percent calling you out," she says. "I have to go to form. Don't freak out. We'll chat later, right?"

"About what?"

"Funny," she says. "Save the jokes for the blog," she adds quietly.

———

DAD

Got another shift tonight. You alright to sort yourself out for dinner?

THE QUIETNESS OF THE HOUSE IS TOO MUCH, SO I'M BARELY THROUGH THE door before I fire up my laptop and find more videos of Mum, letting the sound of her voice fill the house.

Today's interview is on a much smaller stage in a little tent that looks like it's outside somewhere. She's with a couple of other authors who I don't recognise and she looks a little more like the Mum I remember. I check the date. It was only from a year or so before she died.

"These things take time," she says. "That's the thing I say to the people who are right near the beginning of the book and desperately trying to get a guy they like to notice them."

I make myself a cup of tea.

"I remember what it was like with Matthew," she says. "He walked past me time and time again and it was like I wasn't even there. I could barely get my words out whenever I was around him. I was a mess."

I've stopped making the tea and I just staring at the screen, waiting for her to tell me what to do, to divulge a big secret that's going to turn this around for me.

"And then one day everything changed," she says.

79

"Great," I reply.

"I ended up spilling coffee all over myself in the staff room and he was the one that came to my rescue."

"So, what? I need to put myself in danger in order for Grayson to notice me?" I say to the screen.

"I'm begging you all, don't put yourselves in danger for the sake of a guy," she says, which gets a laugh from the audience. It's like she's talking to me. "It may seem like a good idea now, but when you can't wear your lucky blouse anymore, then not so much. But find ways to make an impression that maybe don't get you in too much trouble." She shakes her head. "He didn't notice me, or I thought he didn't. Turns out he'd been noticing me all along and didn't know how to broach it. We don't know what people are thinking."

The conversation goes on and I sit with my cup of tea and watch her. I open a second window and start to type into the blog, updating it with all the things that happened (or didn't happen today.) I even mention the videos of Mum because…well…they're part of it too.

> Hair post is going up tonight.

VICKY

Part one of the hair post. It's not over yet.

> Sure.

LUCAS!

> It's not, it's not, I know!

I send her the link to the video I'm watching, which gets me heart-eye emojis in response. Not only is it weird to have Mum's voice in the house again, it's weird to be sharing her work and talking about her positively. Everything with Dad has always been so strained when it comes to Mum, and when she got brought up at school when I was in Year 7, it was so kids could take the piss. Now I'm getting to celebrate her, and that's magic.

I quickly scroll through my apps, and see a picture Jasmine just posted. She's sitting with Max, Soph, and Krish at her house. I check her stories and there are a few more there too.

I feel sad, excluded.

"Your time will come," Mum's voice is still going. "I know it doesn't seem like it right now, but keep going. Keep your chin up. Keep your eyes open. Keep following the book if you want. And when it happens, tell me all about it."

So I promise myself that I will.

THIRTEEN

BE ALOOF

THIS IS NOT ABOUT BEING A DICK. There are a couple of different ways to be aloof. The first is to 'neg,' a typically male tactic that certain men put way too much stock in. Don't insult the person you're trying to impress. Get a grip.

The second is to play it cool. There are many ways you can do this, but the main one would be to keep it light. You know those jokes you tell with your friends? The way you bounce off of one another? Try some of that with your suitor. At the end of the day, you want to date someone who is your friend. So be friendly. But not too friendly. More on this later.

I DON'T MENTION anything to my friends the next day. I don't want to make things awkward. It looked like they had a good time, and I don't want to ruin that for them because I'm feeling left out.

I do my hair again on Wednesday, a slight adjustment, trying to get it to feel right, to look more natural. But I still catch sight of my reflection and wonder who the hell is looking back at me. I mean, I like it? I think it looks nice, but…I don't know. I might be over-thinking this. (Me? Surely not!)

Maria notices it when I get to work after school.

"It looks nice," she says flatly. "It's out of your face. It's better." She checks her watch. "Now get behind the counter, we're busy."

It's short and sweet, but I'll take it. The fact that it held up with me running here from school is a minor miracle. I'm sweating before I've even started. I'm going to be in a complete state by the time I get to Max's later on tonight.

We power through the school rush. Kids in uniforms I was wearing not five minutes ago, buying iced coffees and hot chocolates and frappés that cost almost as much as I get paid per hour. Wild.

When the lull comes, I am frantically trying to clean up around Vicky. Behind the bar is chaos. I don't even want to look out on the floor because it is going to be disgusting and when Maria sees it, she's going to yell.

"Hello," someone says from beside the till. It's insistent, it's impatient, it's announcing that they are there and I am very much not and that is not acceptable. I don't want to serve them. My throat is scratchy and sore and my feet hurt.

"Oh, I will be with you in just one second," I say, struggling to carry the dirty plates I've grabbed from one end of the bar to the dishwasher.

I swear I hear them sigh. I try to shrug it off. Ultimate ick. Be nice to customer service workers, it isn't hard.

"Sorry, we're just—" The first plate slips from my grip and as I try to catch it, but the other five fall, crashing to the floor and smashing. There is a cheer from some school kids deep in the café, and I can feel my face burning red. "Great."

"You okay?" the voice asks.

"Just another thing," I say, bending down to pick up the shards.

"Be careful, you might cut yourself."

"You're very sweet, and very right," I say, putting the shards down and grabbing a broom. "Sorry, I'll just clean this up and then I'll grab your order. We're short, as I'm sure you can tell from all the—" I lift my head and immediately forget what words are. Grayson Murray is standing on the other side of the counter, a soft smile at the corners of his mouth. "Mess," I finish. I don't know if I'm referring to the state of the bar or myself.

The school rush is long over, and he's still in his uniform, so maybe he was staying late for some reason, or maybe he had detention. Why does the thought of him being a bad boy make me want him more?

"It's okay, you look like you've got your hands full," he says, nodding at the broom in my hand. "You look like you're about to burst into song."

Say something, I think. *Just talk to him. You already did. Just keep going. Make a joke. Come on.*

"I cannot think of a single musical theatre number that would be performed behind a coffee bar with a broom," I say. "Not that you would want to hear it from me."

He laughs, and my heart skips. "Songs in the key of E-Spresso."

"Coffee Crooning."

"Java jazz."

"I think I've run out."

"That's not a coffee pun," Grayson says with a wink.

I do my best to stay on my feet. I can feel Vicky staring at me from the other end of the bar. My heart is pounding so hard I'm surprised it's not cartooning its way out of my chest. I'm talking to him. I'm actually talking to him.

"What can I get you?" I ask, tapping the till screen to wake it up. I can see my reflection and it is not pretty. Good God, what must he think of me right now? He's either seen me startled by the closing of his locker or serving him coffee while looking like a sweaty mess. This is the bad place. Why can't I just bump into him while I'm looking my best like the book wants me to?

Grayson places his order and pays, lingering by the till for a little longer as I pass Vicky the cup and his order.

"What the hell is going on?" she hisses.

"Nothing," I say. "We're just talking."

"You know who that is, right? You haven't bashed your head and have amnesia or something?" she whispers. "That's Grayson Murray."

"Yes," I say, handing her the cup. "And that's his order."

When I get back to the till, he's still there, looking at his phone.

"Your order will be waiting for you at the other end of the bar," I say, for what has to be the millionth time that afternoon.

He pockets his phone and smiles at me. "Taylor, the Latte Boy," he says.

I blink. "Excuse me?"

"That's the song. Taylor, the Latte Boy," he says again. "The coffee shop song."

I nod. It is the last thing that I expect him to say. It's also the last song I would expect someone like Grayson Murray to know. I can't remember the last time I listened to it, it just doesn't come up on shuffle all that often. I'm running the lyrics in my head. But he's already walking away and I know that I'm losing him. I don't want this conversation to be over because who the heck knows when I'm going to get this opportunity again.

"Technically, you should be singing that to me," I say.

He stops and walks back to the counter. Got him.

"Why's that?"

"Well, the person singing it is the customer," I say. "So that makes you Kristen Chenoweth and me Taylor, the Latte Boy." He looks at me blankly. I keep talking. "They've not taught me how to make the coffee yet, so I don't know about that. Maybe next time."

He smiles. "Sure, maybe next time," he says as he looks down at my name tag and smiles. "Bye, Lucas."

My name sounds good in his voice. I want him to say it again.

Grayson heads out of Buttons and into the fading light of the winter afternoon. He looks back in one last time and I wave. He nods and tips his drink to me.

I feel like I'm floating.

"Okay, what the hell was that about?" Vicky asks. "You know you just said several sentences to him, the boy that you could barely speak to literally four days ago."

"I know," I say, watching as he walks away. "I…I don't know what happened. He caught me off guard and then I was being aloof."

"You've read the book!" she exclaims.

"That's the idea!" I reply. "But I was talking to him before I realised it was him, and suddenly we were just talking."

"You were bantering, that was banter. I would go so far as to call that flirting."

"Don't say it, don't even think it," I say, my heart beating so fast that it's practically humming.

It wasn't so bad. I spoke to Grayson, and it maybe wasn't so bad, and all I can hear echoing in the back of my mind is what my mum said on video and in her book. That was very much okay. I did okay.

FOURTEEN

I'M on cloud nine for the rest of my shift. I'm extra smiley with the customers and by the time I'm done at six, I'm exhausted, but I'm not sure I mind. Today feels like a success. I earned some money, and I spoke to the guy I like. What could be better?

When I've said my goodbyes to Vicky, I get changed in the staff room and hurry over to Max's place. They'll have been there since we finished school, doing homework, chatting, that kind of thing. And there is the demon in the back of my mind telling me that they're having way more fun without me.

"You're here! Finally!" Max exclaims as he opens the door. "I wasn't expecting you to show up for another half hour at least. I thought you were the pizza guy."

"Okay, so what you're saying is me being here is a disappointment?"

"Max! Hurry up! We're hungry!" Jasmine yells from the living room.

"I mean, I'm not, but Jasmine might eat you alive. She's been complaining about being hungry since she got here," Max says under his breath. He pulls me into a hug, giving me a tight squeeze before we head inside. *Oh, Max.*

Everyone is already gathered in the living room. There is a movie paused on the TV, papers and books scattered around as they no doubt flitted between actually doing homework and watching.

Julia Roberts is frozen on-screen, which tells me that Soph chose this film. She is sitting on one of the two sofas, and Max goes over to join her. Krish and Jasmine are on the floor, Jasmine with her head in Krish's lap. They all look up as I walk in, saying their hellos. I almost miss Jasmine's disappointment that I'm not carrying a stack of pizza boxes.

"Drinks are in the fridge," Max says. "Do you mind if we unpause the movie?"

"Go ahead," I say. "I've already seen it."

"How do you know what it is?" Krish asks.

"That hairstyle? That backdrop?" I shrug. "It's obvious. Notting Hill, come on, it's a classic."

"Told you he'd know," Soph says.

"Because I'm also just a girl," I say.

"Standing in front of a boy," she continues.

"Asking him to love her!" We finish in unison, descending into cackles, and my anxiety eases a little bit. Oh, what a friend we have in Julia Roberts.

"Can I get anyone anything?" I ask.

"I'll come with you," Jasmine says, bouncing to her feet. It's the last thing that I expect. "I wanted to say thank you," she says as we get out of earshot of everybody else.

"Sure," I say. "Um…why?"

She laughs. "Oh, um, the advice that you gave me the other day?" she says. "Well, you were right. I don't know why I didn't just ask you in the first place."

It's the closest that Jasmine has ever come to giving me a compliment, or really saying anything to me that's nice. We're not close in the way that she and Soph are. I've always felt like, to her, I am just a hanger-on. There is she and Krish, and she and Soph, and I'm just there.

"No problem. Coke?" I ask, getting two glasses out of the cupboard. She nods. "So everything's okay with you two now?"

"Shock, horror, I just needed to communicate with him better," she says with a shrug. "I've never been good at that. Being open has never really been my strong suit."

I finish pouring, and look up at her. She's looking right at me, and

I realise this is her trying to do the same thing with me. She's trying openness and communication. Considering we've never had anything close to that, I appreciate it.

"Well, good for you," I say. "I didn't mean to sound so flippant," I add. "If someone is new to you, it's hard to figure them out. I'm just glad you didn't mind me sticking my oar in."

She snorts and takes one of the glasses. "Of course not," she says. "He's not that hard to figure out, once you've figured him out."

I stare at her blankly. She's not making sense, but at least she's happy.

She raises her glass to me, and I clink mine against it.

"If you ever want to talk about that kind of stuff, you can talk to me, you know?" she says.

I've never thought about talking to Jasmine about anything. We barely talk about the weather, but she's making an effort and it would be rude of me to be shitty in this situation. I can't see a moment in the near future (or even the far future) where I will take her up on her offer, but what's the use in telling her that?

"Sure, that's really nice. Thanks, Jasmine," I reply.

"Like if you ever want to talk about relationship stuff or finding a boy that you like, I'm happy to help," she says. "You've helped me out with my problems. Let me help you out with yours?"

"My problems?"

"You know, being anxious all the time," she says, taking a sip of her drink. "If you put yourself out there, really tried instead of hanging out with us all the time you could find somebody."

It was like having a weird conversation with an aunt at a family gathering who can't figure out why you 'haven't found a nice girl yet.' I can feel my cheeks glowing red.

"And then we could be three couples instead of two and you."

I can't believe she's still talking, let alone about this.

"I mean, we talk about it sometimes, and I know Soph mentioned it to you the other night. It must make you feel a bit uncomfortable, right?"

I nod. I can't even find the words right now.

"You're around two couples all the time. It's just awkward, you know?"

Can she hear herself? Can she actually hear herself? Why aren't I telling her to fuck off? Why am I just nodding along, agreeing with her?

"We could help you with Grayson if you wanted. We know you like him. We've talked about it. We could find a way to set you up if you like—"

I open my mouth to respond but am blessedly interrupted by the doorbell. Jasmine practically skips out of the kitchen and towards the door, greeting the pizza delivery guy like her best friend in the world. I want to throw up.

"Come on, Luc, hurry it up!" Max calls from the living room.

A guy with a backbone would have talked back to Jasmine. A guy who was maybe a little surer of themselves and maybe a little bit more confident might have walked out of the house and not looked back. But I am not that guy. I *so* wish I was that guy, but I'm not.

So I walk into the living room and park myself on the end of the sofa, putting a couple of slices of pizza on a plate while the film continues. While Julia Roberts plays what is arguably one of her greatest roles to date in Notting Hill, I'm thinking about how my friends have all been talking about what a pathetic little saddo I am.

That's what she said, isn't it? They've all been talking about it, about how I could get a guy if I wanted to get a guy, but I'm just not trying hard enough. What Jasmine really just told me is that they're all uncomfortable with me hanging around them all the time, not the other way around. And it sucks. It sucks hard.

We're getting towards the end of the film when I notice that they've stopped laughing, stopped reacting, stopped reaching out to take the final slices of pizza. Julia Roberts and Hugh Grant are talking in a bookshop. They're about to fall in love again, and I realise that I'm the only one who is still awake.

Soph is sleeping on Max, Krish is leaning back against the edge of the sofa with Jasmine asleep on his lap. And I am sitting here, at nine PM, basically alone, watching Notting Hill. I've never felt more single. All I need is a tub of ice cream and the cliché is complete.

The credits roll and I am still sitting there, waiting for someone to wake up, for them to do something, to make a decision. And it strikes me that maybe that's my problem. Why am I always waiting for things to happen?

Everything Mum has said in her book is about doing, not waiting, being front-footed rather than allowing other people to run things.

I think back to the Julia Roberts/Hugh Grant moment in the bookshop. I had this today, didn't I? I had a romcom moment, the beginning of my little story. That was the meet-cute, wasn't it? I'm going to get my romcom ending. I have to. So I make a decision.

I wake them up, and I tell them that I'm leaving, that I'm tired from work, that I have to get up early for school in the morning. Max looks like he's about to follow me to the door, but stops himself, Soph still leaning on him, half asleep. And without another word, I go.

———

DAD ISN'T IN WHEN I GET HOME, SO I HEAD STRAIGHT UPSTAIRS. I'VE barely made it to my bed before I'm doomscrolling, landing on Grayson's Instagram profile and just staring at him. And he's staring back at me, looking all sorts of perfect. There's a selfie he's taken somewhere outdoors earlier in January, before we went back to school, when there was a smattering of snow on the ground.

His cheeks are tinged pink, his red hair is all the more vibrant against the stark white of the background, and he is smiling, laughing.

The screen goes dark. My phone's way of telling me that I've been staring for too long and I need to pull myself together. I see my face in the reflection of the screen and I look absolutely pathetic.

Who cares what Jasmine thinks? Who cares what my friends think? Vicky thinks I can do this, doesn't she? And it's been working. Sure, I've not done a lot more than say a few words to him, but that's more than I'd done this time last week, so that's something.

Suddenly, I remember what it was like to have him say my name. He knows my name now. That has to count for something.

I take Mum's book out of my bag and get back to reading. I'm reading about being aloof, about getting him to want you. Sure, I seem to have managed to do that by accident today, by not realising it was him I was talking to, but surely I can do it again. And I stumble upon gold.

Your opening line is essential. One that worked for me before my husband was "Fancy seeing you here."
Works. Every. Time.

I stand up and walk over to the mirror, leaving the book facedown on my bed. I really do look a state; a full day at school followed by a three-hour shift, followed by a depressing evening with my friends, does not become me. But I push past it.

"Fancy seeing you here," I say to my reflection. "Fancy seeing you here." I try it again and again and again, with different intonations. Now I just have to find a way to say it without stumbling all over it.

I go back to the book, throwing myself back onto my bed to keep reading.

Time to focus. I've got a boy to catch.

FIFTEEN

BE ALOOF (cont.)

There are a lot of dating manuals out there that will tell you to do one of two things. They will either tell you to flirt openly and aggressively with the guy you're trying to bag or they will tell you to ignore him entirely and let him chase you. I can go one better! I remember speeding through book after book after book, trying to find a word or a line to say to get some guy to be interested in me. And those lines just didn't exist, so let me give you a quick crash course on how to be aloof.

Your opening line is essential. One that worked for me before my husband was "Fancy seeing you here."

Works. Every. Time.

I AM on a mission the following morning. Dad isn't up yet when I leave the house, so I message Vicky on my way to school and she joins me halfway there.

"How was last night?"

I take a moment. I want to tell her what happened with my friends, what Jasmine said to me, but I still feel the need to protect them. I know they're not monsters. I feel like they're just looking out for me, but I don't want Vicky to see them in a bad light.

"It was nice," I reply. "I was knackered, though, so did a runner before the night was over. But then ended up reading, didn't I?"

Vicky's eyes light up at this.

"Tell me more."

We join the sea of students in identical uniforms, the volume suddenly going up a few decibels as we compete with everyone's conversations and the queue of cars.

"I watched more interviews. She was talking about the book, and I looked at the sections that she was talking about," I say.

"You skipped ahead?" She almost seems annoyed by it.

"No, not skipped ahead. I just read passages," I reply quickly. "I'm still in order. We're still at the next part of being aloof." I pause for a second. Thoughtful. "Was I aloof yesterday? Does that count?"

"It counts," she says. "I wrote about it like it counts. Did you?"

"Not yet."

"Luc!"

"What?" I say. "No one is reading it anyway."

"*I'm* reading it," she says. "This is an important part of the process here. You've got to be accountable. Homework. Update your blog."

"Okay, okay," I say. "But you really thought I was aloof with Grayson?"

Vicky shakes her head. "You're relentless," she says. "But yes. I think you handled it very well. And now that you've done it once, what's stopping you from doing it again?"

I pretend to think for a moment before letting it hit me like a light-bulb moment. "Oh right, that's it, crippling social anxiety."

"Wrong!" she snaps. "Nothing is stopping you from doing it again. You've got this!" She shrugs off her rucksack and pulls out her copy of the book, opening to a bookmarked page and reading.

"What are you doing? You can't read that here," I say, panicking.

"No one can see what I'm reading, Lucas."

"But what if someone does?" I say. "And if Grayson finds out—"

"He won't find out," Vicky says. "And even if he does, by that point, the two of you will be in such a fun, happy place that he'll just laugh about it. He'll be thankful for it."

She's still flicking through the book, and I'm flicking my gaze left and right, trying to make sure that nobody can see what she's doing.

No one is paying attention to her, but that doesn't stop me meerkating about the place and making myself look unhinged.

"We've made an impression," she says. "You were charming and funny and he waved at you after he left. You might have got him, just like your mum says."

My heart flutters and I feel colour tinge my cheeks. I like that thought very much. More of that, please.

"So the next thing we need to do is keep that going," she says. "He's not just going to ask you out, at least not straight away. Let's establish that connection, let's keep that moving."

"Why can't I ask him out?" I ask.

Vicky raises her eyebrow at me. "You think you can ask him out when you couldn't even talk to him last week?"

"Okay, hypothetically, why can't I ask him out?" She makes a very good point. If anything is going to make me stumble over my words and look like an idiot, that would definitely be it.

Vicky shakes her head. "The man is the one who needs to do the chasing and the asking here."

"But we're both men. That's kind of the whole point."

"Don't even get me started," Vicky groans. "The number of books that are focussed on hettys drives me absolutely nuts." She shakes her head. "It does make for interesting analysis, though."

"I can imagine," I say. "How was your evening?"

She shrugs. "Mum was mad that I was home so late. She thinks I work too hard, but in the same breath will get at me for not doing my homework. Go figure." She shakes her head.

We get to my locker and I start changing my books over, pulling out my English book and putting it in my bag. I still haven't touched Pride and Prejudice, and I know that Mrs Leighton is going to be gunning for me if I don't at least try and read it. I decide I'll make a concerted effort over lunch; I have to. She's my favourite teacher and if I don't start reading it, I'm about to become her least favourite. The perpetual people pleaser in me knows that would be bad. Very bad.

"Good morning."

I slam my locker closed and don't know if I jump at the loud clang or at the fact that Grayson Murray is now standing right in front of me.

Grayson Murray is standing RIGHT IN FRONT OF ME.

There he is, a big smile on his face, a strange sort of recognition, like he's seeing me here for the first time. And maybe he is. Maybe he's just never noticed me before.

Be cool, I think to myself. *Be cool, make a joke, say something funny. What did Mum say?*

'Your opening line is essential and one that worked for me… "Fancy seeing you here."'

"Fancy seeing you here," I say.

He smiles, he even laughs a little bit, and holy shit, my mum might actually be a genius. That piece of advice alone is probably why it sold so well.

"Is that your locker?" he asks.

Damn. More conversation. You can't say 'Fancy seeing you here' again, I think. *Or can I? Deep breaths, Luc, you've got this. SAY SOMETHING!*

"No, it's not," I reply quickly, the sweat no doubt visible on my brow. I think I can feel it dripping down my back. Who turned the heating up? "Found a key, thought I'd try a few out. Not yours, is it?"

He eyes me carefully, possibly trying to figure out if I've made a joke or not. I smile, and when he smiles back, I know that we are, blessedly, on the same page.

"Funny," he says. "How come I've never seen you here before?"

"I'm here every day," I say. "Maybe you just didn't notice."

"Well, now you are the keeper of the coffee, how can I not notice?" he says.

I shrug. "I keep myself to myself." Not exactly a lie, but hardly the truth. I lurk. That's what I do. "But I've noticed you."

"You did?"

"You're Grayson Murray, how can I not notice you?" I say.

He blinks, his cheeks reddening. Okay, maybe that was a little too forward. He smiles though, like he's pleased with himself. Whatever button I just pushed, his ego clearly likes it. Well done me.

"You're sweet," he says, turning to his locker and opening the door.

"Thanks."

With Grayson's face hiding behind the door to his locker, I turn to Vicky and widen my eyes in panic. She's grinning like the Cheshire Cat, apparently enjoying the spectacle of me attempting to flirt with him. She raises her eyebrows at me and gestures at Grayson, who is closing his locker.

I get the impression that I should have gathered myself and left, because the silence that's settled over us isn't altogether comfortable.

"I should probably go to my form class," I say, shouldering my bag and starting towards the opposite corridor. "I guess you'll see me around."

"Now that I know you, I guess I will," he says. "If you want to leave it to chance, that is."

I stop and turn back to him. "Sorry?"

"There's a party a week from Saturday at my house," he says. "Really casual, just a few people coming. You probably know some of them. You'd be more than welcome to join us. Both of you."

I open my mouth to respond, but I have no idea what the bloody hell I'm supposed to say. We haven't covered this part. We'd gotten as far as being aloof, but I have no idea what I'm supposed to do when he asks me to do something.

My brain goes into a sudden spiral. Is it a date? No, of course it isn't a date, he's invited me to a party, other people will be there. Is he just being polite? Why? And now he's staring at me, waiting for a response, and here I am, mouth gaping like a fish. All semblance of cool has melted away.

"Um—I—" I want to say yes, but how do I say, "Absolutely fucking yes, Grayson!" while still being cool and aloof?

"Can't," Vicky interjects. "You were coming with me to that family thing next Saturday, weren't you, Luc?"

I look back at her, my eyes wide, confused, questioning. What is she playing at?

"Um—"

"Typical of you to forget," she says again with a little more force. "My Mum's birthday, she said I could bring somebody."

I'm still fumbling to find words, Velma on the floor scrabbling around for her glasses. What is she doing? *My glasses!*

"That's fine," Grayson says, closing the door to his locker and turning the key. "If you were free, I thought it might be fun." He shrugs. "If you change your mind, just come. It would be good to see you. If you can make it. No pressure."

He's so calm, so collected, like he does this every day. And I'm here getting flustered purple because he's looking at me for once instead of through me. It feels like a miracle. I've flicked a switch somewhere, and it's all suddenly working.

"Alright," I say. "I'll let you know."

He nods. "Okay, you'll let me know," he parrots, raising his eyebrows and smiling at me like I've said something strange.

I don't think he's mocking me, but it's enough to make my cheeks go pink, in case they weren't already luminescent.

"Bye."

"Bye," I say as he walks away, my hand hanging in the air where, for some reason, I have decided it was a good idea to wave to him.

Why am I waving?

Put your arm down, Lucas.

Lucas?

LUCAS!

"Lucas!" Vicky swats at my arm, apparently perfectly in sync with my inner monologue. "Did you see that?"

"Yes," I say, turning to her sharply. "I did see that. Grayson just asked me to do something, and I said no. Surely that was the perfect opportunity to get to know him a little better and now that you turned him down, who's to say he'll ever ask me again?"

"Oh, you're going to that party," Vicky says, starting down the corridor.

Now I'm even more confused.

"If I'm going to the party, then why did you say no?" I ask.

"Lucas, you seem to forget that I've already read the book cover-to-cover," she says. "You're going to that party, but you're not agreeing to go to the party the second he invites you to the party. Do you follow?"

"I literally could not be more lost."

"You're going to the party," she starts again. "But he's not going to know you're going to the party until you show up. The book says that when he asks you out, you need to be unavailable."

"That seems impossible."

"Hence why I made up an event," she says. "We go to the fake event and show up at the party a little late, just like the book says, and that's when you get a chance to get to know him better. And because you're going to the party when he thought you weren't going, he'll be extra pleased to see you there. Your presence is a gift."

She lets out a heavy breath.

I am absolutely floored by this. First smiling and "fancy seeing you here," and now this. Maybe Mum was onto something after all. I mean, the book sold well for a reason, right?

"So, I am going to the party," I say. "He doesn't know it yet."

"Exactly."

"And what am I supposed to do in the meantime?"

Vicky cannot stop herself from smiling. She's giving off big evil villain vibes. I'm half expecting her to cackle maniacally.

"Now, the game begins."

SIXTEEN

GETTING TO KNOW YOU
Make His Interests Your Interests

Now that you're on his radar and are acting aloof (please tell me you're acting aloof) the time has come to make yourself more visible to him than you ever have before.

So, you find out that he enjoys reading books, maybe you read a couple of his favourites so you can talk to him about them. Or you find out he enjoys going to the gym, maybe you start working out, maybe even at the same place in the hope that you'll bump into him.

The theory behind this is that he'll see you as a match, someone he can share his favourite things with. Of course, it is possible that none of your interests will crossover. If that's the case, then maybe this isn't the man for you. But if you want to fake it until you make it, who am I to stop you?

VICKY HAS the next section practically memorised, talking me through it on our way to my form class. I need to figure out what Grayson is interested in. It's never occurred to me before. I thought that was something I would figure out when we actually started hanging out, but the book says to know beforehand.

"I know he likes coffee," I say. He's been in the coffee shop three times now and, because it's Grayson, I know what his order is. "But that's about it."

"Coffee isn't going to be enough," Vicky says, stopping outside my form class. "I have to go or I'm going to be late, but figure it out. Stalk his Instagram or something."

I opt not to tell her that I do that on a daily basis anyway, and he's still an enigma. I may have to figure it out the old-fashioned way and hope that one of our interests aligns somewhere.

But he was disappointed that I wasn't going to his party. Vicky saw it too. So that feels like progress.

———

THE DAY ROLLS BY AND I'M DISTRACTED AS ALL HECK, BUT AT LEAST nothing major is happening today. Just the same old lessons. There are a few classes throughout the day that I share with Grayson and now, instead of not noticing I'm there while I stare at him from across the room, I get a little wave when I walk inside.

It gets weird looks from my friends, especially Max, but I'm not about to question it, nor am I going to explain it. Grayson Murray knows who I am. It feels like a miracle.

"What's that about?" Soph asks, as I sit down in Chemistry. "Since when did you know Grayson?"

I shrug, trying to brush it off, but I can feel my cheeks going pink. "He comes to Buttons," I reply. "I fumbled over his order, obviously made an impression."

Soph shakes her head and tuts at me. "You're a liability."

"Duh, stop acting like you don't already know that."

"But hey," she says, "this is a good sign, right?"

"What do you mean?"

"Well," she says, "if he's waving at you, saying hello at school, who knows what could happen?"

"Yeah," I say. "Maybe."

Her eyes go so wide they look like they're about to pop out of her head. She grabs hold of my arm and squeezes it tight.

"What are you doing?" I ask.

"Lucas, you basically acknowledged that you're going to try and talk to this boy," she says. "Where has this come from?"

I would love to tell her about the book. I'd love to tell her what I've been getting up to with Vicky, but…I can't. She hangs out with Grayson sometimes outside of school, and all it would take is one slip of the tongue and all of this goes away. I want to at least give this a shot first.

"I am now the keeper of the coffee," I say. "He has no choice but to talk to me and…I don't know…when I'm forced to talk to him, I manage to be quite charming."

"Now *that* I have to see!"

"Between the stumbling and fumbling and dropping plates, I can be quite charming."

"You dropped plates?"

"Only five."

"Lucas!" she says with a laugh, before turning back to her work.

We still haven't properly had a chance to chat since she tried to talk to me earlier in the week. I know she said it was all sorted, but there's a part of me that feels bad for not being there for her, and feeling like I've been replaced by Jasmine.

I decide to try and approach it again, even if Mr Edwards, and his way-too-tight trousers, is trying to teach us Chemistry from the front of the room.

"You okay?" I ask under my breath, keeping my gaze on the whiteboard so that it looks like I'm totally focussed on the carbon cycle.

Sophie openly looks at me like I've just grown an extra head. "What, me?"

"No, the person on the next bench," I say dryly. "Of course you."

She shrugs. "Fine, yeah, why?"

I look at her. She's keeping her gaze focussed on the board, taking notes in her perfect, loopy handwriting, trying to look every bit the good student. But even with that, something still isn't quite right. There's a sparkle missing. I can't place it. But if she tells me she's fine, what else can I do?

"Just wondered," I say. "We've not had a lot of time to talk recently."

She shrugs again. "I've been busy," she says. "You've been busy with Vicky. It is what it is."

My anxious brain kicks into high gear because she's brought up Vicky. She's noticed that I've not been around. I mean, I'm glad that she's noticed, I guess. At least I know she's still thinking about me. But now I'm worried that the only reason she's thinking about me is because she hates me.

"We're okay, aren't we?"

"Lucas Cook, see me after class," Mr Edwards calls from the front of the room.

He's stopped writing on the board and is staring at me through his little rectangular glasses. Handsome and intimidating, Mr Edwards is both one of my favourite and least favourite teachers. He's very nice to look at, but if you're not focussing in his class (and I rarely am, let's be real) he will call you out on it. And now I'm in trouble.

The class falls into a deadly silence, a collective knowledge that, for today, Mr Edwards is not to be messed with, and we all go back to focussing on what he's doing at the whiteboard.

I clock Grayson staring at me from the other side of the room, a smirk on his face. At least he finds it funny instead of thinking I'm a dickhead.

Sophie nudges me to get my attention, tapping on the corner of her exercise book. She writes something and then points again.

"Of course we are. <3"

I breathe a sigh of relief and she reaches a finger across the workbench to me, ET style. I press the tip of my index finger to hers and we go back to the lesson. Everything is fine. Thank goodness.

―――――

GROUP CHAT

SOPH

We on for Saturday night?

MAX

Y

KRISH

Y

JASMINE

Of course! Can't wait!

SOPH

Luc?

LUC?

@Lucas Cook?

Sorry, I'm at work.

JASMINE

Saturday night?

No, work late Saturday. And early Sunday morning.
Sorry. Next time?

LUC & MAX

MAX

Boo and hiss to you not coming on Saturday.

Sorry. Work has to come first right now.

Is everything okay?

What do you mean?

You're working a lot. Just checking in.

All good. Have fun on Saturday. I'll try and come
next time?

Good xx

How are YOU?

All good. Just miss you.

You too xx

———

Before I know it, it's the weekend and I'm back at Buttons once again. Grayson even comes in at one point, but Harry is on the till, so they serve him. Even if I did try and speed through the transaction so I had an excuse to talk to him again.

"You know him?" Henry asks.

"Sort of," I say. "Getting to know him. Why?"

Henry hesitates. "No reason."

I feel guilty that I'm not going out with my friends on Saturday, but nobody makes me feel bad about it. And I've not exactly lied, just not told the whole truth. I'm working until about seven on Saturday, but the reason I'm not going out is that I definitely can't afford it. I've not even been paid by Buttons yet and I know Dad needs some of that money.

I feel worse that I've not told Max the whole truth. I'm working on the tills, and realise that I can feel us drifting apart. It makes me unbearably sad, like a weight sitting on my chest. We've been best friends for forever. I can't remember a time in my life without him, and now... Now, I'm not so sure.

It seems to have been forgotten by the time Monday rolls around. There's a little bit of awkwardness in the morning, but I'm fairly sure I'm imagining things.

With me working like a dog over the weekend, I still haven't cracked the spine of Pride and Prejudice. Now, I'm sitting in Mrs Leighton's Monday afternoon class again, the themes inherent in the story being discussed at length by other members of the class, and here I am feeling equal parts unprepared and really, really stupid. This is not how this was supposed to go. *Why, oh why, am I like this?*

"Please make me read this freaking book," I whisper to Sophie.

"You still haven't read it?" she hisses. "How can you not have read it?"

"You haven't read it either!"

"I read the first chapter," she protests. "And watched the Kiera Knightly film. That counts, right?"

"Oh my God."

"Something you'd like to share with the class, Mr Cook?" Mrs Leighton says. The class goes silent, every pair of eyes turning to me as I become more and more tomato-like with every passing second.

First rule of trying not to get noticed by your teacher in class: don't talk to your best friend across the aisle.

"No," I say. "Nothing, sorry."

"No, no," she says, offering me the room like it's a gift rather than an embarrassing punishment. "By all means, Lucas, tell us what scintillating conversation you were having that was more important than your exams, hmm? What were you saying that was more important to you than this book?"

"Sorry, Miss," I say. "Won't happen again."

She breathes a heavy sigh that seems to drag her whole body down, like gravity has its vice-like grip on her.

"I'm not doing this for the good of my health," she says, walking back over to the whiteboard. One tick if you had that particular cliché on your Teacher Bingo Card. "This is your time that you're wasting." Oooh, another one. Two for the price of one, aren't you lucky? "Lucas, if you could stick around after class today, I'd like to have a word."

I turn my attention back to my exercise book as Mrs Leighton continues her lesson, the time dragging on towards the end of the class.

I look towards Grayson at the front of the classroom, studiously paying attention to Mrs Leighton, sometimes even contributing something intelligent. At least I think it's intelligent. I haven't read the book so I couldn't possibly say whether it's actually relevant. Either way, it's something else to distract me as the time goes by.

"What's happening?" Mrs Leighton asks me at the end of the class.

Everyone else has left, the corridor has gone eerily quiet, and Mrs Leighton is giving me Classic Teacher vibes, looking over the top of her glasses at me, disappointment etched in every line on her face.

She's not the kind of teacher who yells, she's the kind of teacher who guilt trips you until you wish you were no longer breathing.

"You're usually so focussed, so here, and this term you've been elsewhere. What's going on, Lucas? How are things at home?"

"I'm sorry," I say. "Things are fine. I've just got a lot on at the moment and it's all getting in the way. Sorry."

She takes her glasses off, folding them and putting them on her desk. "Is there something you want to talk about? Anything I can help with?"

Mrs Leighton is probably the last person I want to talk to about any of this stuff. She's fantastic, she really is, but I'm not about to talk romance with my English teacher. They may be a gay boy's best friend, but not when it comes to—and I cannot stress this enough—*this*.

"Just struggling to juggle it all and consequently fucking it all up," I say flatly, silently cursing myself when I realise I've just sworn in front of a teacher. Irony.

"I'll pretend I didn't hear that," Mrs Leighton says, unable to stop herself from smirking. "It's not an easy book, and it's not an easy class, but you're in top set English for a reason. You just need to apply yourself."

"I know, I just—"

There is a knock at the door, and Grayson pokes his head around the frame to look in. He looks sheepish, and double-takes when he sees me still standing there. Maybe he was expecting me to get a little slap on the wrist and then leave.

"Sorry," he says. "I meant to pick up the assignment from you, Mrs Leighton. I totally forgot."

I blink, a wave of panic suddenly falling over me. Was I really so unfocussed that I missed hearing about an assignment? Shit.

"Calm down, Luc, you didn't miss anything," Mrs Leighton says. "He's talking about the Creative Writing Group assignment for this week. He had to leave early last Wednesday." She pulls a sheet from her desk drawer and hands it to Grayson. "I look forward to seeing what you do with this one, Mr Murray."

"Thanks, Miss," he says.

"You should take a leaf out of his book, Luc," she says. "I still think you should consider the Creative Writing Group. It's not a big commitment and being creative can be a fantastic outlet for stress and worry. Get some of those big thoughts out of that head of yours and on the page. Turn it into art."

"You write?" Grayson says to me.

"A bit," I reply. "Not a lot, mostly for class."

"Convince him to come with you, Grayson," Mrs Leighton pleads. "I've been trying to get him to join us. The more the merrier, right?"

Grayson smiles at me. "It is fun," he says. "Sorry, I feel like we're ganging up on you."

"Gang up on him, Grayson, twist his arm," Mrs Leighton says with a laugh. Her mood has lifted since Grayson has interrupted. I think he might have saved my ass. "Okay, both of you home. Take this with you," she adds, handing me the Creative Writing assignment. "Just in case you change your mind."

"You're relentless," I say.

"And you're not realising your full potential," she says. "I wrote it in your report. Don't think I'm too shy to say it to your face." She winks at me and shoos us out of her classroom. The corridor is absolutely dead, every last student has left the school. How long was I in there?

"Sorry about that," Grayson says. "You don't have to come if you don't want to."

"Do you...do you want me to?" I ask, turning to face him. We're the only ones left in the corridor and there is this strange sort of electricity between us. I can't see it, but by God, I can feel it. Like the push-pull of a magnet.

We lock eyes and I don't know if something is about to happen, but if it is, I can't remember what I had for lunch, or what my breath might smell like. Do I need to stop this and have a mint first or something? Do I even have any?

He shrugs, and it breaks the spell. "You can come if you want," he says. "It's fun."

We stand there in silence for a little while longer. The sheet of paper is getting more and more crumpled in my hand.

"I should probably go," he says, pointing down the corridor. "But maybe I'll see you tomorrow?"

I nod. "If you're lucky."

He lingers for a moment longer. I don't know what it means. Is there anything more to say? I hope there is.

"Bye, then," he says, saluting me awkwardly before turning to leave. I watch him go.

Did that just happen?

SEVENTEEN

"THERE IS no two ways about it, you're absolutely going to that Creative Writing Group," Vicky says as we walk out of school. "It's perfect!"

"Doesn't it feel like I'm intruding?" I say. "I'm barging in on something that Grayson does, something that...I mean, sure I have an interest in it too, but I've spent years telling Mrs Leighton that I don't want to go."

"But it's just fallen into your lap, Luc," Vicky says. "Come on."

She has a very good point, of course. Although, I've been avoiding going to the Creative Writing Group successfully for the last three years, partly for Dad reasons, partly because...I don't know.

I've always thought I was alright at writing. Mrs Leighton has always said so, and so have other teachers, but opening yourself up to be publicly critiqued like that? Add that to my anxious, people-pleasing brain and you can bet your life by the end of the first session I will be crying on the floor.

"What's got you so bent out of shape?" she asks.

"How long have you got?"

"Luc."

"What?"

"I'm being serious."

"Me too," I reply, but I know that won't be enough. She's staring daggers into the side of my head. "It's Dad," I add.

"Yeah, cool, definitely going to need a little more than that," she says, the eye roll implied.

"The Mum connection," I say. Everything always seems to come back to Mum. If she were here, this wouldn't be a problem.

We stop at Vicky's turning, moving out of the way of the other students exiting the school behind us.

"I'm not going to force you to do it," she says. "I don't want you to do anything that's going to hurt your dad, but think about it, okay? It's something you're interested in already, so minimal deception on your part, and you get to hang out with Grayson and learn more about him."

She makes it sound so appealing. I've spent so much time admiring him from afar that every conversation I've had with him feels like some kind of fever dream. But what will Dad say?

"I'll talk to him," I say. "But if he's…really not keen on the idea—"

"We can find something else," Vicky says. "I have no idea what, but we'll figure it out."

———

I CAME HOME TO FIND DAD COOKING UP A STORM IN THE KITCHEN, SO I took that as the perfect excuse not to bother him. I went upstairs and actually committed some time to reading Pride & Prejudice. It turns out the book isn't totally terrible, it just feels like it's written in a totally different language.

I read and make notes until Dad calls me down for dinner. He's made what can only be described as a feast. For some reason, he's decided that tonight is the perfect time to cook the two of us a full roast. There is a hefty joint of pork on the table, more potatoes than either of us could possibly eat, and a mound of vegetables that, when surrounded by all the rest of the food, actually manage to look appetising.

"What's all this?" I ask.

"The phrase you're searching for is, 'Thank you,' and you are very welcome," Dad replies, heading to the fridge and grabbing himself a beer.

He's in a good mood, a really good mood. There must be good

things happening on the work front, because I can't see a way we can afford this otherwise. If there was ever a time for me to have a conversation with him that's even vaguely related to Mum, this is one hundred percent it.

"Tuck in," he says as he sits down. "I think the roast potatoes might be some of my best. I'm not going to tell you how I did it, just taste them first. You're going to die."

"Dad, I have something I want to talk to you about," I say quickly.

The mood in the room suddenly shifts. He's looking at me with this serious Dad expression on his face, brows knitted together, hands pressed to his mouth. He is the living embodiment of the present parent and I feel like I've built this up too much.

"I'm thinking of going to the Creative Writing Group at school," I say.

As quickly as the mood came, it dissipates, like sunshine clearing the early morning mist. Dad lets out a big breath. I have no idea what he was expecting me to say, but I imagine that me wanting to write wasn't in the top ten.

"Not what I thought you were going to say," he says with a chuckle. "Actually, I'm not sure what I thought you were going to say. Last time you looked all serious like that, you told me you were gay."

"I know, I know," I say. "I just…I didn't know how to approach it."

"Okay," he says, nodding. "You've never… We've never… This hasn't come up for a while. Where has this come from?"

I'm not about to sit here and tell my dad that I am doing this because I want to get closer to a boy. I could do without that level of awkwardness, thank you very much.

"Mrs Leighton pulled me aside today after class to talk to me about it," I say. "She said how good my pieces were at the end of last term, but thinks I would benefit from some critique and rewrites."

"Can she not offer you that privately?"

I shrug. "I think she means from my peers, other people who are writing," I say. "And, I don't know, it seems like a good idea. It might look good on my CV and stuff for when I am applying for Uni in a few years. Stuff like this adds up, you know?"

He looks thoughtful, his eyes crinkled, his brow furrowed, his mouth pinched, and I hate all of it. I look away and shovel a few roast potatoes onto my plate, distracting myself until he's managed to process what I've said.

"That makes sense," he says. "I think you should go if you want to go. If you think it will help. You don't need to ask my permission."

He nods. "You're usually with your friends Wednesday anyway, or at work now, right? It makes no difference to me," he says. "You know your mum used to have a Creative Writing Group that she went to." He grabs a serving spoon and starts serving himself some vegetables.

I'm stunned that he's even mentioned her. I don't want to make a thing of it, but it feels like such a big deal right now.

"Oh, yeah?" I say.

"She loved it," he says. "She'd go there—I think it was every Tuesday night. Every week they would present something new and she'd always get so stressed out about it before she went and then always come back absolutely full of beans because it had gone better than she thought. You're having veggies, right?"

"Um—"

"Not a question, Luc. Pass me your plate."

I do as I'm told, and he starts piling broccoli and cabbage next to my roasties.

"She was writing a romcom, something Nora Ephron-y is what she would tell me when I asked her what it was about. She was struggling with the pitch line more than anything. She'd sort of manage to explain it in these big scenes, able to tell me what happens but not what the plot was."

"Oh, no."

"I know, she'd get in such a muddle," he says, smiling fondly at the memory. I can feel myself welling up just listening to him. "She'd been riding the success of the other book for so long, she'd written a few things that hadn't stuck, but that romcom was what she really wanted to be doing."

"How far did she get?"

"I think she was most of the way through the first draft," he says, handing me back my plate. "She was writing it while you were at school. I think I remember her saying she'd nearly finished it

113

when…" He gets this faraway look in his eyes, and scans the table, like the words that have fallen off the edge of his tongue are hiding amongst the cauliflower. The tears come so fast I think they even catch him by surprise. He swallows hard.

"Dad, I'm—"

"I forgot the gravy," he says, jumping to his feet and going back over to the kitchen.

It was going really well for a moment there, wasn't it?

When he comes back with the pot of gravy, he starts to talk about work like the conversation we've just had didn't even happen, but the joy is gone, his smile has vanished, he's gone all serious again. I almost want to try and divert us back, but he's talking so fast that I can't even get a word in.

He's starting at a new restaurant tomorrow night, so he won't be home in the evening, but there will likely be leftovers of this if I want to heat it up. And then he asks me how school was and any mention of Mum drifts out of the kitchen, like it never happened, like she was never even here.

EIGHTEEN

GETTING TO KNOW YOU
Make His Interests Your Interests (Cont.)

A note on how to behave when you're in this setting with him.

The first thing you should do is to get to know your target a little better. You can talk about the activity you're participating in, or not, it's up to you.

The other is an opportunity to observe them outside of their natural habitat, i.e., where you met them. It's one thing to see someone out in a bar or restaurant or even at work, but seeing them in a different setting allows you to observe them a little closer.

You are the David Attenborough of the dating world, a veritable Louis Theroux. Enjoy.

"REALLY? HE JUST TOTALLY SHUT DOWN?" Vicky asks.

"Yep," I say, pulling my coat around myself. "This has to be child abuse, right? I feel like I'm dying out here."

We're sitting outside because Mr Marshall decided that the Geography block is no place for students to spend lunchtime. We should be outside enjoying ourselves, getting Vitamin D (insert penis joke here), and freezing our faces off.

I look over at my friends for reassurance that they are also having a terrible time, only to see that Jasmine and Sophie are huddled close, whispering about something, while Max and Krish are off playing football with Grayson, so at least there's some eye candy happening. Silver lining. He keeps looking over. It's enough to make me feel at least a little bit warm.

"Are you alright?" Vicky asks.

"Me?" I ask. "Yeah, I'm fine. Why would I not be alright?"

"Lucas, seriously, your dad just totally shut down about your mum, again," she says. "We can talk about it if you want. I don't mind."

"He's done it before." I shrug. "But you missed the best part. He actually talked about her. Like, he was excited, smiling and enjoying himself. It was weird but really, really cool. I've not heard him say more than a few words about her in a long time."

"And she'd written a whole other book?"

I nod. "He said it was a romcom. Not altogether surprising, I guess, given her other book," I say. "It's exciting. I wonder what it was like."

"Your mum was a great writer," Vicky says bluntly. "It was probably sensational. If it had ever seen the light of day, maybe she would have had another success on her hands. You never know."

"Maybe."

"Honestly, that's what I think worked about this book," Vicky says. "The storytelling parts of it, where she's talking about how she met your dad and stuff, those are the parts that really pop off the page. The advice itself can be a bit questionable at times, as we know, but the storytelling is sound."

I'm smiling. It's strange to have this now be my default reaction about the book, when just a couple of weeks ago whenever someone brought it up (which, admittedly, wasn't all that often) I felt like I was going to have a heart attack. The change is welcome and I'm beaming at the thought that someone appreciates what Mum made.

"What are you looking so happy about?" Soph says, shuffling over to me, her hands stuffed in her pockets. "It's freezing, be miserable like us."

"Why are you walking like a penguin?"

"They never freeze to death. I figured they must be onto something," she says. "I'm extending the circle."

"Because Jasmine's boring?"

"Rude!" Jasmine snaps, letting out a loud cackle that flies up into the cold air, carried off on the breeze.

I mean, I'm not entirely joking, but at least she took it as such.

"What are you two up to later?" Soph asks.

"Um—" I start.

"I reserve the right to withhold my plans until I know what you're offering," Vicky says with a smirk. "Just in case."

"Smart lady," Sophie replies. "We usually go to one of ours on Wednesdays, sort of a ritual, we do homework—"

"We do not," I interrupt.

"We intend to do homework," Sophie corrects. "And then just hang out and watch a film. But we thought that maybe to combat this horrific weather, a hot beverage was in order. Fancy going to Buttons before we head to Max's?"

"Buttons?" I repeat.

"You know, where you work now so you don't have to hang out with us at the weekends," Jasmine says. There's a smile on her face, but there is definitely something behind those words, something that feels a little sharp, a little stabby.

"I thought it might be fun," Soph says, trying to diffuse things.

"It might be," I say.

"We could use your discount too, Luc," Jasmine adds. "Means we can all go large without feeling like we're breaking the bank."

I try not to be too frosty with Jasmine, but I turn my attention back to Sophie. In the excitement of The Creative Writing Group, I forgot about our Wednesday night study dates.

"I can't tonight," I say. "We could do tomorrow, though? Or the day after?"

"We always hang out on Wednesdays," Sophie says. "That's our thing. Why can't you do tonight?"

"Do what?" Max has appeared at Soph's side, his face bright red either from the cold or the exercise.

He runs a hand through his hair, which is a little damp from sweat and is sticking up wildly. Krish isn't far behind, hands on the back of his head, desperately trying to get the air back into his lungs.

People who voluntarily do exercise are absolutely out of their minds. I keep my eye out for Grayson, but he's disappeared. There was a small part of me that was hoping he'd make his way over here. That would have been nice.

"We were going to go to Buttons tonight before our study sesh, but Lucas has plans, apparently," Jasmine says, her tone pointed again. "Since when do you make plans on a Wednesday? Are you working again?" Her spikiness today is really beginning to rub me up the wrong way.

"Plans?" Krish asks. "Where are you off to, Luc? Got a hot date?"

Soph laughs, as does Jasmine, both of them enjoying the joke a little too much. Knowing that they've been talking about me and my romantic life (or lack thereof) behind my back has me feeling all sorts of sensitive about that right now. I try to shake it off.

"No, nothing like that," I say, putting a brave face on it.

"Then what?" Soph says. "Why don't you want to hang out with us?"

"That's not what it is," I reply, because Sophie actually looks wounded and that's the last thing I want right now. "It's just I'm going to the Creative Writing Group tonight."

"You're what?" Soph says.

"Mrs Leighton asked me to yesterday," I say. Not exactly a lie, but not the whole truth either.

"She asks you every week, Luc, why are you going now?"

"Wait, doesn't Grayson go to that?" Max asks. "Are you going with Grayson?"

"Sort of," I say. "He was there when she asked and he kind of… convinced me to go."

Everyone is looking at me, confused, like this was information that I should have disclosed to them sooner. What difference does it make to them that I'm talking to Grayson? Why are they all acting so weird?

The bell rings from somewhere off in the distance, steadily coming towards us as the rest of the bells catch up. It's like they're on a delay, a wave of noise screaming towards us, telling us to come back inside.

"Tell her you're sick or something," Max says. People have started moving past us now, their conversations threatening to drown us out. "Or that you have work to do. I feel like we never see you anymore."

I stop myself from saying that's because they keep hanging out without me.

"No," I say. "I said I would go, so I'm going."

Sophie looks at me like I'm out of my mind. "You never wanted to go before," she says. "You always said it was stupid and a waste of time."

"Well, maybe it's a waste of time I want to try. I might like it," I say, trying to stand firm.

Sophie shrugs. "Okay," she says. "It won't be the same without you, though."

"We could do it some other time," I say. "Like tomorrow, or even Friday. I just…I can't tonight. I promised."

"It's fine," Soph says, linking arms with Jasmine before starting back towards school. "Come on, we're going to be late. Mr Marshall will do his nut." She's not waiting, she's already walking off and I'm just watching her go.

"I have to get to my form class. You gonna be okay?" Vicky asks quietly.

"Yeah, fine, I'll see you later."

Krish has gone after Jasmine, and Vicky has headed back into school, so I'm standing out in the cold with Max, watching the space where Soph was just a few moments ago.

"I'm sorry I'm not coming tonight," I say to Max. "I didn't think… I sort of forgot and…" I take a breath, trying to steady myself. "I didn't think it would be such a big deal. It's one night."

"We've not seen you for a while," Max says. "I think that's all it is. And the Grayson stuff has come a little out of left field."

"We're just talking."

"But you never did before," Max says. "You couldn't even say two words to him."

"Okay," I say. "So I said two words to him and then it became more than two words and now…"

"Now what?" Max asks. "Are you going out with him or something?"

"No," I say. "We're…talking. That's all. It's one night. I'm just trying something out. Maybe I'll like it, who knows? I'm trying something new and suddenly I'm the bad guy?"

"We just want to see you, Luc," he says. "*I* want to see you."

It's one thing for him to say it over text, but a whole other thing for him to say it to my face. He looks wounded, like he might need me or something. It's not the Max I'm used to. I've always been the one who needs putting back together, the one who needs him. It feels strange.

I want to ask him if he's okay, but we seem to have drifted recently. And he has Soph for that, right?

"Can we go inside? I'm fucking freezing," I say.

Max grabs hold of me and pulls me into a hug, one that I gladly reciprocate. I've missed him. When did everything get so strained?

"What's this for?" I ask.

"I miss you, Luc," he says. "I feel like I never see you anymore."

"I'm a busy boy," I say, trying to keep my tone upbeat even though the thought of Max missing me breaks my heart a bit. "Sorry."

"And you're different," he says.

"I'm different?"

"Yeah," he says, pulling out of the hug to look me in the eye.

"Different how?"

"You're just…less Luc-like," he says. "That sounds bad. I don't mean it to sound bad. You're just changing."

And he's right. Maybe I have changed over the past couple of weeks. Maybe reading this book, trying out different things, and trying to step into my life a little bit more, I am different. Is that so wrong?

"Maybe that's not such a bad thing," I say. "I'm still Lucas, though."

"I know," he says. "Just…don't change too much. I'll miss you even more."

NINETEEN

I DON'T SEE Soph for the rest of the day. We don't have Maths together because I am notoriously shit at numbers and she is some kind of genius at everything so it's the only class in any given week where I don't really know anybody, at least not in the same way I know Soph.

I can't focus on whatever super confusing Maths bullshit Mrs Dhawan is writing on the whiteboard. There are too many letters and too many numbers, and it is all going over my head. Thankfully, she prefers a silent classroom, so I manage to get away with copying notes from the board that I don't have a single hope of understanding and then vanishing quietly as soon as the bell rings. Blessings aplenty.

By the time I make it to Mrs Leighton's class after school, there is already a crowd gathered outside. Grayson included. He is talking to Mr Bird, a teaching assistant who started with the new term. He used to go to school here apparently, not too long ago. I don't remember him. I feel like I would. He's tall, hugely tall in fact, towering over Grayson and therefore towering over me even more. His shoulders are hunched where he's trying to make himself smaller, that much I can tell, but whatever he's talking to Grayson about has him smiling.

"New recruit," he says to Mr Bird as I approach. My cheeks definitely flush pink.

"Aha! Mr Cook, you finally caved," Mr Bird says, his dimples popping in his cheeks as he gives me a smile. "Mrs Leighton is going to be thrilled."

The fact that he seems happy to see me puts me at ease somewhat, but I'm also painfully aware of the fact that I am standing right next to Grayson and our arms are literally touching right now. I mean, there are shirts and blazers and coats between us, but still. I am a mess.

"Sorry, I'm so late!" Mrs Leighton is bustling down the corridor, a stack of papers in her arms, her glasses half hanging off her face. She stops dead when she reaches us. "Lucas, you actually came."

She's so excited to see me here, and I'm feeling more embarrassed by the second that I'm only here because a boy I like is in this class. I feel a bit pathetic.

I wonder if Meatloaf would have crashed a Creative Writing Group in the pursuit of true love or if that fell under, "But I won't do that"?

The tables are rearranged into a circle in the centre of the room, making the whole thing look a little too much like group therapy for my liking. Before I've really had a chance to register what's going on, everyone seems to have found somewhere to sit, and I'm left standing by the door.

"I suppose this saves me the effort of bringing it up," Mrs Leighton says, gesturing to me by the door. "This is Lucas Cook from my Year 11 top set English; he's joining us for the first time today. I've been trying to get him to join us since last year, so never let it be said that I'm a quitter."

"Hello," I say, waving awkwardly, still standing by the door like I'm debating whether or not to make an escape. And I am. There are a few responses, muttered hellos, a couple of waves. Now or never, Lucas, if you're going to run, you need to go now.

"Grab a chair, Lucas, join us," Mrs Leighton says, beckoning me over. "There's a space next to Mr Bird. Shuffle up everybody, shuffle up."

I take a seat next to Mr Bird, which puts me directly opposite Grayson. He's looking at me, a soft smile on his face as we wait for Mrs Leighton to start the session.

"Okay," Mrs Leighton says, clapping her hands. "We're going to start with readings this week. Luc—" She turns her attention to me and my stomach falls into my feet. "Every week we start with readings. What people have been working on over the week based on the prompt, getting us ready for the presentation at the end of half term. I know you didn't get the prompt until yesterday so, for this week, I'll let it slide. But next week we'll start with you."

"Thanks," I reply.

"Grayson," she says. "You're up."

Grayson shifts about in his chair, clearing his throat a couple of times before he starts. He looks up, taking in the faces of his classmates staring back at him. It's probably the first time I've ever seen him look unsure of himself. Whenever he's with his friends or in class, he always looks so confident.

Suddenly I feel like I shouldn't be here, like I'm intruding on some private moment that he has during these classes, a chance to express himself. But I can't leave. I'm stuck. He takes a breath and starts to read.

It's poetry, and I realise that I would have known what was coming had I paid attention to the prompt. He's unsure as he starts, his voice shaking a little, and then he gets into it, finding the rhythm, the words slipping off his tongue and dancing around each of us. He's good. And something about him being good makes me more than a little swoony.

When he finishes, there is a small round of applause before people start giving him feedback, suggestions, ways he could improve it, most of which is prefaced with, "I thought it was really great, but…"

It's hard to be critical because it feels so personal. Were it not my first time, maybe I'd say something about how some of it didn't quite scan or that there were parts that felt a little self-indulgent, but there are others who cover all of that.

He bristles a little at some of the comments, and I can see he wants to respond, but maybe I'm misreading his reactions or something, because he stays quiet and thanks everyone when they're done.

When his feedback is finished, he lets out a big breath and flops back into his chair. He locks eyes with me and mouths, "Phew!"

I give him a thumbs up. It feels awkward and I hate myself the second I've done it, but it makes him smile before he turns his attention to the next student.

It continues like this for the next hour and a half. People reading their pieces, and the others giving feedback. When the session is over, Mrs Leighton gives out the assignment for next week.

Perfectly Imperfect

"Figure out what it means to you," she says. "I'm not expecting perfection, as many of you know, so write from your soul. Or something less cliché and wanky, I don't know."

I do an involuntary gasp at a teacher practically saying a swear word, which makes Mr Bird laugh. My cheeks go red. I look up and Grayson is smiling. I am a tomato.

"That's all for today then. No more than a thousand words," she says over the sound of scraping chairs and tables as the classroom is put back together. "This is the beginning of something that you can continue in your own time if you wish, not your magnum opus. Lucas, don't forget, you're reading first next week. Be prepared."

"I will."

"And please crack the spine of Pride and Prejudice before our next English class or I will be forced to keep you in on your lunch hour to do it," she says, raising an eyebrow at me. It's said in good fun, but I can feel my face turning red.

"Yes, Miss."

"It's not a bad book once you get into it." Grayson has appeared at my side and is talking in a low voice, not wanting Mrs Leighton to hear him. "I mean, it takes a while to get into it because of the language, but once you do, it's great."

"Great?"

"Fine, it's good," he says. "It's not my job to sell you on Pride and Prejudice, but you *do* have to write about it in exam, so it might be a good idea to read it."

"I've read it."

"How much of it?"

"A few pages," I say. It's enough to earn a laugh, which makes my heart flutter a little. "Well done today, by the way," I add, wanting to keep the conversation going. "The poem was…it was beautiful. It didn't feel right to critique it when it seemed so personal."

Grayson shrugs. "You're just saying that. Come on, tell me what you thought. You're the only one who didn't say anything."

"It's my first session."

"Come on," he says, nudging me, the contact sending a little jolt of electricity through me.

"Um…well…there were a few things that felt they could be tightened up," I say cautiously. "They didn't quite fit the rhythm of the rest of the piece, unless the change in rhythm was intentional, in which case tell me to fuck off."

"I'm not going to tell you to fuck off," he says, though his smile seems a little more forced now. "What else?"

"Just what everybody else said," I say, dodging.

"You thought it was self-indulgent?"

"I……I don't know you well enough to make that judgement," I reply, and his smile dwindles a little more and I hate it. "It was really lovely though. I didn't know you were a writer until yesterday."

"Ditto," Grayson replies, his smile returning a little. I've dodged a bullet and I'm glad of that. "I'm looking forward to seeing what you've got next week."

Why does that sound like a threat?

My stomach ties itself in such a hefty knot that I feel like I'm about to throw up. That's right. He's going to hear my work next week. If learning that he's good at writing has made me like him more, then he's going to change his mind about me when he learns mine is shit.

"Don't look so panicked," Grayson says. "Safe space. It's not about perfection, it's about progress."

"You're making it sound like a cult."

He shrugs. "There are worse cults to be in. At least it's not the Drama Club."

I laugh, maybe a little too loudly, and hear Mum's voice telling me to be aloof, to not give away too much, but he's so easy to talk to.

This is definitely where I should make my excuses and leave. I pick up my bag and sling it over my shoulder, making my way towards the door, saying goodbye to Mrs Leighton and Mr Bird as I leave. But he's following me, saying goodbye after I do, joining me in the corridor as I make my way towards the exit.

My heart is pounding so fast that it's practically humming in my chest. I'm walking next to Grayson Murray, and my entire body feels like it's vibrating.

"So, this party on Saturday," Grayson says. "You're totally sure you can't make it?"

"Um…I promised Vicky," I say. "I'd love to, of course, but I told her I'd go."

"That's a shame," Grayson says. "Would've been nice to get to know you outside of school. Maybe we could hang out sometime."

I try to remember what Vicky said, not to be too available, not to be too visible. I don't want him to get bored of me, that's the absolute last thing I want.

"Yeah," I say.

"Maybe at a weekend or something."

"I work," I say, which is true, at least I'm not lying to him. "I just started working at Buttons, the one just outside of school." He nods, he already knows this, of course he does. "And then homework and stuff. Got to read Pride and Prejudice."

"Very true," Grayson says.

Do I sense disappointment? I might be reading into it, but I feel like he is sad about the fact that I'm busy. It's almost definitely wishful thinking on my part.

"You're a busy boy."

I shrug. "The devil makes work for idle hands."

"Oh is that so?" He raises an eyebrow at me, and instantly my face is hotter than the sun. I hate myself. I hate myself so much. "Well, I'll have to catch you at lunchtime or something."

I can't keep up the game for too much longer. I don't want him to think I'm totally uninterested. I've not made myself too available, that much I'm sure, I can still be aloof, right? I can totally do this. I am cool, I am aloof, I am the guy he wants.

"That would be fun," I say as we make our way off the school premises and start down the road. "I'd like that."

"Great," he says, stopping on the corner. "This is me." He points behind him, the opposite direction of where I'm walking. Damn. It's probably for the best. The longer we keep talking to one another, the more likely I am to totally screw this up. "See you tomorrow?"

I smile at him. "Tomorrow."

TWENTY

PLAYING HARD TO GET

This is a classic mainstay of any piece of relationship advice, but let me tell you that it must be used with great caution. You can play so hard to get that you appear ungettable, and not every man is going to have the patience for that.

It's a dangerous game to play. Play it with caution.

LUC & SOPH

SOPH

So, how was it?

?????

Creative Writing Group. How did it go?

It was actually really good! I enjoyed it!

Enjoyed "it" or enjoyed Grayson.

Why not both?

SHAMELESS!

YOU SAID IT!

HA! Are you going to go again?

I think so.

...

How was tonight?

We watched Notting Hill again because everybody missed it last time and they're all heathens who have never seen it before.

So rude.

The rudest.

Big mistake.

Huge! God bless Julia Roberts.

Lord and saviour.

LUC & MAX

MAX

Soph said you had fun at the creative writing group tonight. Glad to hear it! Heard you enjoyed Grayson too. You're shameless.

Leave me be! Let me have nice things.

I'm teasing. Glad you had fun.

———

Saturday rolls around way quicker than I want it to. Dad hasn't really been around since the awkward Mum conversation a few days ago, so I haven't had a chance to talk to him about it. But he's out at work on Saturday night, so…what's the worst that could happen? I'm out with friends like I usually am. It's not a lie, but that low-level buzz of anxiety at not having told him is setting me on edge.

Work during the day on Saturday is fine. Vicky is there, so when

I'm not helping Henry out on the tills or cleaning the floor, we're strategising, figuring out the game plan.

Vicky heads home after our shift to get ready for the party, before coming to mine to help me. She arrives promptly at seven, and I've been a total disaster since the second I ran through the door.

She's wearing a short, emerald green dress that would match her glasses if she weren't wearing contacts tonight. This is Vicky 2.0, this is Night on the Town Vicky. Her hair is more styled than it is at work or school, and she's even wearing makeup. A bold, dark lip and glittery eyeshadow. This is the most glam I've ever seen her and she looks fantastic.

I, on the other hand, have been sitting in my bedroom in sweats for the last thirty minutes because: 1) what the fuck do I wear? 2) who the hell do I think I am, going to a fucking party? and 3) WHAT THE FUCK DO I WEAR?!

"You're not anywhere close to being ready!" Vicky exclaims as I open the door. "We're supposed to be fashionably late, not so late that the party is over."

"If you think I look so shit that we don't have time to rectify it by eight, we might as well give up now."

"Okay, okay, you're having a freakout," she groans, practically pushing me back inside my own house. "Upstairs. We'll get you sorted out. Where's your Dad?"

"Work," I reply, skipping the part where I didn't tell him that I'm going to a party tonight. She doesn't need to know that. Nobody does. "He's always at work."

"Sounds blissful," she says. "I can't get away from my mum. She was fussing around me tonight, trying to get me to change my hair so I could 'meet a nice boy.' She's nuts."

"Sounds like what you're doing to me."

"Do you want my help or not?" she deadpans.

"Very much, please and thank you."

"Okay, so shut up."

We make our way into my bedroom, which…is definitely not in its best state. My wardrobe appears to have exploded, there is a selection of jeans and button-down shirts all over my bed, and yes, the word you're looking for is chaos.

"Lucas Cook, what is this?"

"I was about to ask myself the same question," I reply. "I think I may have lost my mind a little bit."

"You think? Why have you done this? We literally just bought you clothes!"

"I panicked."

She takes a deep breath and surveys the damage. "You're utterly ridiculous, but at least it means that tonight's blog post will be entertaining." She is yet to leave the doorway, possibly afraid of what other horrors await her when she gets inside. Vicky faces me and puts two steadying hands on my shoulders. She has to reach up to do this but, despite her height, I find her incredibly intimidating in this moment.

"Deep breath, Lucas." I follow her. In, out. In, out. "Okay. What have we learned from the book so far?"

"You're never fully dressed without a smile." I can't help but smile because I can actually hear Mum singing it as I say it. She loved that song so much.

"Good. What else?"

"Dress to impress," I say. "And your hair is a hat you never take off."

"Alright," Vicky says. "So get back in there and put on the clothes we spent an entire afternoon picking out for you, then get in that bathroom and do your hair, and finally, and most importantly, smile." I do. "See? This is meant to be fun. If you're not having fun while you're falling in love, then what's the point?"

I hurry back into my room and shut the door behind me, throwing all the other clothes back into my cupboard and just holding onto the ones we picked out the other day. Why am I freaking out? I've done the hard part, right? I've got his attention, now I just have to keep it.

The red checked shirt actually does look really nice on. I forgot how much I liked it. It's been sitting in my cupboard long enough that I've managed to forget. I roll up the sleeves and it looks even nicer. I even undo a couple of the buttons to show off a little bit of my chest. It's a pale bit of white skin, hardly the hairy muscle the guys in the ads had, but it makes it look less preppy. I pair it with some black jeans and a white pair of Converse, and actually look quite nice.

"What's taking so long? Were you crushed under a pile of clothes?"

"Just finished!" I call back.

Vicky opens the door and steps inside, seeming to breathe a sigh of relief at my now much more put-together bedroom.

"That shirt really does suit you," she says. "Excellent choice."

She takes her phone out, her eyes bugging a little bit at the time. "Come on, come on, throw some product in your hair, grab a jacket, and let's go. We're going to be late."

"I thought that was the idea."

"Ignoring you now. I'll be downstairs."

I do as I'm told, turning my hair into that carefully placed messiness that Vicky helped me create. I take a moment to look at myself in the mirror. I think I look good. It's a strange thing for me to even think, and I wouldn't dare say it out loud, but this is the most *me* I've ever looked in my life. It's me, but dialled up to ten, instead of hiding at a three or a four. I could definitely get used to it.

We head out to the party, walking perhaps a little quicker than a stroll, but not as fast as a run because the last thing I want to do is to be all sweaty when we get there. I'm nervous, my heart humming in my chest.

"Remember what your mum said," Vicky says. "You've got this."

We make it to the house, a long garden path lined with trees and flowers leading to a door that is already half open. There is music pouring out into the street, flowing from around the frame and out into the night. I can hear people inside shouting, screaming, singing, having a good time. I've never been to a party like this before.

I step inside first, with Vicky close behind me, and see that a lot of the main lights are off, most of the light coming from lamps dotted down the hallway and in the various rooms. Every door is open, the music somehow managing to come out of every single one of them and hit me like a wall. It practically carries me off my feet.

"Bloody hell," I say. It's sensory overload, so many sights and smells and sounds all at once. There are people dancing, singing at the tops of their lungs, people kissing in corners or up against walls, there is Grayson... I stop dead in the doorway. I can just see into the kitchen from where I am. Grayson is mid-laugh, pure joy sparking across his ruddy face.

When he stops, he looks over and locks eyes with me, bursting into another smile.

"Lucas!" he shouts.

Well, I can't hear him shout it, but I can see his mouth making the sound.

Vicky nudges me in the side. "Got him."

TWENTY-ONE

BE AVAILABLE, BUT NOT TOO AVAILABLE
The Power Of No!

You're all going to think I'm out of my mind here, but when he asks you on a date, you need to say no. I know, it sounds crazy, but at least get to the end of this page before you throw the book out of the window and disregard everything I've said.

As much as you have been anticipating the moment when he finally asks you out, you need to not be too available when the time comes.

There are so many rules out there about never agreeing to go out with someone the same day that they ask you. I say, never agree to go out with someone, period. Be busy, be unavailable, and then make them yours.

"I CAN'T BELIEVE you made it," Grayson says, pulling me into a hug.

I try not to lean into it too much, try not to enjoy the feeling of his big arms around me, the little squeeze. Nope. I'm leaning into it. God, this is a great hug.

He lets go. "Sorry. Overexcited. How come you're here?"

He's having to shout over the music, and my brain isn't working quickly enough to form a response. I'm overwhelmed by everything.

"My mum said it was fine if we wanted to come," Vicky says, yanking me back to reality with a bump.

"The party was wrapping up so we figured we'd swing by," I add. "There's so many people here."

Grayson sighs with his entire body. "It was meant to be a casual thing," he replies. "But one person tells another person and suddenly that person is bringing a friend and then half the year is here. They just want to blow off steam, I guess." He shrugs it off, but if it were me, I'd be freaking out. For Grayson, it's just another day. "But my parents are away and they said to have some people over so…" He says it like it's nothing. I can't imagine being chill about this if it were me.

"Where do we…?" I have no idea what I'm doing here. This is such a huge 'fish out of water' moment that I am about ready to find a smaller pond.

"Follow me," he says, winking at me before heading through the hallway and towards the kitchen.

"I don't recognise half the people here," I whisper to Vicky. "Am I that much of a loser?"

"Do you really want to tug at that thread *now*?" she asks.

The kitchen is the only place that doesn't seem to have followed the lamp policy. The bright white overhead lights are on and people are standing around with drinks, talking and laughing. Grayson leads us over to a group of people, and I'm as surprised to find Max standing amongst them as he is of finding me here. It takes him more than a second to rearrange his face into something more pleasant.

"Lucas!" he says excitedly, hurrying over to me and wrapping me in a hug, which actually succeeds in calming me down a little bit. I don't know why it hadn't occurred to me that he would be here, which must mean that Soph is around somewhere. "What are you doing here? I had no idea you were coming."

"Grayson invited me," I say. "I wasn't sure I'd be able to make it, but…here I am!"

"Let me grab Soph, hang on," he says before slipping into the crowd.

"Have you met everybody?" Grayson asks.

I look at everyone and I recognise them from school and from when we were out the other night, but we've never actually been introduced.

"Apart from Max, no," I say.

Grayson goes around and introduces me to everyone. There's Madhuri, a girl I recognise from my English class who offers me a small wave, Charlotte Couts, who is in my Maths class and insists on being referred to as Char, Dylan, who offers me nothing more than a nod and a smile, and Laurie, who, again, gives me a quick up-down.

"I swear I've seen you around somewhere," Laurie says.

"He's in my English class," Madhuri says, like I'm not even here.

"Oh, okay, cute." Laurie shrugs, turning back to me with a smile. "Nice to meet you then. Is that where you and Grayson met?"

"Nice to meet you too," I say. "Um…sort of." Has he not mentioned me at all? "I work at Buttons."

"Oh, the coffee shop, cute! Well, the more the merrier, I suppose," she says, turning her attention to Vicky, because apparently they know each other already.

How am I this much of an unknown at my own school?

I thought the tension would dissipate once the awkward introductions were out of the way, but it lingers for longer than I would like. They go back to talking about whatever they were talking about, but I can't help feel like I'm intruding on something. The only person who seems to want me here is Grayson, and even then, I'm not sure.

Grayson grabs me a coke, standing painfully close to me as the group continues their conversation from before I arrived. I'm trying to listen, trying to be present, but how am I supposed to do that when Grayson is right next to me looking…well…looking like that?

He's wearing a pair of grey jeans with a pair of black boots, a deep emerald green and white striped shirt which is open with a white vest underneath it. I can see a little bit of orange fuzz across his big chest, and I need to stop staring because this is a public place. His red hair is cut short, and neatly styled to one side, and I swear every time he smiles butterflies dive-bomb my stomach. I really need to calm down.

At one point, Laurie tells a story that has everybody in stitches and he reaches out and grabs hold of my arm. I lock eyes with Vicky, who widens her eyes back. I swear I forget to breathe.

"Lucas!" I turn around to see that Max has found Soph.

She looks confused, surprised, and I think happy to see me? It's hard to tell. Jasmine and Krish follow them, both looking absolutely shocked, like I never go out or something.

"Hey!" I say, turning away from Grayson and the rest of his group to talk to them.

"What are you doing here?" Jasmine says. "I thought Max was kidding."

"Why would he be kidding?" I ask.

"You never come to things like this," Jasmine says.

"I was invited," I say indignantly. "Grayson invited me."

"Grayson invited you?" she repeats, as if it sounds like the most ridiculous thing in the world. My cheeks are burning. "I didn't know things had gotten so serious. First, the Creative Writing Group, now this."

"Jas, drop it," Soph says, coming towards me and playing with my shirt. "Why have I never seen you in this before? Is this new?"

"Yeah, I bought it from Hansens the other day."

"I thought I recognised it! It looks really nice on you!" She does a little gasp. "And look at you with your chest out, you little slut."

I laugh, suddenly feeling a heck of a lot more comfortable. This is more like it. This is the Soph I know and love. Whatever has crawled up Jasmine's ass and died hasn't affected her.

"Well, you know me, if in doubt tits out!" I reply.

She laughs, and it's the most beautiful sound. We've not properly laughed together in ages, there hasn't seemed to be the time. Perhaps whatever's been on her mind has fixed itself.

"You should have said you were coming. We all hung out at mine beforehand," Max says.

"I didn't know I was until a couple of hours ago," I say. "And I had to work so…"

"Yeah," Max says. "Just weird seeing you here. Nice but weird, you know? You never come to parties."

"But hey, I'm here now, right?"

"Come on," Max says. "You should see the rest of the house. It's gorgeous."

I look back at the group I've found myself with, Grayson and his friends. I don't want to go. The book dictates that I shouldn't. There's playing hard to get and then there's just being rude.

"I'm going to hang out here for a bit," I say. "I'll catch up with you later."

Max blinks. It's not the response he was expecting.

"Um…alright," he replies, though he doesn't seem sure. "We'll catch up with you later then."

They disappear into the party and I feel like shit. The conversation with Grayson and his friends has moved on, and I feel like it's sort of a blessing that they didn't have to see my awkwardness with Max. I don't know what's happened, I don't know what it is I've done to upset him, but I can feel it start to overwhelm me in ways that I don't find fun.

I look up at Grayson, who immediately clocks me and looks back. "I'll…I'll be back in a second," I say.

He smiles at me softly. "Okay."

I make my way through the house, drifting past the crowds of people, and start upstairs. I open a couple of doors until I find the bathroom and step inside, taking a moment to get my breath back. It's nice to be in the quiet.

When I'm done, I check myself in the mirror. I'm still pleased with the outfit, though maybe the open shirt is a little much. Maybe I'm overdressed. I try to shake off the feeling that I don't belong. Come on. I've been doing so well. My face is a little bit red, so I splash it with some water before heading back out into the party.

The door across the hall is open a crack. There isn't anybody up here that I can tell, the music from downstairs drifting up so it's a more muffled version of the wall of sound, rather than the actual wall you're faced with downstairs.

I push the door open with my foot and look inside. It's Grayson's bedroom. Much as I would like to say that I can tell because of the books on his shelves, or the way it's decorated, or because I know him so well, or that it's just some kind of sixth sense, that would be bullshit. I know it's his bedroom because I've seen the many, *many* selfies and stories that he's posted from this room.

The deep blue walls and jet black bookcases covered in everything from old hardbacks, to new paperbacks, to Funko Pops, and beyond. They're practically iconic at this point.

It feels strange to be standing in here.

And I realise that I don't want to be in here without Grayson knowing. I don't want this to be how I'm in his bedroom for the first time.

I hurry out and close the door behind me, just as the door to the bathroom opens and I am once again faced with Max.

"Hey," I say.

"What are you doing up here?" he asks. It's so accusatory, so unlike the Max that I know. What's got into him?

"I went to the bathroom," I say. He looks back at the door, insinuating that *he* was just in the bathroom. "And then I just wanted to be somewhere quiet for a little bit. So I went in there."

"Grayson's room?"

"Is it?" I lie. "I didn't know."

"Alright," he says. He looks like he's about to head back downstairs, but he stops himself. "What are you doing with Grayson?"

"What?"

"Are you two dating?"

"Um…I don't know, I—"

"Out of nowhere, you're suddenly talking to him and coming to parties and stuff, it's weird."

"It's weird?" I repeat.

"Not weird, but…not like you," he says. "I'm not trying to be horrible, Luc, this is all coming out wrong, I'm just confused." His hand finds my shoulder and I hate that I still get that early teenage thrill when he touches me. I hate it because Max is asking me questions in a way that he hasn't before. "It's just not like you."

"Okay," I say. "Well, he came into the coffee shop and we started talking and then…it just developed."

"Developed?"

"He finally noticed that we have lockers next to one another," I say with a chuckle. I want to lighten the mood, it all feels so heavy. "And then he invited me here—"

"Why didn't you tell us?"

"Because I…" Because I didn't think they'd care? Is that what I'm about to say? "I don't know why," I say, my voice coming out far quieter than I want it to. "I just didn't think to."

His eyes look a little mournful. We're standing so close to one another, and I'm looking up into his face and wanting him to say something, wanting him to do something.

"Be careful," he says.

I blink. "What?"

"I know Grayson," he says. "He's not... He's... You don't know him like I do, You're...you're a really nice guy, my best friend. I...I don't want you getting hurt. I'd hate to see you hurt, Lucas."

"I'll be careful," I say. "Promise."

He nods, and gives my shoulder a quick squeeze, then takes his hand away. The sudden absence of the heat on my arm sends a chill through me. What he said about Grayson feels like a warning. What is it that I don't know about him? He's always been so nice to me.

"You coming back down?" he asks, smiling, back to the old Max.

"Sure, just give me a minute." I watch him go down the stairs. What am I doing here?

TWENTY-TWO

I GO BACK into the bathroom and splash my face again, trying to get myself to calm down, but it just won't work. No matter how hard I try, I can't stop this tightness in my chest, this desperate need for air.

There is a knock at the door and I shout, "Just a minute," before flushing the toilet, despite not using it, and washing my hands.

"Sorry," I say to whoever is waiting, not hanging around to clock their face. Instead, I practically run downstairs. I get to the door of the kitchen and stop dead.

Grayson is there with his friends, laughing still, standing incredibly close to one of his guy friends—Dylan, I think—so close their foreheads are practically touching. It looks intimate, in front of everybody, and I feel…out of place.

Vicky is with them, part of it all. She fits in perfectly. I look down at my shirt. I'm sticking out for all the wrong reasons. At least, that's what my brain is telling me.

And then there is Max in my head, Max telling me to be careful. What do I need to be careful of? Is this it? Grayson and other boys? Am I losing it? I think I might be.

I can see the doors leading outside where the night has turned dark, where the patio lighting is shining bright and harsh onto the paving slabs. Suddenly I feel like I need to step out there. Maybe it will help.

I take a deep breath and step back into the kitchen, squeezing past people, trying to keep away from Grayson and his friends, stepping out onto the patio and breathing the biggest sigh imaginable.

The air is crisp, cold, and I wish I still had my jacket on because bloody hell is it frosty. It's shaken me awake at least.

My brain is fizzing, trying to figure out what I've done wrong. How have I managed to rub my friends up the wrong way simply by being here? They talked about me trying new things, about putting myself out there, didn't they? They might not have said it to me, but they said it around Jasmine, who couldn't keep her mouth shut. And here I am doing just that and they don't like it?

And then Max telling me to be careful, grilling me about Grayson. What's that about? Why can't he just be happy for me?

The more time that passes, and the more time I spend with this book, the further away from them I end up. I'm not sure I like it, but how do I fix it?

I sit down on a bench, looking out at the darkness of the garden. The lights from the patio can only go so far and the intensity of it means that you're just staring into emptiness. And it's sort of nice.

The sounds of the party get louder and then get quieter again, a door sliding shut. Someone else has probably come out for some air. I can hardly blame them. It was getting pretty hot in there.

"You alright?" I practically jump out of my skin as Grayson appears behind me.

"Yeah, fine," I say. I want to ask him about the other guy, but I don't want to make it weird. "Fine."

"I lost you in there," he says. "Thought you'd gone home."

"I would have said goodbye."

He laughs. "Okay, good," he says. "You alright, though?"

"Yeah, yeah, fine, just felt a bit weird so wanted to come outside."

"Okay," he replies, staying stood there for a moment longer. "Do you want me to go?"

I shrug. "You don't have to. I was just…" What's the best way of saying 'freaking out' without making him run a mile? "Warm. I was just warm."

"Okay," he says again, walking around the bench and taking a seat next to me. I look and see he's not wearing a jacket or anything either.

"You must be freezing!"

141

He shrugs. "I'm alright," he says. "Just wanted to make sure you're okay."

I smile at him in the half dark. He smiles back, the light from the patio only allowing me to see half of his face, which doesn't seem fair somehow.

"That's sweet of you," I say. "Thanks."

"I'm really glad you came," he says. "Sorry there's so many people though."

"What do you mean?"

"Well, I thought if I invited you to this, I'd get a chance to get to know you a bit better," he says. "And then you couldn't come, so I tried to get you to have lunch with me and my friends, and that didn't work…"

"I wanted to come," I say. "I just…couldn't." Not the truth, but not exactly a lie. I mentioned to Vicky he wanted to see me at lunchtime. The book, and in turn Vicky, told me that I couldn't. So that's that.

He narrows his eyes at me like he doesn't quite believe me. "And then you've come to this and there are loads of people here and all of my friends and…" He looks out into the dark.

I'm still staring at him, well, at what I can see of him. The strong line of his jaw, the point of his nose, the shock of fiery hair that disappears into the shadows.

"What?" I say.

"All of my friends are here and there's a room full of people dancing and having a good time, and I want to be out here talking to you," he says, turning back to me.

I feel like I could float off this bench right now, like I need to grab hold of the edge to stop myself because I feel weightless. What did he just say to me? How was that so damn smooth?

"Really?" I ask, cursing the cracking of my voice. "That's…that's good, because I really want to be out here talking to you too."

"It would be awkward if you didn't," he says, his voice low, more like a rumble of thunder. "Maybe we need to find a way that we can actually talk to each other next time, then."

"Next time?"

"Maybe with fewer people around?"

I nod and avert my eyes, which honestly feels like something I should be given a medal for. The hold that this boy has on me is criminal. CRIMINAL!

I try to think of what Mum would say to do in this situation. And maybe now is the moment for a bit of confidence, maybe to call him on it, to be a little more front-footed for once in my life.

"Are you asking me out on a date?"

He clears his throat, like he might have just choked on the air that he's breathing. It's a miracle that he can't see me too well in the dark right now because I know my cheeks are bright red.

"I might be," he says. "If I were asking you out, would you say yes?"

"When?" I ask.

"Sometime this week?" he says. "Maybe Tuesday? I'll message you about it."

"Sounds good to me," I reply.

"So a date."

"A date."

"Sounds nice," he says.

"Very nice," I reply.

A silence falls over us. Well, silence, but for the sounds of the party happening behind us. He reaches across the space between us and takes hold of my hand. I swear to God my heart stops.

I turn to him. He turns to me and smiles. I smile back.

"I'll message you then," he says.

"You don't have my number."

"Then, you'd better give it to me," he says, handing me his phone.

I nod. "Okay." We trade numbers and it feels significant. I feel like I'm going to be thinking of this moment for a long time. This is how we started.

"See you inside?" he asks.

"Sure," I reply.

He squeezes my hand, and I am about to have a freaking heart attack there and then. He stands up and heads back inside and I take a few deep breaths because I feel lightheaded. Did that really just happen? Are we going to go on a date? Really?!

I look out into the dark again and I can practically see my mum giving me an embarrassing thumbs up.

Vicky is decidedly less impressed with my progress on the Grayson front. She wasn't expecting there to be a date so soon, maybe us playing hard to get for a little bit longer before agreeing to go out with him, but he was right there and he was cute and he was asking and I just couldn't help myself.

"You were thinking with what's in your pants," she says as we walk home. "You don't want to admit it, but I know it's the truth. And that's fine, but we've been so good at following the book so far, deviating feels like a misstep."

"The way I see it, there isn't a specific time frame in the book, right?" I say. "So me ending up with a date already isn't a bad thing."

Vicky sighs at me in the dark and I can feel her eyes boring a hole in the side of my head, but I'm not about to give her the satisfaction of telling her to stop.

"You keep telling yourself that," she says. "I still maintain that you were thinking with your pants."

"Well, my pants managed to get me a date."

"I wouldn't advertise that," she replies.

I walk her to her door and wish her a goodnight, telling her that I will see her tomorrow for work, which is unfortunately true.

I am bone tired as I make my way home. Stepping inside, I kick off my shoes and immediately collapse onto the sofa. After everything that happened with Grayson, I went back into the party and joined in with the rest of the group, laughing, joking, getting to know them a little better. I even got to spend a bit more time with Grayson, which was super cute.

I didn't see my friends for the rest of the night. I don't even know when they left. I check my phone and I don't have any messages from them, which makes my chest go all tight again. As my mind drifts back to Grayson, that feeling sort of goes away, or at least quietens down for the time being.

What I've been doing has been working, and so long as I continue to do what Mum says, there is absolutely no way that this can go wrong.

No way at all.

And I keep thinking that, until I hear the front door open and close with a slam.

TWENTY-THREE

SECTION TWO
THE RULES OF DATING
The First Date

Well done, weary traveller, you've made it this far into the book. If you've been following my rules, instructions, and ideas, then you will have him on the hook. Know that I am very proud of you and all you have achieved so far. The next step is arguably the most exciting and nerve-wracking one yet.

The first date.

Casual reminder this is what you've been training for. This is it, your first proper step to not dying alone!

This is where the rules really kick in and where you're going to need to be at your most vigilant. If you're anything like me, you will have had a tendency in your romantic past to let your heart run away with you. That's okay, you're only human. But I'm here to help that not be the case. I'm here to take you through the first date and beyond.

I DON'T KNOW what to do as I hear Dad come in the door. There's no time to bolt upstairs, so I do the next best thing. I throw myself across the sofa and close my eyes, like I've been asleep the whole time.

My heart is beating hard and I don't know how convincing my fake sleeping will be, so I sit up and try to appear groggy.

"Dad?" I call out. Best to make the first move rather than getting caught. "That you?"

"Lucas? You're still up?"

"Barely," I reply, managing to force out a yawn, making sure it's loud enough that he can hear. "What time is it?" *Nice touch.*

"Past midnight," he says. I hear him coming closer and I pull myself up on the sofa as he looks into the living room. "Did you fall asleep down here?"

To say Dad looks like a bit of a wreck right now would be an understatement. His hair is positively wild on top of his head, even his beard looks scruffy. There are bags under his eyes and he's still in his chef whites, a mix of sauces all down the front of them.

"Must have," I say.

"You're dressed," he says. "You been out?"

My stomach contracts. Slight flaw in the plan, I'm in jeans and a shirt.

"Just with friends," I say. "The usual, you know. Must have been more tired from work than I thought. It was pretty full on today." I manage to force another yawn, just to hammer the point home.

He smiles at me, a soft sort of smile, one that could be misconstrued as him being proud of me if you didn't know my dad.

"Come on," he said. "Get yourself up to bed, then. You're back at work tomorrow, aren't you?"

"Yeah," I say. "Bright and early."

"Go get some sleep," he says. "I'll see you tomorrow night."

I get up from the sofa and walk past him, slowly making my way upstairs, trying to make it very clear that I am tired and achy rather than absolutely buzzing off of what happened at Grayson's party tonight. If he isn't buying it, he's not questioning it, which feels like something of a victory.

I hear the TV switch on downstairs before I shut my door. And let out a sigh of relief that I might have managed to get away with it. But it was way too close for comfort.

———

Waking up for work on Sunday is probably one of the worst experiences of my life. The excitement of the night means that I still didn't manage to get to sleep until way after midnight, long after Dad gave up and went upstairs to go to bed. I heard him go and knew that I was going to feel like death at work.

"I want to die," I tell Vicky when she opens the door for me. "Like, fully, just bury me, I beg of you."

"If I bury you, you don't get to go on a date with Grayson."

"Holy wow, suddenly I feel a hundred times better."

Vicky mock gasps. "Oh my God, speedy recovery, I love that for you!"

"I still can't believe it's happening," I say.

"What?"

"He asked me out, Vicky," I say. "He actually asked me out."

"Yes," she says. "Because you did exactly what you were supposed to do, and you followed the book. You made an impression, you made yourself noticeable, you stepped out of the shadow of your friends for five seconds, and lo and behold..."

"Lo and behold," I repeat, before making my way to the counter to serve customers. It's once again a lonely shift for me and Vicky, Maria hiding in back and Henry taking their usual Sunday off. I find myself watching the door, hoping Grayson might walk in. Now wouldn't that be a turn up?

But then I see a face I actually do recognise. And after last night, it's almost the last face I'm expecting.

"Good afternoon, sir. How can I help you?" I say.

"Sir?" Max replies, his face wrinkling. "I don't like that, please don't do that."

"What are you doing here?" I don't know how to be around him. We've not spoken since last night, or if he's messaged, I've been out on the floor and not seen it yet.

"I...wanted coffee," he replies. "And to talk to you, if I can?" He looks over at Vicky, who is cleaning the coffee machine. The lunchtime rush has passed and there are only a couple of customers in the store. She shrugs back at me.

"I can talk for a bit," I say. "Hang on."

I come from around the counter and head out onto the floor,

147

carrying a spray bottle of cleaning product and a cloth so that if Maria happens to come out here, it looks like I'm working.

"What's up?"

"Can you sit?"

I hesitate. "I probably shouldn't."

"Alright then," he replies. "I want to help."

"Sorry?"

"I want to help you with Grayson."

I sigh. Not this again. "Did Soph put you up to this?"

"I know about the book."

Now I really wish I was sitting down. The words hit me so hard that they practically knock me off my feet.

"How did you know?"

"I went looking for it," he says. "After last night, you suddenly being different and talking to Grayson and stuff, I…I felt weird about it. I just did a little bit of digging, fell down a major rabbit hole that took me to Vicky's website, then to yours, and…" He suddenly looks sheepish. "I don't even know if I slept last night because I didn't know what to do."

"Please don't tell him," I say.

"What?"

"Don't tell Grayson," I say. "It's not even really started yet, we've not even been on a date and I…I wanted to try it, I wanted to see if I could win him over and if you tell him he'll never speak to me again and…" I take a few calming breaths, trying to stop my heart running at a hundred miles a second. "I really like him."

I finally look at Max to find he's…smiling? I'd expected him to be annoyed or disappointed in me. Why is he smiling?

"Did you not listen to the part where I said I wanted to help you?" he asks.

"You do?"

"Yes," he says. "I can see how much it means to you and…you're my best friend, Luc, I want to see you happy. I know him better than you do. I can help you out."

"And Soph didn't tell you to do this?"

He hesitates. "Why would she do that?"

"When we were out the other weekend, she basically offered to

148

make me her pet project," I say. "And I love her, but I just…I don't want that. And then Jasmine…" Am I really telling him this? "And then Jasmine talked about how you're all talking about me being single and around two couples and stuff and…"

"You think we're talking about you?" Max says, and the way he says it makes it sound like I'm a massive narcissist. "Maybe Jasmine is, but not to me. I'm just here because I want to help."

"After everything you said last night, why would you want to?"

"What do you mean?"

"You made it sound like Grayson was some kind of monster," I say. "You told me to be careful. Is that why you went digging around for stuff?"

"I just…I know him and…I don't know, he's cute and everything, incredibly flirty with basically everyone, a bit rude too, but maybe you like that, I don't know, *very* into himself. I didn't think he'd be your type," he says.

"Who is my type, then?"

He hesitates again. Does he think I just don't have a type? Does he think I'm not capable of having someone like Grayson like me? Why is this conversation hurting me so much? He is supposed to be my best friend.

"Never mind," I say.

"Come on, Luc, you wouldn't have known how to talk to Grayson in a million years before the other week and suddenly you're at a party on a Saturday night," he says. "I'm not trying to put you down, and I feel like that's how this is coming out. It's just not the Luc that I've known for the past ten years. I'm happy that you're being more outgoing. I would have loved for you to come to those parties with us. You just never really wanted to."

"I was never invited."

"No one is ever invited," Max says. "People just show up. And I'm glad you're showing up, even if it is for Grayson."

"I thought he was your friend?"

"He is my friend," Max says. "And you're my best friend, which is why I want to help you."

I look over at Vicky, who is serving a customer. I'll have to talk to her about it, see what she says. This is her project as much as it is mine.

"I'll ask Vicky," I say. "But if you're going to help with this, you can't tell anyone."

"Not a soul."

"Not even Soph," I say. "It's…it's an experiment. And it's working so far and…I don't want to mess it up."

Max takes his hands out of his pockets, holding them up so I can see them. "I promise I won't tell," he says. "Whether you want my help or not. But I really think you could use it."

"Your faith in me is music to my ears."

"Hey, I know you better than most," he says. "I love you, but you're a walking disaster. We're going to help curb that."

"You're officially banned from this coffee shop."

"Tell me what she says," Max replies. "I really want to help you, Luc. Please let me."

I nod. "I'll let you know," I say. "See you tomorrow?"

"See you tomorrow."

TWENTY-FOUR

"HE WHAT?"

"He knows," I say. "I don't really know how he knows, but he knows, and if he knows, then what are the chances that other people won't find out?"

"I feel like you've been pretty vague so far," Vicky says, scrolling through her phone as we grab our things to leave Buttons. "Maybe he just knows you too well. Keep it vaguer next time."

"Maybe just outright lie."

"No," she says. "Just…less specific details that pin it to you. We can't be too careful."

"And what do you think of him offering to help?"

Vicky thinks for a second. "Well, that's sort of up to you," she says.

"How is it up to me?"

"Max is your friend," she says. "Do you want him to help us get to Grayson?"

"I…"

The truth is, I'm not sure. Max is my best friend and maybe if I hadn't had feelings for him once upon a time, it wouldn't feel so weird. Clearly it's not weird for him, though. He seems to be more than happy to help offload me onto some other guy. Maybe it won't be so bad.

"Look," Vicky says, not enjoying my indecision. "He knows Grayson better than we do, so maybe having him on board will make everything easier. We'll be scrabbling around in the dark a little bit less. You'll have fewer things to overthink."

"Not likely."

"I know, even as I said it, I didn't quite believe it," she says with a smirk. "I'm up for it, if you are."

I take a moment. What's the worst that could happen? He knows Grayson better than me. He will know what makes him tick, surely? And it's Max. He just wants me to be happy.

"I'll text him."

"Good," Vicky says. "And write another post tonight, the party stuff is important. Especially with you skipping pages."

"I'm not skipping pages!"

"You absolutely are, but it is what it is," she says. "It's a guide, not a blueprint. He'll be very useful for your first date, I'm sure of it."

I try not to, but my tired brain is definitely overthinking it. The fact that Grayson hasn't messaged me yet has me thinking that I've imagined the whole thing and that maybe this isn't happening.

I hate that my brain is doing this, but things have been going so well that it feels like it's all got to get pulled out from under me at some point. When is he going to notice that I'm a massive fraud?

"What?" Vicky says as we get to her turning. "What's happening in that big old head of yours?"

I shake it. "Nothing," I lie. "Just…silly thoughts, that's all. Nervous for the date."

"Keep following the book and you'll be fine!"

We go our separate ways and I message Max while I walk.

> You're on the team.

Good. Let's bag you that man.

> I'm going to regret this.

Ha! Hopefully not.

When I get home, I make sure to write my blog post about last night before I forget, and get it posted. Vicky quickly messages me to approve it, and then I get to work on what I'll be presenting at the Creative Writing Group on Wednesday.

Writing is hard. I feel like that's the part that nobody really tells you about. It's one thing to write something for school, when they've literally told you that you need to hit particular key points, but when you just have a little prompt and you have to actually show it to people? I swear it's the living end.

Dad gets in around six, back from a Sunday lunch shift at the new restaurant. He's in good spirits, even if his clothes are covered with spatters of gravy and various sauces.

"Look at you, hard worker," he says as he steps into the kitchen. "I can't remember the last time I saw you sat in the kitchen doing work!"

I mean, the obvious answer to this is that it's because he's usually at work, so he doesn't get a chance to, but it feels cruel to mention it.

"It's like when you were in primary school and would set yourself up a little work station to do your spelling. Do you remember?"

"I try not to," I reply.

"It was cute."

"I beg you to forget this information if I ever bring someone home." I can't imagine Grayson knowing that about me. I'm already such a loser at school, knowing that it extended quite comfortably into my home life would ruin any romantic chances I might have with him.

"I don't need to tell the story, a picture is worth a thousand words," Dad teases, then turns serious. "You...thinking of bringing someone home, Luc?"

I stop what I'm doing, my hands hovering over the keys of my laptop. I look at my dad with wide eyes, a deer in headlights. It gives him an answer, without me having to give him one. He's staring right back at me, apparently unsure what to do or say next. And I need him to say something or we will be stuck here staring at each other in silence for the rest of our lives.

"Wow," he says. *Groundbreaking*. "What's his name?"

"I don't know."

"You don't know his name? Kind of awkward, Luc."

"No, not that. I know his name. It's Grayson, I just don't know if I'm bringing him home, that's all," I say. "I mean, I might be bringing someone home at some point because he might want to go on a date, but I don't know when that will be or even if that would be okay, because we've never discussed anything like that. You and me, I mean. So I guess maybe one day, at some point, I'll bring someone home, if that's okay, and also can I maybe go on a date at some point this week? It might be Tuesday, we're yet to confirm."

I stop talking and take a huge breath. My mouth is dry, I'm definitely sweating through my t-shirt, and Dad is staring at me like I've just spoken to him in another language. And given how fast I was speaking, it's more than likely sounded like I was.

"Luc, that's a lot of information all at once."

"Sorry."

"Are you… dating this boy?" he asks. He's not moved from the door, like he can't, like he's trapped. There is a strange sort of look on his face that I can't place. Is he sad that I'm dating a boy? Is he sad that I'm going on a date? I can't tell.

"No…yes…no…" I stop and think about it, trying to not let my mouth run away with me. "I don't know. Maybe if the date goes well, we will be?"

"Okay," he says, finally taking his eyes off me. And I finally breathe. It's like I was under some kind of spell. He shakes his head, brow creasing before he looks back at me again. "Are you old enough to be dating?"

"Dad."

"What? I don't know," he says. He takes a moment while he goes to the kettle and switches it on. He watches it as it boils. It's only when it clicks off that he speaks again. "No later than ten pm; it's a school night."

I blink. Is it really that easy?

"Really?"

"Tell me what day it is because I might be at work," he says. "When you know. But yes. I think. It feels like the right thing to do." He looks at me and smiles, that kind of smile that tells you they're seeing you as both a six-year-old and a sixteen-year-old at the same time, wondering where the years have gone.

He clears his throat and heads to the fridge, rummaging around, taking things out of his bag and putting them on the shelves, changing the tone. I'm sort of thankful for it.

154

"What did you eat last night?" he asks.

I freeze. The subject change is enough to give me whiplash. "What's that now?"

"I left you soup." He closes the fridge door and turns to look at me. "You didn't want my soup?"

"No," I reply. "It looked great, but I just wasn't all that hungry. I had some cereal." Not a lie, I did inhale some cereal before I left last night.

Dad looks at me curiously for a moment, like the very concept of me having cereal is alien. But he shrugs and goes back to getting things ready for dinner.

Bullet very much dodged.

We talk about how work was, Dad telling me how busy the lunch shift was, how much he's enjoying working there and hopes it can become a more permanent thing so he's not bouncing between restaurants all the time, and I tell him that Maria still won't let me make coffee.

"Don't run before you can walk," he says.

"I walk just fine," I reply. "I can walk with my eyes closed. I know what the coffee is now, at least. I could probably make it."

"How's the writing?" he asks, gesturing at the computer. "I take it that's what you're doing right now, huh?"

I nod. It feels awkward. It shouldn't feel awkward, but it does. Writing is synonymous with Mum and it makes the air so thick that my words almost have to swim through it just to reach him.

"It's not easy," I say. "When I write stuff for school, it's easier than this. I feel like I don't know what I'm doing."

"What's the prompt?"

"Perfectly Imperfect," I reply, feeling silly even saying it out loud.

He stops what he's doing and looks off into the distance, apparently seriously considering it. He smiles. I sort of want to know what he's thinking about. I wonder if it's Mum.

He looks back at me. "What does it make you think of?"

"I don't know."

Truthfully, it makes me think that I need to write something clever and profound because that's what the phrase feels like. It feels like something highbrow and above me. It's intimidating.

155

"Well, I can't tell you what to write," he says. "But your Mum always used to just start writing the first thing that came into her head with things like that. Just go and see what comes out. It might not be what other people write for that prompt, but that's the point, isn't it? In a weird way, that's perfectly imperfect."

He goes back to stacking the fridge like he's not just said something clever and profound that has basically made my jaw drop.

"What do you want for dinner?" he asks.

"I don't know, whatever, I'm easy."

He looks at the fridge and starts taking things out. "Half an hour," he says. "That's how long you've got to do it. You can edit it later, but just write for the next half an hour. I'll be quiet."

I take a deep breath, and write, letting words flow onto the page that I don't even realise I'm thinking and feeling. All the while, Dad is cooking in the background.

I can't help but think this is Mum's doing. Somehow, she's working her magic again. I keep writing. I keep writing until Dad tells me to stop.

TWENTY-FIVE

LUC & GRAYSON

GRAYSON

So…Tuesday?

Who is this?

It's Grayson. This is Lucas, right? I've not got the wrong number.

I know it's you.

Rude.

Please don't cancel.

Haha!

Fine, but only because it's you.

SO…Tuesday? 6 pm?

Perfect.

> TUESDAY! PANIC STATIONS! IT IS HAPPENING ON TUESDAY!

MAX

Oh good, another group chat, exactly what i need ;)

VICKY

Read the chapters on the first date, we'll gather on Tuesday to figure out what to do

MAX

Where?

> Library?

MAX

Perfect.

VICKY

Library!

———

"So that's progress," Vicky says as we walk into school on Monday. "I mean…your dad didn't totally freak out about you going on a date. That has to be a good thing. And then you wrote in front of him. Also a big tick for Matthew Cook."

"Definitely a big tick for Dad," I say. "I thought he was going to flip out."

"He didn't flip out about you going to a party at his house, why would he flip out about you going out with him?"

"Um…well…" I don't know what to say to that. I've barely managed to get the words out before Vicky pounces on them.

"He knew that you went to the party, right?"

"Not exactly."

"LUCAS!"

"What?" I say. "He wasn't going to be in, I'd not seen him, he knows I'm usually out with my friends on weekends, so what's the difference?"

"The difference is, if something bad had happened, he wouldn't have known where you were or what you were up to," she says. "Christ, I shouldn't have to explain that to you. We're the same age." She shakes her head. "My parents freaked out at me getting in after midnight."

"But they knew you were going out."

"Yeah, and they knew I was going to be back around midnight," Vicky says, shaking her head. "But my mum just wanted the drama, I think. She wanted to smell my breath and told my dad I'd been drinking and, 'How could I raise a party animal? What am I going to do?'" She shakes her head again. "Parents."

"What did your dad say?"

"My dad told her she was overreacting," she says. "Which took the heat off me because...well...then the heat was now squarely on him for criticising her."

"Big tick for Mr Jones."

"Big tick for Dad, indeed."

I'm oddly nervous on my way to the Geography block. I didn't bump into Grayson at my locker, and I don't know if that would have made things better or worse after his message yesterday about the date. But the thought of seeing my friends this morning is making my chest feel tight.

I've not really spoken to any of them, apart from Max, since what happened on Saturday and...well...I'm not sure how they are feeling about me. I only had messages off Soph yesterday to make sure I got home alright. The group chat has been silent.

Jasmine and Soph are acting fairly normal, but there is something in the air, something that no one is saying. Until Jasmine says it.

"Where did you go on Saturday?" she asks.

"Huh?"

"You didn't say goodbye," she says. "Did you duck out early?"

I try to laugh it off. "I'm not sure," I say. "I had to get home by midnight, so I left a little before twelve. Didn't want to turn into a pumpkin. What time did you guys leave?"

Jasmine shrugs. "I think we left around one? Is that right, Soph?"

"Oh God, I don't know," Soph replies, her gaze not quite finding mine. I feel like she's upset about something, but I might be projecting. "I think I was passed out on the sofa before midnight. Sad I didn't get to see you all night, though," she adds. "I never get to hang with you at parties. It would have been nice."

"Maybe the next one?" I offer.

It gets her to smile, so maybe I'm imagining her being mad.

"Look at you, you're turning into a party animal."

"Hardly!" I say. "But please pretend that you've not seen that shirt again next time you see me wearing it; you know my wardrobe is limited."

"I'll put on a performance that would make Mrs Hartman give a standing O."

"That's all I ask," I say. "So, what did I miss? Anything fun?"

The bell rings for form and everybody gets up. Soph immediately links my arm.

"You missed out on a couple of spats from people whose names you probably don't know, no offence," she says. "Nothing major. What about you?"

I open my mouth to tell her about what happened with Grayson when Max appears. Distracted, her arm unhooks from mine and joins with his as they walk to their usual seats.

I'm frozen by the door as I watch them walk arm in arm to their chairs, talking conspiratorially as they go.

"Come on, Mr Cook," Mr Marshall's thunder rumble of a voice comes from behind me. "Can't stand around all day. Keep moving."

"Sorry, sir," I say, making my way over to my usual desk behind the couples. Got to keep moving.

———

IT'S A WONDER I MANAGE TO GET ANYTHING DONE AT SCHOOL FOR THE rest of Monday.

That night, Dad confirms that it's fine for me to go, once again reiterating that he wants me home by ten because it's a school night.

"And I'd like to meet him," he adds. "Is he coming to pick you up?"

"I think so, but Dad—"

"I should get to meet the boy who's taking my son out," he says

160

with a strange sense of pride that actually makes me feel a bit warm inside.

I mean, he's probably about to embarrass me so hard that Grayson will cancel the date there and then, but at least he's taking an interest.

———

"Fancy seeing you here," Max says as I get to the library on Tuesday.

Why does that make my heart flutter? Those words really are powerful.

"You've read it!" I say.

"Bits and bobs," he says. "So, do we have a game plan, here?" Max asks. I'd half expected him to blow it off to hang out with Soph and everybody else, but he showed up and he's ready for action. Even if the words 'game plan' give me anxiety.

Max doesn't know that Vicky and I already had a strategy chat on the way to school this morning. I didn't want to pull him away from Soph too much, just in case she gets suspicious.

"So you've read the book?" Vicky asks Max, sending a perfectly arched eyebrow across the table at him.

"I read the first date part," he replies. "Didn't have time to read all of it."

"Slow reader?"

"Busy man."

"Fine," she replies, turning back to me. "Our best option at this point is to follow it to the letter. Stay aloof, keep it light, be bubbly, like what your mum says. Don't talk about anything too serious."

"But what if—?"

"No buts," she says. "If he tries to talk about something too deep, move the conversation on and stay light." She turns to Max. "Anything to add?"

"Grayson isn't that complicated," Max says. "He's...he's a little bit into how he looks, which you might have noticed, so if you acknowledge that, you'll make him feel good."

"I'll likely be drooling, so big tick in that box."

"Gross," Vicky says.

"Seconded," Max adds. "Be yourself."

"Terrible advice!" Vicky snaps, earning her a loud shush from Ms Harris, the librarian. She lowers her voice and looks dead into my eyes. "Be the best version of you, the 'fancy seeing you here' version of you." She turns back to Max. "Read the book."

"Duly noted."

When I get home in the afternoon, I am in a bit of a state. Dad doesn't bother me, probably because he can sense my mood. I was almost tempted to go back to the shop that Vicky and I went to in town and pick up a different shirt because I finally got paid from Buttons last Friday, but know I'll need money for the date tonight, and money for Dad. So one of my old shirts will have to do. I sent the options to Vicky, and she approved one to wear tonight, a dark green shirt that I got Christmas before last that just about still fits.

I shower once, and then again because I stress myself out. I take my time doing my hair and putting my outfit on, sending Vicky a selfie before Grayson arrives.

VICKY

YOU LOOK GREAT! FOLLOW THE RULES! BE GOOD! DON'T DO ANYTHING STUPID!

I WILL TRY!

But it's me. Chances are I'm going to do something stupid.

MANIFESTING THAT YOU DON'T!

It's going to take more than manifesting because right now I am a nervous wreck, and as time ticks on, it's only getting worse. My phone buzzes again, and I wonder if it's Vicky with more advice, but see that it's Max.

MAX

Smash it tonight. Be your charming self and you'll be grand.

Vicky is going to kill you.

162

I've known you longer. If he doesn't like you for you, he doesn't deserve you. Text me later. Tell me how it goes.

When I know Grayson is going to be arriving soon, I go downstairs and take a seat in the kitchen, trying not to worry.

"You look like you're about to be sent out to face the firing squad," Dad says, sitting at his computer at the dining table in his chef whites.

"Shut up."

"You need to calm down."

"You need to shut up."

Dad scoffs. "Touché, save some of that scintillating chat for Graham."

"GRAYSON!"

He puts his hands up. "Alright, alright!"

The doorbell rings, and I look over at Dad. He's smiling at me.

"Showtime," he says.

TWENTY-SIX

The First Date (Cont.)

You're about to put a lot of pressure on this. I know you are, because I used to do the same thing. You just need to follow the rules that I've laid out in this chapter, and you will be absolutely fine. These are tried and tested. I went through a lot of guys and made a lot of mistakes before I ended up with Matthew. I've made mistakes, so you don't have to.

MY HEART IS in my mouth as I walk to the door. I check myself in the mirror in the hallway one more time. The hair is like I practised, the shirt looks alright, my face looks a little bit red, but that's the absolute terror I feel because Grayson Murray is on the other side of the door.

Deep breath.

"I thought you'd changed your mind or something," he says, a smile sitting lazily on his face.

He's wearing a grey denim button down and a pair of black jeans. His ginger hair, that I'm used to seeing a little bit fussed at school, is swept over to one side like it was on Saturday. He looks like he's made an effort and it's more than enough to make me go all swoony.

"Gosh, you look great."

He snorts. "'Gosh'?! What are we in, Downton Abbey or something?"

"Sorry," I breathe. "You do look great, though."

"Thanks," he replies, his smile getting a little bigger.

He's actually here. He's actually standing at my door. No take backs. No big prank at my expense. Grayson is here.

"Come on in!" Dad's voice rings through the house.

Before I can go full Admiral Akbar and tell Grayson, "It's a trap!" he is stepping inside. More fool him.

I take him to the kitchen where Dad has closed his computer and is, instead, watching the door for Grayson's arrival. To say that every second of this is killing me is an understatement.

"Lovely to meet you," Grayson says.

"Graham, wasn't it?" Dad says, a smirk tugging at the corners of his mouth.

"Grayson, Dad," I reply. I'm trying to keep my tone light, but really I'm begging for Dad to just stop and let us leave.

"That's right, that's right," he says, nodding and fixing his eyes on the two of us.

It's painfully awkward. I have no idea what to say, and I can practically hear my dad's inner monologue whirring as he tries to come up with either a witty remark or something that will embarrass me to the point of death.

"You've got a really lovely home," Grayson says, and the fact that he is trying to fill this painful silence only succeeds in making me like him even more.

"And what are your intentions with my Lucas?"

Grayson's eyes go wide. "Um-well-I thought we'd…we'd get some dinner and—"

"He's kidding," I say. But suddenly I'm unsure. "You're kidding, right?"

"An attempt was made."

"I think it failed."

"Noted," Dad says.

"Can we go?" I ask. "We've got a reservation and—"

"Of course, of course, go," Dad says. "Home by ten, please."

I practically shove Grayson out of the door and into the coolness of the January night. He's smiling as we wander down the garden path. I, on the other hand, am on fire.

"What?" I ask.

"Your Dad's funny," he says. "And you're bright red."

"It was warm in there."

"It absolutely was not, you were embarrassed," Grayson says. "Bold of you to let me even come inside on the first date."

"Bold of you to assume that I had any choice in the matter," I say. "Dad called your name and you practically ran past me. If you were hoping for embarrassing stories, you were fresh out of luck."

"Ah, so it's your mum that has all the juicy stuff, huh?" he asks with a laugh. But I don't laugh back. I can't.

"My Mum is…dead," I say. It comes out way blunter than I mean it to. So blunt, it's like I've just smacked Grayson in the face because he fully stops walking, eyes wide, mouth hanging open.

"Are you joking? If that's a joke, you're sick."

"Not a joke."

"So she really is…"

"Yeah," I reply.

"Christ, shit, oh God, Lucas, I'm so sorry," he says. "I didn't mean to…I didn't think, I just…I thought that maybe she was out or… Why…why didn't you say anything?"

"I don't often lead with it, to be honest," I say.

"Of course," he says. "I'm…I'm sorry I brought it up."

"It's okay, not your fault," I reply.

"How long ago did she…?"

The funny thing about talking about dead people is that people suddenly struggle to even say the word. Like it's too harsh to say that somebody is dead when…that's what they are.

"She died about seven years ago," I say. "Hit by a van on her way to pick me up from school. Not my favourite day."

"Sure," Grayson says. "I'm sorry. I'll stop talking about it."

"We don't have to," I reply. "I don't get to talk about her all that often. If you want to hear about my mum, we can talk about her."

I suddenly remember one of the rules for the first date: avoid anything too serious. I'm breaking that by talking about the woman who wrote that rule in the first place. Nice one, Lucas, barely out of the gate and we're already striking out.

"Or we can talk about how embarrassing my dad is. That, I can talk about for days."

"Believe me, you don't get the monopoly on embarrassing parents."

"Says the boy whose parents let him have a party while they were away on some trip?" I reply. "Sure, your parents seem totally embarrassing and not at all way cooler than my dad could ever hope to be."

The topic has swerved, and I feel my breath start to ease in my chest. Why do I get the feeling that following these rules is going to be easier said than done?

––––––

RIGBY'S STEAKHOUSE IS DEFINITELY ON THE FANCIER END OF THE restaurant scale. I don't know what I was expecting, but I didn't check the menu and now I realise how much of an error that was.

The tablecloths are white, giving me anxiety about spillages, and the waiting staff are all in white shirts with black ties, so smartly dressed that the fact we're both there in jeans makes me feel uncomfortable. As we are taken through the restaurant to our table, we pass middle-aged couples drinking expensive looking wine and eating their meals by candlelight, probably looking at me, wondering if I've wandered in by accident.

"Your waiter will be with you shortly," we are told before the fancy-looking man walks back to his position at the front.

I take off my coat and hang it on the back of my chair. The lights are low, the candles are lit, and everything about this place screams ROMANCE ROMANCE ROMANCE in big pink neon letters with a love heart where the "O" should be.

"This is nice," I say, keeping my voice low. It's quiet. So quiet that even whispering feels like it's disturbing the people a few tables over.

"I Googled it," Grayson replies. "Apparently it's good for…you know…first dates."

"Oh."

We stare at each other for a second. There is a part of me that is trying to follow the rules, trying to remember to:

Make eye contact. It shows that you're interested in what they're saying and what they're doing.
    Mimic their body language, so you appear more compatible.

But neither one of us is saying anything. We're just staring at each other, hands beneath the table, waiting for something to happen.

"Can I get you two started with some drinks?" Our waitress has arrived. Her voice is posh and clipped. Either they're not from this part of Essex or they're very much putting it on. Her black hair is pulled back into a high ponytail that pulls her face back to make her look so severe, I swear they're mad at me before we've even ordered.

"We've not had a chance to look yet," Grayson says, his voice coming out a little sharp. Even I'm taken aback by it. It gets him a stiff smile before the waitress saunters off in the direction of the kitchen. He looks over at me. "Something I said?"

Probably how you said it, I think. But I don't want to upset him.

"How dare you not be ready two seconds after sitting down!" I say. "Unacceptable."

"Wow, worst diner ever."

"Confirmed."

We pick up the menus and my jaw drops. I have to rearrange my face because I don't want Grayson to see, but the food is expensive. I don't have this much money on me. I maybe have enough for a couple of sides and a drink, but this is way out of my price range. I knew I should have checked. Why didn't I check?

"It's a good menu, right? We've been here loads," he says, a big smile on his face. "And not too expensive."

"Sure," I say, the intense awkwardness of the moment invading my entire body. I can't afford this. Not by a long shot. I stare at the menu, at the stupidly high numbers. What am I going to do?

"So, what did your mum do?" Grayson asks. He's put his menu down. Has he already decided? Fuck. "You said we could talk about her. Sorry if that's weird."

"Um…it's not weird," I say, but my brain is screaming how against the rules it is.

Don't talk about anything too serious on the first date. Keep it light.

Talking about my dead Mum is definitely not light. "She…she was a writer. Anyway, what are you getting, because I—?"

"Really?" He says. "That's so cool, I had no idea. Did she write anything I would know?"

My brain goes to full panic stations because all it would take was a simple Google search and he would know about Mum's book, and then the torture begins again.

"No," I say. "She always wanted to, but never quite made it. She's a failed actor too," I add with a laugh, though even I can tell it sounds hollow.

The last thing I want to do is talk about my mum negatively and here I am making a stupid joke. Why am I like this?

"So is that why you took so long to come to the Creative Writing Group?" Grayson asks. "Because of your mum?"

"Huh?"

"Well, it must remind you of her, right? I bet it must be pretty difficult to go to something that's tied so closely to her." His eyes widen suddenly. "And I'm really sorry if me bringing her up now means that you're having a tough time. God, I'm stupid."

"No, no," I say. "That's…that's not why. It's because…" And we're floating ever closer to serious territory again and I need to not do this. The rules say not to talk about serious stuff, to keep it light, keep it conversational, but all I want to do is talk about Mum right now and I — "I just need to go to the bathroom," I say quickly. "I won't be a second."

Nothing ruins the flow of conversation like a last-minute trip to the ladies' room!

It might be against the rules, but I need to get out of there. Now.

I get up from the table and hurry to the back of the restaurant, dipping into the brightly lit, stark white bathroom where I finally feel

169

like I can take a breath. I mean, it's a breath that smells a little unpleasant, but at least I feel less sweaty now.

I pull my phone out and call Vicky. She picks up on the first ring. "What did you do?"

Apparently, "Hello," is too simple.

"I'm fine thanks, how are you?" I reply.

"Jokes can wait. What have you done?"

"What makes you think I've done something?"

I can see the look on her face without needing to see it. Looking over her glasses at me, lips pursed, judgement radiating from her so intensely it makes me die.

"You don't want me to answer that question," she says.

"He keeps trying to talk about serious stuff," I say. "The book says to avoid the serious stuff when it comes up."

"Then avoid it."

"He's relentless."

"Then make it about him," she says. "You can do this, you've talked to him before."

"I've talked to him in a school corridor with you as my witness, someone to punch me if I say something stupid," I say. "Here, it's just me and I am in full panic stations. What if I say something stupid?"

"You're going to say something stupid."

I stop, mouth open. I was about to argue with her, but she seems to be agreeing with me. And frankly, I don't like that either.

"Wow, Vicky, way to kick a man while he's down."

Vicky sighs. I can hear her shuffling about on the other end of the phone. "You're going to say something stupid, you're going to make a tit of yourself, you're going to overthink what happens tonight into oblivion," she says. "But that doesn't mean it's going to go badly. You're a person, not a bloody robot, and you need to accept that this might not be a perfect first date. It might be a bit of a struggle. Did you even read the section on first dates?"

"Yes."

"And what did your mum say?"

No matter what happens tonight, try and enjoy it. I think following

170

these rules will help you do that, but be in the moment and listen to him and respond to what he says. Let it flow.

"To go with it."

"So go with it!" Vicky says. "If you don't want to talk about what he's talking about, change the subject and try something else. Make it about him."

I nod. "Okay." I let out a breath. "I should probably get back."

"Yes, because you've broken another rule by being in the bathroom."

I blink. "Huh?"

"'*Nothing spoils the flow of conversation like a last-minute trip to the ladies' room*,'" Vicky says.

"I shouldn't be on this date with him. I shouldn't be in this fancy restaurant. All of this seems wrong," I blurt out. "He's good-looking and nice and I've liked him for forever and the only reason he's noticed me is because—"

"Is because you made yourself noticeable," Vicky interrupts firmly. "You deserve this, Luc. He wants to go out with you. He wants to get to know you better. That's a good thing."

"Am I not lying to him?"

"No," she says. "You've just been the most upgraded and confident version of yourself. You've been you, turned up to eleven. You can do this."

I take a breath to try and calm myself. "I'm a disaster."

"You're a work in progress," she says. "Now get back out there and make that boy fall in love with you. Don't let me down, soldier."

I check myself in the mirror first. The hair is still good, the shirt still good, the face is a little bit shinier than I would like, but the lighting is dim, so I'll probably be alright.

"Let it flow," I say. "Just let it flow."

I step out of the bathroom and start back to the table.

"Lucas?"

I turn sharply to the door of the kitchen. Standing in chef whites, a surprised look on his face that is no doubt a mirror of mine, is my dad.

"What the fuck are you doing here?" I ask.

171

TWENTY-SEVEN

HIDE THE CRAZY

One of the most important rules of your first date (and your subsequent dates) is to hide the crazy. Nobody is perfect, that's not what I'm trying to suggest. We all have our little idiosyncrasies that make us who we are. Maybe it's a small thing, maybe it's quite a big thing, but the first date is not the place to air that.

You want this man to fall in love with every part of you and eventually he will. But first you need to hide those slightly more intense parts of yourself, the parts that will make him run a mile. You'll thank me later.

"LANGUAGE, LUC," Dad hisses.

"Fine. What the *hell* are you doing here?" I ask, annoyed that now, of all times, is the moment he's going to pull me up on my language. "I thought you were working tonight."

He gestures to himself. "You think I'm wearing this for fun? This is where I'm working tonight," he says. He looks over my shoulder towards the dining area. "Is this where you're having your date with Graham?"

"Grayson, Dad. Are you doing that on purpose?"

"It's an unusual name."

"It's a *great* name."

"Bit pricey here, isn't it?" Dad says, scrunching his nose.

"Well, I know that now." I've gone from super calm, I'm totally going to do this Lucas, to sweaty Lucas in the space of a few seconds. I hate this. Why is this happening to me?

"Do you want me to—"

"It's fine."

"I can help. I can—"

"Dad, please, I'm just going to go back to the table," I say. "It's fine. I'll…I'll see you at home."

I dread to think how red my face is right now. With a deep breath, I try to steady myself and head back over to the table.

"That took a while," Grayson says. "Everything okay?"

He thinks I've pooped. Oh my God. I'm on a first date with a beautiful boy and he thinks that I've gone to the bathroom to take a massive sh—

"Phone call," I say quickly. "When I was done in the bathroom, I got a phone call. Max, you know Max, he was struggling with a homework thing and decided to call me to ask about it. I think he's fine now."

"Okay," Grayson says, suddenly a little stiff. "You and Max are close, huh?"

"He's my best friend," I say. "You know Max, you two hang out all the time."

"Yeah, he's a good player," Grayson replies.

Apparently, Max is not a topic he wants to talk about. And now I really want to know why.

"Just can't survive without me sometimes, that boy," I say, laughing a little too hard, a little too loudly. The dirty looks come flying from all directions and I really don't want to be here right now. *Focus on him,* I think. *Focus on Grayson.* "How are you?" I ask.

He blinks, confused. We've been on this date for more than half an hour and I'm only just asking him how he is. Am I the worst date ever? It's possible.

"I'm alright," he says. "The waiter came over again. She really wants us to order some drinks."

"I could definitely use a drink," I say. "I'm parched."

Grayson looks around. "Just wait, we're never going to see her again now."

The waiter appears at the opposite end of the restaurant, a tray balanced on her hands so daintily that it looks like it's floating. She glides in our direction and places a drink in front of each of us.

"Here you go," she says. "From the kitchen."

Oh Christ, I think.

"For the young lovers," she continues, raising an eyebrow at the two of us. She vanishes again, quickly reappearing with two long white candles. She lights them both and puts them on the table. Suddenly we've gone from being in dim light to being lit up by orange-yellow light and...gosh it's nice to be able to properly see Grayson's face.

He looks so calm, like this happens to him all the time. He's used to candlelit dinners in fancy restaurants, while I feel so out of place it's like I'm the sheep among all these wolves.

"That's...actually much better," he says. "I can see your face now."

I've gone from red to...whatever the heck is redder than red. I am a tomato. I am a beetroot. My face is a volcano about to erupt.

"A-a-a-a-a-and I can see yours," I say. "Hello, Grayson's face."

He laughs. I don't know if he's laughing at me or with me, so I laugh too, hoping he thinks I've made a joke instead of making an ass of myself.

"We should probably look at ordering something before she comes back and decides she hates us again," Grayson whispers, the candles flickering, his breath drifting across the table and hitting my face.

Why am I enjoying him breathing on me? Am I really that love-starved?

Yes. Yes, you are.

The waiter, as if summoned by Grayson's whisper, reappears with a small arrangement of flowers that she sets between the two candles. They're red, just like my embarrassed face, and beautifully arranged. I've never had my breath taken away by a flower arrangement, but here I am, speechless. If this goes well, I want to take them home. I want to remember what these flowers look like.

"Did you do all this?" I ask.

Grayson shakes his head. "Maybe they noticed the date vibes and thought we needed a little push in the right direction."

I look over towards the kitchen and see Dad watching us. He gives me a thumbs up. I quickly look back at Grayson, who looks concerned at the panicked look on my face.

"You okay?"

"Um…" I stammer. "Phone is ringing again, will you give me a second?"

"Hang up, it's only Max," Grayson snaps, rolling his eyes.

"I'll just be a second."

I take my phone out of my pocket and pretend to answer it as I walk back towards the kitchen. Dad stays there, waiting for me to arrive.

"What are you doing?" he hisses. "You shouldn't be answering the phone at the dinner table."

"I'm not," I hiss back, putting the phone in my pocket. "You need to stop. You need to leave me alone. We're doing fine."

"You were barely speaking to one another. I was trying to help set the mood."

"Stop trying to help," I say. "We're going to be okay. I just want this to go well, please don't do anything else."

"Luc, I'm just—"

"Dad, please," I say. "I like this boy, okay? I like him a lot, and I just want this to go well."

Dad swallows and nods and, for the first time, I feel like he's actually heard me. I look back over to the table to where Grayson is sitting. I can only see the back of his head, but I am overcome by the feeling of wanting this to work out. The book has been so successful so far, it got me talking to him, it got me here. If I can just keep this casual, if I can just not put too much pressure on it, then maybe we'll be okay.

"I'll see you later," I say, before taking a deep breath and going back over to the table. "Okay, phone is on silent now," I say, pulling Grayson's focus to me. "No more interruptions. So…what were we talking about?"

"I don't think we'd even really started yet," he says with a smile.

God, it really is good to see his face. "But I'm an open book you can ask—"

I'm interrupted by the sound of instruments tuning up, of strings being plucked. There is shuffling nearby, the sound of people walking in our direction. I look around and see that a string quartet has set up nearby, two men and two women in black suits, readying themselves to start playing.

My gaze snaps back over to the kitchen. Is he fucking joking? But Dad isn't there. Maybe this is just what they do, maybe I'm over-thinking this.

One of the women counts them in and as one they start to play a song that I vaguely recognise. It's a little squeakier than I remember it, but I can hear the lyrics playing out in my head. What is that song?

"Is that…is that Ed Sheeran?" Grayson says quietly.

I don't know if he loses points for knowing that this song is an Ed Sheeran song. I think he's right, though. It sounds just whiny enough to be an Ed Sheeran song, though that could just be because it's being played on violins and such.

"I hate Ed Sheeran," Grayson whispers, a wicked smile on his face.

One million points to Grayson. He wins. Ed Sheeran is trash, and Grayson is everything.

"He's the soul sucking worst," I say with a chuckle, which makes him laugh too. But even with our mutual hatred of Ed Sheeran, I'm still painfully aware that there is a romantic song being played at a candlelit dinner with flowers and I am suddenly feeling the pressure to make this good, despite what Mum said in her book.

I want this to go well, I really want this to go well, and I want to follow her rules, but suddenly the restaurant is putting all of this extra pressure on us for it to go well. Is the universe interfering in my life right now or—?

"Compliments of the chef!" The voice pulls me back to reality so quickly that it's a wonder I don't fall off my chair. I see Dad standing next to the table, a tray in his hands and a smile plastered across his face. He sets the tray down on the edge of the table, and the food looks great, but what the hell is he doing?

"Dad, what are you doing?" I ask.

"I'm trying to help," he says quietly, through gritted teeth, like Grayson isn't right there and can't hear every single word he's saying.

"Did you do all of this?" I ask, gesturing to the string quartet that have now moved on to what I *think* is a different Ed Sheeran song, but I can't tell. Either all of his songs sound the same or they all sound the same from a string quartet.

"Like I said, Luc, trying to help," he says.

"I thought I recognised you," Grayson says. "I didn't know you worked here." He turns to me. "Why didn't you say something?"

"I didn't know he worked here either," I reply, which sounds stupid. And it's a weird enough statement that even Grayson looks confused by it. "No, I mean, he works at lots of places, I didn't realise this was one of them."

"Well, thanks for the food," Grayson says. "And the candles. Did you…did you get us a string quartet?"

"I just sent them over," Dad says.

He looks so pleased with himself. Like this is his crowning moment as he waits for someone to give him the Dad of the Year award, but all it's succeeding in doing is making me feel more uncomfortable than I've ever felt in my life. My dad is standing at the table while I try and win over this guy that I've had a crush on for goodness knows how many years and I just can't take any of it.

The tray is overloaded, even I can see that. And I feel like I see the disaster happen before it even does. Dad picks up a plate, which knocks a jug, which immediately flies towards me, sending sauce flying all over my shirt.

It's hot. It is burning my skin.

In a panic, I get up.

Grayson looks at me, alarmed.

Dad does the same.

"Shit," I say, grabbing a napkin off the table, that ultimately knocks my drink. "Sorry, fuck."

"Language."

"Dad!"

I step away from the table. But it's not a clean getaway by any stretch of the imagination. The table cloth is too long and I catch it with my foot. I trip, pulling it with me, the drinks, the food, the flowers, the candles, all of it clattering to the ground.

The string quartet stops so suddenly it's like their instruments have broken, all of them backing away. And then I feel the heat.

The tablecloth is on fire, because of course it is.

I scramble to my feet, trying to get away from it when an ear-piercing alarm rings through the restaurant.

No sooner have my hands slammed over my ears, the sprinklers turn on. There are screams from the other diners, from the restaurant staff, but not from me. I stand there and let the sprinklers soak me.

When Vicky told me I would do something stupid tonight, I get the feeling even she didn't think it was going to be this bad.

TWENTY-EIGHT

DON'T LET THEM SEE YOU SWEAT

Physically, spiritually, or psychologically. Trust me. It's just not cute.

THE WALK home is a cold one. Despite the towels given to us by the fire brigade when they arrived, we are soaked through to the bone. Grayson is at my side, shivering as much as me, maybe even more because at least I have the endless warmth of my embarrassment to keep me from turning into a little Luc-cicle.

He walks me to my door, something I definitely don't deserve, given how much of a disaster this was. I'd half expected him to get picked up by his parents then and there and we'd go back to never speaking to one another. It was fun while it lasted.

"Well, goodnight, Lu," he says. "See you tomorrow."

I nod. "Night."

And this is the moment in the movie where, at the end of a perfect evening, or at least one that didn't end in a literal fire, the two romantic leads would kiss. Or maybe the kiss would have happened in the restaurant under the sprinklers, or across the table after the dessert, but I can tell by the way that he gives me an awkward wave that I'm not even getting a pitiful hug tonight.

I watch Grayson walk away from my house and down the street. He doesn't even look back. And I don't really blame him for that.

Lu, I think. *God, it would have been cute if he started calling me Lu.*

In the hallway, I strip off my soaking wet clothes, carrying them through to the utility room and hanging them up. I take a quick shower to try and warm myself up, pulling on some sweats, before heading downstairs and getting myself something to eat.

Cereal was not what I thought I would be having tonight.

I haven't messaged Vicky. That's the last thing I want to do right now, because messaging Vicky will be admitting defeat. That can wait until morning.

I open my laptop and start to type a blog post. The disaster of the evening flows from my fingers with more ease than even I anticipated and my Cheerios are soggy by the time I get to the end of it.

Vicky will probably see this the second I post it, and will want to talk about it. She'll tell me what the "game plan" is to fix it, but I don't want to think about fixing it right now. I just want to wallow for a little while longer, think about what this night could have been had Dad not literally appeared to fuck everything up.

It's definitely over this time. There's just no way, after literally setting a restaurant on fire, that Grayson is going to want to go out with me again.

I hear the door open and close.

Dad doesn't call out.

He walks into the kitchen, in his normal clothes rather than his chef whites, which he's carrying in a plastic bag at his side. They are dripping onto the hardwood floors, and he is looking at me, fifty shades of incredibly unimpressed. I do not love this journey for me, not at all.

"What the heck was that all about?" he asks, putting the plastic bag down and fishing out his chef whites.

"Dad, I'm—"

"I was trying to help," he said. "I thought I could help make the night a little better. You looked like you didn't want to be there."

"I *did* want to be there."

"Well, I doubt Grayson knew that," Dad replied.

"Thank you for getting his name right."

"Thank you for not being able to take a joke." He takes the chef

180

whites over to the kitchen sink and starts wringing them out. "You're out of your mind, Luc, the overreaction—"

"Overreaction? Dad, you were butting in."

"I was trying to help."

"You were embarrassing me!" I reply, my voice getting a little high, a little squeaky. "I was trying to get to know this boy, trying to… I don't know…just trying. And then you come barrelling in, throwing flowers at us and candles and…and what the fuck were you doing with a string quartet?"

"I was trying to set the mood," Dad says. "And watch your language."

"Fuck my language."

"I mean it, Luc, don't talk to me like that."

"I asked you to leave me alone," I say. "I specifically went over to you and asked you because I wanted to do this myself and you just couldn't resist making it shit for me."

"Luc—"

"You embarrassed me in front of a boy I really like in the name of helping, which you weren't, by the way, and you're telling me not to talk to you like this? How do you want me to talk to you, Dad? You want me to thank you for fucking up my life?"

"Now you're just being dramatic." Dad walks away from the sink and hangs his clothes over the backs of the chairs, shaking his head, mumbling something in a tone that sounds more like a rumbling of thunder than it does words.

"I'm not being dramatic, I'm telling you how I feel."

He turns to me. "Alright, then. Tell me how you feel."

I blink, caught off guard by him staring me right in the face and asking to hear from me, his eyes blazing.

"You shouldn't have done what you did tonight," I say. My voice is quiet. I've lost my fire because it's been eclipsed by his. "You…you should have left us to it, let me do my own thing."

"Well, I'm sorry for taking an interest in my son's life."

It's like I can feel an elastic band in my head snapping. "That makes a change," I say. It doesn't come out with the conviction that I actually feel, it just sounds a little bit sad. I want to yell it at him, want to smack him in the face with the words, but they just drift from my mouth to his ears. But the way his face crumples tells me that it had the desired effect. He looks crushed.

Good.

"Lucas, I—"

"You shouldn't have got involved," I say.

"I wanted to help. Why can't you understand that?"

"I do understand that," I snap. "I understand it, but you shouldn't have done it, you ruined it. You ruined my first date with a boy by… by…by doing too much. You should have left it. I'm going to bed." I grab my laptop and start out of the kitchen.

"Lucas, we are talking about this."

"No we're not, goodnight."

"Lucas!" he calls after me as I walk up the stairs, but I'm not listening.

I slam my bedroom door. It's childish, I know, but it gets the point across because he stops calling my name.

I half expect him to come up the stairs and open the door to yell at me some more, to make sure we talk about it. That feels like the kind of thing a parent should do. But he doesn't. He's given up. Of course.

When I pick up my phone, I see that I have a message from Vicky hovering on the screen.

VICKY

Saw the blog post. You alright?

The truth is, I want to be alright, but I'm really not. I wanted tonight to go well, and maybe I put too much pressure on myself, on it, maybe I wanted it too badly, but all that did was end up embarrassing me, and subsequently, Grayson.

I'm fine. Just tired. Talk tomorrow? Xx

My phone buzzes again and I'm ready to say goodnight to Vicky when I see it's from Max.

MAX

How did it go? The fact you've not messaged yet tells me that it went well?

Oh Max, how wrong you are.

Not quite. Total disaster. I'll tell you all about it tomorrow.

I put my phone on my bedside table and get ready for bed, climbing beneath my covers and waiting for my brain to get tired and switch itself off so I'll stop replaying the night over and over again in my head. I really did mess it up. I had an opportunity with Grayson Murray and I messed it up.

I can blame Dad all I like, but he was right, I overreacted. Maybe if I hadn't, I wouldn't have almost set fire to Rigby's.

Christ, I set fire to a restaurant. Why am I such a disaster?

Far too late to tug at that thread, I think.

I open my laptop one more time and go back to the piece I was writing for the Creative Writing Group session tomorrow. It is practically finished, but I hate it now. Am I really going to go tomorrow? Am I really going to do this? Why bother if this is already over?

I close it again and put it on my desk. I've embarrassed myself enough, surely.

There is a tapping at my window and I freeze. I am about to ignore it, thinking I've imagined it, when it comes again.

Why is there a stupid romcom part of my brain that insists it's Grayson going full *Say Anything* and is standing outside with a boombox over his head?

Cautiously, I cross the room, inching my curtain open until I see a figure sitting outside my window, his phone lighting up his face.

"Max?" I say, maybe a little too loud.

He looks up. "Let me in!" he mouths.

I open the window.

"Fancy seeing you here," he says.

"Don't," I say. "What the fuck are you doing outside my window?"

He looks at me blankly, like it's the most obvious thing in the world. "Because I felt like you needed me," he says. "I can go home if you want."

The smart move would be to tell him to go home, to tell him that I'm fine and that I don't want to talk about it, but that would be a lie.

He's done this a couple of times before, usually when something was going shit for me and he was coming around to help. I can even remember the first time he did it.

Seven years ago.

It was the night after Mum died.

My dad must have called his mum or something. They only live down the road, and suddenly he was here, and he'd climbed up the tree outside my house so he could get to my bedroom window, all because he wanted to make sure that I was okay.

"I probably could have knocked."

"You definitely couldn't have," I reply. "Got into a fight with Dad, too. Icing on the cake."

"Jesus," Max says, climbing inside. I close the window behind him. "You really decided to set fire to everything tonight."

"When I tell you what happened, you'll realise why that is a really poor choice of words."

We sit on the floor, and it's like we're kids again. But we're not playing with toys or drawing or doing homework, we're talking about the boy who I've just gone out on a date with and the restaurant that I almost burned down. When did we get so grown up?

"You're such a disaster," he says with a laugh. "How…I mean… literally how?"

"I wish I knew, I really do," I say.

"I feel like I could put you in a padded room and you'd still find a way to do something stupid."

"I am not that bad."

"You're right," Max says. "You're worse."

"I hate you."

"Sure you do," he says. "If you hated me, you wouldn't have opened the window. You would have called the police."

"Who's to say they're not on their way now?"

"Busted."

"Damn."

A silence falls between us for a second, but at least I'm smiling now. Even if it's just for a moment. Until I see Grayson tomorrow and he starts blanking me again, at least I'm managing to laugh about my absolute wreck of a life.

He shuffles closer, and I lean my head on his shoulder. He leans his head on top of mine. And we just sit.

"So it didn't work out," he says quietly. "You'll figure it out. Maybe…maybe he's just not the right guy for you."

"But I thought he was."

"I know," Max says. "But he's out there, somewhere. I promise."

"So you found Soph and suddenly you're the oracle on romance?"

"Shut up," he says. "Look, I know it seems shitty now, but at some point, it will just be a funny story that you tell people."

"Please don't tell Soph," I say. "If this is going to be a funny story I tell people, can it please be a funny story I tell people in a couple of weeks?"

"You really think you'll be able to stop Grayson from telling literally every single one of his friends?"

I let out a groan. "You're not helping," I say, lifting my head to look at him. "You really think he'd do that?"

"I don't know," he says. "His group of friends seem to laugh all the time. They've got to be laughing at something. I'm pretty sure Dylan isn't bringing the jokes."

"Shade."

"He's a dickhead."

"I get that impression," I say. "He barely spoke to me at the party."

"Dylan?" Max says.

"Yeah," I reply. "Who did you think I meant?"

"Just making sure," Max replies. "He's a dickhead."

He takes his phone out of his pocket and checks it, quickly tapping a few times before he puts it back. I'm pretty sure he's texting Soph, and suddenly I feel like I'm intruding in my own bedroom. Which is stupid. He came over here.

"So, you're okay?" Max says, looking at me.

"Yeah," I say. "You didn't have to come over, you know."

"I feel like I did," he replies. "If I hadn't, I probably would have called you, and you wouldn't have answered because phone calls make you anxious and then…" He smiles. "I would have come over anyway, I guess."

"No Soph tonight, then?"

"School night," he says. "And she was doing something with her family."

"Okay," I say. "I'm okay. Thank you. It…it means a lot."

He shrugs like it's nothing, like he didn't just walk ten minutes and climb up a tree for me at ten o'clock at night. He gets to his feet and I follow suit. Before I know it, he's pulled me into a hug.

It's the perfect Max hug, squeezy, telling me that he's here for me if I need him. Which I always knew, I guess. He's been there for me for pretty much my whole life. I'm suddenly incredibly glad he's helping me with Grayson.

"Thanks," I say into his shoulder.

"Welcome," he replies. "Right, I'm going to climb back down. Listen for a crash. I've not done this for a while."

I wait while he leaves, watching as he walks off down the road and back towards his house. I try not to let my brain spiral about Grayson. Whatever happens tomorrow, I guess I'll be okay. Maybe this is my sign to let it all go. I had my shot, and I blew it. It is what it is.

I'm done.

Goodbye, Grayson Murray.

TWENTY-NINE

LUC & SOPH

Did you go on a date with Grayson Murray last
night?

Lucas Cook, I need a response.

———

I don't see Dad the following morning. His chef whites are still
hanging on the back of the chairs in the dining room, and his
computer is open on the dining room table, some papers sitting
around it.

It only takes me a second to realise that they're bills that need
paying, big red stamps at the top of each one telling him just how
urgent they are.

I can't imagine the small amount of money that I gave him from
my first paycheck, even denting this. And he wouldn't have been
paid for a full shift last night after everything that happened. In the
AITA, I think I am coming out as the asshole here.

VICKY

I'm outside

I grab my things and head out to see Vicky shivering on the street corner.

"That was more than two minutes," she says when I reach her. I pull her into a hug, giving her the tightest squeeze I can manage. It's a combination of wanting to warm her up and making myself feel better.

"Morning," I grumble.

"Wow," she says. "Not even a good on that morning."

"There's nothing good about it," I say. "You read the post."

"It was delightfully vague," she replies. "Which I understand for the anonymity of it all, but…come on now. I'm gagging to hear."

"About my massive fail?"

"No, what's got you looking so defeated?" she asks. "What happened?"

"What didn't happen?" I reply.

We start the walk to school and I explain everything that happened the previous night. She doesn't say a word, doesn't butt in, doesn't even try to add her wisdom or her two cents. She just listens to me, and I couldn't be more grateful for that.

"Your dad fucked it, huh?" she says when I'm done.

"Yes and no," I reply. I'm feeling bad about how I went off at him, even though he did make me feel like shit. The fact that I didn't get to see him this morning to clear the air definitely has me feeling worse. "He tried to help, but didn't listen to me when I asked him not to," I say. "His heart was in the right place. It all just went wrong."

"The clumsiness is genetic, then?"

"Apparently so," I say. "It's a wonder he has all of his fingers, given that he works in a kitchen."

"I wouldn't trust you with a butter knife," Vicky replies. "And you're okay?"

"Max came over," I say.

"He did?"

"He messaged to see how it went, and I think my response was vague and chaotic enough that he felt the need to check in."

Vicky "Hmmms" and nods her head.

"What?"

"He's just a surprise, that's all," she says. "Straight boys can be considerate."

"He's not straight."

A pause. "I see."

"What do you see?" I ask.

"Nothing, nothing at all," she replies. "It's sweet of him to come over and check in, though," she adds. "Did he make you feel better?"

"He got me to laugh about it?" I say.

"Before you spiralled again."

"Duh."

"Great," she says. "So, what are we going to do here?"

I look at her, confused. "What do you mean?"

"Well, there has to be a way that we bounce back from this, no?" she says. "It can't be over."

"Why can't it be over?"

"It was one bad date."

"It was horrific," I say. "We barely knew what to say to one another, then my dad fucked it up. Did you miss the part where I set the restaurant on fire?"

Vicky snorts at that.

"VICKY!"

"What?"

"You laughing isn't helping!"

"Come on, Luc, it's kind of funny," she manages. "How many people do you know who would go to the fanciest restaurant in town and end up with the fire brigade being called?"

I can't keep the hint of a smile off my face. "Good point, well made," I say. "I'm a total disaster. You see why I think it might be over?"

"Did you message him?"

"No."

"Then how do you know?!" She groans. "Come on, Luc, where is your fighting spirit?"

"I think it drowned when the sprinklers went off," I say.

"We could—"

"You should have seen his face, Vicky," I interrupt. "He seems to be taking it as a sign, and maybe I should too."

She opens her mouth to say something else, but seems to think better of it. I take it as an opportunity to change the subject and I ask her how she is and how the blog is going.

"The book updates are good," she says. "I'm not pressuring you to keep going, but the content is chef's kiss. I've thought of some great ways to update the tips based on your…mishaps, and ways to decode what it means exactly."

"Oh, yeah?"

"Yeah!" She keeps talking about it, letting me know how good the book has been for her blog. Eventually, we are at my locker and my brain has drifted to Grayson once again. "And there's the sad boy again," she says.

"What?"

"Keep your chin up, Luc," she says. "So it didn't work out with Grayson, there are plenty more fish in the sea or something less cliché."

I snort. "Thanks. That's what Max said." I sigh. "Maybe he's just not right for me."

"Maybe. And you've learned things, right? You just apply that to the next guy," she says. "It's found you once, it will find you again."

She heads off to her form class and I open my locker, swapping some of my books over. The bell rings and I know that I'm taking too long to do this, but Mr Marshall will understand, or at least I hope he will. Who knows? Maybe he'll reprimand me for being late and then I'll just cry. It's a lucky dip.

I close my locker door and the one next to me slams at the same time. I jump. I'm pretty sure I scream, then all of my books are on the floor.

"Great," I say, getting onto my knees and gathering them up.

"Hey."

And there's that voice that I've grown to like so much over the last couple of weeks. Is he talking to me?

I look at the shoes first, scuffed, black, my eyes tracing up the black trousers to the untucked shirt and up to his face. Which is looking right at me. I half expected him to be talking to Max or one of his other friends. Why on earth is he talking to me after everything that happened last night?

"You alright down there?" he asks.

"Um…yeah," I say. "Just…being my usual clumsy self, you know."

"At least nothing's on fire this time." I wince at the memory. "Sorry, bad joke."

"Not even a joke," I reply. "Just a reference I would like to forget."

"I think I'm going to be reminding you of that forever," he says.

I grab my books and get to my feet. "I'm…I'm sorry about last night," I say. "Sorry about Dad, and about freaking, and about… well…about setting the restaurant on fire."

"I still can't believe you did that," he says, chuckling. "It's so…I don't know. It's so you."

I laugh. "I hate that. Why does a disaster of that magnitude have to be *so me*?"

His turn to laugh now.

The silence that pushes its way between us is horrible. It hate it. It's suffocating.

"So—"

"Well—"

We start trying to talk at the same time, then both stop.

"You go first," I say.

"About last night," he says.

"Yeah."

"That…wasn't good," he chuckles. "I mean, as disastrous dates go, that one has to go down in the history books, surely."

"I'll say."

"So I think we need a do-over." He says it like it's the simplest thing in the world, like I didn't just set the restaurant on fire last night, like I didn't just make myself look like a total disaster in front of him.

"What?"

"We need a do-over," he says. "That doesn't count. Let's call it a dry run."

"It wasn't dry."

"A sopping wet run," he corrects. "What are you doing tonight?"

The second bell rings and now we're both officially late, but neither one of us shows any sign of moving.

I stare at him, dumbstruck.

Hello, Grayson Murray.

THIRTY

BE ALOOF (Cont.)

By all means, you should be pleased to see him, especially if you're bumping into him by chance. (And by chance I mean, in a perfectly choreographed way that means you are the brightest spark in his day.) So when you see him, you act surprised, you give him some of your attention but not all of it. This is not me suggesting that he will get bored of you, but this is just a way of making him always want more of your time but not being able to quite get it. Let him become addicted to you.

LUC & VICKY

> Grayson wants a do-over

Since when?!

> Since literally two minutes ago when I bumped into him at my locker.

YES! OKAY! GAME PLAN! How are you feeling?

> How do you think I'm feeling?

You're freaking.

Duh.

Fully losing it.

Ding ding ding!

Deep breath, we'll go over it later. GOLDEN opportunity!

———

It's the last thing that I was expecting to happen this morning, but the possibility of a do-over has my brain fizzing at such a high frequency that I can barely focus all day. To say that school is an absolute disaster would be an understatement.

Which is to say, I'm an absolute disaster, school is just happening around me. Lessons are passing me by, anyone trying to get my attention might as well not bother.

"So, tonight?" Grayson said. "I'll pick you up after Creative Writing Group? Maybe we go somewhere less high pressure."

"Okay, so it wasn't just me that felt like Rigby's Steakhouse was not the move."

"One hundred percent not the move."

"I am not a fancy person, Grayson."

He laughs. "Sorry, I forget sometimes not everyone can afford somewhere like that." He caught himself and readjusted. "I mean, I just wanted to go someplace nice."

"Anywhere we go will be someplace nice," I replied.

Then he looked at me all goo-goo-eyed and asked me to meet him in the canteen for lunch. So now I'm freaking out over that.

I am meeting Grayson.

In the canteen.

FOR LUNCH.

"If you're going to the canteen, I'm coming with you," Vicky says, when she meets me after my fourth-period Geography class.

"Why do you need to come with me?" I ask.

"Because I'm going to stop you doing anything stupid," she says. "Like usual."

"Where were you last night?"

"If I thought for a single second you were going to set a restaurant on fire, I would have been there just to get video footage."

"I hate you."

"You love me," she corrects. "And don't you forget it."

We open the doors to the canteen and are hit by a wall of noise. A combination of kids talking loudly over each other, plates clattering, and card machines beeping. It is a mess of activity and I am reminded why my friends and I never, under any circumstances, come to the canteen. It is only in times of pure desperation.

The lighting is homophobic to say the least, yellow, grimy, stark, and just makes the already filthy-looking walls appear all the worse. There is graffiti, tiny notes left on it, honest-to-God handprints, and food stains. It is not a good look. How this place doesn't have a hygiene rating of minus twelve is beyond me.

The benches aren't much better. White table tops are surrounded by red, circular chairs that are attached in such a way that no one can be truly comfortable for a prolonged period of time. They don't want us to stay in here. They want us to eat our food and leave, but this is the only sanctuary in winter. And that's grim.

My heart is beating double in my chest as we make our way across the canteen to where Grayson is sitting with his friends. And my friends. It takes me a second to clock them sitting with him, chatting like they're here every day when…when usually they're in the Geography block with me. Though, when was the last time I spent a lunch break there?

I've hardly seen them at all today. Wednesday is not a day where many of our classes cross over, and me being late to form this morning didn't help matters.

"What are you doing here?" Jasmine says.

"I was looking for Grayson," I say. "Is this where you've been—?"

"While you've been in the library or whatever, yeah," she says, turning back to Krish. I guess that's the end of that then.

"He said to come and meet him for lunch," I say, trying to be bold, trying to take control of the situation. I'm sick of Jasmine trying to make me feel bad about this, about myself.

"Oh," she says. "That's new."

"We're going out tonight," I say.

"Again," Grayson adds. "So, not that new."

He gets up from his seat and there's a moment where I think he's about to hug me or something, and my face is suddenly on fire. But he squeezes past me.

"Need coffee. I'll be back."

I watch him go, Soph suddenly appearing in my line of sight, Max at her side. Her face bursts into a smile, his twists in confusion.

"Here you are!" Soph exclaims. "I messaged you."

I remember the message from this morning that I definitely wasn't ready to respond to and take out my phone to see more have arrived since.

SOPH

Are you lost?

??????

Okay, now I feel like an asshole.

"Sorry, phone was on silent," I say.

"Sure," she says, brightly. "Okay, so tonight we were thinking of going for Pretty Woman. They actually enjoyed Notting Hill last week after we slept through it the week before."

"You slept through Notting Hill?" Vicky says, a little too loudly. I think she's ready to go to the mat on this one. "It's a classic."

Soph rolls her eyes and laughs. "Oh my God, you two are made for each other. How were you not friends before now?! So, you in? Vicky, you should come too!"

"I've got Creative Writing Group," I say. "And then a date with Grayson."

Max blinks. Sophie's jaw drops.

"Be cool," I say quietly.

"I can't, this is insane," she hisses. "I thought you went out last night."

"We did. Big disaster."

"He set the restaurant on fire," Vicky says.

"Thanks."

"You're welcome."

"Wait, what? Rewind! When did this all happen?" She is giddy.

"I said be cool. This is the opposite of cool." I'm looking between her and Max. I thought he might have told her about it. Something weird happens when one of your best friends gets into a relationship, suddenly anything you share with them isn't shared with them singular, it's shared with the couple. They are one entity. One brain.

But I asked him not to, and he didn't, and I'm pleased about that.

"I'm surprised that you're cool," she says. "You should be freaking out right now."

"I am freaking out, but I'm trying to be cool because he's going to be back any second."

"I need FULL details," she says. "Promise?"

She holds out her finger towards me. I press it with my own. "Promise."

She's about to walk away when she stops. "When did all of this start?" she asks. "Last time I checked, you guys were just talking. Did something happen on Saturday? I feel like I've totally missed something here."

I open my mouth to respond, but only air comes out. I want to be able to talk to her about this, but suddenly, out of nowhere, there is this distance between us. I wish I knew where it had come from, and more than that, I wish I knew how I was supposed to stop it.

"Luc?"

"We got to talking on Saturday," I say. "Like, properly talking and then…last night…and then tonight."

She nods, forcing a smile onto her face. I can tell it's strained, that she doesn't want to talk about this now.

"We need a bit of a catch-up, huh?"

"Yeah," I say.

"Okay then," she says. She walks away and goes to sit with Jasmine and Krish, engaging them in conversation. Max leans in close.

"What the hell is happening? I thought—"

"He asked for a do-over," I say, fizzing with excitement.

Max smiles, but the smile doesn't quite reach his eyes. "Alright then," he says. "We've got some work to do, huh?"

"Totally."

Grayson comes back and we actually sit together and have lunch. My friends are there, but I can feel that strange distance between us, like we're having lunch together but we're not actually in the same place. I keep looking at Soph, trying to catch her eye, but she's deep in conversation with Max or with Jasmine and I'm so far away from them it hurts.

———

WHEN I STAND TO READ MY PIECE DURING CREATIVE WRITING GROUP AT the end of the day, I honestly feel like I have the eyes of the whole world on me. Apparently, the way everybody sat last week was the seating plan, because I'm once again opposite Grayson and it's making me sweat.

But his smile is encouraging and I have a feeling that even if this is the worst thing I've ever written, he's still going to be nice about it. Let's be honest, if he's willing to talk to me after I almost burned a restaurant to the ground, what's a bit of writing going to do?

"Whenever you're ready, Lucas," Mrs Leighton says, raising her eyebrows at me.

Apparently, I've been standing here quietly for too long. *That's enough psyching yourself up now, Lucas, get on with it.*

After one last deep breath, I start to read.

The piece ended up coming in a rush of inspiration. I took Dad's advice, much as I don't want to admit it just now, and wrote without thinking too much about it. What came out was about Mum.

Understandably, I think, she's been on my mind a lot lately, so writing about a day at the seaside that ended up being a total washout felt right. It didn't stop us from sitting on the beach under an umbrella, from having fish and chips in the freezing cold, from having a perfect day in imperfect weather.

As I read, it almost feels too personal, like I'm reaching a little too deep, but I'm reliving it in my head as the words come out of my mouth. I can see us under a bright yellow umbrella, I can feel the chill in the air, taste the salt of the sea on my tongue.

"It's a little on the nose," is the first comment I get.

I stand there and take it as well as I can, graciously, with a smile, trying to pull myself out of the headspace that is thinking about Mum, so I don't just break down and cry.

"Something a little more figurative might work to make it less... obvious."

"I liked it," Mrs Leighton says. "A good beginning, potentially something to read at the end of term if you wanted to develop it further. Could definitely do with some more detail in there, some of the finer points being given a little more poignancy, a little more weight, but there are some gorgeous images in it."

Mrs Leighton is looking at me with a 'proud parent' sort of smile. This was what she was hoping for. She was hoping to get my creative juice flowing and get me making stuff. She's got her way.

It only occurs to me as I stand there that she knows Mum has died, that it would be in my file somewhere or it was probably mentioned to her by another teacher at some point. Maybe she's just being nice.

Mrs Leighton opens it up to the rest of the group, each of whom gives feedback, varying in levels of actual usefulness. There are some good suggestions on where to take it next, and some that tell me that, while they were hearing the words, they weren't really listening.

"Just Grayson, now," Mrs Leighton says. "Thoughts, questions, comments."

My heart is in my mouth. Literally, it feels like. I turn my attention to my notebook, furiously scribbling down the critiques I've already been given.

"It can't have been easy to write," Grayson says softly. "It felt very personal, very true to life. It made me wonder if I've had days like that with my mum, you know? I think Mrs Leighton is right, more detail. I want to be able to taste the fish and chips, smell the salt of the sea, all of that."

I'm staring across the circle at Grayson and he's staring right back, but this time, there is something more to it. It's as if he isn't looking at me, it's more like he's looking into me, seeing beyond the Lucas that I've been trying to show him. And he's not cowering away from it. He's smiling at me. And I get the feeling that things might be about to start going right.

THIRTY-ONE

BE CHAMPAGNE IN HUMAN FORM

It's not easy being sparkling. It takes effort, it takes courage, and it is one of the many things that it is good to be on a first date. Keep the conversation flowing, but as I said previously in this chapter, be sure to keep it light. You don't want to talk about anything too serious like death or war on a date, nothing will harsh someone's buzz like talking about plague and famine.

So the alternative is to be like a fizzing glass of champagne. Be sweet, be sparkly, be a little dry, be addictive. Be something that they enjoy.

WHILE I CAN HARDLY SAY for certain whether Dad will be at this restaurant tonight, I'm pretty sure he wouldn't even dare try to "help" again.

We've come to Lamberti's. When Grayson suggested it, I practically jumped with glee. 1) As we have already established, the food is to die for, and 2) it is well within my price range. A third bonus reason appears as we arrive—there is actually noise. And not a string quartet in sight.

Bingo.

Vicky and Max came over after school to go over the rules one more time, sure beyond all reasonable doubt that the reason last night went so horribly was because I didn't follow the rules closely enough.

"You got sloppy."

"What I've got is an embarrassing Dad who couldn't resist an opportunity to make me look like an asshole in front of Graham."

"Graham?" Max asked.

"He kept calling him Graham. I think it was supposed to be a joke," I say. Vicky was cracking up. "What?"

She shrugged. "Your Dad's funny."

"Get out of my house."

Now, Grayson and I are seated by the window, looking out onto the rest of the entertainment complex, and people heading out for the evening. Weirdly, I feel like we're on display, like we're being watched as people pass. But no one is looking at me. Well, no one apart from Grayson. He obviously knows the eye contact rule too.

"What?" I ask.

"You look nice," he says.

I try to hold back the cheesiest grin. "So do you," I reply.

And he does. It's a different shirt than last night (maybe his hasn't dried yet either), a deep blue colour that brings out his eyes. Honestly, how dare he look consistently good so often?

I'm already noticing a tick in Grayson. Whenever I've told him he looks good, he feels the need to check again, this time his reflection in the window we're sitting next to. He fiddles with his hair, undoes another button on his shirt, only turning back to me when he's completely satisfied.

"So," he says, a little louder than before, his voice serious, businesslike. "This is a do-over date. Last night was a total blip and didn't count." There's a smile tugging at the corners of his mouth. "But please know that I will never let you forget it."

"Please let me forget it," I reply. "There is nothing I want more than to pretend that it never happened."

"Which part?"

"The part where I made an ass of myself."

His smile gets bigger. "You want to forget the whole thing?"

"I hate you, I'm leaving," I reply, but I don't move an inch. He knows I'm not going anywhere, but it makes him laugh. "Have you been here before?"

"A couple times," he says. "You?"

"Far more times than I care to admit," I reply.

And suddenly we're talking through the menu. I'm showing him my favourite dishes and he's showing me his, and we're deciding what to get. There seems to be a silent understanding that we're not getting garlic bread, which makes my heart do a small flip.

If you must eat on your first date (which I don't recommend!) don't get anything breathy. The lasting memory of the night should be you, not what you ate.

Mum's voice in my head again. But the fact that he avoids it too bodes well. What if he kisses me? What if I kiss him? What were the rules on kissing? I try to remember.

I pull my phone out under the table and text Vicky.

> RULES ON KISSING?!

The three dots appear instantly.

> You're supposed to let the man do it.

> WE ARE BOTH MEN. THAT IS KIND OF THE POINT!

> Duh!

> Play it by ear

> And stop messaging me. It might not be a rule in the book, but it's just bad manners.

"Everything okay?" Grayson asks.

Apparently, I'm not nearly as subtle as I think I am.

"Fine," I say. "Just...checking my...um..." I remember how he reacted to Max last night. "Dad."

"Huh?"

"He wasn't home when I got ready tonight. I wanted to make sure he knew I was out," I say. "So he didn't wait up."

202

Grayson snorts. "You think I'm going to keep you out late?"

"You're twisting my words to make me get all flustered."

"Because it's so easy!" he says.

"I really will leave, you know," I say. "Then you'll end up sat here eating pizza all by yourself."

"More for me."

"So rude."

"You love it."

And I kind of do. This is the kind of stuff you don't get to see in films and on TV. A gay character is far too often sitting off to the side, a catalyst for the straight character to do something. Right now, I'm having a main character moment, and it's all because of Mum's book. She's got me living some kind of romcom dream.

Our drinks arrive and we order our mains with a waiter who is way more bubbly and kind than the one we had last night. She actually seems to want us here, which is kind of nice.

"Where did we get to last night?" Grayson asks. "Conversation wise."

"Oh, I thought this was a do-over and last night didn't count?"

"Right, I did say that," Grayson replies. "Tell me about yourself."

I open my mouth and try to come up with a witty response, but my brain won't engage quickly enough. I can't say "Fancy seeing you here" because as much as the third time is a charm, we arrived together and that would just be weird. I'm holding eye contact like the rules say to, mimicking his body language, leaning forward, hand on chin. He smiles. I smile.

"I go to Southford Secondary School," I say. "I'm okay at most things. There are two classes I enjoy: Biology, because Mr Edwards is a DILF and English, because Mrs Leighton is a gay icon waiting to happen. But I've still not finished Pride & Prejudice and I'm very aware that I am one slip-up away from her actually realising it."

"She definitely knows."

"She does not."

"Lu, she told you to crack the spine the other day, she knows," Grayson says flatly. "And you do that thing in class whenever she asks a question about the book where you suddenly look all studious, like you're taking notes and stuff. It's *so* obvious."

I sit back. "You've been watching me in class?"

It catches him off guard. He takes his eyes away from me and his mouth flaps open and closed like a fish as he tries to work out a response.

"Got me," he says.

"That's cute."

He shrugs. "So are you."

The pizza arrives, which is a damn good thing because if I look at him any longer, I think I might break. There is something really funny to me about how we both slowly reach for the knife and fork. If I were out with my friends, I would be picking up these pizza slices with my hands, but there's something about being across from Grayson. He can obviously feel it too, which means we're cautiously cutting each slice into bite-size pieces, tiptoeing around the fact that pizza is meant to be picked up.

"Your piece today was beautiful," he says suddenly. "I...don't know what I was expecting. I mean, Mrs Leighton has been pushing you to come, so I assumed you would be good, but I wasn't expecting that."

"Unexpected in a good way?"

"Well, doesn't that just about sum you up?" he says.

Damn, he's smooth and I am mush.

"I meant what I said. It can't have been easy to write about," he continues. "And after what we started talking about on Monday, I'm sort of glad that you let me know a little bit more about you. About her."

"Where did we get to?" I ask.

"You were telling me about your mum," he says. "When your dad...you know...decided we needed to be more romantic." He puts a bite of his pizza in his mouth, eyeing me expectantly, waiting for me to talk.

And I want to. After the fight with Dad last night, after him ignoring her again, I want to talk about her, but I know it's against the rules.

"I don't remember her that well," I reply, slicing my pizza. Which is probably the most honest I've ever been about her and even though I can hear Vicky's voice in my head telling me not to talk about it, and Mum's voice telling me to keep it light, my own inner monologue is telling me to open up. "I wish I did, but she died when I was quite young and the more time that goes by, the harder it is to remember her. That's the weird thing about memories. You're not actually remembering it, you're remembering the remembering of something, and that gets more and more diluted every time you think about it. So I can still see her face because of pictures, but I can't really remember her voice all that well."

That last part isn't entirely true anymore. Since I found those videos of her online, I can actually hear her voice clearer than ever, but the point still stands. I remember the memory of her rather than her in reality.

"That must be hard," Grayson says. "I'm quite close with my parents, so…I can't imagine what that must be like."

"Some days are better than others," I say. "There are times when it really hurts and I miss her, and there are other times when…everything is fine. Most days are fine, by the way. It's just not the kind of thing you get over in a hurry. Or ever, really."

I swerve to a safer topic, but I have this warm feeling in my chest from Mum coming up in a conversation and it not ending in chaos or heartache. That was nice.

We talk about school a little, about our friends, and about the places where they crossover. I find myself asking a lot of questions about his friendship group, about his family, about school. And I am quickly realising that even though I've been admiring him from afar for the last four years, I don't really know much about him.

He and Max play sports together sometimes, which is where that crossover in the friendship groups comes from, and again he wonders aloud how we haven't spent time together before. I don't have the heart to tell him that he practically looked through me when we were all out the other night, and that he didn't know I existed until I had the coffee.

I keep asking questions, and he keeps answering them, and I feel like I'm doing a good job of keeping the conversation going, even if he isn't asking me many questions back.

He has an older brother and a younger one who are so chaotic that he seems to be the balance in the middle, and two parents who—he pauses a little before he says this—care about him a lot.

I want to know what he means by that. I want to dig into it a little bit more, but when he changes the subject to how good the food is, that tells me he doesn't want to get into it right now and he'll talk when he's ready.

We split a dessert, which shouldn't be a big deal, but my brain makes it the biggest deal imaginable. There's something about our spoons clashing as we each dive into a bowl of gelato that makes us look lovesick and ridiculous, and if anyone is walking past and happens to look in the window, I hope that's what they see.

We split the bill and ride back together on the bus, leaning into each other, sharing a pair of headphones and listening to music. His taste isn't the worst. There's some musical theatre in there, but not nearly enough. There are some girl groups but, again, not nearly enough. I will take it upon myself to educate him.

At one point he takes my hand, and it's like everything explodes into full colour. The lights on the inside of the bus are brighter, the music that's playing seems to swell and grow. Bernadette Peters is singing Being Alive from Company and Grayson Murray is holding my hand. It feels like the world stops spinning for a second.

"Somebody hold me too close…"

He's still holding my hand when we get off the bus, still holding it as we walk from the bus stop to my house, which is blessedly, still dark. No Dad here to ruin it. No Dad here to know that I was out again. No Dad here to notice.

"I think that was a success," he says quietly, like he's trying to keep that between us if he can.

I can't help but smile. "Me too," I reply. "I think, after a false start, we might actually be quite good at the date night thing."

"Cocky."

"Tell me I'm wrong."

He shrugs. "I can't."

We're outside my front door and the cinematic thing would be to invite him in for coffee or something, but 1) I don't drink coffee, and 2) everyone knows that inviting someone in for coffee is the old person equivalent of Netflix and Chill, which is basically code for sex. Facts.

"I'll see you tomorrow then," I say.

"Yeah," he replies, all breathy.

And there is that electric feeling again. I don't know whether to make the move or to wait for him to do it, and I can already feel myself overthinking this into oblivion, to the point where I know I will screw it up. I can't screw this up.

He lets go of my hand, and it sort of surprises me. I'm about to make a joke about it when his hands find my waist and he pulls me in closer. Our bodies are pressed together, two thin layers of fabric between us. I don't have time to overthink it. He leans down and I lift my chin a little, our lips meeting.

And the world around me explodes into fireworks.

THIRTY-TWO

IT'S IN HIS KISS (That's Where It Is)

If you want to know if he loves you so, Cher is the one who said it best. You'll know when you kiss him, you'll know if he feels the way you feel. And you'll certainly know how you feel about him.
   Take your time, take it slow, breathe it in. A kiss can't lie.

WHEN WE BREAK off the kiss, I'm seeing stars. He stares down at me, eyes big and wide, a soft smile on his face. I think I'm smiling back, but my face feels numb. Did that just happen? Wow. Fuck. Wow.

"Tomorrow then?" he says softly.

"Tomorrow."

He leans down and gives me one more kiss, a light peck on the lips that leaves me wanting more. And without another word, he walks down the path to my house and disappears into the night. I hurry inside, barely able to catch my breath.

I pull my phone out of my pocket.

LUC, MAX & VICKY

WE KISSED!

WTH?!

> **WE KISSED!! I KISSED A BOY!**

VICKY

Did you like it?

> **YEP!**

VICKY

I was making a joke.

> **I WAS IGNORING IT.**

VICKY

Katy Perry song? Are you sure you're gay?

> **VICKYYYYYYY!**

VICKY

Is your keyboard stuck or something?

> **Stop being such a killjoy!**

I tell her how the date went in far too much detail. She doesn't need to know what we ordered or what music was playing but, let's be real, it sets the mood. It's ambiance.

She messages back with the appropriate levels of enthusiasm, even resorting to caps when I get to the kissing part. Job done.

VICKY

Very proud of you.

Now read on. This is just the beginning.

And don't forget to update the blog. Given that last we heard, you were giving up, they're going to gag over this.

She's not wrong. I need to update the blog. I need to tell them all about this. But not yet.

I hurry upstairs and practically throw myself onto my bed, the biggest smile on my face. I feel like I'm shaking with glee. I can still smell him, I can still taste him, the memory so clear in my brain I wish I could screen record it and keep it forever.

I take Mum's book out of my schoolbag and flick to the next section.

After the first date, no contact for three days.

I blink and read it again. It's something that I've seen done in films loads of times, playing hard to get by making yourself unavailable, but surely it's not something that people do in real life. Is it?

Absence makes the heart grow fonder and while you're definitely going to want to see him as soon as possible (so long as the date has gone well) being too available can be off-putting. Do your best to not see him for at least three days following your date. Or, if you must see him, limit your contact.

Even though we've been playing a game this whole time, this feels like a brand-new level. I wasn't comfortable pretending I was unavailable for his party, but this feels worse. What am I going to do, just ignore him at school?

She's right about one thing. I want to spend time with him. If I wasn't shit-scared about what might happen if I invited him into an empty house, he'd probably still be here now.

Don't think about that, I think. *Save it for later.*

THREE DAYS?!

VICKY
Sorry, them's the rules.

That's torture.

VICKY
It's the rules!

VICKY!

VICKY
RULES!

Sorry for the delay. Well done for not burning
anything down. Hope it was a good kiss.

Max's message at the end isn't much of anything. I don't know
what I expected. Praise? More than that, at least. Maybe he's with
Soph and can't talk right now.

My phone buzzes again in my hand. This time it's not Vicky
messaging, or Max adding anything, but Grayson. My heart is in my
mouth. The last few messages we sent were just arranging tonight.
Very formal, very to the point.

GRAYSON

I had a great time tonight. Score one for do-overs.

Sorry for messaging so fast. I know that's not cool.

Self-aware boy is self-aware. God, he's good.

I flick through Mum's book until I find the page on text messages.
It's not nearly as extensive as I hoped it would be, barely even a page,
the section on phone calls in the pages prior was at least three.

*Texting is a very impersonal medium. Why text someone when you
can call them?*

Why call someone when you text? The thought of phoning
Grayson right now makes me want to throw up. Between the
awkward silences and pauses and not knowing what to say, I would
rather shove bamboo under my fingernails than call him. Ever.

*Your characters are limited, so you need to be concise. Shorten words
where you can. U instead of you. Gr8 instead of great.*

The fact that my mum wrote this makes me want to kill myself.
This has to be an early edition of the book. Who the hell messages like
that? Give me full sentences or give me death.

But I would always opt to call. The sound of his voice can be so much more telling than the tone of a text. Think of it as an extension of your date. But make sure he's the one who calls you first.

I switch to the chat that's just me and Vicky, not wanting to disturb Max's night with Soph.

> Mum wants me to call Grayson.

What?

> The text message section is woefully undercooked. I think this is an old edition.

The book is old, Lucas. What do you expect? People used to call more than message. I know it seems crazy. Why are you asking about messages? Did he message you?

> Just now.

Right.

> Where does this fall as far as contact goes?

The three dots appear on the screen and disappear. It happens again. Suddenly, my phone starts ringing. So much for me never talking to anyone on the phone.

"Why are you calling me?"

"Hello to you too," Vicky says.

"Hello," I say. "Why are you calling me?"

"You're in a crisis, I'm on my way," she says. "Metaphorically speaking. I'm literally in my PJs in a face mask right now."

"Great," I say. "And you're calling me because—"

"Your Mum can't help you with this one, so it falls to me," she says dramatically. "What's he sent you?"

I put her on loudspeaker and read her the message.

"And the book says no contact for three days," I add. "So yeah, you're right, I'm in a crisis."

Vicky takes a moment. I can practically hear the cogs whirring in her head as she thinks it through. Grayson is going off-script, and it's making it even harder for me to figure out how to proceed. I know what my instincts are telling me, but if this book has taught me anything, it's that my instincts are wrong.

"Keep it civil," she says.

"Wait, you want me to message back?"

"Yes."

"But the rules—"

"The rules say no contact, but it was written in a time before everyone was available literally all the time on their phones," she says. "You don't want to seem rude. Nothing too gushy, but at least let him know that you're into it, into him."

"Have I not made it obvious?"

She sighs. "If you're following the book, then yes," she replies. "But subtly. So continue that. Let him know you've had a good time, but don't give everything away. Cool it on the emojis."

"What makes you think I'll overuse emojis?"

"I've messaged you enough to know you're more than partial to them," she says.

I start to type out a response, then stop.

"This all feels a little bit game play-y," I say. There is a strange sort of tension that grips my chest. "I just want to be able to tell him that I like him, that I had a great time. I'm an emotional person. Why should I have to hide that?"

"Because the book says to," Vicky says. "And if there's one thing that all of these books have in common, it's that too much exuberance might scare a guy off."

"I don't mind exuberance," I say. "I'd kill to have a guy telling me how much he liked me. That's all anyone wants, isn't it?"

Vicky sighs, the phone speaker distorting slightly. "Maybe," she says. "But you've got to follow the book here, Luc. And the messaging section is practically non-existent so…I'm making a judgement call. Nothing too over the top."

> Me too. We should do it again soon.

> Maybe we'll get it right first time this time around.

"How's that?" I ask before I send it.

"Perfect. Now put your phone down," she says. "One message will do for now."

"Thanks," I say, closing the messaging app and taking Vicky off speaker. "What happens next?"

"Well, no more contact," she says. "So you can stalk to your heart's content, but don't talk to him. Give him space. Let him miss you."

There is a quip sitting in my head, one about there being a first time for everything or how that would be dreamy, but I don't say it. Because after tonight, maybe it's a possibility. But I have no idea how the hell I'm supposed to stop myself from seeing Grayson tomorrow when we literally have school together. I thought things were about to get uncomplicated. Apparently not.

THIRTY-THREE

ABSENCE MAKES THE HEART GROW FONDER (cont.)

As a great signer once sang, you don't know what you've got until it's gone, and right now you need to make sure he realises what he's missing. Make yourself a little more unavailable than you would like. Trust me, I know this is going to be difficult. When I first started dating Matthew, I wanted to see him every minute of every day, but Lord knows that wasn't feasible, at least not if I wanted him to want me.

So hide your heart for a little while longer and become a little more elusive. It will all pay off in the end.

I'M like Gaymes Bond when I get to school the following morning. There is danger around every corner, the potential for Grayson at every turn, and I'll be damned if I'm going to break yet another rule and screw up Vicky's experiment.

I've already had messages from Vicky this morning telling me that I needed to be careful when I was heading into school today. And also a little nudge that I need to update the blog, because after the disastrous date post, we've gained a little bit of attention.

> We're hardly setting the world on fire here, but there
> are at least ten people who have sent me a message
> asking what the heck is going on!

It was enough to stroke my ego and get me to draft a post on my way to school this morning. I'll check it over at lunch maybe, and post it later. I can't believe anyone is even interested. Trust people to only give a shit when things are going wrong. I'll tell them that the book is working and that I've kissed him, and they'll all vanish again.

As I make my way to my locker, I can see up ahead that he's there waiting. It's sweet. My heart flutters when I see he's watching for me, not sure which direction I'm going to be coming from.

I have to resist the urge to hurtle down the corridor at breakneck speed and wrap myself up in those big arms, maybe even manage to get myself another kiss out of it, but there's Mum's voice in my head again.

Absence makes the heart grow fonder.

He looks my way, and I'm almost certain that I've been spotted, so I turn around. My heart is beating double-time in my chest and my palms are sweating, as I slip into the nearest classroom and hide behind the door, peering out into the corridor to see if he's followed me.

I can just about make out his shape at the other end of the corridor, still watching, still waiting. He's not coming this way. Crisis averted. If he's not growing fond of me right this very second, I'm going to be pissed.

"Can I help you, Mr Cook?"

I practically jump out of my skin at the voice, slamming the door to see Mr Edwards sitting behind his desk. There are students in here, Year 7s by the rabbit-in-headlights looks they're giving me. Hello. I am the headlights.

He's waiting for me to respond, his bespectacled eyes drilling into me in a way that would normally make me giggly because, as previously mentioned, DILF, but today I'd just like the ground to swallow me whole.

"Um…I'm…I shouldn't be…I'm sorry."

"Any particular reason you're disturbing my form class?"

"There…there was a wasp," I say. "In the corridor. Big wasp. And I'm…I'm allergic. And didn't want to, you know, go full Violet Beauregarde and swell up to the size of a, well, giant blueberry and…die."

I wish I were dead. He's staring at me like I've just spoken to him in Elvish or something.

He opens his mouth to say something when the bell rings. He changes tact. "Go to your form class, Mr Cook. I'll see you this afternoon."

"Yes, sir. Thank you, sir," I reply and scurry out of the classroom and into the corridor.

"Lucas!" I jump again. I hate this morning. This morning is not the one. I want to go home.

Vicky is bent double beside me in the corridor, apparently thrilled that she's scared the absolute shit out of me. I forget why we became friends.

"How goes the avoidance?"

"I just told Mr Edwards that I was being chased by a wasp," I reply.

Vicky blinks. "You've lost me."

"Grayson was waiting for me at my locker."

"So you got chased by a wasp?"

"No, I went into Mr Edwards's classroom."

"Why?"

"To avoid Grayson."

"He has a form class in there."

"I know that *now*," I respond through gritted teeth. I would love to say that this is the most embarrassed I have ever been, but every time I say that, something else seems to come along to top it. At least I didn't set anything on fire this time around. "But I had to avoid him." I look down the corridor. "He's gone, and I'm late."

Vicky shrugged. "What's a few minutes between friends?" she says. "You got my messages this morning?"

"Yes," I reply. "And I've drafted the date redo post, so that can go up later for the ten people who've asked."

"Everybody starts somewhere," she says. "There are people who

217

are loving this, Luc, whether or not they're messaging me about it. Have you been keeping up to date with your stats?"

"I choose not to look," I reply. "It's depressing to know that the only people reading it are you and me."

Vicky raises an eyebrow at me. "You might want to look again."

I take out my phone as we reach my locker and I check my blog's stats. The disastrous date post is by far the most popular thing I've put on there, with over three hundred people having read it. The other posts are doing alright, but there's something about looking at that little spike, which gives my brain a hit of happiness that I've never felt before. This is coming from someone who posts on Instagram once every two months and gets about twenty likes, and that's on a good day. This is something else.

"People really like it," I say. "Well, they like me fucking things up."

"Alright, negative," Vicky says, rolling her eyes. "I'd say that they like you trying to better yourself, trying to make a difference in your life. And they'll love it even more when you come back and talk about the re-do. They'll lose it."

I open my locker, swapping out books and putting them in my bag. I can't believe people actually care. I know they're a bunch of strangers, but there's something about them taking an interest in my life that makes me...I don't know...happy, I guess.

"Grayson."

"Lucas," I correct.

"No, Grayson is coming," Vicky says. "Other end of the corridor, do something."

I can see him in the distance, Madhuri at his side. They are coming from the direction of my form class, blocking my way. Have I missed registration already? Fuck's sake. Why am I like this? I'm going to be in trouble now.

"LUCAS!" Vicky barks. "Grayson is approaching. Do something."

I slam my locker closed, staring at Vicky for guidance.

"What are you waiting for? Go!"

I'm pretty sure he's seen me because he's picking up the pace, and I'm panicking. It seems ridiculous. Even as I do it, I feel stupid, but my legs take over before my brain can engage. I throw my bag over my shoulders and run down a different corridor. It's not the direction I need to go in to get to registration, but I can take the long way around. I'm already late, what's another five minutes?

For fuck's sake, Mum, this had better work!

———

I AM LATE FOR MY FORM CLASS, SO LATE THAT MR MARSHALL HOLDS ME back at the end to talk to me about it. He saw me walking through the school gates that morning and was "shocked and appalled" that my time management was so poor that I couldn't make it to his form class on time. Form class is compulsory blah blah blah. I'm ninety percent sure that he has no idea who any of us are. I'm not trying to be a bitch here, (okay maybe a little bit) but why do teachers only take an actual interest in you when you're doing anything less than average?

I drop Max a message during first break when I realise that he isn't in school today, just asking him how he is. But I don't get a response. Soph says he started feeling sick last night and said he probably wouldn't be in today.

"You should check the friend group chat," she says in a way that I don't think is meant to be pointed, but definitely feels that way. "He put it in there this morning."

Sure enough, it's right there in black and white.

MAX

Feel rough today. Won't be in. If someone could grab homework, that would get Mum off my back for taking the day off.

Lunch was pretty much a non-event. Even though Grayson messaged to invite me to have lunch with him and his friends in the canteen, Vicky said not to respond and to join her in the library. It meant I actually read some of Pride & Prejudice between waves of guilt that I was point-blank ignoring Grayson.

If you'd told me at the start of this that I would be deliberately dodging the boy whose attention I've been wanting for the past few years, I would have called you a liar and a damn fool. Now, I am the damn fool who isn't replying to his messages. Because Mum said so. Weird.

The good thing is that the latest blog post has Vicky's approval and has now gone live, so if anyone wants to know what it's like to kiss Grayson then that information is now available, cleverly disguised and hopefully undetectable to anyone who knows either of us.

The fact that I make it to the end of the day without a Grayson encounter feels borderline miraculous. But the final gauntlet is yet to be run. Biology with Mr Edwards.

I can tell that Mr Edwards is paying extra close attention to me as I walk into his class. I head to my usual seat with Soph, right at the back of the classroom, out of sight of literally anyone else in the room apart from the big man himself. (Mr Edwards, not God.)

Grayson turns around to try and catch my eye, but I look past him at the board, watching Mr Edwards talk about...something. Okay, so maybe I'm trying so hard not to pay attention to Grayson that I'm inadvertently paying attention to him rather than Mr Edwards. It's fine, exams aren't until May, I'll be over this by then. I can revise...I try and focus on the board... "The Human Nervous System."

I'm the most nervous human I know, this will be a piece of cake.

The final bell of the day rings and, once again, I can feel Grayson's eyes on me. In my periphery, I can see that he's turned his attention to me as he packs up his things. I can't fail at this gauntlet. If I can get out of this room fast enough and get myself to Buttons, I'll have made it one day. Then I just have to figure out how the heck I'm going to make it through Friday, then it's the weekend and by Monday I can talk to him as much as I like.

Dating is stressful.

"Do you want to borrow my notes?" Soph asks as we pack up our things. Grayson is on the move. He is approaching. No, no, no, no, *no!*

"Huh?"

"You barely wrote anything down," she says. "Have you suddenly become a Biology genius or..." She wants to know what's going on.

"I was just distracted," I say, "and tired."

"Yeah, I imagine you are," she says, widening her eyes. "Come on,

Luc, I'm waiting for the details of your hot date last night. Max said it went well?"

So he *is* talking to her about it? I don't know what to do with this information. Or maybe it's because he got those messages while he was with her. He had to say something. I hope he's still keeping the book a secret.

Grayson has been stopped by Laurie on the way over. He's gesturing a little too wildly for my liking and the way he keeps pointing over his shoulder has me thinking that he's talking about me, which is great for my already anxious brain. I really don't think Laurie likes me.

"Grayson was looking for you over lunch," Soph says. "I told him you had detention because you were late this morning. I don't know if that's true or not, but…you know…no one likes to feel like they're being ignored or avoided."

"Yeah," I say, still watching Grayson getting ever closer.

"So?" she says. "Hot date? How did it go? I was waiting for messages last night."

He's ditched Laurie, and he's on the way over, and I need to do something drastic or I'm going to fuck all of this up. I put my hands on Soph's shoulders and look her directly in the eyes.

"A promise between friends means never having to give a reason, right?" I say.

"Why are you quoting Phoebe Buffay at me?"

"You believe that for us, right?"

"Sure."

"I promise I will tell you everything," I say. "But can you please distract Grayson so I can get to work?"

She sighs so heavily that it's like her entire body is being dragged towards the ground. "Lucas, what are you doing? If you're messing this boy around—"

"I promise you I'm not, but I literally start in like ten minutes and I can't be late or I'll lose this job, please, Soph?"

She's mulling it over. It feels like the slowest few seconds of my life as she comes to a decision. She shakes her head, and I almost think she's going to say no when she puts out her finger towards me. "I've got you, bestie."

I press my finger against hers. "I love you so much. Thank you."

She turns around and I hear her say, "Grayson, oh my GOD!" as I grab my bag and make a break for the door. Grayson calls after me as the door to Mr Edwards' biology room slams behind me, but I have to ignore it. I have to ignore the pull of my heart, telling me to go and talk to the beautiful broad-shouldered boy who actually knows I exist and wants to talk to me.

I said I would follow the rules, so I will. I don't look back. I hurry out of school at a run and towards Buttons, the decision weighing heavily on my heart.

It's not a lie that I need to get to work. Maria was very clear that if I wasn't working Wednesday nights because of this school thing, she was going to need me to make up the hours on Thursdays. But my shift doesn't start until three-thirty. School lets out at three. Ditching Grayson feels like bad karma. It feels like it is one hundred percent going to bite me in the ass.

I make it to Buttons and have plenty of time to put on my black shirt and black trousers. I even have time to take a breath and steady myself before I make my way behind the counter to join Henry as we deal with the onslaught of school kids bursting through the door for their overpriced drinks.

Blessedly, I don't have much time to think about what I've done to Grayson. All I'm thinking about is how I can avoid him again tomorrow without it looking suspicious. We have a couple of classes together on a Friday. It's going to be way harder than it was today, that much is for sure.

"Hey, what can I—?" I freeze mid-phrase. Standing on the other side of the counter, a tight-lipped smile on his face, is Grayson. I look to his left, to his right, none of his friends are with him. They're outside. I can see them waiting. "What can I get you?" I say, fixing my customer-facing smile in place.

"An explanation?" he replies, laughing a little bit. He's trying to keep it light, but I can see that he's stressing out. I know I would be. I practically ran away from him earlier. It's not like I've been subtle about it.

"For what?" I ask, guilt burning in my chest.

Just tell him about the book, I think. *Tell him what's going on, why you did it. Why are you fucking this up?*

"Lu," he says, and the cute shortening of my name has me melting. No one calls me Lu but him. To everyone else, it's Luc. Or Lucas. To him, I'm Lu. "Please?"

"What?"

He shakes his head. "Forget it then. Nevermind."

"No, no, no, no, *no!*" I say under my breath, hurrying out from behind the counter to stop him before he can get to the door. "Wait."

"What for?" he says.

"For…for your order," I say. "You wanted an explanation and I'm going to give it to you."

He folds his arms. It somehow makes him look bigger, broader. I'm trying to think of what the heck I'm supposed to say to make this right, to make it better. Mum didn't cover this part in the book. She told me to play the game, so I played it, and it feels like I'm about to lose. Game over.

He sighs. "If you're not into it, you just have to say."

"No, I—"

"I thought the date went well. I had a good time," he says. "I'm not about playing games. I don't like having to chase someone. I want to get to know you better. But if you want to call it off, we can be friends." He nods, like he's trying to convince himself.

I open my mouth, but the words die on my tongue. If I tell him about the book, I am so sure it will just make him hate me. He can't ever find out about that. If he does, I know it will be over for us. For good. So I need to think of something else. Something that isn't entirely a lie but doesn't give him the whole truth.

But I can't think of anything.

My brain can't work quickly enough and there is no Vicky here to save me, no Mum advice floating around in my head telling me what line goes here, and what the heck I'm supposed to say to make him stay.

Because Grayson is walking away from me.

He's walking to the door of Buttons.

He's walking through it.

And I see my chances with him disappear down the street.

223

THIRTY-FOUR

LUC & SOPH

> Babes, are you about?

SOPH

...

Sorry. Busy just now. Tomorrow though?

Dinner at Jasmine's tonight. Long overdue girls' night.

I don't know what to say back. She's busy. When is she not busy? I thought that maybe she would be able to help. I don't know why. Maybe I feel like I owe her one for distracting Grayson for me, even if it has all blown up in my face.

> Oooh, have fun!

Face masks. Shitty films. Totally not a Thursday thing, but felt like I needed it.

> Have fun. See you tomorrow.

Nothing comes back after that.

I pocket my phone and continue my walk home. The shift was

pretty horrible after Grayson left. I like Henry, but they're not the biggest conversationalist, so without Vicky there, I had way too much time paddling around in my head, so now I'm practically swimming in my sadness.

LUC & MAX

> Hope you're okay. Missed you today. I may have fucked things up with Grayson.

> Again.

My phone starts ringing. If Max's name wasn't emblazoned across the front of the screen, I probably would have ignored it. But I pick up.

"Hello?" I say.

"Why do you sound confused when you can see who's calling you?"

"Because you're calling me," I say. "Why are you calling me?"

"Your messages were giving 'spiralling out of control,'" he says. "Tell me what happened."

He doesn't sound sick, is the first thing I think. But what was I expecting? Him to be talking with a blocked nose or whatever? Either way, he sounds fine.

I talk him through everything that happened, following the rules, trying not to talk to him.

"Those rules are insane," he says.

"I know."

"Have you ever considered just being yourself?"

"Being myself didn't get him to notice me. Nobody noticed invisible Luc," I say. "And I am being myself. It's just myself dialled up to eleven."

"Okay," Max replies, though I can hear in his voice that he doesn't quite believe me. I feel this almost uncontrollable urge to try and convince him. "Maybe you should just talk to him tomorrow."

"But I'm not supposed to—"

"Shut up for a second," he says. "This book was written in an age before people were constantly on their phones, constantly contactable, right?"

I stay silent.

"Okay, please respond."

"I thought I was meant to shut up."

"Stop being obtuse."

"Right," I answer.

"And it definitely wasn't written for someone who is in secondary school," he says. "You are bound to see him around. Trying to avoid him is stupid."

"I almost managed it."

"No, you didn't," Max says. "Because now he's upset, right?"

I sigh. "Right."

"So talk to him tomorrow," he says. "Explain that you were being an idiot and then…" He takes a breath, it distorts the phone. "Then, hopefully, you two can move on."

I take a breath. "Thanks, Max," I say. "You're the best."

"I have my moments."

"How come you weren't at school today?"

"Um…I just didn't feel up to it," he says. "Needed the day to myself, I think."

I wait for him to elaborate. He doesn't. "Anything I can help with?"

He chuckles. "No, don't worry," he says. "You're very sweet to ask, though."

Max says he will see me tomorrow, so I guess whatever kept him at home today is over now, and we say our goodbyes. I hope he's alright.

The house is quiet when I get home. I missed a message from Dad earlier, telling me that he was out tonight. We've not really talked since what happened on Tuesday night. We just seem to keep missing each other. I can't tell if it's by design or not.

I follow orders from Vicky and I head upstairs and I write out a post. I am torn between following the rules, and doing as Max suggested, and just talking to Grayson tomorrow. In my heart of hearts, I know Max is right, but maybe I need to see this through. I don't know.

The book has no solutions for this part going wrong. I read all around it and there is nothing. There is talk of the second date, there is talk of the third date and all the things that come with that. It assumes that you're successful and you're just carrying on. I am not. Because I let the boy of my dreams walk away this afternoon and I feel positively lousy about it.

———

I MAKE MY WAY TO SCHOOL THE FOLLOWING MORNING, PRAYING FOR THE day to be over and for the weekend to take me into the loving arms of two exceptionally busy days at work so I can just not think about what happened with Grayson. That's what I need right now. I can't believe how badly I fucked this up.

I tell myself that if I see him at my locker this morning, I'll apologise, but he's not there, so I revert to my usual routine and make my way to the Geography block to see my friends.

They're all already there, in the middle of some conversation or other that promptly stops when I round the corner. My anxious brain immediately assumes that they're talking about me.

Soph isn't there, and it's the first question that I want to ask. And then I see Grayson with Laurie and Dylan. And I want the ground to open up and swallow me whole. What are they doing? Did they all come here to ambush me or something?

"Hey, Lu," he says.

"Hey," I reply. "You okay?"

"Been better," he says.

"Can I… Can I talk to you?" I ask.

He seems reluctant, looking at Laurie, who takes her time looking at him and then at me. Why does this have anything to do with her? What has Laurie been saying to him? Eventually Laurie nods, Dylan not taking his eyes off me.

"Sure," he says.

We walk a little way away from where everyone is sitting, and I can feel their eyes on us both and I hate it. I want to walk further away; I don't want them to see this because I already feel like I might break.

"I just… I wanted to…" I can't find the words. I want to explain

227

what happened, but how can I explain what happened without giving away everything that's been happening with the book?

"Come on, Lu," he says, softly. "What the hell happened yesterday?"

Suddenly Jasmine is at my side. "You need my help," she says. "And I owe you one, so consider this a freebie."

I turn to her sharply. This isn't her moment. I need her to walk away. "Jasmine—"

"Something has clearly happened here," she says. "Grayson is here like a sad sack, whispering with Laurie, you're looking like a lost puppy. And now you're all like 'Hey,' 'Hey,' Come on! You're bringing the whole mood down."

"Jasmine, stop it," I say. To Grayson, I mumble, "Sorry."

"I'm helping," she insists. "Come on, Luc, you've liked him forever. You've basically been obsessed with him and you're just going to let all of this go because something happened?"

"Jasmine, please stop talking—"

"No, you're better than this, Luc. And you helped me with Krish, so now I'm helping you with this." She turns to Grayson. "He likes you, he's basically your biggest fan, he's just too stupid to say anything about it."

I'm burning up and I want to yell at her to stop, to butt out, but she genuinely thinks that what she's doing is helping. And she's still talking, but the blood is pumping so hard in my ears that I just can't take it anymore. So I walk.

I just walk.

There are tears in my eyes and I can barely see where I'm going. I know I'm sniffling and crying and being a total mess and people are looking at me, but I just keep walking.

And I walk until I feel a hand land heavily on my shoulder.

It startles me into turning around.

"Luc!" It's Max. Max has followed me and he's standing right in front of me, his eyes all big and wide and hopeful and concerned and—

"Lu!"

Grayson. He's a couple of steps behind Max, but he's there. They both followed me. Why did they both follow me?

228

I look between them. Grayson staring daggers into the back of Max's head.

"Max, can you give me and Grayson a minute?" I say quietly.

He opens his mouth to respond but stops, almost like what I've said has startled him. He blinks. He shakes it off and smiles.

"Sure," he whispers. "I'll be around the corner if you need me."

"Thanks," I reply.

Grayson watches Max walk away, waiting a few seconds before he comes any closer to me. He looks at me and then at Max, and what I wouldn't give to know what he's thinking right now.

"I'm sorry," I say.

Grayson takes a breath. "What for?"

"I-I don't know," I say. "Sorry for Jasmine, sorry for me yesterday, sorry for all of it. And sorry that this is over."

He blinks again. That's really caught him off guard for some reason.

"What do you mean, this is over?"

"Well, come on, I've…I've tried to play it cool, tried to be aloof, and I scared you off yesterday and now Jasmine has shown me to be…I don't know…some kind of freak who is obsessed with you or whatever." I stop. I take a breath. I sniff. God, I must look disgusting right now. "So, it's over."

"It's not over," he says. "So you like me…I like that you like me. I want you to like me. Why wouldn't I want you to like me?" He pauses and takes me in. "Is that what yesterday was all about?" he asks. "You were trying to play it cool?"

"I-I got scared," I say. "I mean…look at you."

"Look at me?"

"Yes," I insist. "You're tall and broad-shouldered and everybody likes you. Everybody wants to be friends with you. Basically, everybody is. That's intimidating."

"Why?"

"Because why would…" And I realise I'm being more honest than I should be. The early part of a relationship should be light and fun and breezy, not filled with the little bits of trauma that you carry around with you on the daily. But faced with losing Grayson, my mouth is running before my brain can stop me. "Because why would someone like you be interested in someone like me?"

I see the words as they hit him, as he processes them. His arms unfold and his face softens as he realises that I'm not as cool as I seem.

"Lu—"

"No, Grayson, come on," I say. "I'm not fishing here, but up until a week ago you couldn't have picked me out of a lineup and...I got scared that all it would take is for you to see who I am, who I really am, and you would run a mile. And I didn't want that, so the best thing to do was to keep you at arm's length in the hope that... that you would miss me." I chuckle. "It sounds so stupid saying it out loud."

The first bell rings and this boy is going to absolutely ruin my attendance record. I say ruin, but it wasn't exactly stellar to begin with.

"Well, I did," Grayson says. "I missed you yesterday. Look, maybe I didn't notice you before, sure. But this confident boy suddenly appeared in my life and was making jokes with me and looking at me...looking at me like nobody has really looked at me before."

"You're really pretty."

He laughs. "Thanks, you're pretty too," he says. "Cute, actually. And charming, and funny, and I didn't get to see that before, and now I do, and I like that." He pauses. "When did you...? How long have you...?"

I take a deep, shuddering breath. Apparently I've not finished crying over this because tears are coming without me meaning them too. Ugh. Why am I this person?

"I'd always thought you were hot," I say, laughing a little. "I just didn't realise it when I was like thirteen. Then you came out and were, like, this idol to me. And then...then you saved me."

"I saved you?"

"I was being bullied in Year 9 after I came out," I say. "A bunch of arseholes decided that I was worth kicking the shit out of at lunchtime. And you were there, and you pulled them off me and told them to leave me the fuck alone and—"

"And you ripped my shirt," he says, the recognition crossing his face. "My mum was so mad."

230

"I'm sorry," I say. "But that was it. If I wasn't obsessed with you before, I was from then on. And it…it's never not been weird that you and my friends know each other, but you've…you've never known me."

I don't know where this falls under Mum's rules. I'm fairly sure it breaks every single one of them because this is so deep and so serious, but he still isn't running away.

"Well, I know you now," he says. "And want to keep getting to know you. I missed you yesterday, so when I got a chance I tried to talk to you but… Did you send Soph to distract me?"

"I might have."

He laughs. "I should have figured that," he says. "She started talking about what the Biology homework was and then tried to talk to me about how interesting it all was. No one cares about what Mr Edwards has to say. No one is listening."

"He missed a button on his shirt."

"I know," Grayson says. "I think he did it on purpose."

"He must know!" I say, which makes him laugh. "I'm sorry. That was stupid. What I did, I mean."

"It's alright," he says, reaching out and taking hold of my arm. My entire body reacts to it, a chill running over every inch of me. "And, for what it's worth, I like that you like me."

"You do?"

"I like you too, Lu," he says. "I hate that it rhymes."

"Cringe."

"Yes," he replies. "And I'm sorry I didn't notice you sooner." He gives my arm a squeeze and I am weak. "So…again? Another date?"

"Yes," I say, maybe a little too quickly, and it's Grayson's turn to laugh at me. "Or something less eager."

"I'll message you later," he says. "Which one will this be? Is this two or three because of the do-over?"

"Oh, three, definitely," I say. "I might want to forget about the first one, but that's legacy work right there. We'll be dining out on that anecdote for years."

"Just not dining out at that restaurant."

"I think I'll be banned for life."

"With good reason."

He steps a little closer to me, looking around the corridor before he leans down to kiss me. I lift my chin and kiss him back. It's different from that first kiss. It's less tentative. His hands find my hips and I find myself pressing my body into him. I can feel things. He can *definitely* feel things. My face immediately feels hot. What is this boy doing to me?

"I'll message you later to arrange date number three," he says before heading down the corridor.

The phrase 'date number three' is sticking in my head for some reason. I don't know why, but it's like somewhere off in the distance there is an alarm going off. I can't ignore it because it's too loud, but I can't place where it's coming from.

I'm sure there was something about the third date in Mum's book. I just can't remember what it is. I wait until I'm definitely sure that he has gone and I take the book out.

I go straight for the table of contents, past the "Playing Hard To Get" part that I have clearly failed dramatically at, and there it is.

The Third Date: Insert cheesy sexy music here. Bow chicka wow wow etc. etc.

"Oh, God."

THIRTY-FIVE

THE THIRD DATE
Insert cheesy sex music here. **Bow chicka wow wow, etc., etc.**

It is a truth universally acknowledged that by the time you get to the third date, you know whether or not you like this man. And I will tell you something for nothing. He will be expecting sex.

It's the conventional time for such things to kick off and while you don't have to engage in it (No is a full sentence!) you may want to. This is the time.

I SPEND the rest of the morning wanting to throw up. You hear about it in films, you see it on TV, why did I not think that Grayson might expect sex on the third date? I kissed a boy for the first time and now I have to think about what is going where and who is doing what?

Much as I want to put it out of my head, I simply can't.

Have I thought about sex before? Of course I have. I'm a sixteen-year-old gay boy who is confidently nowhere on the asexual spectrum. I want to do it. I just…I don't know if I'm ready. Nor do I know how. They don't teach these kinds of things in school. Not for the queer population, anyway. It's always for the hettys, which means my only frame of reference for gay sex is porn and…that's not so much educational as it is…recreational.

> Library at lunch?

MAX

Thought you'd want to hang with Grayson in the canteen or something?

VICKY

Wait. What happened?

> Please?

VICKY

I'll be late, but I'll be there.

MAX

Snap.

Distraction seems like the only way to go. I jump on a computer in the library, intending to write an update on how the playing hard-to-get part of the book is going. The short version is, "Not well, I've fucked it," but I can't imagine that will be acceptable for a full post.

"Christ, you're working on the blog," Vicky says as she appears at my side. "Feel like I've had to drag you kicking and screaming to do that recently. You alright?"

"I'm very much not alright," I say. "We have a problem."

"What kind of problem?"

"Grayson wants to have sex with me," I say, just as the library goes more silent than I thought was humanly possible.

Mrs Singh stares at me from her desk. I stare back. She whispers something to Ms Harris. I hate my life.

"Okay, we're going to use our indoor voices," Vicky whispers. "He wants to have sex with you?"

"Who wants to have sex with you?" Max says as he appears.

Another dirty look comes from Mrs Singh and now I regret ever opening my mouth.

"You need to sound a little bit less surprised by the idea."

"Not surprised," he says. "I'm sure you're perfectly—"

"Don't finish that sentence."

"Don't be offended."

"What do I do?"

"Hold on now," Vicky says. "Three deep breaths and we can continue talking because I feel like you're on the verge of a cardiac arrest or something."

Together we deep breathe three times. If anything, it makes me feel worse.

"What makes you think he wants to have sex with you?" she asks. "Did he say that?"

"Not exactly?"

"Lucas, clarity, please, I'm hungry and don't want to use up my whole lunch break talking you off a ledge," she says. "How's the view from up there?"

"Beautiful," I say. "Good weather too."

"Glad to hear it," she replies. "Now please tell us what's going on?"

I sigh. "He asked me to go out on what he's calling a 'third date.'"

"So everything went alright when you talked this morning?" Max says. "You didn't come back, so I wasn't sure."

"Wait, wait, wait, I thought you were supposed to be avoiding him?"

"Can we deal with one of my screw-ups at a time, please?"

"There's so many, I'm starting to lose track," she teases.

I explain everything that happened yesterday and everything that happened this morning, going into a little more detail because I realise walking away to have a panic attack straight after means that this is the first Max is hearing of it too.

"Why didn't you tell me this last night?"

"I didn't want to be annoying."

"You're an idiot."

"A well-established fact at this point," I say. "But he called it a third date and the third date implies sex."

"According to who?"

"The book," I say. "The book says that the third date is the sex date and I don't know if I'm ready for—"

"Lucas," Max interrupts. "I need you to take a moment and take a few more deep breaths because you're totally overthinking this."

I pause. "That doesn't sound like me, are you sure?" I reply.

"We'll work on the stand-up set another time," he says. "But please know that you are freaking out over nothing. Bring it up with Grayson. If he's expecting sex on the third date when he's not brought it up with you at all, he's kind of a dick. All you've done is kiss, right?"

"But the book—"

"Could be wrong," he says, looking to Vicky for confirmation. She nods. "It's been wrong in the past. Quite recently, in fact. Clearly, you trying to fully avoid Grayson was a shit idea."

"Seconded," Vicky adds.

"So it could be wrong again. You freaking out about it certainly isn't going to help. Talk to him, let him know how you're feeling, communicate."

The thought of doing that, of actually talking to him about it, calms me down a touch. When we talked earlier, it had felt good. That openness had been needed and, if anything, it brought us a little closer. Or at least it stopped us from breaking up.

"Okay," I say. "I…I guess I can do that. We've not actually arranged the date yet, so maybe when he brings it up, I can…talk to him about it."

"Good," Max says. "Now, are we calm?"

"As calm as I usually am," I say.

"So that's a no," Max says with a smirk.

"Are we good?" Vicky says. "Nice work on calming him down."

"I've got over a decade of practice," he replies.

Vicky eyes him carefully, giving him a knowing sort of nod. And now I feel like they've been talking about me behind my back and I hate it.

"Can we go get some lunch now?" Vicky asks. "I'm dying."

"Sure," I say. "And sorry."

"For what?"

"For panicking."

"You're sorry for being yourself?" she says as we make our way out of the library.

"Rude."

"You'll be fine," she replies. "By the way, I have something to tell you."

"What?"

"June is coming back," Vicky says, and she seems genuinely happy about it.

We've barely talked about June, because...well...it's an awkward thing to bring up. Any time June is mentioned she quickly moves the topic on. It's clearly a sore subject.

"And how do you feel about that?"

Vicky takes a heavy breath. "I don't know," she says. "We've been messaging and stuff, on and off. She's coming back to see family for a couple of weeks and she wants to see me. So that's nice."

"Very nice."

"And she wants to meet you."

I blink. "What do you mean? Why does she want to meet me?"

"Because you're my friend and I talk about you," she says, like it's the most obvious thing in the world. "And she's been reading the blog, which is kind of cool because I thought she'd totally abandoned it and didn't even think about it anymore, and because of that, she kind of knows who you are."

"Wait, hold on, what?" I say, stopping, my heart in my mouth. "I thought we were supposed to be keeping my identity a secret?"

"We are," Vicky says.

"But if June knows—"

"June isn't going to tell anybody," Vicky says. "She just asked who it was I was working on it with. She was interested. She still really likes the blog and loves what I'm doing with it."

She seems so pleased with herself, so pleased that June is still interested in the blog and in what she's doing. It's sweet, and I don't want to be the person to rain on this particular parade because she's happy.

"I promise you, it's fine," Vicky says. "Look, she wants to meet you, okay? She loves what we're doing and she just wants to see who are. Can we?"

I don't want to ruin this for her. But I am also unspeakably nervous that suddenly the secret that was just between the three of us has extended to four people. I don't want to get found out here.

But I take a breath, and try to still the frantic drumming in my chest.

"I'd love to meet her," I say. "Just tell me when."

"She's back next Friday," she says. "So then?"

"Sure."

But I'm not sure. I couldn't be more unsure if I tried.

———

LUC & SOPH

> You okay? You weren't in school today.

SOPH

...

All good.

I make my way home to find that Dad is already there. There is noise coming from the kitchen and this is the first time I've seen him since Monday. Which already makes me feel weird.

"Luc? Is that you?"

I don't know who he's expecting. Like, I really don't know. I'm the only other person with a key.

"Yep!"

"Marco!"

"Polo!"

"Marco!"

I follow his voice to the kitchen and see that he's at the table once again, those same papers around him, that same defeated look on his face.

"Tea?" I say.

"Please."

When he looks up at me, I can't help but notice how exhausted he looks. His hair looks a little greasy, his eyes sunken. He's wearing his chef whites, but they are stained with the sauce of what looks like a very busy lunch shift.

"You alright?" I ask, as I put the kettle on.

"Fine," he replies, forcing a smile onto his face. "Long day. After a long night. Not had time to think, let alone do anything else. How was school?"

"School was…school," I say.

"Did you talk to Grayson?" he asks. "Is everything alright there?"

I nod. "Yeah, I think so."

"I'm sorry about the other night."

"Me too," I say.

"Having a tough time at the moment, Luc, you know that," he says. "Got a lot on and I'm just trying to…to do the right things."

The kettle boils and I turn around and make two cups of tea. I hand him his and he wraps his hands around it. He looks happier just to have it in his hand. Never underestimate the healing powers of a cup of tea.

"I just…I wanted things to be perfect and—"

"Nothing's perfect, Luc," Dad says. "Not a damn thing."

"I know, Dad, I just—"

"At least everything's okay," he says. "I'm really sorry, I have to keep going through all this before I head out to work again tonight. I've got some calls to make." He picks up his phone and starts dialling, and it's like I'm not even there anymore. So I take my tea and I go.

THIRTY-SIX

WELCOME TO THE HONEYMOON

So you've got the guy. Well done you. If you've made it this far in the book, then I imagine there have been many stumbling blocks along the way. The course of true love never runs smoothly, but you've got him. Now, you've got to keep him.

But don't forget to enjoy your time together as well. You are in the honeymoon phase. Everything they do will be cute. Everything they do will be adorable. Everything they do will set your heart on fire. Tread carefully.

LUC & GRAYSON

GRAYSON

Sorry if kissing you at school today was a step too far

I just…I wanted you to know that everything was alright, and that felt like a good way to do it. If it was too much, I won't do it again.

> I wish you would. It was nice. And thank you for not hating me for avoiding you yesterday.

Grayson and I talked late into the night, to the point where when I wake up the following day, I'm fairly sure I haven't slept. It's...not ideal, especially when I have a full weekend at work ahead of me.

In the interest of doing the right thing, I pick up an extra shift on Saturday, staying later so I can earn a bit of extra money. Dad looked so stressed last night. It won't be a lot, but it will be something.

Grayson meets me before school on Monday morning. I know it's totally in the wrong direction for him, and he's pretty much had to walk past the school to get to me, so that makes it all the sweeter when he messages me in the morning to say he's outside.

"You're doing all the right things here," I say as I meet him on the corner.

He pulls me into a kiss and I swear this has to be some kind of dream because how on earth is this happening to me right now?

"Good morning," he says.

"Good morning, yourself," I say, giving him another quick peck before we start our walk to school. "How was your weekend?" I ask.

"You know how my weekend was," he replies. When I wasn't at work, we barely stopped messaging. But there's something about hearing it from him rather than reading about it that makes me press him for an answer. "A busy one for everybody else but me, I think," he adds. "Brothers off at clubs and things, me just doing homework. How's Pride & Prejudice?"

"I plead the fifth."

"Lucas!"

"What?"

"You're going to fail English!" He says. "Do I need to sit you down and read it to you?"

"Why does that actually sound like a good idea?"

He chuckles and shakes his head. "You want me to read to you?"

"I don't know."

"So for our third date, you'll come over to my house and I'll read you Pride and Prejudice," he says with a laugh.

We've not talked about date number three yet, so my panic has subsided somewhat. I want to bring it up, want to talk to him about this tiny, low-level buzz of anxiety that's hanging around at the back of my head, but I also don't want to ruin what's going on right now. I don't want to ruin my time with him by bringing up something awkward.

"Something like that," I reply.

He takes hold of my hand as we walk into school. There are people looking, pointing, whispering. I guess it's not every day you see two guys walking around school holding hands. But I don't feel unsafe. Because Grayson is there.

"So I'm thinking Friday," he says when we get to our lockers. It takes me a second to register what he's talking about. "For a date. If you're free."

"Um—"

"The weekend is kind of packed with family stuff," he adds quickly. "But otherwise next weekend—"

"No, um, Friday works," I say. "After school?"

"Much as I'd like to take Friday off, I can't imagine they'd let that slide."

"Rude."

"I know," he says.

We collect our things and close our lockers. Awkwardly, we stand in the corridor, a couple of people walking around us, some going to their lockers, some on their way to their form classes. It's cliché, but I can barely see them, with Grayson looking down at me, a soft smile dancing across his lips.

Without a word, we lean in, that magnet pulling us closer to one another, closer still, our lips almost touching—

And the bell rings.

We stop millimetres from each other. I can feel his breath on my face.

"Saved by the bell," he whispers. It comes out like a growl and I swear my knees go weak.

"Something like that," I reply.

242

He gives me a quick kiss, soft, fleeting, leaving me wanting more.

"Lunch?" he asks.

"Sure."

I make my way to the Geography block, surprised to see that Soph isn't there again. Max seems out of place with just Krish and Jasmine. I'm so used to seeing them as a foursome that it takes me a second to recalibrate.

"Where's—?"

"Where have you been?" Max asks. "I swear I saw you walking in with Grayson this morning."

"You probably did," I reply. "He walked me to my locker and… then the first bell went."

I expect a comment from Max, maybe even a joke or a congratulations, but all I get is an "Oh" before his attention is pulled back to his phone.

"I suppose you should be thanking me, huh?" Jasmine piped up, and it's taking every bit of my willpower not to look at her like she's got two heads.

"What?"

"Well, if I hadn't chimed in, you two would still be on the rocks," she says. "You wouldn't be going out. So you're welcome. Guess we're even now."

"Um—"

"It's just so weird to see you two together," Jasmine continues. "Not trying to be rude or anything, but…you're so quiet, Luc. I didn't think you had it in you."

It's almost a compliment. It's almost saying congratulations and well done, but mostly it's backhanded and somehow I still can't find the strength to snap back at her. If Soph were here, maybe she would have stepped in. Maybe she wouldn't. I can't be sure anymore.

"Congratulations, Luc," Krish says. "You two look cute together."

He's a man of few words, but I appreciate it.

"Where's Soph?" I ask. "She wasn't in on Friday either. Is she alright?"

"Um—" Max starts.

"She's fine," Jasmine says quickly. "Saturday night was a bit rough for her, but she's doing alright. Just not feeling good."

And I'm about to look at Max for confirmation, wondering why this information isn't coming from him, when I realise what Jasmine has said.

"Saturday night?" I say.

"Yeah," Krish says. "We were out on Saturday night." The second bell rings and he gets to his feet. "You know, the usual. Pizza, film, we even hung out in the arcade for a bit afterwards. It was alright. Shame you couldn't make it."

Couldn't make it, I think. *I wasn't even asked! I didn't even know.*

I throw my brave face back on. "Yeah, shame," I say, wondering who said I couldn't make it. Maybe Soph. Maybe Max. Maybe they just didn't want to ask.

"You too, Max," Krish says.

I look at Max, who quickly looks up from his phone and throws Krish a tight-lipped smile. So Max didn't even go.

I type out a message to Soph, a quick, "You okay?" but find myself doubting whether to even send it. Jasmine says that she's fine. I look through the last few messages we've sent to one another. They're not really anything. Maybe I shouldn't be doing this for her anymore. Maybe I shouldn't be checking in. Maybe she doesn't want me to.

The bell rings and we all turn to head to our form room. I touch Max on the arm as he is about to walk past.

"Is everything alright with you and Soph?" I ask.

"Yeah," he says. "She's going through some stuff. Makes things… weird, I guess."

"You weren't out on Saturday?"

He shakes his head. "I had…stuff to deal with."

"Do you want to talk about it?"

He opens his mouth to respond, but seems to change his mind mid-thought. "I'm alright," he says. "But thanks."

He walks past me and into Mr Marshall's classroom. Much as I want to press him on it, I'm sure he'll come to me if he needs to talk. At least, I hope he knows I'm here if he needs me.

I fire off a message to Vicky.

Grayson date is Friday. Need a game plan. You free at break?

A throat is cleared nearby, and I look up to see Mr Marshall waiting by the door. He gestures to the phone, and I put it away. He rolls his eyes before ushering me inside.

―――――

"She was really excited to meet you," Vicky says when she meets me on break. "But we can totally rearrange. She's still here next week."

"Wait, what are we talking about?"

"June!" She says impatiently. "We're supposed hang out with her on Friday."

"Shit, yes, we were. I'm sorry," I say. "I've been so wrapped up with Grayson and third date stuff and Dad, it totally slipped my mind."

"It's fine," she says. "I've already rearranged for next Wednesday." But I feel like a dickhead.

"And how is all that?" I ask.

"What?"

"June."

Vicky opens her mouth to respond, but seems to change her mind. "It's okay," she replies. "It's awkward, I guess. She's still with her partner, which is great, they're very happy together, it's just...I don't know where I fit with her anymore and it's kind of hard to reconcile when we've only really spoken on and off for the past few months, you know?"

"Sure," I say. "But when you're together, does it feel normal?"

"Like old times," she says. "Which, in a way, makes it weirder. It me wonder why we let stuff get between us, you know? You said you're worried about your dad. Everything okay at home?"

"He's struggling, I think," I say. "He's still worried about money, which makes me worried about money."

"Yeah, I noticed you signing up for all the overtime," Vicky says. "You better be taking care of yourself, Luc."

I shrug. "I'm doing my best," I say, which is almost the truth. But I don't want to talk about this anymore. I want to focus on happier things. "Grayson. Third date. What do I do?"

245

Vicky takes a breath.

"You carry on doing everything that you've been doing so far," she says. "Follow the rules, light and bubbly, sparkling wine, body language, eye contact, all of that, follow those impulses."

"And the sex stuff?"

Vicky groans. "Talk. To. Him." she says. "Communication is key. It's the biggest thing missing from that book. It's all about hiding stuff and enhancing stuff and minimising stuff. The one thing it doesn't seem to say is that you have to talk. So talk to him. It will be fine."

I can only hope she's right.

THIRTY-SEVEN

THE THIRD DATE
Insert cheesy sex music here. **Bow chicka wow wow, etc., etc. (Cont.)**

You likely know each other pretty well by now. But you'll continue to learn about each other as you become closer. Remember all the rules that got you the guy in the first place. It is essential they stay in play until you're ready.

Stay aloof, dear one. Stay aloof.

THE REST of the week is fairly hectic for me. I see Grayson a lot, which is very nice, even if it means I'm seeing my friends less. When I've been around them, they don't seem...like they want me there, which is hard to deal with.

Soph came back to school towards the end of the week, but we've not really had a chance to sit down and talk. Any time I've been around her, she's been with Jasmine and there hasn't been a moment. Sometimes they've been there with Grayson and his other friends over lunch, and it's kind of satisfying how easily I've slotted in with Madhuri and Char. Laurie still doesn't seem keen. Dylan definitely hates me, but like Max said, he's a dickhead.

Now that Max has mentioned it, I can see the weirdness between him and Soph. They don't seem to be as touchy-feely as they were before, quite as in each other's pockets. If I'm in the library doing book stuff, Max is there with me, and so is Vicky, usually. I want to ask him what's going on but... He'd tell me, wouldn't he?

I'm trying to do what Mum says, trying to stay aloof. But Grayson is the one holding my hand. He's the one who can't seem to stay away from me. When he offers to walk me home, I can't help but say yes. I find him intoxicating, and I just want to spend every waking moment with him. But I know I shouldn't, I know Mum would advise against it, so I don't.

Dad still seems to be pretty exhausted and distant. He has to head out to work almost immediately as I get in.

Grayson and I decide to meet at FUNTERTAINMENT on Friday night. I've not seen Dad to tell him what's going on, but I got a nice text message saying, "WORKING TONIGHT" so it's not like he's about to miss me.

I've run out of clothes. I'm re-wearing what I wore on our first disastrous date and hoping that the outfit choice isn't some kind of bad omen.

VICKY

You look great, don't overthink it, talk to him about
the sex thing.

'The sex thing' hasn't come up yet. We have talked about it being the third date, we've had Madhuri and Char making ooh-ing and kissy noises at the mention of it being the third date, but no one has actually mentioned the possibility of sex, which makes me tense.

But that's sort of my default so...

I'm waiting outside the cinema for him, having just got off the bus, when a car pulls up and drops him off. Whatever is happening in the car sounds like the epitome of chaos. There's a younger teen in the back, wearing a red and white striped football kit, who is shouting about something, and a woman, I assume to be Grayson's Mum, yelling back from the front seat. Grayson looks thoroughly embarrassed.

He catches my eye, and I quickly look away so he doesn't think I've heard.

"Sorry about that," he says as he approaches. "My family is..." He waves his hands in the air, giving the impression of them being rather a lot.

I get it. I mean, I get it in the figurative sense. Personally, I think our house could do with a little more chaos.

He waves at them as his mum drives away. I catch sight again of her fiery-hair, her eyebrows practically vertical, saying something to the boy in the back. She doesn't see Grayson's wave, and I feel bad for him.

"It's fine," I say. "Is everything okay?"

"I'd rather not talk about it," he says firmly, drawing a harsh line under the conversation. He is still watching the car go, like she might stop and reverse and wave at him or something.

It's probably the first time I've seen him anything less than confident, anything less than front-footed. And I need to do something about it.

I step a little closer to him and nudge him with my hip. It's enough to throw him off balance and it looks like he's about to fall, which is enough to make him laugh. He looks at me, smiling, dimples popping, eyes sparkling a little bit. That's the Grayson I know. But there is that part of me, however small, that wants to go back and help the sad Grayson, and figure out what's going on there.

"Hello," he says. "You look nice."

Before I can even think of a response, he's wrapped me up in his arms and planted a kiss on my lips. I let myself melt into it. There's been a lot of kisses this week, fleeting pecks between classes, at our lockers, before lunch, after lunch, during lunch, whenever we can, really. But this is different. There's no one around, so I don't feel like I'm on display. It's just a bunch of strangers walking by while I breathe Grayson in.

"You look nicer," I say when we part. "That was nice."

"Stop saying nice."

"It's nice."

"Stupid," he says, rolling his eyes and giving me one last peck on the lips.

We head into the cinema and get tickets for *CHASING LOVE.* It's literally the only thing that's on right now because neither of us was sensible enough to do some research.

"When did you see this?" he asks.

"When you did," I reply.

"What?"

"I was there, Grayson," I say. "When you saw it with Max and Soph and everybody, I was there too. I was just…quiet."

He shakes his head. "Now I feel like an arsehole."

"You're not an arsehole," I say. "I'm just…I was just good at being invisible. Not so much now."

He takes my hand. "I'm very happy about that."

The film is way better the second time around. Somehow the romance feels less cheesy, even if the moment where she does The Turn and suddenly the love interest notices her makes me laugh, because that really didn't work for me. At least, not without a little, "Fancy seeing you here," thrown in.

We're about halfway through the film when it happens.

Grayson reaches down and takes hold of my hand. I couldn't tell you what part of the film it is, because fireworks are exploding in my head. I'm sitting in a cinema holding hands with a really, *really* handsome boy, and… How did this happen? How did we get here?

I keep my focus on the screen. I want to be able to act casually, act aloof, just let this really wonderful thing happen to me.

We're leaning into each other, trying to get as close as we can with the physical barrier of the armrest between us. I can see him looking at me out of the corner of my eye. I know he's looking. And I think he knows I know he's looking because he's smiling at me.

"What?" I whisper, turning to face him.

"You look really good."

"In the dark?" I reply, raising an eyebrow.

He lets out a breath, the smallest laugh. "I can see your face."

"Unlucky."

"Stop it, you're getting me all flustered," he says, leaning closer still.

I follow suit because I know what's coming and, even though we kissed outside, I can't get enough of him. I just want to be around him all the time. I want to be holding his hand, kissing his face. Just being near him is enough.

We miss quite a lot of the second half of the film, but it doesn't matter given we've both seen it before. We talk about everything else that happens in the film on our way out, the cheesy romantic ending, the grand romantic gesture to get the guy. Classic romcom tropes that I absolutely live for.

"I still don't like the ending," Grayson says.

"What do you mean? It's sweet."

"How?"

"Everything that she wanted had been right in front of her the whole time, she just couldn't see it."

"But we've spent a whole film getting to know the other guy," Grayson says. "And he's supposed to be *the* guy and then he's just not?"

"Sometimes that's life, I guess," I say.

"At least my parents will think I came here to watch a film rather than to just kiss you," he says as we get outside.

"You came here to kiss me?"

"Duh."

"It's not *duh*, this is new to me!" I say, suddenly nervous that I've said too much. We make our way to the bus stop and sit down.

"So, what now?" he asks.

"I don't know," I reply. "The bus is in five minutes. I don't know where else there is to go where they won't want ID to let us inside."

"You could come back to mine?" he says. I freeze. "It's still early. Time for another film, at least."

"Um…I don't…I don't know," I reply.

"You can ask your dad," he says. "See if he's okay with it."

I snort. "He won't care."

"I'm sure he will."

"It's not that, though," I say. "I just…I mean…I can't…I don't… I've never."

"Lu, what?" he asks.

"I don't want to have sex with you!" I say quickly, and way, *way* too loud.

Someone walking past looks at the two of us like we've just grown an extra head each. Someone else starts laughing.

Grayson is speechless. Understandably, I think.

"I'm…um…I…I'm…"

"It's not that I don't want to ever have sex with you, it's just that tonight, I mean, it's the third date and the third date means sex, doesn't it?" I say. Someone has started the engine in my mouth and it's running at a million miles an hour, smashing through any silence it comes into contact with. "And I wanted to talk to you about it sooner, wanted to bring it up at a point that, you know, wasn't here, but I was having such a nice time that I forgot, and now you've invited me back to yours to 'watch a film' and we all know what that means."

"D-d-d-d-do we?" Grayson stammers. "Are you okay?"

"Not really," I say, running out of breath. I lean forward, putting my head in my hands. Everything has been so smooth so far. Why is it my brain has decided to act up now and make me look mad in front of him? There is a literal rule about hiding the crazy, and here I am displaying mine, not just for Grayson, but the whole of Funtertainment to see.

His hand lands on my back and he rubs it in small circular motions. I take a few deep breaths, the two of us treading water in the silence for a few moments.

"Better?" he says.

"Much." I sit up straight again, but I can't bring myself to look at him. My stomach is in knots.

"Can I speak?" he says.

"Yes."

"Without you freaking out?"

"Hold up now, I don't think I can promise that," I reply.

"I've never had sex before," he says.

It's so plain, so matter of fact. It hadn't occurred to me. He's…I mean… He's so handsome and everybody loves him and I assumed that he would have had a boyfriend somewhere, or hooked up with someone from school at some point. There's no way we're the only boys who like boys, statistically that makes no sense.

"Have I thought about it? Yes," he says. "With you? Maybe, but we've not been going out very long and…I don't know…" He turns to look at me. I can't bring myself to look at him; I feel like if I do, I might combust. "But you're my first proper boyfriend. I've kissed other guys before, but I've never been with someone. So…yeah. There you go. I don't want to have sex with you either." I face him and see that he's smirking. "At least not yet."

I have to look away because there is a strange feeling buzzing throughout my body. It was him saying "not yet." It's that little smirk on his face that always makes me weak. And then there was the other thing he said.

"Did you just call me your boyfriend?" I ask.

His eyes go wide and his mouth drops open. "I mean...I know we've not talked about it, and we've not actually said it to one another yet, but I thought...I don't know...I figured...I was just... Okay, my turn to take some deep breaths."

"I'm your boyfriend," I say. "I mean, I'm your boyfriend if you want me to be your boyfriend. I want you to be mine."

"You do?"

"It's because you're so nice."

"Enough of the nice," he groans, but he's smiling the whole time, positively beaming. "So, what now?" he asks. "We can get the bus and then I can walk you home."

I take a steadying breath. "Let's go back to yours."

THIRTY-EIGHT

"BEFORE WE GO INSIDE, I need to tell you something incredibly important." Grayson has turned to me on his doorstep and is looking down at me all seriously. How he manages to still be so handsome when his eyebrows are knitted together and his forehead is all crinkled tells you exactly how smitten I am right now.

"Go on."

"My family is…strange," he says, struggling with the last word.

"Okay. Isn't everybody's?"

"Yes, but—"

"You met my dad. I'd hardly call him normal."

"Lu, you've got to listen to me," he says. "It's a little wild in there. You heard what was happening in the car. It's not a normal house."

I don't know whether he's trying to make me nervous or if it's just a casual warning, but as he takes his keys out of his pocket, there are butterflies dive-bombing my stomach, making me feel more than a little bit panicky.

The last time I was at Grayson's house was for the party when he ended up asking me out. But I am more nervous this time around. It's one thing to walk into a house that's packed to the rafters with other kids from school, especially when I was pretty sure there wasn't a single person paying attention to me. But knowing that his family is here this time, that they know we've been on a date… What if they hate me? What if I say something stupid? What if—?

I run out of time for what-ifs because Grayson has opened the door and is walking inside, and it would be too weird if I didn't follow him in.

As we step inside, the house is alive with activity, but in a totally different way than the party. There is no music, there is no laughing and screaming. There are voices in the deeper recesses of the house talking animatedly about something. There are dogs barking. There are at least two people fighting one room over. It's a different kind of chaos, but I don't hate it. The house is alive.

He kicks his shoes off, putting them on the rack by the door, so I do the same. A black Labrador rounds the corner and bounds over to him, jumping to greet him, tail wagging a million miles a minute, tongue hanging out of its mouth.

"Hey puppy, hey puppy, how are you doing, puppy? How are you?" He's talking baby talk to the dog.

ALERT!

HE IS TALKING BABY TALK TO THE DOG.

The dog, who is almost certainly not a puppy.

Is there anything cuter than a really hot guy with a dog?

Allow me to answer that for you. There is nothing cuter than a really hot guy with a dog.

He looks over at me. "You're staring."

"You have a dog."

"We have two," he says with a grin, sinking to the floor to fuss with the dog. "This is Molly, she loves people, the other is Tallulah. She hates anyone and anything that comes near her. Look." He gestures over to a door where another black lab is watching us. I might be imagining it, but I'm fairly sure I'm being sneered at. She turns around and walks away. "See? Hateful."

"Grayson, is that you?" A woman's voice comes from deeper in the house. It manages to break through the hubbub happening one room over, noise that I assume is coming from Grayson's brothers. The house seems to go quiet at her voice. I can hear footsteps, and immediately I tense up.

"Yeah, I'm here with Lucas," he says, getting to his feet. It almost sounds like a warning. 'I'm here with Lucas' definitely means 'be on your best behaviour and hide the baby pictures.'

She appears where Tallulah had just been, a red-headed vision in a black floral maxi dress. She has Grayson's face, just rounder and a bit chubbier rather than square-jawed. There is a big smile on her face, and I wonder what conversation they'd had before he left the house earlier this evening.

"It's so nice to meet you," she says, walking towards me, still smiling, positively giddy. "Are you a hugger? I like to hug, but if you're not a hugger, it's fine."

"I could go for a hug."

"Oh, wonderful!" She reaches out and gives me a big squeeze.

I can't remember the last time I had a hug like that. Hugs from friends are one thing, hugs from Grayson are a totally different scenario, but that was a parent hug, a mama bear kind of hug. Now is not the time to cry about this.

"It's so nice to meet you," she says. "I'm sorry I didn't stick around earlier. I had the boys in the car. I was the taxi tonight."

"Mum—"

"What?" she says. "That's not embarrassing. One had football practice, one had a music lesson, and this one had a date. My boys are busy, busy, busy, and now two of them are FIGHTING IN THE LIVING ROOM AND NEED TO STOP BEFORE I COME IN THERE!" The noise one room away stops again. She holds. Mission accomplished. She turns back to us. "We were just having some dinner. Have you both eaten?"

"I'm okay," I say.

"Did you get popcorn?"

"Of course," Grayson replies.

"Salty or sweet?"

I say sweet as Grayson says salty. His mum puts a finger on her nose and points at me. "You're a man after my own heart, Lucas. Sweet is always the way to go."

"Wrong," Grayson announces.

"I did everything right, Lucas. I raised him with good manners, but he still insists on salted popcorn."

"Heathen."

"Couldn't agree more," she says. "So what have you kids got planned, hmmm?"

My face immediately goes red and I look at Grayson, panicked. He seems entirely unaffected by it.

"Well, I was thinking we'd go upstairs, maybe watch a film or something?"

"Door open."

"Mum!" His face goes so red so fast that I only just catch the switch.

"I know what it's like to be young."

"MUM!"

"Gray!" she calls out over the sound of Grayson's brothers bickering again.

It's only when a response comes back yelling, "What?" that I realise she isn't talking to Grayson.

"Come meet Lucas."

Grayson looks at me, panic in his eyes. He wants to disappear, he wants the ground to swallow him up, and there is something adorable about seeing him on the back foot for once.

I hear a chair scrape in the kitchen. Grayson is vibrating next to me, one hundred percent on edge. I reach out and, out of sight of his mum, give his hand a quick squeeze. He looks at me, and I can see him relax a fraction.

He lets go of my hand the second a man, who is easily twice the size of his mum, appears in the doorframe. Another redhead, but with a strong jaw, broad shoulders, and a barrel chest. A cheesy grin practically glows beneath his ginger beard as he clocks the two of us.

"Lucas!" His voice is like a rumble of thunder. "Lovely to meet you. We've heard a lot about you."

"You have?"

"Oh yes," he says. "Lucas did this, Lucas said that, can I do this with Lucas? We never hear the end of it."

"Dad!"

"Not trying to embarrass you, son," he says. "I managed to convince your Mum to put away the photo albums."

"Photo albums?" I say.

"I'll make sure you see them next time," his mum stage whispers.

"We're going upstairs now," Grayson says. "Come on, Lu."

"Door open," his Dad booms.

"I know!"

The noise in the house erupts once again, a dog starts barking, the rumble of thunder I met downstairs seems to burst into life, lightning cracking through the downstairs. Grayson leads me away from the chaos, his hand in mine, practically dragging me up the stairs. I'm falling over myself when he gets me into his bedroom and closes the door.

"I thought they said door open," I say.

"With all that noise downstairs, you want the door open?" Grayson replies. "We'll barely be able to hear ourselves think."

He leans his back against the door and takes a couple of deep breaths. It's the nervous, sad Grayson that got out of that car back at the cinema just a few short hours ago.

I'm starting to see that the Grayson I've watched from afar, that I've seen living his best life on Instagram stories, that's not the real Grayson, not by a long shot. This is him.

"You okay?" I ask tentatively.

"They're just a lot," he says. "And…and I don't really have people over when they're here because…well…" He gestures around himself, referencing the chaos we experienced downstairs.

"They're fine," I say. "Your house is so different from mine."

"A mess?"

"No," I say. "It's…alive. It's lived in. There are people living in it."

"You do know that you live in your house, right? That your dad lives there with you?"

I shrug. "It's just quiet a lot of the time. He's never there. Your parents are here. And they're clearly very interested in what you're getting up to."

Grayson laughs. "That's what I get for actually doing something for once."

"What do you mean?"

"Oh, come *on*," he says. "You heard my brothers down there. I'm the quiet one. I'm actually doing something, so they're all interested."

"You do all sorts of stuff," I say.

"I do?"

"You play rugby on the school team, you're part of the Creative Writing Group, you throw parties for your friends, you…" I trail off because he's looking at me curiously. "You pull bullies off of little gay boys in Year 9 who had just come out."

A soft smile drifts across his face. "You noticed all of that?"

"Of course I've noticed all of that. Have you seen you?" I say. "How could anyone not notice you?"

He walks over to me and wraps me in his arms, planting a kiss on my lips.

"I'm glad you noticed," he says.

"I'm glad you noticed that I noticed."

He kisses me again.

"I do a lot of things, but they aren't things that require my parents to do anything. My brother is a footballing protégé and a nightmare in college. He's struggling. My younger brother is going to be the next Sondheim or some—"

"Did you just reference Sondheim?"

"Hey, I do listen to you, you know," he says. "So he's taking up a lot of my parents' attention. The two of them seem to compete for it, hence the rough-housing and fighting and the noise. And then I'm just in the middle. Dependable, reliable Grayson. Good grades, good behaviour, good boy."

"They notice," I say. Grayson doesn't look convinced. "They do! They're probably grateful that you're so easy to deal with."

"They don't."

"If they didn't notice, they wouldn't have asked how our date went. They were ready to come and talk to you before they knew I was with you," I say. "They notice. They care. Trust me."

"Alright," he says. "I trust you."

He leans down, and he kisses me again. Slowly, he leads me over to his bed, the two of us stumbling over our feet as we try to keep kissing while we move.

We lie down on his bed and he's on top, leading the charge, and there is something so magical (and incredibly hot, let's not lie here) about seeing him looking down at me.

"What?" he asks. "Is something wrong?"

"No," I reply. "Nothing at all."

We keep kissing until we can't anymore, stopping until we get a second head of steam, and then starting all over again. I forget how many times this repeats. I can't get enough of him.

What feels like minutes later there are hands on my shoulders, shaking me, and I hear my name, but it sounds so far away.

"Lucas?" It's not a voice I recognise. "Lucas." I open my eyes and there's a woman standing over me, red hair, round, open face, her eyes pleading with me. "Lucas, sweetie, you have to wake up. It's late."

I couldn't tell you when I fell asleep, when the world just fell away, but when I open my eyes, I'm lying on Grayson's chest. I've definitely drooled a little bit, and heat warms my cheeks. I wipe my mouth on the back of my hand and look up to see if he's noticed. He's still asleep, but stirring now. And I feel a little bit creepy, but I can't help but watch him for just a few seconds. He looks so peaceful, so serene.

"Lucas, I'm sorry, I noticed the light was still on when Gray and I came up to bed." I'd forgotten that Grayson's Mum is standing over us, and I'm cuddling her son, on his bed, and this definitely doesn't look good.

"Jesus, I'm sorry, I didn't mean to… We fell asleep," I say.

She laughs a little, but it feels a little forced. "I can see that," she says. "You should probably be getting home. Do you want me to call your Dad and let him know you're on your way?"

And it dawns on me like I've run face-first into a brick wall.

I grab my phone and see a slew of missed calls on the Lock Screen.

Dad emblazoned across it over and over and over again.

The time reads a little after midnight, and I am in big trouble.

THIRTY-NINE

"WHAT? WHAT'S HAPPENING?"

Grayson is still a little groggy, his eyes still adjusting to the light, so they're barely managing to follow me as I tear around the room trying to find my bag.

Where the hell is my bag?

"Grayson, Lucas has to go." His mum's voice is more serious now.

We were found in a compromising position. I don't want to know what she's thinking right now. Grayson sits up a little straighter, his face suddenly bright red.

"Where's my bag? Did I bring a jacket?"

"Why are you panicking?" He swings his legs over the side of the bed and looks at me like I'm out of my mind. He's not clocked the time yet, he's not realised what's happened. He doesn't know, how could he? I've not told him.

"It's quarter past twelve," I say.

His eyes widen. "What?!"

"I can give you a lift if you want?" Grayson's Mum says.

"I'll be fine," I say. "I'll walk. It will be okay."

"I'll walk him, I'll take the dogs," Grayson says. "Thanks, Mum."

"We fell asleep," I say. "My Dad has been trying to call me, and I didn't hear it, and—"

"Your Dad? Did he not know you were here?"

"No."

"At all?"

"No!" I say.

"LUCAS!"

"I can't right now," I say. "He didn't know we were out tonight, he certainly didn't know I was going to fall asleep here. Fuck. FUCK!"

"Calm down, you're acting crazy," Grayson says, getting up from the bed and putting his hands on my shoulders to steady me. It goes some way to bringing me back to reality, but certainly not enough. My phone starts ringing again. DAD is on the front of the screen and my heart rate quickens at the sight of it. I reject the call.

"Lu!"

"I can't talk to him right now, not in front of you, I just…" I look around. "Where's my bag?!"

"You need to calm down. You're losing it." He sounds aggressive, not like the Grayson that I've come to know. Why is he being like this? "He'll understand."

"You don't know him."

"You're freaking out. Calm down, for goodness sake."

"Stop telling me what I'm doing!" I shrug his hands off my shoulders. "I'm trying to figure this out!"

"I'm trying to help, and you're acting like a nutcase."

"I'm not."

"You can't go home like this!"

"What are you going to do, keep me here?"

His face twists into something akin to disgust and the pit in my stomach gets deeper.

"What is wrong with you?"

"Stop yelling at me!" I shout. "Where is my bag?"

He stops and takes a few deep breaths.

"It's downstairs, so is your jacket." Grayson follows me downstairs. He grabs my jacket off the hook and hands me my bag, face set, hard lined, the two of us standing in the hallway staring at one another. How did we go from passionately kissing one another to having absolutely no idea what to do with ourselves? Did I do this? Did I imagine it?

His hands are on my shoulders again and I'm looking up into his face. His face is stony, like he's angry at me, like he hates me, and I can see my panicked expression reflected back at me.

He leans in just as I say, "I have to go," which stops him in his tracks. How can he be thinking of kissing me right now?

"Okay," he says flatly. "Let me just get some shoes on and grab the dogs and—"

"No, I don't think you should," I say. I don't know if I want him to. "Dad is going to be losing his mind."

"Lucas, let me come with you, we can explain—"

"I'll message you later," I interrupt. "At least, I will if I'm still alive."

"Lu—"

"Joking."

"Bad joke," he says.

I give him a quick peck on the cheek and leave the house, my phone already ringing in my pocket again. I take it out and answer.

"LUCAS!" Dad's voice down the phone is so loud it practically smacks me in the face. "Lucas, is that you? Where are you? Where have you been?"

"I was at Grayson's," I say. "I'm fine. I'm coming—"

"Get home now."

"I was about to say I'm coming home."

"Don't talk back to me," he says. "I'll see you soon."

Dad doesn't say goodbye. He just hangs up, the phone going dead in my hand. My heart feels so heavy in my chest that it's like I'm dragging it home, every step taking a monumental effort as my brain spirals into every single scenario waiting for me when I open that front door.

The house looks threatening somehow when I reach it. Looming large against the dark. And I hate that the place I'm supposed to call home feels this way. Even if it is my fault.

It's icy cold as I step inside. Either it's my imagination or it's another way we're trying to tighten our belts.

"Dad?" I call. There is a definite shake in my voice. I don't know if it will stop Dad from ripping me to pieces the second he lays eyes on me.

"Kitchen!" he calls back.

263

No Marco.

No Polo.

This is way more serious than Marco Polo.

Dad is sitting at the kitchen table. He's wearing his chef whites, though they're more grey than white at this point, a couple of stains on the jacket. His hair is greasy, pulled back and out of his face, and bloody hell does he look tired. How long has he been awake today? Has he been looking for me since he got home from work? It certainly looks that way.

"Where the bloody hell were you tonight?" he growls.

"Out."

His fist lands heavily on the table. "Fuck's sake, Lucas, I know that much," he barks. He takes a second to breathe, to regain a little bit of control.

Dad isn't normally one to shout and scream. He doesn't yell. It's not his style. Not that there's ever really been a reason for him to scream at me. He normally goes for the silent treatment, laced with a bit of parental disappointment. It usually does the trick. Apparently, we're way past that now.

"Where were you?"

"Out with Grayson," I say. "We went out to see a film, then I went back to his—"

"Bloody hell."

"What?"

"You went back to his house?"

"Yes, we went back to his house."

"And then what?"

I know what he's thinking. There's something accusatory about his tone. He's already made up his mind.

"We fell asleep."

"Do you think I was born yesterday?"

"Dad—"

"You really expect me to believe that you went over to the boy's house, stayed the night, and that nothing happened?"

"I didn't stay the night," I say, though it's not far from the truth given it's half past midnight. "We fell asleep."

"Lucas, I'm not stupid," Dad snaps. "Were you safe?"

264

"Nothing happened!"

"Why are you lying to me?"

"I'm not lying to you, Dad. Nothing happened!" I can hear the desperation in my voice, the pleading. "We were kissing, and we fell asleep."

"Answer the question, Lucas, were you safe?"

"While we were kissing and having a nap?" I snap. "Yes, Dad, we wore rubbers on our lips and kept our clothes on the whole time."

"You've got to be careful, Lucas. You can't just be staying out at all hours of the night with boys you barely know."

"It was an accident. Nothing happened."

"You're sixteen!"

"I know that!"

"Do you, Lucas?" Dad barks. "Because if you knew that, then maybe you would have been considerate enough to let your father know where the hell you'd been all night? No note, no text, not a fucking thing."

"I'm sorry."

"Are you?" he barks. "I had no idea where my son was, no idea what he's been doing with himself at all hours of the night. What else have you been up to? Any other late nights I don't know about?"

I open my mouth to respond, but I don't want to lie right now. I'm already in enough shit.

"I went to a party weekend before last," I say. "At Grayson's house."

He is staring at me, his eyes wide, blazing, like he's looking at someone he doesn't even know anymore. And I can feel everything coming tumbling down around me.

"So you've been lying?"

"When am I supposed to have told you?" I say.

"Message me."

"So I can have a text relationship with my dad? Alright then," I say.

"Lucas."

"I'm sorry I didn't tell you, Dad, but tonight was an accident, nothing happened. I'm sorry."

"You don't sound very sorry to me," he says. "After everything

265

this family has been through, you would think that maybe you'd be a little more thoughtful."

He isn't listening to a word I'm saying, or he's just ignoring it. I can't tell which. But that last comment is enough to have my blood boiling so much I feel like I'm about to erupt.

"Is that a comment about Mum?" Dad's face goes dark. "So you're allowed to bring her up, but whenever I do, I get shut down?"

"I just mean that I don't want to lose you too," Dad says, tears pooling in his eyes. "I was so worried tonight, Lucas. I came home, and you were nowhere to be found. I called you, I messaged you, I didn't get a damn thing back from you. I called Max. He had no idea where you were. I called the police..." He shakes his head. "I've already lost so much."

"And I haven't?"

"Of course you have."

"Then why don't we ever talk about her?" My voice is louder than I mean it to be, but it's been building for such a long time. "We rattle around in this big old house and it's like she was never even here."

"Lucas—"

"You took down all her pictures, you hid her books, you've hidden her away from me, Dad." I'm crying. I don't want to, it feels like it's weakening everything I say, but I'm feeling so many things right now that I can't keep a lid on any of it. "I barely remember what she looks like, what she sounds like. You act like she never even existed."

"Of course she existed."

"Then why do we constantly pretend that she doesn't?!" My voice cracks. I'm shouting. I'm raging against my dad. "Why did you take her out of this house? We never talk about her, never visit her grave, never visit Nana. I know you're hurting, but you've never stopped to consider what I might be feeling, that maybe I'm hurting too. It fucking sucks, Dad. I miss her. I miss her every day, and there's no one for me to talk to about it."

"You can talk to me."

"No, Dad, I can't! Every time I bring her up, you shut down, or you change the subject, you just leave me out in the cold."

"Lucas, that's not fair."

266

"Yeah, Dad, it isn't," I say. "I can't talk to you."

"And right now you're making it impossible for me to talk to you," Dad snaps. "You come home from God knows where—"

"I told you where I was."

"And now you're the one who's shouting at me?" he finishes. "You're not above punishment, Lucas. You're sixteen years old and you can't be staying out until the early hours of the morning, doing God knows what, with God knows who."

"Nothing happened!"

"I don't believe you."

"Clearly! I told you that you don't listen to me and here you are proving it over and over and over again."

"You're not seeing him anymore," he says flatly.

"What?"

"Grounded," he replies. "So fucking grounded, Lucas."

"NOTHING. HAPPENED!" I yell. "Why don't you believe me?"

"Go to bed, Lucas."

"Get fucked!"

"Bed! Now!"

I storm up the stairs, making sure to stomp every step of the way. Maybe I'm waking the neighbours, maybe I don't care because I'm trying to make a point. I slam my door and throw myself onto my bed. There's so much spinning around in my mind right now that I barely know where to start.

LUC & GRAYSON

> I'm sorry about tonight. See you tomorrow? xx

I wait for him to reply. I watch it go from "Delivered" to "Read" and still I wait. Nothing. I check my other messages.

LUC & MAX

MAX

> Your dad called here in a panic. Are you okay? What happened with Grayson?

267

Please tell me you're okay!

LUCAS!

LUCAS!!

The messages are from a couple of hours ago, and I doubt he'll be awake, but I message him back so at least when he wakes up in the morning he'll know I'm okay.

I'm fine. It's a long story. I'll explain tomorrow.

I barely have a chance to put my phone down before it moves to "read" and the three dots pop up. Did he wait up to check that I'm okay?

MAX

Did something happen with Grayson? Sorry. I know it's late but I just need to know he didn't do anything to you.

He didn't do anything at all.

It's not entirely true. The way he acted when I was leaving wasn't exactly ideal. He loses points for that. But he offered to walk me home. That counts for something?

I didn't tell Dad I was going out tonight, and then went to Grayson's after we saw the film. Nothing happened. You know, like that. But we fell asleep and then it was past midnight and I wasn't home and Dad panicked.

You're an idiot.

But I'm glad you're okay. Don't you have work tomorrow?

Ewww. Yes. That's going to be fun. Have to be up in less than six hours.

Hate that for you.

Same.

Thanks for checking in though. I'm sorry if I worried you.

Super worried. But I'm glad you're okay. Sleep tight.

I message back saying "Sleep tight" and then put my phone on my bedside table. I lie back on my bed and stare up at the ceiling, trying to make my way through the wreckage in my head and find a restful place.

It's not a total surprise that Dad wouldn't listen to what I was saying, wouldn't believe me. I didn't tell him where I was going, but when was I supposed to do that? He's never here.

And then there's Mum.

I know he's hurting. I know that's why he never talks about her and refuses to engage with me when I bring her up, but she's my mum. I don't want to forget her.

I grab my laptop and pull it up onto the bed beside me, scrolling back through all the videos that I've watched far too many times at this point. There are parts I'm sure I could quote verbatim.

I press play, and listen to Mum's voice as I fall asleep.

FORTY

I'VE BARELY SLEPT, replaying the previous night in my head. How did it go from something so joyful to something so horrible so quickly? Even the way Grayson reacted to me leaving makes me feel all sorts of weird about everything.

The house is quiet when I make it downstairs. I half expect Dad to be down there ready for round two, but he's nowhere to be seen. I head to work, praying for death on swift wings because damn, I am tired.

"Morning."

I look up as I walk out the door, surprised to see that someone is waiting for me at the end of the path. And I can't stop the smile that bursts across my face.

I lock the door and walk towards Max, who is wrapped up in a coat and scarf, looking about as awake as I feel right now.

"Fancy seeing you here," I say.

"Wow, that's the saddest that phrase has ever sounded."

"What are you doing here?"

"Felt like you needed me this morning," he says. "And I wanted to make sure you're okay."

"You checked in last night."

"And you're a notorious overthinker and liar," he replies with a smirk. "Felt like the right thing to do was to come and make sure."

I'm tired enough that Max just saying that makes me want to cry. I don't know what I did to deserve him, but he's always been there for me when I've needed him. Even when I didn't know that I needed him. As he pulls me into a hug, it takes every bit of strength I have not to burst into tears.

"I was about to ask how you were getting on, but I take it not well, given you're squeezing the life out of me."

I let go. "Sorry," I say. "Needed that, I think."

"It's alright, it's why I came," he says. "Do you want to talk about what happened? You don't have to if you don't want to, but I'm here if you do."

I check my phone. Still nothing from Grayson, nothing from anybody, and I see that I've got a little bit of time before I have to be at work.

I start at the beginning of the date, at the part where it was all going rather well, all the way up until we were kissing and we fell asleep and…it descended into chaos.

"He yelled at you?"

"He raised his voice," I say. "He acted like I was being crazy trying to get out of the house. His relationship with his parents is obviously different to mine."

"Well, he told them where he was, for a start."

"Alright, judgment."

"I think that judgment is necessary given the situation you've ended up in," he says. "At least me and Vicky knew where you were, otherwise…"

"What? Why are we treating Grayson like he's some kind of monster?"

"I'm not," he says. "I just mean…I don't know. Don't you think you're having to work pretty hard just to get this off the ground?"

"What do you mean?"

"Well, you're changing yourself, you're buying new clothes, you're staying out late and not telling your dad…" Max shakes his head. "Don't get me wrong, I like that you're more confident. It's like the rest of the world gets to see how brilliant you are, but the other stuff… You're having to work very hard for this."

"You don't think love is worth it?"

"Do you think what you have with Grayson is love?"

271

"Well…" I don't know how to respond to that. It's way too early to say that it's love, that much I know. We've been on three dates, one of which was a washout due to various reasons, including a visit from the fire brigade. But it could be, couldn't it? "Why are you saying this?"

"I'm not trying to upset you or put you off him," Max says. "But you're having to do a lot of the legwork to get into his good graces. He didn't tell his friends about you until you showed up at the party. You were having to ask all the questions on the do-over date. And then the yelling…"

"What are you saying?" There is a catch in my voice and I hate that it's there because it makes me sound like I'm too emotional, like I'm overly invested in something that's barely started.

"I don't want you to lose who you are for a guy," Max says. "Because who you are, or who you were before you started using the book, was already pretty great."

"But not great enough for him to notice me," I say. "I wasn't worth knowing before the book told me what to do."

"Yes you were," Max says.

I don't know how to respond to that, and I wish I could come up with some witty reply, but I can't, so we carry on towards Buttons.

"Who's that?" Max asks, nodding up ahead.

I look outside the front of the shop and, lo-and-behold, there is Grayson. He's wearing an oversized hoodie and a pair of jogging bottoms. He looks cosy, like he's come here in his pyjamas. To see me. He's leaning against the glass-front of the shop and stands as soon as he sees me, leaving a smudge that either Vicky or I will have to clean later during the post-lunch lull.

"What are you doing here?" I ask.

"I wanted to see how last night went," he says. "I don't think you left in the best state and…I don't know…you seemed pretty spooked."

"You didn't reply to my message."

He shrugs. "It was late and…my head was all over the place." He turns his attention to Max. "You alright?"

"Yeah," Max says. "Was just making sure he was alright."

"Alright."

"Alright."

Too many people have said the word alright and now it seems like no one is in any way alright.

The door to the café opens, Vicky looking out at the three of us, confusion written all over her face. She locks eyes with me.

"You alright?"

Jesus Christ.

I have to resist the urge to laugh. "Fine, I won't be long."

"Maria says to open," Vicky says. "So I'd keep whatever this is brief."

"Sure."

"I'm going to get a coffee," Max says, giving my arm a quick squeeze before following Vicky inside.

I turn my attention back to Grayson, who doesn't look particularly happy. "What?" I say.

"You told him what happened?"

"He wanted to know if I was okay," I say. "He's my best friend, and I needed someone to talk to. Last night was a lot."

"It was," he says. "We messed up." He lets out a breath. "Did you... Did you fight?"

I nod, taking a shuddering breath. I don't want to cry in front of him. So much of the book is about holding back these parts of yourself, hiding the bits that might scare him off. I'm supposed to be this perfect version of Lucas around him, but every time we hang out I get closer and closer to the Lucas that can't seem to cope with day-to-day life, the Lucas that suddenly feels like he has no idea what he's doing.

He must see that I'm about to shatter because suddenly his arms are around me and he's holding me as tightly as he can. I resist it at first, arms by my sides—don't get too attached, let him come to you, play hard to get, be aloof—but I can't stop myself.

I wrap my arms around him and let myself silently cry onto his chest for a minute. He squeezes tighter when he can feel that I'm sobbing. And even when I stop, I don't want to let go of him because then he's going to see me all red-faced and chaotic.

"You going to be okay?" he asks.

I nod.

"Is that a yes?"

"Yes," I say, my voice muffled by his chest. I pull away. "I'm sorry. You've dragged yourself out of bed this morning to come and see me and I've just cried all over you. God, I'm a mess."

"You're not a mess."

I raise an eyebrow at him. "I'm a bit of a mess."

"Okay, a bit, but nothing you can't handle," he says. "You should probably go inside, right?" I nod. "Message me later?"

"Sure," I say. "I'm…I'm not allowed to see you anymore."

He blinks, looking wounded. "Weird way to break up with me, but fine—"

"No, no, no, I didn't mean it like that," I say. "I just mean…when my dad was yelling last night, he said that I wasn't allowed to see you anymore. It doesn't make any sense to me given that nothing happened, but he doesn't believe me, so…" I watch as Grayson soaks this information up, breathes it in.

"Do you want to keep seeing me?" He says.

"Of course I do," I reply, maybe a little too quickly. Mum would scold me for that, I'm sure.

"Then we'll make it work," he replies. "It took me long enough to get you, Lucas. Don't flake out on me now."

He smiles at me and I give him the strongest smile I can muster, which still feels pretty weak. I'm mostly relieved that he hasn't done a runner.

He heads off home and I make my way into the café, ready to face the onslaught of Saturday morning customers that will be charging through those doors in the next few minutes. If I'm honest with myself, I'm grateful for the distraction.

———

"Jesus, Luc, I'm sorry." It's taken me a little while to tell Vicky the full story. Between serving customers, I'd been giving her snippets of it, but now she's heard the whole thing. Everything from Grayson and I having a fantastic date and the two of us getting closer, right up to falling asleep at Grayson's, then Dad getting mad. "Hardly how you wanted to end the night."

I raise an eyebrow at her. "Is that judgment?"

"No, paranoid," she says, rolling her eyes. "I just mean that it would have been nice for you to finish the evening with Grayson without you getting yelled at. You actually fell asleep?"

"Yes," I say. I'm even getting exasperated with Vicky. "We talked about sex, and how neither one of us feels ready for that right now, and we were just kissing and stuff. If his Mum hadn't come in to check on us, I probably would have been there until the morning."

"And then you would have been in even bigger trouble," Max adds. He's been sitting at the bar with his coffee so he could chime in.

"Dad would have sent the army or something, I'm sure," I say. With the immediate glare off it, I can see what I've done wrong and how much I've screwed up. I just don't like the way he handled it. "I don't know what to do."

"So how did that all shake down last night?"

"I'm grounded," I say. "No friends, no Grayson, just work and school. The end."

"For how long?"

"He didn't say."

"Well, it's been nice knowing you," she says with a laugh. "Guess the experiment is over then, huh?"

"Hardly," I say. "Grayson doesn't seem to be scared off by any of this. We've still got a book to finish."

Max takes a long sip of his coffee. Vicky takes a deep breath and goes back to cleaning the counter. There is something that she isn't saying.

"What?" I ask, even though I know I'm not going to want to hear it.

"Don't hate me for this."

"How could I?"

"Maybe we should cool it with the book stuff for now," she says.

I'm about to protest when Max says, "She might be right, Luc."

"Hear me out before you say anything, okay?" she says, talking quickly so I don't have a chance to interrupt her. "I'm not saying that I have all the answers here, but this book has got you into trouble with your dad a couple of times now. I don't want you following it to the detriment of your relationship with him. That would suck. Sure, you might end up with Grayson, but at what cost?"

275

"At what cost?" I repeat. "When did we step into a romcom?"

"Lucas."

"I can have it all here, Vicky, I know I can," I say. "And the book has been pretty successful so far. Sure, there have been a couple of fuck-ups along the way. I've slipped up because Grayson is too bloody charming and I'm too bloody besotted, but I've made so much progress over the past few weeks. We're really getting somewhere. I'd hate to throw that away."

"I'm not saying throw it away, I'm saying cool off," she says. "Great as the book is, I don't want you to get into even more trouble."

"I'll be fine," I say. "Remember how it was at the start when you were the one telling me to trust the process? This is the time for us to do that. We've come way too far to let up now. Grayson is my boyfriend. We've got the guy, now we've just got to keep him."

Vicky hesitates. "Only if you're sure."

I nod. "I'm very sure. June can help too, right?"

"Alright then," she says. "Let's lock him in."

FORTY-ONE

THE REST of my day is pretty quiet, all things considered. Vicky and I spend a little bit of time over our lunch break figuring out a game plan for what to do with Grayson going forward. Not being allowed to leave the house to see him complicates things, but there are plenty of ways to work around those at school. There is still the Creative Writing Group and the time we get to spend on lunch breaks. That, according to Vicky at least, is something we can work with.

"Especially if you really take your time walking home," Vicky says. "And he drops you off around the corner from your house."

"You want me to lie?"

"I don't want your dad to rip Grayson's head off," she says. "You sure you still want to do this?"

I think back to what Grayson said before I walked into work that morning. He'd made it pretty clear that he didn't want me to bail on this and that was reason enough for me not to. Like he said, it had taken us long enough to get to this point. Why stop now? Obviously, that time has been more like four years for me versus a few weeks for him, but it is what it is.

"Yeah, I want to do this," I say. "Just have to be careful around Dad. And maybe Max."

"What do you mean?"

I explain what Max said to me on my way to work, how he was

questioning if it was worth it, about us not being right for one another.

"Do you think you're right for each other?"

"I think so," I say. "I have to believe that. We've already put so much effort into this and—"

"This isn't about the effort we've put in," she says. "If you're having doubts, then maybe it's not worth it."

"It is," I say.

"He's looking out for you," Vicky says. "He's known you for, what, more than ten years? And he's your best friend. He's seen you hurting before, when your mum died, and he's probably trying to prevent something like that from happening again. He cares about you."

"I can't wrap myself in cotton wool."

"No one is saying you should," Vicky replies. "He's just trying to make sure you're not getting your heart stomped on."

"I'm not," I say. *At least I don't think I am.*

Monday rolls around and Grayson meets me around the corner from my house, just like Vicky and I discussed. It's enough for us to still get a chance to be couple, still get to spend a bit of time together, but without my dad's eyes on me.

Over the weekend he seemed to make a point of taking shifts that meant he saw me get home from work, like if he didn't see me walk in the house I'd be off doing "God knows what, with God knows who" as he so delicately put it.

How did our entire relationship fall apart because of one slip-up? Not that I need to be reminded of it, but perhaps our relationship wasn't all that strong to begin with.

That sounds about right.

There is a strange unease when Grayson meets me. I don't know if it's because I feel like I'm having to be careful or if maybe he's losing interest, but I try and push through it.

"I hope your Mum doesn't hate me," I say as we walk to school.

He looks at me, well and truly confused by what I've just said. "Why would she hate you?"

"Because I ran out of your house at breakneck speed on Friday night, I barely said goodbye or anything."

"I explained it all to her."

I eye him carefully. "All? All, like how?"

He smirks. "I left out the part where you'd not told your dad where you were," he says. "And I just went with the bit where we fell asleep. I did end up getting a sex chat, though."

"Oh shit, I'm sorry."

"At least it wasn't just you on the business end of that," he says. "So if we ever do decide to have sex, I have enough condoms and lube to last us a lifetime."

I choke on the air I'm breathing. "Are you freaking serious?"

Grayson nodded. "When Mum got home from work yesterday, she handed me a bag from Superdrug that was practically overflowing. She was very pleased with herself. I, on the other hand, wanted the ground to open up and for a creature to drag me to hell."

"To make use of the condoms?"

"LU!"

"What? It's nice! At least she's being supportive," I say. "Dad's wasn't so much a talk as it was a slut shaming and telling me to be careful."

"He's just looking out for you."

"He's only looking out for me because I fucked up," I say. "He couldn't have been less interested before that."

The line is enough to bring our conversation to a crashing halt, and I realise that I've broken yet another rule in Mum's book because we're in the deepest, darkest wood of a very serious topic. That's not what we need.

"I don't want him to hate me," Grayson says. "And if this gets around the school…" He shakes his head. "I'm not saying we need to play it low-key or anything, but I don't want people getting the wrong idea about me."

"The wrong idea?"

"Optics. Thinking I'm some kind of bad boy," he says. "That's not what I want. I'm a nice guy, a good person, fun to have at parties, that kind of thing. I don't want people to think I'm turning into… I don't know what."

I'm trying to find the thread of what he's saying, but I just can't seem to grasp it.

"What do you mean?"

"I just want to be careful," he says as we get to our lockers. "So we'll walk to and from school and stuff, but if your dad starts to get a sniff of us being together or whatever, I don't…I don't want to be part of all that drama."

"Okay," I say, because I don't really know how to unpack that. Maybe he's starting to lose interest if the slightest whiff of drama, something that is usually so absent from my life, is enough to push him away. "See you at lunch?" I add.

"Sure thing," he says, giving me a quick kiss. Then he walks away, and for some reason that leaves me hurting.

————

It's definitely hard to focus on schoolwork after that. My head is swimming, and I'm drowning in questions about whether Grayson is even still interested, or if he's finding a reason to pull away from me.

"Lucas Cook, the board is over here, not out the window," Mrs Dhawan barks.

Oh yeah, Maths. Never my strong suit.

By some divine miracle, I manage to make it to lunchtime unscathed, my last lesson was Geography (grim), so I'm spat out straight into the Geography block where my friends are already waiting.

"Well, look who it is!" Jasmine remarks, as I walk towards them. Either there is a little bit of venom in her voice or I'm imagining it because…well…it's Jasmine. The rest of my class is filing out of the Geography block around me, eager to get to the canteen for lunch. I'm pretty eager to see Grayson, but there's no harm in waiting for a few minutes.

"Where have you been?" Jasmine asks, a fake sort of smile on her face, like she's caught me out or something.

"What do you mean?" I ask. "I was just in Geography."

"You didn't reply to any of our messages over the weekend."

I blink and look at Soph, who isn't looking at me. She's literally looking at my feet instead of my face. I'm looking for Max, who is nowhere to be seen. Krish is standing silently next to Jasmine. Is Max even in school today? I don't know. My head has been elsewhere.

"The weekend was hectic," I say. "Sorry, there was stuff happening at home and—"

"It's fine," Soph says quickly. "Drop it, Jasmine. It doesn't matter."

It cuts deeper, like she's driving the knife in further by being indifferent. I try to shake it off.

"Still sorry though," I say. "You all okay?"

"We're fine," Jasmine says. I missed the moment where she started speaking for the entire group, but sure. "You up to much this week?"

"I've got Creative Writing Group on Wednesday and work over the weekend," I say. "That's about it."

She rolls her eyes. "We were going to ask you to hang out."

"Has everybody else suddenly lost the power of speech? What's going on here?"

"You haven't been around, Luc!" Jasmine snaps. "We've all been messaging you, calling you, but you're always at work or you're with Grayson."

"You haven't all been messaging me. I missed a few messages."

"And you never come to Wednesday night study sessions anymore."

"Because I have Creative Writing Group."

"With Grayson."

"Yeah and about fifteen other people," I snap. "What are you getting at here?"

"That you just don't seem to care about us anymore," she says. "Before I even had a chance to invite you out this weekend, you've already called it off by saying you have to work."

"I do have to work."

"So what about after?"

"I can't."

"Why?"

"Because I'm grounded, Jasmine. What is with the third degree?" I look to Soph to back me up, but she's gone from looking at her shoes to looking at me with a look of pure disgust on her face. "Are you hearing this?"

281

"Jasmine, let it go," Soph says. "Can you just… Can you give us a minute?"

Jasmine doesn't seem sure that she wants to go anywhere, standing solidly at Sophie's side. Krish is being quiet, apparently as exasperated by this situation as I am.

"Please," Sophie adds.

Jasmine sighs. "We'll be around the corner," she says before walking away.

"I've wanted to talk to you," she says. "I've been messaging you and trying to catch you at school, but…you've just been busy."

"What do you want to talk to me about? If you need me, Soph, I'm there," I say.

"But you're not," she replies. "And I'm not trying to accuse you of anything, alright? I didn't want to shout or argue, that was just Jasmine being Jasmine, but I…I thought I wanted to have this conversation, but actually I think I just need a bit of space right now."

"Space? Soph—"

"Like a break," she says. "I thought I wanted to talk to you about this, but I just want time."

"Time?" I say. "How much time?"

"I don't know," she breathes. "There's a lot going on at the moment and you used to be the person that I'd turn to with things like that, but…I don't think I can this time. I'm sorry."

She walks away from me, turning the corner where I hear Jasmine say something, though I can't quite make out what. How can this be happening? How can everything be falling apart?

I take out my phone, intending to phone Max, but I don't know if I can. This is about Sophie. I can't go complaining to him about something that's happened with our friends, with his girlfriend. I put it away and go to the canteen.

It's only as I see Grayson that I realise what a state I must look, because I'm barely three steps in before he's wrapping me in his arms and whisking me outside.

"It's going to be okay," he says.

"It's just more drama," I reply.

"You seem to be a magnet for it," he says. "Try and shake it off."

Everything is falling apart, and I have no idea how I'm supposed to fix it.

FORTY-TWO

LUC & VICKY

You sure you're okay?

> Fine. It sucks but I'll be alright.

> I don't think any of them are too keen on speaking to me right now. And Soph says she needs time.

She'll come around.

What actually happened?

I spent the rest of lunch with Grayson. We sat outside for a while, to make sure that I could face being around his friends without having a massive breakdown. He's good like that. He didn't want to go back inside until he was a hundred percent sure that I was okay. Which was sweet.

The rest of the school day sort of went by in a blur. I couldn't stop thinking about how Soph had looked at me. It was like we didn't even know each other anymore, which properly sucked.

Tuesday was much of the same. I didn't have them to talk to, to hang out with. Even though we were sitting right next to each other in English, it was like we were a million miles apart. It was made even more pronounced by her keeping her back to me for the entire lesson.

I tried to remember the last time we'd hung out, just the two of us. Even now, lying in bed chatting to Vicky over messages, I can't pinpoint it. We used to be so close. What happened?

Max isn't at school, but he's tried phoning me a couple of times since the fight. I think Sophie must have spoken to him about it and he's probably calling to have a go. I don't think I can take losing him too.

> A lot of stuff. Some yelling. Mostly just Soph telling me she can't talk to me about what she's going through rn.

Oh Luc. I'm sorry. Maybe June can help with that too?

> I don't think I want to talk about it.

Then we can talk book stuff. Grayson stuff.

> Perfect.

———

"Can I hang out with Vicky after school tomorrow night?" I ask Dad when I get downstairs for dinner.

Since our fight, he's had this annoying habit of making sure he's there when I wake up and when I get home from school. We've even taken to having dinner together every night. He's gone full prison warden and I don't care for it. All it's really made me do is worry about the mortgage payments. He doesn't seem to be working as much.

"Good evening to you too," he says, not turning around as he dishes up. "Did you get your homework done?"

"Yes," I lie.

"Did you have a good day at school?"

"Yes," I lie.

"Can I get anything more than monosyllables?"

"Are you going to answer my question?"

He looks up at this, raising an eyebrow at me. To say it's been tense since the weekend would be the understatement of the century. It feels like we're on the edge of a fight every single day, like one false move is going to send us into another shouting match.

"Sure," he says. "Are you going to be here or at hers?"

"Meeting here," I say. "Then a coffee shop in town, I think. Maybe at Vicky's house."

"Let me know," he says. "If it's at Vicky's, I want to call her parents to make sure."

"You don't trust me?"

"Trust is earned."

"I've done nothing to break your trust."

"Do you really want to get into this right before dinner?"

"No, because you won't fucking listen to me anyway."

"Language, Lucas."

"We've got bigger problems than my language, Dad."

The doorbell rings. I move to go and answer it.

"Don't walk away from me."

"I'm answering the door."

"We were talking."

"No we weren't," I reply, slamming the door to the hallway to really drive the point home. I open the door to find Max standing there, eyes wide, eyebrows raised.

"Please don't tell me you could hear us fighting?" I ask.

"No, but the door slam was quite something," he replies. "The birds on the power lines actually flew away. It was very cinematic."

"I could do without cinematic right now," I say. "Are you alright?"

"I've been trying to call you."

"I know."

"You haven't answered."

"I know."

"Have I done something to upset you?" he asks. "I wanted to call and make sure you were okay after everything that had happened at school."

I blink. "You're not upset with me?"

"For what?"

"Duh, for what happened with Soph," I say. "And Jasmine, I guess. There was yelling. Things were said. A lot of other things weren't said."

"That's why you weren't answering the phone?"

"I wanted to talk to you about it, Max, but you and Soph are together. I couldn't come to you about her, or even our friends, it didn't seem right," I say, the words coming out in a rush. "Sorry."

"Don't apologise," he says, a ghost of a smile crossing his face. "And don't think for a second that you can't talk to me about stuff."

"She's your girlfriend, Max."

"She's going through a tough time at the moment," he says. "And so are you. And I'm… Well, I'm supposed to be your best friend. So you can talk to me if you need to. About anything."

I let out a heavy breath, the weight I'd been feeling on my chest dissipating like it's nothing at all.

"Thanks," I say. "Sorry for not saying anything sooner."

"Apology accepted," he says. "Do you need to go back in there for round two?"

I groan. "Probably."

"Are you going to get in more trouble if you stay here?"

"Definitely."

He chuckles. "He's still being hard on you?"

"I'm locked in my tower, apart from school and work," I say.

"Agony."

"Misery."

"Woe."

"And it cuts like a knife," I say. "I'm lucky he's even letting me go to Creative Writing Group."

"Well, he clearly doesn't know Grayson's in it," he says, putting a finger to his lips. "Your secret is safe with me."

"You're a good friend."

"Best friend," he corrects.

"Oh yeah," I say.

"You should let me read some of your writing some time," he says. "If you…if you want to."

No one outside of the Creative Writing Group has read any of my

287

writing before. Not even Vicky, blog posts aside. It makes me feel too exposed to even think of Max reading my work.

"I can see the panic in your eyes," he says. "You don't have to."

"No, no," I say. "I want to. It's just...new."

"I can't promise I can give you any kind of critique," he replies. "English is not my strong suit."

"Kind words and adoration will go a long way," I say.

"That I can do," he replies. "I should let you go."

"Okay."

"See you tomorrow?"

"If you bother to show up for school, maybe."

He laughs. "Alright, snarky," he replies. "See you tomorrow."

"Okay." I watch him go, desperately not wanting to go back inside and spend another evening feeling awkward and tense with Dad. But at least I've got Max. Thank goodness I've got Max.

FORTY-THREE

LUC & MAX

MAX

You were resisting Creative Writing Group for what reason?

So you don't hate it?

It's brilliant. Why weren't you doing it before?

I don't know. Dad didn't want me to. I didn't want to hurt him.

You're out of your mind. You need to be doing this.

Max was good on his promise to read the work that I sent him and it's enough to sustain me, get me through the day until Creative Writing Group.

Wednesdays have quickly become my favourite day of the week. If you'd told me a couple of months ago that I'd be excited about it, I probably would have called you a liar. But after limping through another day at school where my long-time friends basically ignored me, it is exactly what I need.

Max did come in today, and he spent time with me and Vicky in the library over lunch. I don't know where he was during morning break. My guess is that he was with Soph and...I don't think I'm wanted there right now.

The group of familiar faces that smile at me as I line up with them is heartwarming. Having Grayson at my side is even better. We still don't sit next to one another. I think it's because everyone's seats are pretty well established and we don't want to mess with it. Also there's something cute about getting to sit across from each other in the circle. It means I actually get to watch him read his pieces.

"Okay," Mrs Leighton says. "*Missing* was our prompt for this week. I'm sure you've all been working hard on your pieces, as usual, and I can't wait to hear what you've come up with."

The only reason I've been working hard on my piece this week is because doing my homework downstairs in the kitchen while Dad makes dinner is practically court-mandated at this point.

"First up, we have Lucas."

I'm always nervous to read in front of people. It's the one thing that I struggle with. There's something about the impending critique that makes me want to throw myself out of the window just so I don't have to do it.

I clear my throat. "I hate this part," I say.

"Stop apologising," Mr Bird says quietly from my side. "Go on."

I barely remember her, but she's everywhere I go. She's in my eyes as I laugh a little too hard, she's in my voice when I talk, she's part of what made me and yet I don't know her.

She vanished from the house seven years ago and never came back.

I waited for her at the school gates and she never came.

I waited for her at home and she never came.

I waited for her every day and she never came.

Dad told me where she'd gone, and I didn't believe him. I thought it was a lie, a cruel joke that would be met with a, "Got you, fooled you, you should see your face!" But that part definitely never came.

What followed were tears that threatened to drown me, both my own and of those around me. People talking in hushed whispers about who I would be, where I would go, how we would cope.

We didn't cope. We still aren't coping.

But she is still there.

Even though her picture isn't on the walls, she is still there. Even though her name never passes my father's lips, she is still there. Even though every part of her has been scrubbed from the house, there are times her essence rings through it like the sound of a bell.

"That's all I managed," I say, my voice smaller than it had been when I was reading the piece. The room is silent. And there is a small part of me, the smallest, that can almost feel Mum somewhere nearby having heard that.

"That was beautiful," Mrs Leighton says. "Honest, raw, heartfelt, it's what I've been waiting for from you," she adds. "Please note that I'm not asking any of you to dig deep into your souls and bare them to us for the sake of art, that's not what I want at all. But I'm glad you felt you could share that with us, Lucas. Does anyone else have any critiques?"

The critiques start to roll in. The initial approval from Mrs Leighton means that I don't feel so bad about getting critiques from everybody else in the room. I take notes while they talk and thank them for their time. But I can't help notice that Grayson has stayed quiet.

We move on to the next people, moving around the room. Grayson critiques everybody else, but he hasn't critiqued me.

"We're just two weeks away from our presentation," Mrs Leighton says at the end of the session. "Next week, if possible, I'd love to hear what you're thinking of reading. I know that eliminates the element of surprise, but I'm sure you all want feedback before showings. See you next week."

Grayson is quiet as we make our way out of the classroom.

"Everything okay?" I ask.

He takes my hand and walks me in the opposite direction of the exit. We're already nearly two hours past school closing, the last thing I want to do is get locked in here. I hate being here from nine to three, I don't want to be here all night.

He doesn't seem to be going anywhere in particular, walking me toward the perimeter of the school and dawdling, his hand in mine. I don't want to break the spell by talking, by being annoying, but I feel like I have to because…well…what are we doing walking around an empty school at dusk?

My phone buzzes in my pocket, but I ignore it.

"Grayson?" I say slowly. "You okay?"

"That piece was…just so beautiful," he says. "I'm annoyed that I can't think of a better word because Mrs Leighton said that, but it was so…beautiful."

"Thank you," I say. It means so much coming from him. To know that he thinks I'm good at this thing that I really enjoy. That's what's beautiful. The fact that he's holding my hand and wants to spend more time with me than we've been allowed. That's beautiful.

"And it was nice to hear you talk about your mum," he says. "You know you don't talk about her all that often, right?"

"I know."

"We can talk about her more if you want to? I don't want you to feel like you have to or anything," he says. "But if you ever want to talk about her or…I don't know…see if we can find the pictures that your dad has hidden away, then…we can do that."

I smile at him and lean into him because everything he's doing and saying right now is one hundred percent the right thing, and I just can't get enough of him.

"Thank you," I say. "I may actually take you up on that. Max said it was a good piece, I just don't think I quite believed him until I actually heard it from everybody in the group."

"Max read it?"

I nod. "I sent it to him last night," I say. "He's never read anything of mine before and he asked, so…" A weird tension has pushed its way between us. "Are you alright?"

"Yeah," he says. "I just didn't know he read your writing."

"He doesn't," I say. "He just read this piece."

He shrugs. "Okay then," he says. "I'd happily read your pieces early if you need help with them."

"Okay," I say. "We can do that if you want. But then it's spoilers, isn't it?"

"Do you not want me reading them?"

"No. That's—"

"But you want Max to read them?"

"Why are you making this weird?" I ask. "He just wanted to read something I'd written. It's not that serious."

"It's serious to me," he says. "I'd love to read more of your work."

"Okay," I reply. "We can do that." But suddenly I feel awkward. What is it about Max that makes him get like this? I thought they were friends. They play sports together, and I swear they used to hang out together before me and Grayson got together.

Walking in an uncomfortable silence, I'm about to take my usual route home, not wanting to prolong the awkwardness, but he pulls me in a different direction. He's smiling again, not letting go of my hand.

"What?" I say.

"Come on," he replies. "Not yet."

He takes me down a different side street and we keep walking, the daylight fading as we wander, talking, occasionally stopping to kiss. My phone keeps buzzing in my pocket, probably Dad wondering where I am. But I'll be home when I'm home. I'm not stopping this. I can't believe this is happening.

He walks me through the side streets of Southford, around routes I don't know. Before I know it, we're walking past his house. There is a moment where I think he's going to invite me inside or something, but we just keep walking.

"You do know that was your place?" I say. "You could fully have just gone home right now."

"I don't want to go home yet," he says. "Do you?"

"Not even a little bit."

We keep walking until we reach my road, where I stop.

"What?" he asks.

"I have a feeling that if Dad sees me with you, he'll lose his shit."

"Okay," he says. "You okay?"

"Very," I say.

He leans in again and I know that my lips are a little chapped from where we've been kissing and kissing and kissing, but I can't help having just one more. I can't get enough of him. Someone pinch me.

I watch him as he walks away, taking his phone out of his pocket, and putting it to his ear. I laugh at the thought of his mum looking out the window and seeing us walking past, only for us not to come inside.

It is only as I walk away that I take my phone out of my pocket to see who's been dialling me this whole time. I freeze as I see the number of missed calls on the screen.

Vicky.

FORTY-FOUR

I HURRY down my road and find her sitting outside my house, the lights are off where Dad must have gone to work, and she's just waiting. How long has she been there?

She looks up as I approach, her eyes big behind her glasses.

"Vicky, I'm so—"

"Don't worry about it," she says quickly. "It's fine."

"It's not fine. I was meant to be back here after Creative Writing Group to see you and I totally forgot," I say.

"Was it something important?" she asks.

I blink. "What?"

"The reason you weren't here, was it important?"

I open my mouth to respond, but can't seem to get the words out. On the one hand, that walk home with Grayson was what I needed and I'm excited to talk to her about it, but on the other…I totally blew her off.

"No," I say. "I was walking home with Grayson."

She lets out a heavy breath, her gaze turning skyward. "And you just forgot about me?"

"I…I didn't mean to, Vicky, I—"

"It's okay," she says in a way that definitely makes it seem like it isn't. I can see that she's hurt and I hate that it's my fault. "I've been here before."

She brushes past me.

"What are you talking about?"

She turns back and looks at me. "This is what happened with June."

"With June?" I repeat. "Where's June?"

"We were going to meet her," Vicky says. "She's waiting for us."

"Right."

Vicky nods, and I can see that there are tears in her eyes.

"It was more than just her going to university that stopped her doing Love Me Nots," Vicky says.

This is a story that Vicky hasn't told me before. Whenever June had come up in conversation in the past, she'd brushed it off, tried to play it off as something that didn't matter, even though I could see it still hurt her.

"I told you she had a girlfriend. Well, that girlfriend was at University, and that meant that June wanted to spend more time at Uni than she did at home, which meant less time for me, less time for Love Me Nots." She sighs. "She really does Love Me Not. And now it's happening with you."

"Vicky—"

"Lucas, don't make excuses," she says. "I get it. The relationship becomes the priority. I've seen it happen. This ain't my first rodeo. It even happened to you with your friends." That hits harder than anything else she's already said, like a punch to the gut. "Don't take it too hard, Luc. I'm not trying to hurt you here. It just happens. I'll see you tomorrow at school, okay?"

"Vicky, don't go," I say. "Come inside. We can still go through the book, figure out the next move."

"You don't need me anymore," she says. "You've got him. Clearly. Enjoy him. It's fine, honestly. I'll see you tomorrow."

I call after her, but she doesn't turn around. It stings to watch her leave. It stings more to know that she's hurting because of me, because of all the memories that I brought back about June. I hate that I've done that to her.

I step through the front door and see that there are lights on in the kitchen. I can hear Dad shuffling around in there. Because there were no lights on in the hallway, I'd assumed that he'd gone out, but obviously not. I follow the sound.

"Evening. No Vicky?"

"She was outside," I say. "But she changed her mind."

"Oh," Dad seems confused. "Why's that?"

There is no way for me to respond truthfully without prompting further questions and the last thing I want to do is talk about this with Dad. "She's got a headache," I say. "So she decided to go home."

"Oh, that's a shame," Dad says. "Maybe some other day."

"Yeah, maybe," I reply. I make myself a cup of tea because that feels like the only thing that will help right now. "Do you want tea?" I ask.

Dad looks up, mock startled. "To what do I owe the pleasure?"

It's something akin to a peace offering, even if I do still think he's a bit of a dick.

"It's a cup of tea. Don't overthink it," I say.

"Sure thing," he says. "But don't make it too strong. I know what you're like."

"The way you have your tea is criminal," I say. "It should be an offence."

"Let me have it milky, Luc," he says. "It's my one vice."

"I'd rather you smoked."

He laughs, and it's the first fragment of joy that's made its way into this house since Friday night. It's not much, but it's a start. I make the tea and take it over to the kitchen table.

"What? No biscuits?" he asks with a smirk.

"Do we have biscuits?"

Dad thinks about it for a second. "Good point, well made," he says. "Can't remember the last time we had biscuits."

"Probably when I made them in food tech."

"Those weren't biscuits, they were weaponry," he says, which makes me laugh. "It's late."

I stop, the kitchen cupboard open. I stare into it.

"What?"

"It's late," he says flatly. "Where have you been?"

"At school."

"Luc—"

"Come on, Dad," I say, closing the kitchen cupboard.

"What?"

"It's…" I don't want to fight again, I don't want to keep fighting. "It's quite a way to ask that."

"What were you expecting?"

"I don't know, something less accusatory."

"Accusatory? I was asking why my son was home late," Dad says, raising his voice a little. "I think I'm allowed to do that, given what's been happening around here recently."

"Oh my God, NOTHING HAPPENED!"

"Don't shout at me!"

"Don't shout at ME!" I retort.

"Lucas Cook, this is not the way I want things to be in this house. You shouldn't be treating me like this."

"And you shouldn't be treating me like a prisoner," I say.

"I'm not."

"Well, suddenly you're here all the time, Dad," I say. "That's not a fucking coincidence."

"Language!"

"Piss off."

I storm upstairs because I just can't take it anymore. He's calling after me, but I'm having none of it. I slam my door to really drive the point home that I am done.

I open my laptop, ready to do my usual tab switching between half-arseing schoolwork. I need to work on things for the Creative Writing Group presentation. I want what I submit to be good. I'm tempted to use what I read today, but everyone's heard it now. I wonder if I have time to come up with something different.

I put on one of Mum's videos in the background, still keeping the volume down just in case Dad happens to hear it. I'm still protecting him, even after everything. But I push those thoughts out of my head and I just start writing, and I don't stop until I'm done.

FORTY-FIVE

I LOSE TRACK OF TIME, but I think I have a piece that might work for the presentation. I'm not sure if it's quite right, but maybe, with some feedback and tweaking, it could work. It's hard to say.

I message Grayson at one point to talk to him about it, message Vicky at another, but neither of them replies. I didn't expect Vicky to, but seeing that Grayson hasn't even replied by morning doesn't spark joy.

I can hear Dad downstairs, clattering around. I was hoping he'd still be asleep so I could just gather myself and go, but apparently he has other ideas. If he's woken up to ambush me, then I'm not here for it.

"Morning," I say as I shuffle into the kitchen. There is a cup of tea on the side, a couple of slices of toast in the toaster. Dad already has his in front of him. "These for me?" I ask.

"My turn for a peace offering, I think," he says. "You get your homework done?"

I shrug. "I did enough," I say.

"Enough?"

"Enough that I won't get in trouble, but not so much that the teachers will start having high expectations of me."

"Heaven forbid," Dad says, rolling his eyes. "Are you in tonight?"

I narrow my eyes at him. "I'm still grounded, aren't I?"

He chuckles. "Oh yeah, forgot about that," he says. "I don't want to fight with you, Luc. I really don't."

"Neither do I."

"Okay then," he says. "You don't have a Creative Writing Group thing or anything?"

I shake my head. "That's Wednesday," I say.

"So you're in tonight."

"Yes."

"Okay," he says. "I'm not working tonight, so I thought I'd make dinner again if you fancy it. We'll try it without the shouting."

I look at him warily. I'm waiting for the catch, but no catch comes. He's just offering to make dinner. Maybe he really is ready to stop fighting, and he's just letting this fall out from underneath us rather than us dragging it on. There has been so much tension in the house since my first date with Grayson. It actually feels good to be able to let it go.

"Yeah, okay," I say. "I'll be back around four."

"Okay then," he says. "I'll see you tonight. Have a good day."

"You too."

I take my phone out and message Grayson again, telling him that things seem to be better and maybe I won't be grounded for too much longer. He reads it but doesn't reply. The three dots appear for a second, but then they vanish.

I don't expect Vicky to show up for us to walk to school together after everything that happened last night, so I message her another apology.

As I walk through the school, I can't help but feel a little bit uneasy. It feels like people are looking at me funny. I check my reflection, but there's nothing on my face. I start to wonder if people have heard about what happened with my friends earlier in the week. It was quite the shouting match. Maybe it's finally spread to the lower parts of the school, so now everybody knows about it.

I don't love it for me. The last time I was getting this much attention was when I came out and that ended with me getting punched in the face. I'd rather not have a repeat if I can help it.

I'd usually just message Vicky or Sophie about this straight away, but I guess those avenues aren't available to me just now. I drop Max a message.

> People are looking at me funny. I need you to tell me I'm crazy.

I watch it get read. And I watch the three dots appear and then vanish. He obviously changed his mind. I make my way to my locker, to try and find the safety of Grayson.

He's waiting for me when I get there, his broad frame visible as students open and close the door to the corridor. Just the sight of him puts a smile on my face. I can't help it.

"Morning!" I say brightly as I reach him, because he's not looking my way. Maybe he was expecting me to come from somewhere else. "You okay? You didn't message me this morning."

"I didn't want to," he says. His voice is tight, like he's talking through gritted teeth. "I didn't feel like it."

"Okay," I say. "Do I get a good morning kiss?"

"Well, that depends, Lucas. Do you love me or do you love me not?" he says, finally turning around to face me.

I feel my entire world collapse around me, the walls feel like they're literally crumbling down around my ears.

"What do you mean by that?"

"What do you *think* I mean, Lu?" he asks, raising his voice a little. He slams his locker closed and I flinch. "You tell me what I mean by that."

I take a breath, trying to steady myself because suddenly it feels like the world is spinning. "What do you know?"

"What do I know?" he repeats, incredulous. "You're asking me what I know so that you can spin a different lie, Lucas—what the fuck?"

People are stopping in the corridor to watch. When did my relationship become a spectator sport?

Probably when you started posting all the details online, I think.

"I know that you've been writing about me," he says. "Writing about us. I know you've been using some book, your mum's book, 'Don't die alone' or some bullshit like that."

"It wasn't bullshit—"

301

"You've been following advice, you've been using tips, you've been playing games, all to try and get me?"

"Yes, Grayson, to try and get you, because I liked you," I say. "I like you, I really bloody like you, and I had no idea how to go about it, no idea how to approach you and then this book and..." I don't want to bring Vicky into this if I can help it.

"And Vicky put you up to it?"

"She didn't put me up to it," I say. "She asked if I wanted to try it and part of the book was documenting the experience, so I...I documented it."

"Online! For all the world to see!"

"I changed the names, I changed the actual dates, I was just doing what the book told me to—"

"It's not difficult to work out, Lucas," he snaps. "I read it and knew it was about us. I knew all the little details, and I knew all the little things you did, all the things you tried to get me to fall for you, and now here we are."

"Here we are, what?"

"I fell for you, and for the lies you were spinning."

"They weren't lies, Grayson, I promise they—"

"Then what would you call them?" he shouts. "You manipulated me, you played games, you messed with my head to try and get me to like you, to go out with you. And you won, okay? This great big experiment to get me to like you, and you fucking won, okay? I hope you're happy." He shakes his head. "I didn't even know who you were a couple of weeks ago. I didn't care."

"Grayson—"

"I didn't," he says. "You showed up out of nowhere and I thought you were sweet, I thought you were different, but I knew there was something wrong. My friends kept telling me it was weird, and I ignored it because...I don't know why. Because you were manipulating me, I guess. But I knew."

"What do you mean?"

"The way you are with your friends, just ditching them like that."

"What?"

"And the way you are with Max."

"What about Max?"

"Oh, come on, Luc," he says, shaking his head, and I wish I knew what he was getting at.

A silence pushes its way between us and I can feel this darkness in my chest, this gathering black thundercloud.

"Did you read all of it?" I ask.

"Every word," he says. "And I'm starting to wonder how much of what we had was real. How much of it was what I was actually feeling and how much of it was what you wanted me to feel? You really played me. Reading it snapped me out of it."

"What do you—?"

"I didn't notice you before, Lucas," he says. "Nobody did. You were just this quiet kid in the corner, lurking, watching. I didn't notice you before because you clearly weren't worth noticing." He looks me up and down, disgusted. "And now, I know why."

He turns and walks away, and as the door swings shut behind him, I feel my heart splinter and shatter in my chest. *What have I done?*

My chest feels like someone has reached into it with a giant spoon and scooped everything out. I feel hollow, empty, and all that's left are storm clouds swirling around.

I message Vicky.

No response.

I call her and, by some miracle, she picks up.

"What are you—?"

"Grayson knows," I say quickly. I can hardly catch my breath. "Grayson knows about the blog. He knows about everything."

"What? When did you—?"

"Did you tell him?"

There is silence on the end of the line. I check the phone to make sure I haven't lost her. Now would not be the time for my shitty phone to die on me.

"Hello? Vicky?"

"Are you really asking me that question?"

"Are you really avoiding it?" I ask.

Vicky sighs, her breath distorting the sound. "I didn't tell him, Lucas. I promised you it would remain anonymous, and that's exactly what I did. If he found out, then he either found out by chance or somebody else figured it out and told him. And I don't appreciate you accusing me of telling him. Why would I do that?"

"I'm not accusing you, I'm sorry, I just wanted to check, I—"

"No, Lucas, you're trying to cover your own back now," she says. "And I think it's pretty shitty of you to blow me off time and time again and then suddenly think I'd sell you down the river because I was upset. Our friendship means more than that."

"I know Vicky, I just thought—"

"You thought that I'd want revenge and retaliate," she interrupts. "Well, I didn't. Have a nice life, Lucas."

She hangs up and when I try to call her back, it goes straight to voicemail. I am about to walk towards the Geography block. My friends are all there, sitting in their usual spots, lost in each other even as I round the corner and say, "Hello."

They look up at me and I can see the disgust passing across each of their faces. Sophie gets up and starts away from me.

"Wait, hang on, I can explain!"

"You don't need to explain a thing," Jasmine says, her voice venomous. "You've shown exactly who you are, Lucas, and now the whole school knows. Or at least they will do by the end of the day. What's wrong with you?"

"Did you tell everyone?"

She shakes her head. "No," she says. "I heard about it, though. And I want you to know that what you've done to Grayson is disgusting. You should be ashamed of yourself." She walks away, with Krish following suit.

I'm left alone in the Geography block, my mind racing, my heart beating so hard and fast in my chest that it hurts. Tears are streaming down my face, and I just don't seem to be able to stop them. No matter how hard I try, they just keep coming.

The bell rings, loud, obnoxious, a screaming sensory overload, and I can't take it anymore. I just can't take it.

I walk out of the Geography block and around the outside of the school towards the exit, and I just keep walking.

FORTY-SIX

NOBODY STOPS me on the way out. I'd half expected there to be a teacher running after me or some member of staff telling me that I should be in my form class, but maybe walking with this much purpose means that you get left alone.

I don't know where I'm going.

My feet keep walking, but I don't know where they're heading. I can't go home. What if Dad found out about the blog? Everything seemed like it was going so well this morning. This throws all of that out of the window.

I take my phone out and check through the messages. There is one sitting there from him, waiting for me to read it. I don't want to. If he knows, I don't want to know. I've lost my boyfriend, I've lost my friends, I can't lose my dad too. Everything is falling apart, I can feel it. It's like every step I take I leave disaster in my wake.

While my brain doesn't seem to know where I'm going, my feet must do because it isn't long until I've walked all the way through town and to the church, then on to the cemetery, through the various gravestones to one that I haven't seen in several years. One that I should have been at weekly, if not monthly. I certainly should have been here far more than I have.

Let's add guilt to the awful feelings currently swirling around my chest.

Now, I really can't stop the tears.

I drop to my knees, crying until my head hurts. There are people staring at me, people watching me breakdown on the grass, but no one comes anywhere near me. They just watch. They probably see it all the time.

None of this would have happened if she were still here. None of it. Everything would be easier if she were still around.

I have no idea how I'm supposed to fix any of this, how I'm supposed to make it better. My friends won't talk to me, the boy that I like thinks I'm scum, and when Dad realises what's happened... I don't want to think about what will happen.

I can hear her voice in my head, replaying all the things that I've listened to her say over the past few weeks. The questions she's answered on her book tours, at book festivals, what she'd written in that book. I followed it all and still managed to get it all so wrong. What was meant to bring me love and help me find someone has only succeeded in making things worse.

And she's not even here to answer for it.

It's the most I've thought about Mum since she died, the closest I've ever felt to her, and yet here I am crying my eyes out at her grave like she literally died yesterday. As much as I can pretend that I'm okay a lot of the time, or feel okay with her not being around, somehow getting closer to her has made her feel even further away.

If she were here, maybe I could talk to her about all of this. If she were here, my and Dad's relationship might be better. If she were here, everything would be different.

"Why aren't you here?" I whimper. I don't know how loud it comes out, but there's something about saying it out loud that just makes me feel better, like a catharsis. So I keep talking. "I miss you so much. Where did you go? Why did you have to go? Why aren't you still here? It's not fair."

"I agree. It's not fair."

I practically jump out of my skin. I don't know how long I've been sitting here, how long I've been crying, how long this person has been watching me. I turn to face them and I can hardly believe my eyes.

It's my mum.

I know that can't be true, that my eyes have got to be playing tricks on me because that's not possible.

I wipe my tears away and see that it's not. The woman standing in front of me is much older, her hair a shock of white and cut short, her face wrinkled, her eyes magnified by a pair of glasses. It takes me a second to figure out who it is.

"Nana," I say.

I can't remember the last time I saw her. When I was growing up, we used to see her all the time. She lives on the other side of town, much closer to the cemetery than we do. Dad would take me there sometimes when he had to work. Or she'd come to our house so she could look after me. It was another thing that stopped after Mum died. I was old enough to take care of myself, and Dad never made the effort to keep in touch.

I can't really blame him for all of that. I could have called or done something. I just didn't.

"Luc," she says, her face crunching into a smile. "What are you doing here? Shouldn't you be at school?" She takes in my uniform. It's a rhetorical question.

"I…I didn't want to be there today," I say, getting to my feet.

She raises a drawn-on eyebrow at me. "Sounds like there's a bit of a story in that," she replies. "Does your father—?"

"No," I interrupt. "Things are happening at school. I didn't want to be there, and… I'm sorry. I'll go."

"Now, now, young man, you don't need to be going anywhere just yet," she says. She's carrying two bunches of flowers. Pansies, I think. She lays one down on Mum's grave, and then the other on the one next to it. Grandad. "I don't see you here very often. Do you visit?"

I shake my head. "No."

"Why's that?"

I shrug. "I…I don't know," I say. "I think I'm waiting for Dad to want to come. He…he never does. So I don't either, because…"

Her hand finds my shoulder, and she gives it a squeeze. I take it as an invitation and I step forward and hug her. Suddenly I'm crying again. It only makes her squeeze tighter.

She knows what I mean. She gets where I'm coming from. This is the kind of conversation I should be having with Dad. This is the kind of understanding we should have. One where we both know what the other has been through. We've both lost someone. It's not just him. He doesn't have a monopoly on pain.

"Come on, you," she says, pulling away from the hug and looking up at me, her eyes a little misty behind her glasses. I didn't realise how much taller I am now. I wonder if this is what it would be like with Mum. I forget how tall she was. "We'll get you back to mine. Can't have you going back to school looking like that, eh?"

Her house isn't far. It's been a while since I've been there, but as we walk, there are parts of the route I remember; the trees that line her road, which are covered in blossoms in the spring but look haggard and threatening in the winter, her neighbours' front gardens that don't seem to have changed. There is so much here that has stayed the same, but at the same time, it feels like everything has changed.

Even Nana's house looks the same. The same well-kept front garden with plants around the border, the rhododendron bush out front, the same pink door that I remember Dad picking me up to knock on when I was small.

It even looks the same inside. It's maybe had a fresh coat of paint, but it's the same furniture that's always been there, same dresser in the hallway, same full-length mirror by the door. Time has stood still.

I catch sight of my reflection and can't quite believe how much of a mess I am. It's a good thing the cemetery isn't far from where Nana lives. There were likely more than a few people who would have been freaked out by my appearance.

"I'll just clean myself up and then I'll go," I say.

"Nonsense," she says. "I'm making tea. Now, remind me, you still like Rich Tea biscuits, right?"

"Yes, but you don't—"

"I bought some yesterday," she says. "It was almost like I knew I'd bump into you. Go on, get yourself cleaned up, I'll make the tea. Come on."

I'm not upstairs long, just long enough to splash my face and make myself look somewhat presentable, but by the time I get back downstairs there is a pot of tea on the table (in the same china she's always had) and a plate of Rich Tea biscuits laid out in front of us.

"There," she says. "Much better."

"You really don't have to," I say. "I should probably get back to school. They're probably wondering where I am."

She shrugs. "Let them wonder," she replies. "I've not seen you in a long time, young man. I think this is just as important as anything they could teach you at that school, wouldn't you agree?" There is a playful smirk tugging at the corners of her mouth.

I'm not about to tell her she's wrong. I really want those biscuits.

I take a seat at the dining table with her and she pours the tea.

"Tea solves everything," she says as she picks up a little ceramic jug of milk. "You're just milk, right?"

"Just a splash."

"Strong enough for the spoon to stand up in," she says with a knowing nod. "That's the only way to have it."

"Try telling Dad that," I reply.

"Oh, the way that man had his tea made me die," she replies with a laugh. "I couldn't watch when he poured all that milk in."

"Makes me sick."

"Your Mum always had her tea nice and strong," Nana says. "She'd have two cups every morning, one before she went out to school, and then one that she'd take in a flask. So really it was more like one cup and then a whole pot to herself every day."

"She must have been wide awake."

"Always on the go, she never stopped," she says. The smile fades, moving from something happy to something a little bit sadder. "She would be gutted that she didn't get to see you grow up, Luc. She was going to give it one more try with the writing, see if she could make it work. Then she was going to stop. She was going to spend more time with you and Matthew, that's what she always said. And then..."

And then.

She just never came and picked me up. I was sat there for hours wondering where she was. Teachers had no idea. I was just waiting in my classroom, like I'd been abandoned. It was Dad who came to get me, Dad who had to break the news to me. It didn't make any sense in my head. How could she just be gone? Where did she go? Why would she just vanish like that?

"Do you miss her?" I ask.

"Every day," she says without hesitation. "I think about her when I wake up, I think about her before I go to sleep, at various points throughout the day she'll just appear in my head because I'll hear a song she used to love listening to or see something in a shop that she might have liked. Do you?"

"Of course," I say. "But Dad doesn't talk about her…ever."

"He doesn't?" Her brows knit together at that. "Why not?"

"Because it hurts him to even think about her," I say. "So I think he'd rather not. There are no pictures of her in the house. We never talk about her, and whenever I do, it just…it just blows up or it vanishes."

"Why didn't you go to school today?" she asks.

I take a sip of my tea, even though it's definitely still too hot. Who needs a tongue anyway? And then I tell her everything that happened over the past month or so. All of it. In the name of getting closer to Mum? Sort of. That was a byproduct, I guess.

"You seem to have got yourself into a bit of a pickle," she says.

"A bit? More like a whole jar of pickles," I say. "I don't know what I'm supposed to do."

"About which part?"

I laugh, because if I don't laugh, I'll just start crying again. "Any of it," I say.

The doorbell rings and Nana flinches. "Let me just get that," she says, getting to her feet.

I hear voices at the front door, though I can't quite make out what they're saying. One is much deeper than the other. The door closes and two sets of footsteps make their way through the kitchen and into the dining room.

She reappears in the doorframe with Dad standing a little way behind her, his face red, his eyes wet. He looks broken. It's a face I remember from all those years ago, and it hurts me to see him like this again.

"I think you two have a lot to talk about," Nana says. "I'll be in the living room. Take your time."

FORTY-SEVEN

DAD WALKS into the dining room and takes the seat that Nana had just been sitting in. I'm not surprised that he's here. Maybe I should be, I don't know.

I check my phone and see that it's almost midday. I've missed three classes already and didn't register or call in sick, so they would have been in touch with Dad.

"Did Nana call you?" I ask.

He nods. "I'd already been called by the school and had no idea where you were, so when she called me I...I came straight over."

"Okay," I say. "I'm sorry."

"For which part?" he asks.

"All of it?"

He pours himself a cup of tea, glugging half the milk jug into it so it practically goes white. It really does make me feel a bit sick.

"Where do you want to start?" he asks.

I start at the beginning. I tell him everything about Vicky reading the book, about how much I've liked Grayson for the past few years and how it was an opportunity, how Max was helping, and how I didn't tell him because he never wants to talk about Mum and then how I ended up ditching my friends in favour of Grayson and hurting everybody in the process, including Grayson. And I tell him about the blog, and he averts his gaze.

"What?" I say.

"I had a message from someone telling me about that," he says. "I…I read it. It's…it's quite good."

"Quite good?"

"The way you write," he says. "It's very clearly you, very clearly your voice." He takes a breath. "I wish you would have told me what you were doing."

"Dad, I couldn't do that."

"Why not?"

"Because, Dad," I say. And it's not because it would have been weird and embarrassing, which it definitely would have been. It's the thing that hurts the most. "Because I can't talk to you."

"Lucas." The word comes out barely above a whisper.

He actually looks wounded, almost surprised, and it has the blood suddenly boiling in my body again, because how can he not realise what our relationship is like? How can he be so blind?

"You can always talk to me," he says.

"No, I can't," I reply.

"Lucas—"

"No, Dad, I can't. How can you not see that?" I say. "Whenever I try to talk about Mum, you shut down. I can't even start talking about her because you go all quiet and want to move on to something else. Or we just sit in silence."

"It's hard for me."

"It's hard for me too, Dad," I say. "She was your wife, I know, but she was my mum, and I've spent the last few years feeling like I'm forgetting who she is. I didn't tell you what was happening with the book because you caught me reading it and freaked out over it. That's why I hid it. I…I didn't want you to have to think about her…dying alone."

"What?"

"Well, she did, didn't she?" I say. "After everything."

Dad takes a moment. He sips his disgusting-looking cup of tea and looks me dead in the eyes. "I never want you to feel like you can't talk to me," he says. "We shared that experience when Olivia died, and I…I shouldn't shut you out. I should be trying to keep her memory alive. She'd be so disappointed in me."

"Dad—"

"She would," he says. "I know her well enough to know that she would. She'd say, 'Typical Matthew, not wanting to talk about things,' because that's how I always was. I wasn't happy she was on the road so much while you were growing up, but I bottled it up and then it came out in a big argument when, if I'd just mentioned it earlier, we could have avoided all of that hurt. And here I am bottling things up and hurting you in the process. That's the last thing I want to do, Luc." He shakes his head. "She would know exactly what to do in this situation," he continues. "She always knew what to do."

It's then that I realise Dad and I are more similar than I thought. He talks about how he's been bottling up all of his feelings and I've been doing that too, with my friends, even with him to a degree. Maybe if I'd talked to him about all this Mum stuff, then we wouldn't have made it to this point, maybe things would be okay. Maybe I wouldn't have fucked it up so badly with my friends if I'd told them how they were making me feel.

"I'm sorry, Dad," I say. "I didn't mean to hurt you."

"I didn't mean to hurt you either," he says. "And I didn't mean to keep Olivia from you. That wasn't the way I should have handled it. We should talk about her, of course we should, we should have her in the house because…she's your mum."

"I'd like that," I say, fighting back the tears again. Why am I fighting them? Why am I trying to be strong right now? "I'm sorry."

"What for?"

"For keeping things to myself too, I guess?" I say. "I just…I miss her a lot and, God, all of that anger, me shouting at you, I didn't want to, I just…I don't know how to deal with it sometimes and it's hard and…" I can't make words happen past the tears anymore, past the lump in my throat.

And then Dad does the last thing I expect him to do.

He gets up out of his chair and he pulls me to my feet to wrap me in a hug.

It's a shock. I can't remember the last time my dad hugged me, can't remember the last time he gave me that big, parental squeeze that tells you everything is going to be alright.

I need this. I can't begin to put into words just how much I need this.

I hug him back. I don't know how long we stay there, but it's long enough for the crying to subside, for my breathing to level out.

"You okay?" he asks.

I nod. "Think so."

He pulls out of the hug, but keeps his hands on my shoulders, looking me right in the eye. "If you ever need to talk to me about this, or anything else," he says, "please speak to me. I know I'm not the easiest to talk to. Christ knows I've been shit for the past seven years, but please? Okay? Promise me."

"I promise."

"And she didn't die alone, Lucas," he says, his eyes locked on mine, watery, unable to hold the emotion back. "She had us. Alright? You understand that?"

"Yes," I say. "Sorry."

"It's alright."

"And you've not been shit."

"I'm not winning any awards."

"But you've not been shit," I repeat.

"Okay, so while we're here and we're laying everything out, what happened with Grayson?" he asks when he sits back down.

"Nothing happened," I say. "I promise you, nothing happened. And now I don't know if it ever will."

He locks eyes with me, like he's waiting for me to blink, searching for a reason to not believe what I'm telling him. I think he's about to argue with me, but then he just nods.

"Okay," he says. "What makes you say that?"

"He said some pretty awful things when he found out, so I can't imagine he'll ever want to even look at me again, and…I don't know. I don't think he's who I thought he was," I say. "I think I built him up in my head."

"What do you mean?"

"It's hard to explain," I say. "I thought he was perfect."

Everything that I've been through with him suddenly feels like it's in a sharper focus, the moments where he wasn't quite what I hoped he would be. Have I been ignoring them the entire time, all because I wanted it to be right?

Why wasn't it right?

"It's possible," Dad says, "that his reaction to the book stuff is just a bit extreme because it shocked him. And apart from that, nobody is perfect. Nobody at all."

"I know," I say. "I just...I don't know. My head feels all fuzzy right now and I don't know what to do."

It's strange to say out loud, because what were the last two months for? I've spent all this time chasing him and for what?

"What are you going to do about all this?"

"God, I don't know," I say. "I definitely fucked up."

"Yep," Dad replies. "And language, by the way. I'll let it slide, but come on, this is your Nana's house."

"Messed up, then," I say. "None of my friends want to speak to me."

"Not even Max?"

"I...I don't know about Max," I say.

"He's your best friend," Dad says. "He's been there for you through everything else. Why would he stop being there for you now? He cares about you, Lucas."

"But he's the only other person who knew about the website and he's been so helpful in all of this," I say. "What if he was..." It doesn't bear thinking about. "I don't want to lose him, too."

And I'm crying again. The very thought of losing Max, the thought of him betraying me is too much. He's the only person in my life who has been there when things have been at their very, very worst and if he's done that to me...

"I don't think Max would do something like that to you," Dad replies. "A boy who climbs trees in the middle of the night to come and see you, who meets you outside at six-thirty in the morning on a Saturday, who calls you and calls you and calls you because he wants to make sure you're okay, is not the kind of boy who would do that."

I think of everything Max has done for me since the Grayson stuff started. He's been more Max in the past month and a half than he's been since he got with Sophie and it means the absolute world to have him like that, to have him at my side. It makes me realise just how much I've missed him, just how much he means to me.

"You know about all that?"

"You really think I don't notice a damn thing, don't you?" Dad

316

says. "He's your best friend for a reason." He takes another sip of his tea. "Damn, this is a good cuppa."

"It really isn't, Dad. Who are you trying to fool?"

He laughs, and any residual tension in the air seems to ease, carried away on the sound.

"And your friends?"

"I've been shit to them," I say.

Dad doesn't seem so sure. "Yes and no," he replies. "They did the same to you. But I'm not much of an 'eye for an eye' person."

"I didn't do it on purpose."

He smiles. "I know you didn't," he says. "Neither did they. But I'm sure you can still fix it."

I groan. "There's so much that needs fixing," I say. "I've broken so many things."

"Then start picking up the pieces and putting them back together one thing at a time," he says. "Did you get to the end of the book?"

"No."

"Well, it might be worth carrying on with it," he says. "It does have a happy ending, after all."

He's not wrong, it did. Even if it did end with us like this, broken, at my Nana's dining table with one of us drinking a positively heinous cup of tea. But I still have one question burning in the back of my mind.

"Who told you?" I ask.

He blinks. "Who told me what?"

"About the blog."

He shakes his head, and there's a moment where I think he isn't going to tell me.

"Sophie."

FORTY-EIGHT

IT HITS me like a brick wall. And I wonder if that's what Max tried to call me about. I wonder if he wanted to warn me. I wonder if that's why Soph couldn't even look at me, because even she wasn't expecting the fallout to be quite so catastrophic.

It takes a little more coaxing from Dad to get me to leave Nana's house. She makes me promise to come back more often, and I'm pretty sure my dad is due a bollocking off her for everything he's done.

I hope she's not too hard on him. We're making progress here.

Dad drives me back to school. He takes me to reception and makes up some excuse about me not feeling well and not getting a chance to call in, which they properly lambast him for, but I'm not suspended for not showing up, so there's that.

I check my phone and see I have messages from Max.

Where are you?

I heard what happened. Please talk to me.

Lucas?

It's almost lunchtime by the time I get there, and there is a part of me that wants to speak to Grayson, but I know that's not the right course of action. At least not now. He made it abundantly clear this morning that he wants nothing to do with me, and…maybe that's the right call. I don't know. I still have some thinking to do in that regard.

Instead, I make my way to the Geography block, knowing that my friends will be there pretty much the second the bell rings. My heart is humming in my chest, but they are the ones I need to make things right with first. If I can.

I sit in our usual spot, knee bouncing, head spinning, waiting for them to round the corner.

Jasmine appears first, mid-conversation, mid-laugh, her face dropping the second she lays eyes on me. She rolls her eyes and shakes her head. Soph is next. She stops dead. Eyes wide. Deer in headlights. I wonder if anyone else knows that Sophie is the one who told.

She turns around as if she's about to leave.

"Wait, Soph, can we talk about this? Please?"

"I don't want to talk," she says. "I'm going outside. Jas, are you coming?"

Jasmine follows her out of the Geography block, walking right by me, Krish in tow. And then Max rounds the corner and just stares at me. He's just standing there, watching them all walk away. He turns his attention back to me. And in a way, it's better this way. He's who I need to talk to first.

"Did you tell her?" I ask.

"No," he says.

"You swear?"

"I can't believe you're asking me to swear on this, Luc, come on," Max says, and I can see the frustration on his face. "She asked me about it and I wasn't about to lie to her."

"So you confirmed it?"

"I did," he says. "I didn't want to lie to her."

"Why did she tell Grayson?"

"I don't know," Max says. "I didn't want it all to blow up like this. But I'm…I'm glad she did."

"What?"

"I'm glad," he says. "I'm angry at her for doing it, but I'm glad it's out in the open."

I stare at him, incredulous. "You can't be serious," I say. "Grayson

319

is furious with me. He's probably never going to speak to me again. You should have heard the things he said to me earlier, Max."

"I did hear," he says. "Well, I heard secondhand, but I heard he was pretty rotten to you."

"He was."

"Alright then," Max says. "I didn't want it to be true, but do you want to hear the rest of it?"

"Do I?"

"How he's been saying awful things about you around school, cosying up to Dylan, trying to make himself seem as much the victim as possible?" Max shook his head. "It makes me sick. I don't get it."

"What are you even getting at?"

"Don't you see that he's not right for you, Lucas?" he says. "He seems like he's the nicest guy on the planet, everybody's best friend, but he's not all he seems. He's far too into himself, he puts way too much stock into what his friends think and who his friends are, constantly puts them down for sport, like it's funny or something. He's an arsehole."

"Why are you saying this? He's your friend," I say. "And you were helping me try and hook up with him. Where the hell is this coming from?"

"Yeah, that was stupid," he says. "I don't know what I was think-ing. Overcompensating, I guess."

"For?"

He stares at me like I've suddenly grown an extra head. "You can't be serious."

"What?"

He sighs. "Lucas Cook, you are the most frustrating person I have ever met in my entire life."

"Thanks?"

"You go on and on about how Grayson never noticed you before, how he never paid any attention to you, and here you are doing the same thing to me."

My mouth falls open. And I don't know what to say. He can't mean what I think he means. He can't.

"Do you need me to spell it out for you?" Max asks. "I like you. Okay? I think I've always liked you like that, but never did anything about it because, well, we were young and stupid and I didn't think you liked me in the same way. Then I was with Soph, and now I've had to watch you chase this boy who doesn't deserve you, who isn't right for you."

"And you're right for me?"

"Yes!" he shouts. "I mean. I think I am. I feel like I am."

"You can't be serious." My head is spinning. I can hardly catch my breath. All this time he's liked me?

"I am serious."

"Why didn't you tell me?"

"I don't know!"

"Because if you'd have bloody said something, then maybe…" What am I about to say? What stupidity is about to leave my mouth?

"Finish that sentence."

"I can't."

"Lucas!"

"If you'd have bloody said something, then maybe I could have told you that I like you too," I say. "I've liked you for years, but I didn't think for a second you'd like me back, or think about me that way."

"How could I not?"

"Well, you went off with Sophie for a start," I say. "Wait, what about Soph?"

"You're so oblivious to all of this, aren't you, Luc?" he says, shaking his head. "We broke up before Christmas."

"Before Christmas?"

"It wasn't working."

"What? Why?"

Max swallows hard, looking at me like he has the weight of the world on his shoulders. I can see the tears in his eyes, how hard he's fighting to keep them back.

"It was never meant to be me and Soph," he says. "I love her. I love her a lot, but she's my friend. She's not… She's not you." He takes a breath to steady himself.

"But you were still all over each other all the time," I say. "You were still acting like a couple."

"It didn't end in chaos and fire," Max says. "It ended because it ended, and we wanted to stay friends, and that was our way of staying friends. She tried to help me through what I was feeling for you. She told me to stay away from you, told me it would be easier on me while all the Grayson stuff was going on, but I couldn't help myself."

"Why didn't you say anything?"

"Because if I told you, then I'd have to tell you that I like you as more than a friend and…I was just too scared to do something like that," he says. "I tried to make it easier, tried to be friendlier with you, tried to get things back to how they were before I was with Soph, but then you were chasing after Grayson and…"

"And what?"

"I wanted to help."

"But if you like me, then why the hell were you helping me be with someone else?"

He shrugs, and even he seems a bit surprised by the answer. "Because I want you to be happy. Even if that's not with me." He sighs. "But I can't help you anymore," he adds. "I can't help you be with someone who…who isn't right for you. I just can't. Not anymore."

"Max—"

"You can be with him if you want," he says. "But I'm not helping you anymore. It's hurting me too much to watch you go back to him over and over again. I can't watch you pretend to be someone else, to not be yourself, to lie to him."

"I didn't, Max. No matter what you think, I never lied to Grayson," I say. I don't know why I'm defending myself right now. I just suddenly feel like I need to have my guard up. I can't stand this. "What we had was real. I know it was. I was there. I was part of it. You weren't."

"Fine," he says. "But I know you. And I feel like I know you well enough to know that he was seeing the highlights, not the real Lucas."

"Maybe that's a good thing."

"It's not," Max says. "Because the best thing about you is every single bit of you, good, bad, anxious, up, down, every single bit. And if he doesn't want all of you, then he doesn't deserve any of you."

FORTY-NINE

SECTION THREE
KEEPING HIM
"Besides, Which You See,
I Have Confidence In Me"

So you've got him. Now what?

It feels like I should say this is where the game begins. Quite the opposite, in fact. This is where any game playing ends. This is where you get to embrace who you've become during this process and keep that guy in your grasp. (Assuming, of course, you haven't come to realise that, like most men, he's the worst. Fingers crossed. I'm rooting for you.)

THE REST of the school day flies by. I'm supposed to sit near Sophie for Biology but by the time I get to the classroom she's moved, which tells me that she still isn't ready to talk. I don't want to push it. Much as I want to fix things between us, the last thing I want to do is make her feel uncomfortable. It will only push her further away.

More than anything, I want to know why she did it. And I want to know why she kept everything about her and Max from me. I feel like I've been kept in the dark for a long time, and I just want to know why.

I'm still trying to process everything that Max told me. For the longest time, I liked him and I never did anything about it. I never crossed that line. When he got with Soph, I decided that it wasn't the time and it never would be. Now I don't know what to do. I feel lost.

Then, there's Grayson. I still have feelings for him, even after everything he said this morning. He might not feel it right now, but what happened between us was real. At least, it felt like it was.

When I get home, it's blissful for the house to not feel as tense. Dad isn't going to work tonight, I think it's because he's worried about me, but also because he wants to make a start on us being better with one another, which I appreciate.

"Lucas?" he calls out as I close the door.

It's a small thing, but the fact that yelling to each other through the house has been reinstated brings my heart rate down a few clicks.

"Hey, Dad!"

"Marco!"

"Polo!"

"Marco!"

"Polo!"

I follow the sound of his voice to the kitchen, where the smell of freshly baked cookies hits me. There are piles of them on cooling racks across the kitchen counter, gooey, golden brown, and delicious-looking.

"What's all this?"

"We talked about biscuits yesterday and I couldn't remember the last time I baked cookies," he says. "So I made these."

"You've had a day off from being a chef, so you've spent it...being a chef?" I say.

"I mean, sure, if you put it like that, it sounds nuts," he says. "Do you want these biscuits or not?"

He puts some on a plate and carries them over to the table. I make tea and we sit in the silence for a little while, surrounded by the smell of freshly baked biscuits.

"So," he says. "Do you want to talk about your mum?"

The question is so jarring that it knocks any other words out of my head. It's the last thing I expected him to say.

"We don't have to start right now," I say. "It's just nice to know that the option is there."

"Okay," he says, taking a bite of the biscuit. "She used to hate it when I baked."

"What?"

"Seriously," he says. "She loved the end product, she loved the way it made the house smell, but she *hated* when I baked because I always made a mess."

I look over at the kitchen, to the mixing bowl in the sink, the mixing spoons on the side in bits of flour and discarded bits of dough.

"Do you blame her? This is chaos."

"But the cookies are good, right?" he says, taking another bite.

He's not wrong. The cookies are good. Definitely worth a little bit of chaos.

"How did the day go?" he asks. "The rest of it, I mean. Did you figure things out?"

"No," I say. "If anything, it all just got more confusing."

"Tell me about it," he says.

I talk him through what happened with Max and I watch his face as I tell him how Max feels, how he's felt for a long time. And how I had felt that way too.

"You're surprised that he likes you?"

"Dad!"

"What? It's obvious."

"To everyone?"

He shrugs. "To me," he says. "Come on, Luc, window climbing? Late-night phone calls? Early morning pick-ups when you're sad?" He pauses meaningfully. "So…?"

"I don't know," I reply. "I'm still going through it all. It's…not what I was expecting."

"But you care about Max?"

"More than anything," I say.

"Then what's stopping you?"

"Grayson," I reply. "The fear it could all fall apart, that it would ruin our friendship." I shake my head. "I need more time, I think. What about you? How was your day? Between all the baking, I mean."

"You really don't want to talk about it?" he says. "Because we can, if you want to."

"Some other time?" I say. "I…I need to think."

He nods. "Okay then," he says, taking a breath. "Well, here's something to take your mind off it. I read some of Olivia's book."

It's the last thing that I expect him to say. The very, very last thing.

"You did?"

"She was a bloody good writer, your mum," he says.

"Are you about to try and give me love-life advice?" I ask.

"No," he says. "I am, however, about to tell you, once again, to keep reading. There's a really lovely bit in there that I think will help you. No spoilers."

"Dad—"

"What?"

"What does it say?"

He sighs. "You're no fun," he says. "There's a really lovely chapter that your mum put in there at the end of section three. It's almost like an afterword. And it's about letting go."

A lump forms in my throat. "Letting go?"

"Yes," he replies, his voice cracking over the words. "Because some things don't work out the way you plan them to, no matter how many rules you follow, no matter what you try. Sometimes things last for a few days, weeks, years. Even then, sometimes they're cut short. It's rare for things to last a lifetime. It's like she was writing it to me, Lucas."

"She didn't know she was going to—"

"I know," he interrupts. "But it was what I've needed to hear for a very, *very* long time. And it's all in her voice too. She was practically reading it to me."

"You remember what her voice sounds like?"

"I feel like I do," he says. "I'm probably remembering wrong, though."

"There are videos online," I say. "I…I've watched a lot of them. She did loads of tour stuff for the book, loads of interviews."

He looks like I've just told him he's won the lottery. His eyes fill with tears almost instantly.

"I'll have to look them up," he manages to say, before taking a quick breath to stop himself from getting so upset. "But you need to finish the book. And…whatever it is that you find in there, whatever you think is the right thing to do, it's the right thing to do because that's the choice you've made." He smiles. "Listen to your heart, cheesy and vomit-inducing as it sounds."

"But what if I don't know what it's saying?"

"Then you're not listening hard enough."

FIFTY

THE ART OF LETTING GO AND FINDING PEACE

I've been in many relationships in my life and I feel like I learned something from each and every one of them. Some of them lasted for a couple of years, some of them lasted for a couple of weeks, some of them didn't even last until the end of the night. But each one had a lesson. Even if the lesson was just to not go out again with someone you meet on the street.

A lot of these things come along and they surprise us with how significant they feel, how poignant, and so often I talk to my girlfriends and they tell me how trash the person was that they just broke up with. That's their way of dealing with it. Chaos. Fire. Burn it to the ground. But not everything ends like that.

Sometimes things end too soon, or abruptly, or feel like they do. Maybe they weren't right in the first place. Or maybe something got in the way. But we have to learn to let go of things sometimes, because holding onto them forever will only cause us more pain.

Feel your feelings. Let it affect you. Take a deep breath. And make your next move.

I HEAD UPSTAIRS and take out Mum's book. It's kind of nice to not have to hide it or feel like I'm sneaking around with it anymore.

But I just want to get to the end of it. Dad has a good point. It has a happy ending, after all.

THE SLOW REVEAL

We've talked about The Turn; now let's talk about the slow reveal.

At the end of the day, these are all great ways to get somebody interested in you. They're eye-catching, they're pulling focus to you because that's what getting into a relationship is about, getting the right person's attention.

It is very likely that you won't have made it to this point in the book because 1) you will have realised that the guy you're chasing isn't actually worth your time, or 2) you took my ideas and thoughts too far and ended up showing your other half an entirely fake persona.

Did I show Grayson an entirely fake version of myself? I try and think back to when he saw the worst of me, the parts that I try to keep hidden, and how he wasn't quite so keen on them.

Is Max right? Have I been lying the whole time?

And while I've been doing that, have I been neglecting Max

Confidence is what I've been trying to teach you in this book. Confidence in who you are, confidence in what you bring to the table.

Have there been games? Yes. Have there been moments that were maybe a little questionable? Absolutely. But so long as you have stayed true to you, then there's no reason this new relationship cannot work for you. And slowly, it is time to show him who you really are.

That's what's sticking in my head.

Have I been true to myself?

Who knows who I really am? Warts and all?

With Mum's voice in my head, I open up my laptop and I start to write. I write about everything that has happened in the past week. I write about following the book and about how much it meant to get that wisdom from my mum. I'm careful to keep Vicky out of it because I don't want anybody to hate her because of this. She's done nothing wrong. I'm the one who ended up pushing it. I'm the one who wanted to keep going.

I know that Grayson might read this. I know that Max might read it. I know that Vicky probably will too, but if nothing else, it spurs me on, to be as honest as possible about all of it.

I post it and go back to reading Mum's book. I'm nearly at the end of it when my phone rings. I half hoped it would be Grayson's name flashing across the screen, old habits dying hard, but it's Vicky, and that's more than good enough for me.

"Hey," I say. It feels miraculous that after a few days of being totally blanked, she's actually calling me. "You alright?"

"Yeah, are you?" she says. "Normally it takes a good few rings for you to psych yourself up to answer the phone."

"Needs must," I say.

A pause. A significant one. *Hey, Luc,* I think, *now would be a really good time to say you're sorry.*

"Good post," Vicky says, before I can. "First one I think you've managed without any major spelling errors."

"I had to get one at some point," I say. "I'm really sorry."

"For what?"

"For totally ditching you for Grayson," I say.

"It happens," she replies. "And I know you're going to say that it shouldn't or something like that, but it happens, okay? People fall for someone and they want to spend every waking moment with them. It's a thing that happens. I wish it didn't, but when someone thinks they've found their person, it can't really be helped."

"But I should have been more considerate," I say. "Especially as I've had it happen to me."

"Maybe," she says.

"I'm also sorry for accusing you of telling him," I say. "I didn't think it was you. I just panicked."

"I know."

"So there," I say. "I understand if you don't want to be my friend anymore, but at least I got the chance to say I'm sorry. So thank you for listening to me at least."

"Lucas," she says. "I don't want to fight with you about this. I was

330

upset that you blew me off because it reminded me of June and then when you were talking at me yesterday, I…I didn't like it. But…it made me talk to June."

"What?"

"I still went to see her yesterday, and I was…I was so angry, so upset with you, you dickhead."

"Sorry again."

"It's alright," she says, laughing. "But it meant that I talked to her, and I told her how she made me feel and…she actually apologised for it. It was…good. I think we'll be better now."

"Glad to hear it," I say. "Sorry it had to come from me being a dickhead, though."

"It's fine," she says. "You're a dickhead most of the time anyway, why break a habit?"

"I'll let that slide."

"Because it's true," she says. "I just needed some space. And you gave me that, which I appreciate. We're supposed to be friends, I think. The universe threw us together in that shitty coffee shop for some reason. I'd like to think that this is it." She takes a breath. "So, what happened? School was dramatic today."

"You don't know the half of it," I say.

"Want to fill me in?"

I tell her what happened with me leaving school, what happened with Soph, with Max, with Dad, every little detail, and how I am completely and utterly clueless about what to do next.

"That's very sweet of Max," she says. "I sort of figured."

"What?"

"You're pretty oblivious, Luc, but I'm not. You should see the way he looks at you."

"Shut up," I say, but I can't keep the smile off my face. I can't help it. There's something about the thought of Max Carter holding a candle for me that just makes me smile.

"You don't want me to shut up," she says. "You want me to go on and on about how goo-goo-eyed he is for you and how he sacrifices basically everything to be around you."

"You really need to shut up because this isn't helping," I say, though maybe it is.

"What's the plan?" she asks.

Her saying those words has my heart fluttering. There is an idea forming in the back of my brain. Small for now, but growing.

"I don't know," I say. "I have a lot of apologising to do. I never meant to hurt anyone. And I seem to have succeeded in hurting literally everyone."

"I know," she says. "Keep reading. You'll figure something out."

We say our goodbyes and I pick up Mum's book and keep reading, her voice in my head, the idea bubbling away. I think I know what I have to do.

FIFTY-ONE

OWNING YOUR SH!T

Maybe this is the sort of disclaimer that should be at the start of the book, but if you've lied to your significant other at any point during this process, you are going to need to own that at some point. Maybe you pretended to like sports or a particular football team. That's going to take some undoing.

I remember telling my Matthew that I loved football, and it took a solid two years to undo. We went to matches together, and while I enjoyed spending the time with him, being around all of those men for a whole afternoon was too much for me. He wanted to go to the FA Cup Final, and I broke down and told him to go with a friend. It was awkward. I said sorry a lot. Get it out of the way now. PLEASE DON'T LIE.

LUC & SOPH

> I think we need to talk.

SOPH

…

I think we do too. I'm heading in early. Geography block?

I stayed up way later than I should have, but once I caught hold of the idea, I didn't want to let it go. I carried on reading Mum's book, getting all the way to the end. I even ended up chatting over messages with Vicky about it afterwards. She'd already read it cover to cover, and knew exactly what I was getting at.

When I'd finished it, I opened my laptop and just started writing. I couldn't stop myself. It was like everything in Mum's book, everything that had happened over the past couple of days, had finally given me the impetus to actually write something for the presentation.

I sent it over to Vicky, who sent it back, correcting all of my spelling errors. I sent it to her again, but she didn't reply, so I was fairly sure she'd gone to sleep.

I head downstairs the following morning to find that Dad is surrounded by papers once again, his laptop open, his glasses on. He looks up as I enter.

"Morning," he says. He looks a little less stressed today, but the sight of all those papers has me feeling more than a little anxious.

"I can send more money if you need me to," I say.

He takes his glasses off and looks at me. "What?"

"The bills and stuff," I say. "If it's stressing you out and we're still struggling, I can—"

"Don't worry," he interrupts. "We're fine. The pay from all those odd jobs is rolling in now, and what you're sending is fine."

"Dad—"

"I mean it," he says. "If I feel like I need more, I promise to let you know. But we're fine." He puts his glasses back on and he goes back to reading whatever he's reading. I make him a cup of tea and make some to put in a flask for myself, smiling at what Nana said yesterday about Mum taking a flask with her to school. Tea likely isn't genetic, but it's strange that I've been doing this without knowing she did the same thing.

"You're heading out early," he says.

"I'm going to talk to Soph," I say. "Figured I should do it now before my brain fully wakes up and convinces me it's a bad idea."

"It's definitely a good idea," Dad says. "Good luck."

—————

WALKING INTO SCHOOL FEELS EXTRA AWKWARD TODAY. MAYBE I'M imagining it, but I'm sure I can feel people watching me as I go. When I make it to my locker, Grayson is already there.

I need to own my shit, is all I can think as I walk towards him.

"Morning," I say. Nothing comes back. I can't really blame him. "I know you probably don't want to talk to me," I continue regardless, as he rummages in his locker. "But I wanted to apologise. What I did was wrong. I shouldn't have lied to get to you. I should have just been myself, even though you didn't notice me when I was just myself."

He slams his locker door and looks me square in the face. I think for a moment he's going to say something, but whatever words he has die on his tongue.

"The truth is, I like you, or liked you, I don't know," I say. "And what I did was done out of love or a want for love, and I'm sorry. I didn't mean to hurt you."

"Well, you did," Grayson says, firmly.

"I'm sorry for that," I say.

"Okay," he replies. "I'm sorry for not noticing you. I think if I had…things would have been very different."

"I agree." Maybe. Because there's a part of me that still wonders if I built him up in my head. That the Grayson I saw wasn't the real one. Not really.

"Okay," he says again. "Are you done?"

That question carries more weight than maybe even he knows. I'm suddenly not sure if I am. When I don't answer, he just sighs and walks away, heading down the corridor and out of sight.

Am I done?

I don't have time to overthink it, so I make my way to the Geography block to where Sophie said she would be. The fact that she's sitting there, staring right at me, tells me that maybe there is a way through this. I just have a lot of questions, and I hope she can provide the answers.

"Hey," I say as I sit down.

"Hey." It's not a lot, but it feels like a novelty.

"You okay?"

She looks at me, exasperated.

"Let me start slow," I say. "I'm building up to the serious stuff."

"Oh goody," she deadpans. "I don't think I've been okay for a while."

"Oh, Soph—"

"No, no, no, I don't want sympathy. I don't deserve sympathy," she says. "I did a shitty thing and I shouldn't have done it." She pauses. "Max hates me."

"Max doesn't hate you."

"We had a fight last night," she says. "The whole time we were in a relationship, we never really fought. Anything that wasn't working we just talked about, even us breaking up. But I screwed up this time."

"Why didn't you tell me about the breakup?"

"Max wanted to keep it quiet for a bit," she says. "I didn't know why at first, but I just went along with it because I thought…I thought that maybe he would change his mind. Then I realised what it was."

"What was it?"

"You really want me to say it?" she says, shaking her head. "And when I realised what it was, I confronted him about it and he said that he wasn't ready to face those feelings yet, and you were after Grayson anyway and…" She sighs and reaches out, taking hold of my hand. I let her. "I told him to stay away, told him not to get involved, but then he wanted to and…I sort of encouraged it, because I thought that maybe helping you find happiness would help him move on, or something stupid like that."

"And it didn't."

"I saw how much he was hurting," she says. "Just being around you and not being able to tell you how he felt, and helping you with Grayson who, incidentally, he really doesn't like. He was hurting, and I did something stupid. I didn't mean to hurt you."

"Yeah, there's been a lot of that going around," I say.

"But I mean it," she says. "I feel like I've had to pull away from you because I was protecting Max, and then I've had to watch him hurt himself over and over and over again, while you've been chasing after Grayson…" She shakes her head again. "I should have stepped in sooner, maybe even spoken to him about it, but I didn't. I found out about the website, saw what you'd been writing, and…I saw a way out."

"For who?"

"Very clever," she says. "For both of us, I suppose. I could stop pretending with him, which would protect me in the long run. And he could… He could at least tell you how he feels." Her eyes widen. "Bloody hell, he did tell you, didn't he? I've not totally rained on that parade?"

"He told me yesterday."

"And?"

"And…" And what? He's my best friend in the whole world, he means everything to me and, sure, I had a crush on him for a long time but, in a weird way, we've just become closer since then. What if it all goes wrong?

And then there's Grayson…

"Is that you overthinking it?" she says, nudging me. "I know you like him."

"Sophie—"

"You had a crush on him long before we got together," she says. "I didn't know he felt the same way, had no idea. I just knew what I wanted. I wanted him. Maybe that makes me a bad person. I just…I thought he liked me the way that you liked him, if that makes sense. Quiet, unrequited." She sighs. "I'm not saying he didn't. I just think he likes you more."

"Soph—"

"I'm not trying to be maudlin or get sympathy or whatever," she says. "I think that's just a fact. He's been holding a candle for you for all this time. When we fell apart, and when I figured it out, I thought he was going to do something. Instead, he…he tried to set you up with someone else."

"He said he wanted me to be happy."

"He's an idiot."

"He's sweet."

She laughs. "You're made for each other."

The silence that pushes its way between us is something I can't

337

explain. There is a tension to it, an unsteadiness. We're treading on new ground here, and neither one of us really knows how to proceed.

"What are you going to do?"

"About what?"

"The question of the day," she says. "Grayson. Max. Everything."

"I don't know," I say. "It all feels so up in the air. I apologised to Grayson."

"Good."

"He took it badly."

Sophie snorts. "I don't think he's the guy we thought he was," she says. "Or hoped he was. The image is a little less perfect and polished, I think."

"Isn't everyone's?"

She rolls her eyes. "How poetic."

"I don't know what to do," I say, which is the truth. I have a germ of an idea, and that idea has been committed to paper, but am I going to do anything about it? Is it worth the risk?

"Whatever you decide," she says. "I'm backing you. And if you're worried about me regarding Max, don't."

"But—"

"Don't," she says. "Some things just aren't meant to be. Me and Max weren't meant to be."

Soph gives me a soft smile, one that doesn't quite do enough to mask the unsteadiness she feels, but it tells me that she means what she's saying. I pull her into a hug, and we stay like that until the first bell rings and we have to file into Mr Marshall's classroom.

I've got some figuring out to do. A lot of it.

FIFTY-TWO

"WAIT, so this piece you're writing is the big plan?" Vicky says when I meet her at lunch. I'd dropped her a message about what happened with Soph, and how we've managed to smooth things over.

"I think so?" I reply.

"Grand romantic gesture?"

"Yes."

"It's a little cheesy, and very cliché," she says. "I guess this is your equivalent of standing outside his bedroom window with a boombox over your head."

"Something like that," I say. "If he likes it, great. If he doesn't…"

"If he doesn't like it, it will still be a great piece, and at least you'll know either way," Vicky says. "Seriously, I don't know why you resisted this Creative Writing Group for so long. You clearly have a knack for it."

"You don't know why? Do I need to tell you about all my Dad-problems again?"

"Oh yeah, forgot about that," she says. "How is all that, by the way?"

"It's actually alright," I say. "We talked about Mum last night. It looks like he's going to try and talk to me about her and stuff."

"Great."

"And how are you?"

She pauses, eyeing me carefully. "Fine… Why? What have you done?"

"Nothing," I say. "I just mean…with the June stuff. How are you coping with all of that?"

"We messaged last night," she says. "We're back on track, I think. I'm glad I told her. So thanks for being a dickhead."

"The alternate theme song to Golden Girls."

"Thank you for being a dickhead," Vicky sings, then adds, "I think she wants to be friends again."

"And you're okay with that?"

Vicky shrugs. "I want to be friends with her."

I nod, because I understand that. It's what I'm trying to do. Keeping feelings bottled up is never a good idea because…it ends like this, going around and fixing things. There are still things to fix, but I will get there. Just have to keep going.

———

"How did it go?" Dad calls as I walk into the kitchen. He has a big stack of papers next to him at the table, his is laptop open, his glasses on. I swear he's not moved since this morning. "I've been on the edge of my seat all day."

"You have not."

"No, but you walked in and I remembered that no one at school is talking to you, so… you know…" He looks at me, interested. "How are you?"

"Things with Vicky are fine," I say. "Things with Soph…will be okay."

"Will be?"

"There's work to be done," I say. "But we'll work it out."

"And Max? Grayson?" And isn't that the question of the day? I must make a face because Dad winces. "What?"

"I'm writing something," I say.

Dad shakes his head and closes the lid of his laptop.

"What?!"

"That is the most Olivia thing you could do," he says. His

mentioning Mum is still a little bit jarring, but he's trying, and I appreciate that. "What did you write?"

"We've got this Creative Writing Group presentation a week from Wednesday," I say.

He perks up. "Did you tell me about that?"

"No, I—"

"Can I come?"

"Dad, you don't need to come to it."

"Why didn't you tell me?"

"Because of Mum," I say. "Creative Writing Group stuff always made things weird between us, and I didn't think you'd want to be around it." He looks defeated, like I've properly knocked the wind out of his sails. "But if you're okay with it and you don't have to work, you can come. It's at four-thirty, after school."

"I'll be there with bells on."

"Please tell me you don't mean that literally."

"What are you writing?" he asks.

The fact that he won't confirm that he's not going to wear bells fills me with trepidation, but I let it slide. If he shows up wearing literal bells, I'm emancipating.

"It's a work in progress," I say. "Something for me to read out at the presentation. If he shows up."

"You don't think he's going to show up?"

"I don't know," I say. "We'll have to wait and see."

"Don't lose hope," Dad says. "There's still time."

He turns back to his computer, opens it, and starts tapping away.

"Is everything okay?" I ask.

"Why do you ask?"

"You've barely moved all day," I say. "Surely that means whatever you're looking at must be serious."

He laughs. "It started that way, yes. I've been reading."

I blink. "Reading what?"

He taps the larger stack of papers next to him. "This is your mum's book."

"God, you have an old printed-out version of it?"

"No," he says. "This is the romcom she was writing before she died."

It's like I've had the breath knocked out of me.

"Oh."

"I went into the attic and was looking through all the stuff I packed up when...well...after," he says. "I found a couple of family pictures, the books that I put up there, and then...this." He looks a little bit misty eyed. "It turns out, she didn't get to finish it."

"What?"

"She made it all the way to the end, but didn't get to write the happy ending," he says. "I've been going through old files, hard drives, all sorts to see if I can find it, but it's just not there."

"That's...that's really sad," I say. I don't know why it hurts me that these imaginary people who I didn't know about didn't get to have their happy ending, but it does.

"She worked so hard on it," he says. "Every week she took it to her focus group, trying to get to the end. She was doing it for herself, I think, rather than for anybody else. It was important to her." He picks it up. "She got almost all the way to the end and then just...stopped. You should read it."

I blink. "I should?"

He smiles. "I think if she knew everything that you'd been doing, she'd probably want you to," he says. He takes a breath and steadies himself. "Right, remind me what time this thing is next week."

"Four-thirty on Wednesday," I say. "But Dad, you don't have to—"

"I'm coming," he says. "If you want me to."

"Of course I do."

"Good," he says. "I think Liv would want me to be there too."

FIFTY-THREE

THE GRAND ROMANTIC GESTURE

Only to be used in times of true desperation, the Grand Romantic Gesture is your one-time-only opportunity to win the heart of your one true love, if you happened to mess it up somewhere along the way.

This is your Mr Darcy in the rain. This is your thousand yellow daisies. This is your Harry running to the New Year's Eve Party to kiss Sally at midnight. You've got one shot. Don't mess it up.

"SO, DID YOU READ IT?"

It's practically the first thing that Vicky asks when I see her at work the next day.

I told her about the manuscript last night. I couldn't keep it in. I took a picture and sent it to her. The barrage of messages I got from her afterwards were borderline insane.

"Yeah," I say. "I basically stayed up all night."

"And?"

"It's killer," I say. "Like…it's brilliant, really and truly brilliant."

"But…?" It's like she could sense it on the air.

"It's not finished," I say. "She never finished it."

"Where does it end?"

"Right where you don't want it to," I say. "Dad said it just stopped, and he's right. The main character is torn between two guys, and we get right up to the point where she's ready to make this grand romantic gesture and then…nothing."

"Nothing?"

"Nothing."

"Not a hint?" she asks, incredulous. "No notes saying how it ends?"

"No," I reply. "It could go either way. No happy ending. It's…it's a killer."

"Maybe a little bit more so, when you're currently living it," Vicky says.

"Thanks for that."

"Well, you're going to write yours," she says.

"I'm trying," I say. "We'll see if it lands."

Vicky wraps her arm around my waist and leans her head on my shoulder.

"What's this for?" I ask.

"A little bit of affection to try and make you feel better," she says. "One way or another, people will see it and it will be great. Something will happen."

"This is not the time for hugging, this is the time for working!" Maria's voice snaps us both to attention and we split apart to carry on with our shifts.

"The one time she actually bothers to come out here on a Saturday," Vicky grumbles.

———

ON MONDAY AT SCHOOL, THINGS FEEL LIKE THEY'VE IMPROVED A LITTLE from the tail end of last week. Jasmine is still on guard with me, so is Krish, which I don't enjoy so much, but things with Soph seem to be steadily moving back to normal. We're talking at least, so that's something. But I'm still hanging out with Vicky at lunch and during break times. I don't want to push too hard. I don't want to cause any more upset. I think Soph needs time as much as I do.

I see Max wandering around school, I see him hanging out with Soph, Jasmine, and Krish, and I start to wonder if everything is okay.

We've not spoken in a few days and I have no idea what that means for us. Maybe he's changed his mind.

Grayson doesn't show up to the Creative Writing Group session on Wednesday. I've seen him around school, almost bumped into him at my locker, but we haven't talked. I thought tonight would have been the perfect opportunity, but when I'm lining up I can feel that he's not coming.

I find myself watching the door, watching the space where he normally sits and not really focussing on anyone else's pieces, which definitely makes me the arsehole in this situation. I still listen, I still try to offer feedback, but I know I'm not one hundred percent here.

"Lucas Cook," Mrs Leighton says, when I'm still there after everyone else has left. "Everything alright? You want to talk a little more about your piece?"

"Um—"

"Because I really do think it's good," she says, packing up her things. "You could tighten it up in a few places, maybe cut *some* of the repetition so you don't labour the point too much, but it's all there."

"It's not that," I say. "Have you… Have you heard from Grayson?"

Mrs Leighton breathes a heavy sigh. "He's pulled out," she says.

"No," I say. "Why?"

"He didn't say why," she replies. "He just didn't want to do it anymore, didn't want to read next week. He said he might come back next term, but he's got some things going on that he's dealing with."

"Oh."

"Things that I think you maybe know more about than I do," she says.

And I know that she knows. And I hate that she knows, because I'm the arsehole here.

"Something like that," I reply. "I fucked up."

"Yeah, you did," she says. "And what are you going to do about it?"

"I've apologised," I say.

Mrs Leighton gathers her things and we start walking out of the classroom. "That's something," she says. "I look forward to hearing it next week. It's a great piece. Heartfelt. I think…I think if the right person hears it, it will have the desired effect." She winks at me. "Goodbye, Lucas."

I'm beaming. My Mum never got to write her happy ending, but I have a chance at writing mine. I can't just let it slide past. Not if I can help it.

FIFTY-FOUR

THE GRAND ROMANTIC GESTURE (Cont.)

It won't always work. It's a cinematic trope for a reason. Our lives are not films, much as we would like them to be. We don't always get the happy ending that we want or feel we deserve, so don't put too much stock in this. It's all or nothing and, when it comes to matters of the heart, you owe it to yourself to at least try.

LUC & SOPH

SOPH

This is amazing

Thank you

He'll love it.

I want him to hear it. I would message to invite him, but I don't know if he'll come.

He'll come.

Will you ask him? Please?

You think he'll come if I ask him?

Yes.

I'll try.

Please? He needs to hear this.

Seeing Grayson around school, getting dirty looks from him and his friends, is just a reminder of everything I did to him. I feel rotten. Worse than rotten.

And seeing Max is somehow worse still. We can't even seem to hold eye contact without it being awkward or uncomfortable, and I wish I could bring myself to do something about it.

When Wednesday rolls around, I have no idea if Sophie is going to follow through, but I know she will have asked, and that's all that matters.

For the presentation, we are in the black box drama studio, a much bigger space than Mrs Leighton's English classroom, with a small stage set up to one side where we'll all stand and read our pieces. I've never been to one of these before, but it seems fairly well attended. There are parents, teachers, and students, though not many students, but a nice selection.

"I don't think he's coming," I say to Vicky, looking around.

"No," she replies. "Not to make you feel worse, but me either. I've checked with Soph. He's nowhere to be seen."

I look out over the crowd and I can see Dad chatting with other parents, Mrs Leighton schmoozing with various members of the faculty, Mr Bird standing over by a student dressed head to toe in black, rummaging through wires, trying to get everything set up for the event. He's not here. He's not coming. Grand romantic gesture failed.

I try to look at the positives. My friends have shown up. Even Jasmine came, which is actually the biggest surprise of the evening. We've not really spoken since everything went down. I'm sure we will at some point. That moment isn't now. Personally, not talking to her has been remarkably peaceful, but when I think things like that I know I'm just being a little bitch.

"You're going to be fine," Vicky says quietly.

"What?"

"Whether he's here or not, it's a great piece," she says. "You should be very proud of it. Not to sound cheesy here, but I reckon your mum would be."

"Mum probably would have done a better job at the grand romantic gesture," I say. "She would have got him here."

"He'll come around," she says. "If it's meant to be, it will be."

There is the sound of microphone feedback around the room that pulls the attention of the audience to the tiny stage. Mrs Leighton is standing on it in a pair of jeans and a flowy leopard print blouse. She's wearing a matching scrunchie in her hair, and even her glasses look like leopard print. Mrs Leighton will always be a style icon.

"Good afternoon, everyone," she says, her voice sounding less harsh and authoritative in this environment. She's more chill, which is strange. "I'm very excited that you're all here. Our students have been working incredibly hard over the course of this half term, and I'm sure they're all thrilled to be sharing their work with you this afternoon."

My stomach drops as I realise I'm going to have to read in front of all of these people. It might be a silly thing to only just now realise, but in agreeing to do this, I've potentially set myself up to look like a complete asshole. Great.

Well done, Luc. Here comes the anxiety sweats.

"Christ, I don't think I can do this," I say quietly.

"You're going to be fine," Mr Bird says. The way he's suddenly appeared at my side is enough to make me jump, which has him chuckling and shaking his head. "You've done this loads this term. What's the difference?"

"Faces I don't recognise."

"Faces you might never have to see again."

"Very true," I say. "I just…I wanted someone else to be here."

Mr Bird shrugs. "We can't always get what we want," he says. "What's that Shakespeare quote?"

"To throw up or not to throw up, that is the question?"

He laughs again. "I was more thinking, 'The course of true love never did run smooth,' but that too," he says. "And for what it's worth, I would say to *not* throw up is the answer to that one."

"First up, we have someone who joined us for the first time this

349

term," she says. "I've been trying to convince him to join us for a long time though, so I'm very excited to be introducing Lucas Cook."

There is applause, but the blood is pumping so loud in my ears that I can barely hear it. It takes Vicky giving me a little nudge to make me start walking to the stage. I stumble as I step onto the little podium, my pieces of paper in my hand. I'm gripping them so tightly that they are shaking, my fingers leaving sweaty indents on the pages.

Pull it together, I say to myself.

I look out at the crowd and can see Dad standing near the back, absolutely beaming. I'm pretty sure he has tears in his eyes. This is probably a big deal for him. I know it is for me. I'm glad he's here.

"Hello," I say into the microphone. Christ, is that really what my voice sounds like? Massive apologies to literally everyone who knows me; that's awful. "My name is Lucas Cook, and this piece is called—"

There is movement at the door to the drama studio. It opens and a couple of latecomers step through. It's enough to stop me mid-sentence. Amid a small collection of people, I see two faces. Grayson. And then Max.

Shit.

FIFTY-FIVE

THEY SNEAK in at the back and really don't pull anybody's focus, apart from mine. For everybody else, I'm standing up here like a twat, just not saying anything, but for me, the entire world has stood still. I watch as they move further into the room, standing at the back of the waiting audience.

He came, I thought. *He actually came.*

The thought races through my head that he probably didn't come here for me, that he came because Soph asked, but all the same he is here. And he's going to hear my piece. That's all I wanted.

"It's called 'Fancy,'" I say, my voice barely making it to the microphone. I see Mrs Leighton off to one side, directing me to project my voice more. I wish we'd had a dress rehearsal, a tech run, anything, because I feel like I'm floundering.

I clear my throat and shuffle my papers, reading the first line over and over and over again before I can finally vocalise it. My heart needs to calm down or this will be my first and only reading. Jesus.

"Fancy seeing you here." The words come so easily to me, directed, instructed, from her pen, to my mouth, to his ears. And the way he smiles, it's like my entire world has been brightened, like the sun has risen on a day that I didn't realise had been quite so cloudy.

"Fancy seeing you here." It comes back to me differently, and I

feel their power flow through me. It's like I've been waiting to hear them from you all my life. And when I hear them, something shifts.

"Fancy seeing you here." In this place where we've stood together ten, fifteen, twenty, a hundred times, in this place that I know so well, that you know so well, that we haven't discovered together, but apart.

"Fancy seeing you here." This person who has meant so much to me for so long, but means more to me now than I ever thought they could. Crazy.

"Fancy seeing you here." Here in my life. Here at my side. Here with your hand in mine? Maybe.

Fancy seeing you happy.
Fancy seeing you hurt.
Fancy seeing you with me.
Fancy seeing you without.

I am looking up after every line. I am waiting to see a reaction. His eyes are wide, his mouth open, but maybe that's because I just keep looking at him, because I can't stop.

"Fancy seeing you here." It's a line from a book. It's a piece of dialogue in a movie. It's a romcom waiting to happen.

"Fancy seeing you here." It was never my line, but I used it anyway. Now it feels like it might be ours, after all.

Fancy seeing you finally seeing me the way I've seen you.
Fancy seeing you walking away.
Fancy seeing you here.
Maybe I'll see you again.

"Thank you," I say into the microphone.

There is applause, and it's nice to hear. It's different from how it is in Creative Writing Group sessions. There, it's much more muted, politeness more than anything else, an appreciation of someone else's work before it gets torn to shreds. Here, it's just a lot of love.

I look out at the sea of faces and see Soph, who is absolutely beaming. She widens her eyes and emphatically moves her head to indicate that it worked, he's here, she asked and it happened.

Vicky gives me a thumbs up. Dad is crying, which is definitely a jarring image. Grayson is clapping, but he's not looking at me, he's looking at the ground. Max looks like he's about to cry.

"Thank you so much for that stirring performance, Lucas," Mrs Leighton says. "Next to the stage we have…"

————

THE AFTERNOON CONTINUES WITH READING AFTER READING, EACH ONE seeming to explore a different genre, a different style. It's nice to see people really in their element, really showing off what they love to do. Even though I've heard all the pieces before, it's nice to hear them in this setting. They're different with this crowd, different in this space.

When the last person has performed, we all end up on stage again for one final bow and then Mrs Leighton does a small speech about being proud of us and she gets a little misty-eyed.

"Now, go and mingle, go meet your adoring public. Thank you so much for coming," she says. "We'll be back at the end of next half term, so please, if you enjoyed this evening, do join us again."

There is another round of applause, one that's for all of us and for Mrs Leighton too. She takes a bow. She really is loving this, which is sweet. And with that, we all depart, heading off to see the various people in the crowd who came to see us.

Dad finds me first, his eyes misty again, his face looking like it's about to crumple just looking at me. He takes a deep breath and steadies himself.

"I'm…I'm very proud of you," he says, barely managing to get the words out. Not because they're hard to say or anything, at least I don't think that's what it is, but because he means them, and he clearly feels overcome by it all. "That piece was…beautiful. You know, that's the first thing your mum said to me when we met?"

I smile. "I know," I reply.

"You do?"

"It's in the book, Dad," I say.

"So…" he says, looking around before lowering his voice. "Did it work?"

"I don't know yet," I whisper. "I should probably go and find out."

"Your mum would have loved it," Dad says quietly. "I mean, she would have loved it because it referenced her and, I love your mum, I do, but she loved herself more." I can't help but laugh. "But she'd be proud to see you writing and to see you up there reading it too. She hated reading out loud. Didn't think anyone wanted to hear from her."

"They definitely did," I say.

"I'm still sorry about all that, Luc," he continues. "I never wanted to hide her from you, or make you feel like I didn't care about her."

"It's okay," I say. "You had your reasons. Same way I had mine for wanting to find out more."

"Things will be better," he says. "I promise."

"Okay," I say. And I know that they will because the last week or so has been so different to how things have been over the past seven years. It's like I can feel her with me, and I don't have to hide that. It's nice.

"But go and talk to your legions of fans," Dad says. "I shouldn't be over here cramping your style."

"You're not cramping my style," I say.

"It's okay," Dad replies, holding his hands up. "I'll go and talk to some of the other parents, leave you to it."

He vanishes into the crowd, and I find myself looking around for a familiar face. It's possible he left. Maybe he doesn't want to talk after all.

"He's by the door." Vicky's voice startles me. "Assuming you're not looking for me."

"What did you think?" I say, spinning around to face her.

She shrugs. "You were okay, I guess," she replies with a smirk. "Good that he came, right?"

"Even better that he hasn't left yet," I reply.

"Agreed," she says. "You ready for this?"

I look over at the door. Almost like he can feel my eyes on him, he looks up at me. He smiles.

"That feels like a signal," she says. "Go get him."

"What if I say something stupid?"

"I feel like that's kind of a foregone conclusion at this point," Vicky says. "But you wanted him to be here, you got him here, you did the boombox outside the window thing, and now…now, you've got to see if it worked."

I take a deep breath.

"What if it hasn't?"

"Then you'll survive," Vicky says. "But there's only one way to find out."

I snake my way through the crowd and I am feeling every cinematic beat of the moment as I go, like we're at some crowded party and I'm having to make my way around people to catch this boy who is fully illuminated by some imaginary spotlight.

He keeps looking in my direction, fleeting glances, subtle, but I see them. If he's looking for an opportunity to run, this would definitely be it.

"Fancy seeing you here."

ACKNOWLEDGMENTS

To quote a great prophet - it's been a while.

If I'm totally honest, I wasn't sure this book would ever see the light of day, I didn't know if I would ever get to write a set of acknowledgements again. I think that's why the ones in Boy Queen are so long! This book took me two years to write, and then after a turbulent submission process it took my another year before I decided I was going to do anything with it, so this story has been sitting in my head for a long while. I only hope it was worth the wait!

I want to thank my editor Hanna for all of your kind words and thoughtful notes on this book. You are a wonder! I loved it when I wrote it, I loved it when I spent time editing it, but sometimes the longer you spend with book the less sure you are that it is doing what you want it to. You gave me renewed belief in it, so thank you.

Thank you to Michael for giving me faith in myself when I didn't have it and telling me that there would be another book one day even when I was so sure there never would be. Here it is. About damn time! You were right, because of course you were! Thank goodness for you.

To Chris, who was the first person to read this book and gave me so much faith in it and so many useful notes - this ending is your fault, I need everyone reading this to know that! I am very grateful have you as a friend and a sounding board and a writing partner (get back to work! Ha!) And to Jon, who was the second person to read this book and also had so much faith in it, and in me. Your constant kind words and unwavering belief in my ability is everything, I don't know if you realise quite how important those words are to me. Thank you.

Mum, you've listened to me talk about this more than most and you've been telling me to back myself and to get a new story out there pretty much since Boy Queen came out. It took a while, but it's here. Thank you for listening to me constantly talk about my dreams, and never telling me that I'm dreaming too big.

My drag family, you are all perfect...too perfect in fact. Stop that. But don't. Get away from me. But obviously don't. You're all stars (you are a-a-all sta-a-ars!) so thank you for just being you.

I want to thank Harrold-Vincent Villanueva for all of your work on the cover. It has been an absolute joy watching it come to life and it just looks so unbelievably stunning I cannot actually cope with how gorgeous it is!

To everyone who read and loved Boy Queen, to everyone who has sent messages of excitement ahead of me writing something new and has asked for a new book, thank you thank you thank you. I really hope you like this one! To everyone who is brand new to me (hello there!) and took a chance on this book, I really hope you like it too!

And finally to Jordan. You listen to me talk about book stuff more than anyone should have to. Thank you for listening, for talking me down, talking me up, and generally just being solid ground when I feel like I'm walking on sand. Love you much.

ABOUT THE AUTHOR

George Lester is author of YA novels *Boy Queen* and *Don't Die Alone, Lucas Cook!*, an actor and a drag queen based in London. When he's not living in a world of words, he's living his best life in the biggest wig imaginable as drag queen That Girl. In 2023, following protests at a Drag Storytime event, That Girl was named Pink News Drag Artist of the Year 2023 for her community work and went on to write and star in multi-award nominated show, THAT GIRL VS THE WORLD, which premiered at The Bridge House Theatre in 2024. George lives in Twickenham with his partner, is obsessed with romcoms of all kinds (gloriously classic to deliciously trashy), and, if pushed, would probably say that they *were* on a break but Ross still shouldn't have done what he did.

instagram.com/TheGeorgeLester
tiktok.com/@ThatGirlDrag

www.ingramcontent.com/pod-product-compliance
Ingram Content Group UK Ltd.
Pitfield, Milton Keynes, MK11 3LW, UK
UKHW042149060225
454777UK00004B/387